Mated by Midnight

The Complete Trilogy

Heather Hildenbrand

Falls Gazette

Mated By Midnight

Heather Hildenbrand

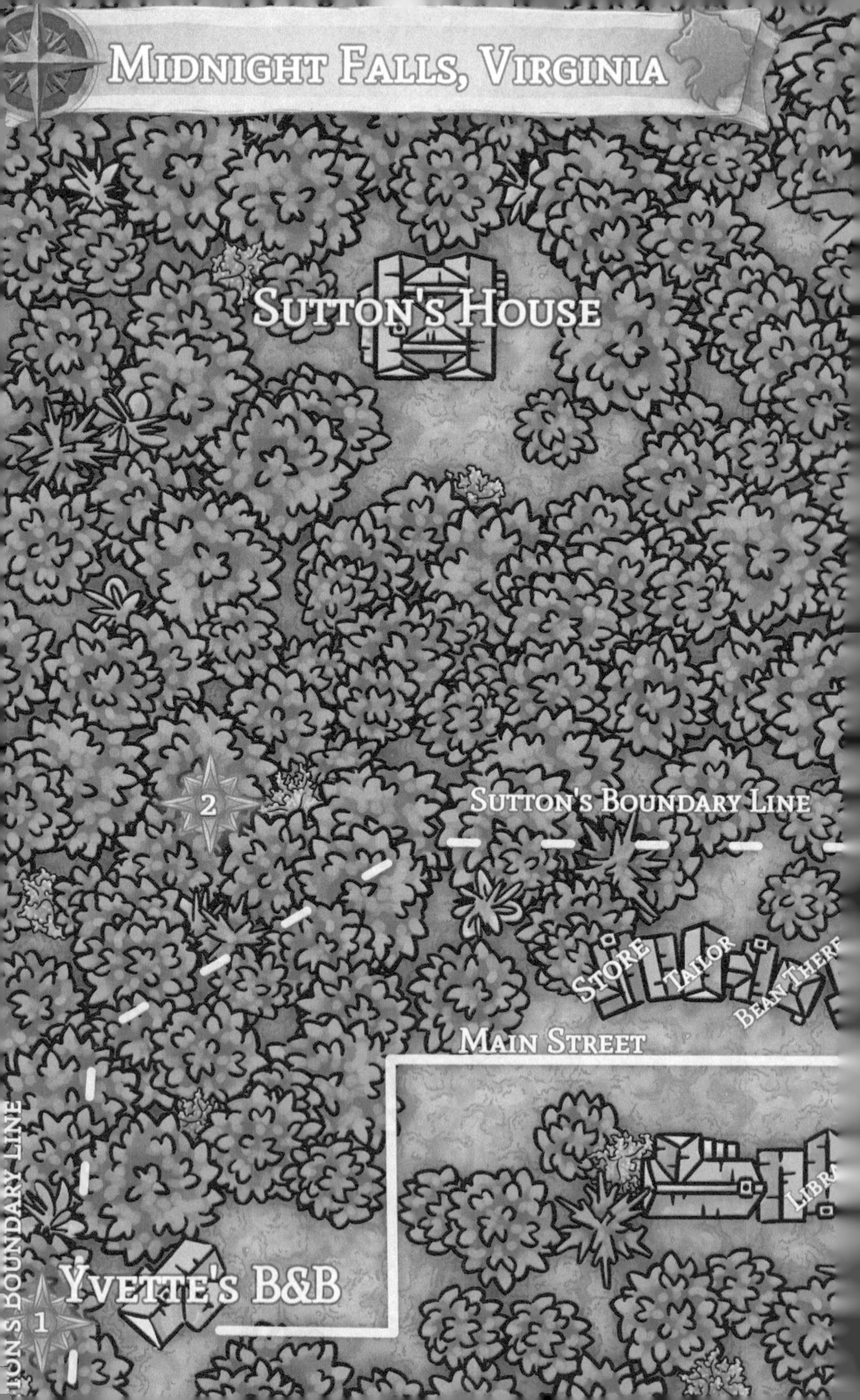

Midnight Falls, Virginia

Sutton's House

2

Sutton's Boundary Line

Store

Tailor

Main Street

Yvette's B&B

1

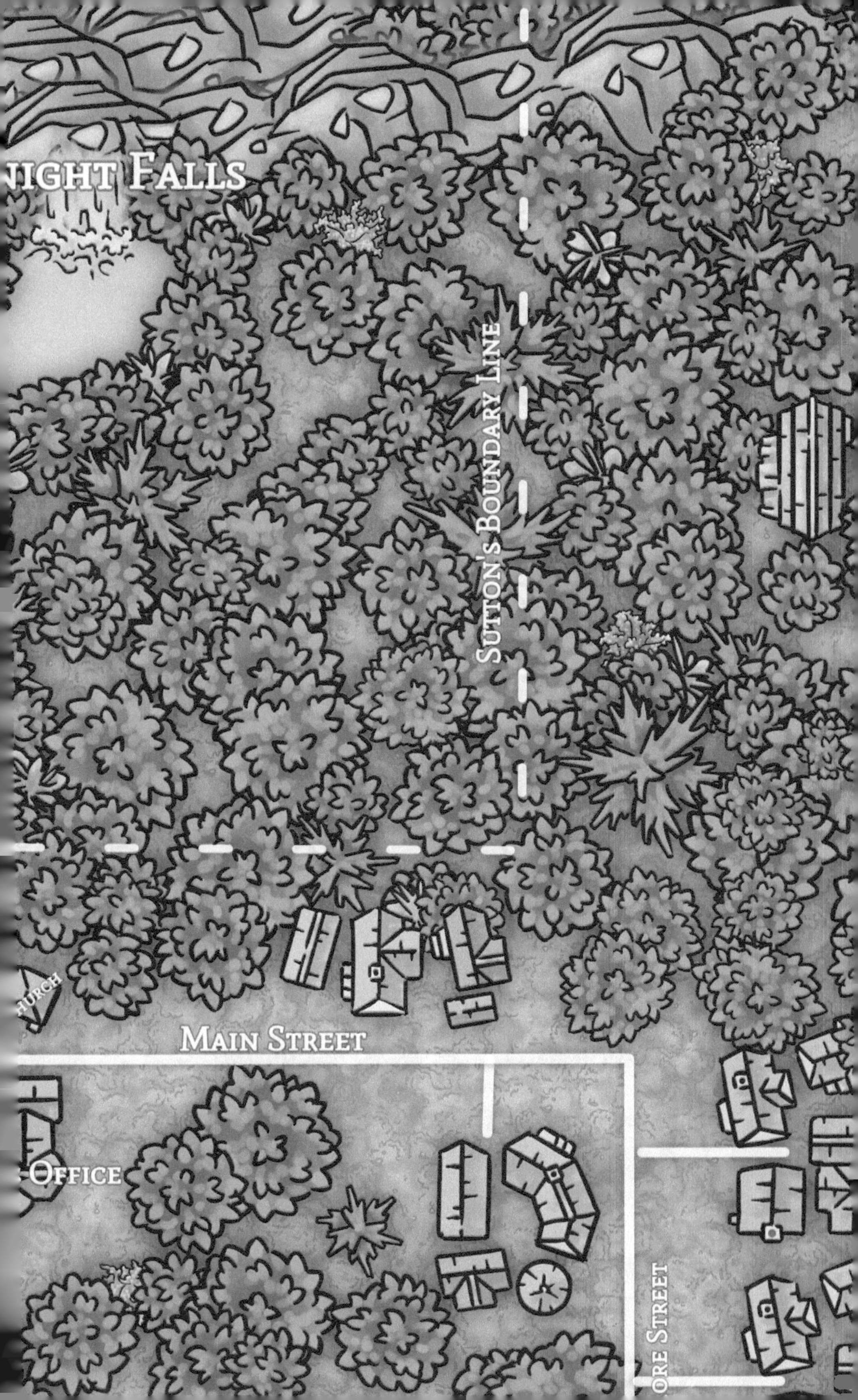

Falls
Sutton's Boundary Line
Main Street
Office
Street

Midnight Cursed
Midnight Hunted
Midnight Hunted
Mated by Midnight Series
By Heather Hildenbrand

Edited by Dawn Y
Cover Design by Pretty Indie

Midnight Cursed

Falls Gazette

Chapter One

Once upon a time, I loved living in New York City. Bright lights, bustling streets, activity literally everywhere you look. Back in college, this city had seemed perfect for someone like me. Someone who seeks a story out like a dog searches the yard for a bone. Every stone turned over; every needle separated from the haystack.

Journalism or subterfuge—that's what my brothers always predicted for my career. I usually followed that up with a middle finger, provided my mother wasn't watching. It doesn't matter how old a girl gets; you're never quite old enough to flip your own mother the bird and have your father hear about it.

As far back as I can remember, I've always wanted to know it all. Solve the mystery. Get to the truth. And in college, studying journalism only fed my passion for separating fact from fiction. Or, even better, the everyday monotony from the flashy and exciting. Those are the needles in the haystack I'm after. Even if the haystack I'm currently assigned to involves such riveting drama as which hot dog cart is at war with which taco truck. And that's just this week—

next week, it could be the coffee cart at odds with the mobile juice bar. See what I mean? *Riveting.*

When I landed my dream job at the *Times* straight out of college, I thought I'd "made it." But after two years on the back page of the Local's Section, I'm just not sure anymore. And that uncertainty has made me wonder if the grass is, in fact, greener. Every day, the city lights lose a bit more of their luster, waning alongside my excitement for journalism.

Maybe soured is more accurate. Yeah, soured is a pretty damn good word for this particular journalistic dry spell. What was once a passion has turned into a job. And isn't that depressing as hell?

"That had *better* be coffee in your hand, Serenity Kellis."

Armed with a smile, I turn toward Allison, my best friend in the entire world. Rocking red *Chuck Taylors* and navy-blue hair, she looks like a beautiful, female version of *Sonic The Hedgehog*. "You know it is." I offer her a paper cup, and she takes it, not wasting any time before tipping it up and drinking.

"I cannot believe you talked me into this," she groans.

"It's not *that* early," I tell her as I loop my free arm through hers and guide her toward the large iron archway of New York's food truck park. Trees canopy over the top of us, casting shadows over the sidewalk.

"It's before eight. It's early."

I supposed there's no need to mention that I've been up since four. "Listen, when my contact says there's something to see, there's something to see." Even as I say the words, I also send up a silent plea that they're the truth. While things in the food truck world can certainly get dramatic, most of the time, "something to see" is really just a lewd statement written in washable paint on the side of one of the carts. Just once, I'd kill for permanent ink. At least, then there'd be a reason for the theatrics.

"Yeah. Well, agree to disagree. But since I'm here—for which you owe me, I might add—the least you can do is entertain me. What's new in RoscoeVille?"

I sigh. I don't mean to…it just comes out. And like the investigative journalist she is, Allison whirls on me and points her index finger at me.

"What is it? Do we get to kill him? Bury the body? You just say the word. I've already got a shovel and—"

Chuckling, I shake my head. She's never been a fan of Roscoe. Says he's far too arrogant to be any good. "It's nothing like that. He's just been distant lately, and I think that's screwing with my head when it comes to planning the wedding."

"You know, it's not too late to run," she tells me. "You've got a month. We can hop on a plane, head to Mexico; they'll never find us."

I don't say it out loud, but the idea of running? It's something that has crossed my mind. Even if I know I won't ever go through with it. After all, I have the ideal life: steady job, handsome fiancé, New York apartment. It doesn't get better than that, right?

"I picked up my dress yesterday, and we settled on our song."

"Please tell me you talked him out of *When A Man Loves A Woman*."

"He loves that song, so I figured, since I got my pick of the cake, I should give him something."

"But he doesn't even want to use the original," she complains.

"The Blasters are a good cover band."

She glares at me, soft brown eyes unwavering. "Ser, this is your wedding. *Wedding.* Arguably the single most important day of your life, and dude is *loaded*. There is no reason he can't afford an actual band."

"He wants to make sure we're saving for our future," I remind her, even as the words sting. When I was a child, I'd dreamt of a big, beautiful, fairy tale wedding. Flowers, a string quartet, champagne fountains—all of it. But even as disappointing as it is, now that I'm an adult, I can understand the practicality of ensuring we don't dump all of our savings into a single day.

And since my parents had to put five of us siblings through college, we aren't exactly rolling in extra wedding funds. Not that I would have let them pay for anything more than the rehearsal dinner they forced me into, anyway. I don't buy into the old-world dowry traditions. This is my wedding, *my* day, and while I appreciate their help, it's up to Roscoe and me to afford everything.

"Future, smuture. I know you, Ser. You're going to regret this one day."

I don't answer her. It's an old argument, anyway, and Allison takes my silence for the cue it is and lets it go. For now.

Overhead, a bird chirps loudly, and even though the busy street is merely a few yards behind us, the loud honks of impatient drivers seem to fade away. It's refreshing, and even when I'm not working on a story that brings me to the park, I run here at least twice a week rather than being stuck on my treadmill.

"So this is what the outside looks like?"

I glance over at Allison, who's pretending to be awestruck by the view around us. "I'm surprised you can still see the sun with those damn windshields over your eyes."

She turns toward me, her massive blue-rimmed sunglasses taking up most of her face. "Hey, seeing as how my job description doesn't actually let me outside, I need to take every precaution."

I chuckle. "Next time, we'll be sure to bring a big umbrella, too."

"Good."

The pavilion ahead is concrete with steel picnic tables arranged in neat lines. Food carts line the area with the bigger trucks toward the back of the lot. I can already smell the delicate aroma of coffee and the mouthwatering scents of what are likely breakfast tacos, featuring varying forms of bacon and sausage.

"Thank goodness! 'Bout fucking time we get someone with some common sense here!" Bill Palter steps out from behind his taco cart and throws his hands up in the air.

"She ain't one of us," Mallse Adams retorts, barely throwing a half glance my way through his sheet of thick, black bangs. His Cajun food truck is parked next to Bill's.

I give him a wounded look. "That hurts, Mallse."

"It's the damned truth."

"So, what's going on here?" I ask Bill, knowing if anyone's going to talk, it's him.

"Better make sure it's off the record, Bill," Mallse warns. "Else you'll piss Candie off!"

"Who's Candie?" Allison leans over and asks quietly.

"The burger lady," I tell her. "Think of this like the food truck mob, and she's the head of the family."

"Oh, shit."

"Yup." I turn my attention back to Bill, who's looking even more nervous. "What you got for me?"

"I-I-I think you oughta know the authorities are on their way."

"Okay."

"But I wanted you to have the first look-see because I think you'll do right by me when this gets out."

"I appreciate your trust in me, Bill."

His gaze shifts to Mallse, who merely stuffs his hands into his red hoodie, then back to me. "Come on, then."

I follow Bill off the concrete path and into the trees. Birds chirp from inside the canopy of leaves overhead. The branches are thick enough to blot out the sunlight, plunging everything into shadows.

"Is this guy going to kill us?" Allison questions loudly.

"Of course, not," Bill shoots back. "But I-I-I need you t-t-to see this before..." he trails off as we step up to the edge of a small creekbank.

"Holy shit," Allison's words are drowned out by the sound of my own pulse hammering in my ears.

I smile; my grin savage and triumphant. This is *exactly* what I've been waiting for. The creek bed is full of hamburger buns, patties, ketchup and mustard packets, and cans of sodas. What used to be Candie's cart is now nothing more than planks of broken wood and shredded fabric of her red and white checkered canopy.

"Did you do this?" I turn to Bill, trying my best to keep any judgment off my face. I don't care who did what at this point, only that I get a story good enough to make it off the back page.

He shakes his head adamantly. "I know she's going to think I-I-I did, though. She's g-g-gonna kill me, Serenity."

"Nah, don't worry." I pull out my phone and start snapping pictures. To be completely truthful, she might have him offed over this. From what I've gathered, Candie is one of the most connected street vendors in New York. And trust me, that is saying something.

"She's g-g-gonna think I did it. We got bad blood…bad blood," he repeats.

Allison taps my shoulder.

"What is it?"

"Your girl have cotton-candy pink hair?" Allison asks.

"Yes, why?"

She points to the left, and my gaze follows her gesture to some bushes off to the side. Bushes with a bit of pink hair sticking out from the bottom. "Oh no." My stomach twists as I realize exactly what it is I'm looking at. And, for some reason, my earlier thought about killing for something more permanent pops back into my mind, making me feel like shit, even as I know I couldn't have willed this into existence.

"What is it?" Bill scans the bushes then lets out a blood-chilling scream as he jumps back. "No! No! Tell me that ain't C-C-Candie!"

I take cautious steps forward, ensuring I don't step on anything that could be evidence. Carefully, I reach out and pull back the branches to reveal a pale, very-dead Candie Calico. Lips blue, throat lined with red. Clear homicide. I let go of the branches and straighten again, frowning. Beside me, Allison whispers, "Oh shit, oh shit, oh shit," over and over again. But me? I say nothing.

Seems like I'm too calm, right? After all, how many dead bodies could I have seen? Well, you'd be surprised. With parents who worked themselves to the bone when I was younger, I ended up in the back of a cruiser, riding along with my brother through the first few years of his career.

Though, if I'm being honest, this is the first time I've arrived prior to police tape and crime scene investigators. My stomach rolls as I reach for my phone and unlock the screen. With my heart beating louder than a drumline, I tap on Steven's contact information at the top of my favorites list.

"Who you callin'?" Bill demands.

"My brother," I tell him.

His eyes widen in panic, which makes it clear he remembers who—and what—my brother is.

"Aw, hell no. No damned way I'm sticking around! I ain't going to jail!"

Bill spins on his heel and disappears into the tree line before my brother's deep, "What's up," comes through my phone.

"I've got a dead body."

He's silent, and then, dead pan, he says, "A dead body."

"Yes. The hamburger cart owner at the food truck alley."

He's silent again.

"Come on, Steven, don't be a dick. The local cops are on their way here, and they don't realize they're walking into a homicide investigation. I know how you love when they trample all over evidence."

He groans. "Fine, but you'd better not be fucking with me."

"That was one time, and it was for your surprise birthday party."

"Fool me once," he adds. "Where exactly?"

"Food truck alley."

"You said that already," he reminds me. "Where in the food truck alley? I can't imagine there's a dead body in the middle of the pavilion."

"We took a path into the trees directly off the parking lot and found her stashed in the bushes. I'll drop a pin for you."

"On my way."

After shoving my phone back into my pocket, I inch a little closer to try to get a look at a small patch of fabric on the ground beside her body.

"What are you doing?" Allison hisses.

"I wanna see what this is."

"Steven's going to be pissed when he gets here and you've screwed with stuff."

"I'm being careful." I pull the sleeve of my sweater down and crouch right beside the body; then, using my shirt-covered hand, I gently nudge some leaves away as sirens scream in the distance. The small patch of red fabric is nothing by itself, except for the fact that I know exactly where I've seen it. "Shit."

"What?"

I straighten and shake my head. The woman might have been a massive pain in the ass, but she was a person. And now she's been murdered. No one deserves this. Turning to Allison, I clear my throat. "I know who killed her."

Falls Gazette

Chapter Two

Standing damn near seven-foot-tall, Steven is intimidating all on his own. Add to that the gun, badge, and leather jacket, and he's terrified more than a handful of my boyfriends over the years. But even though he's the oldest of my brothers, he's never tried to shield me from life.

Death, though, is another matter.

"What the hell are you doing back here?" he demands as he shoves through the brush and into the small clearing where Bill left us.

I gesture to the mess of buns and condiments. "My contact wanted to show me the contents of the cart."

He removes his sunglasses and glares at me with crystal-blue eyes that are nearly the same shade as my own. "So you followed a strange man back here? Away from the safety of the public park? Have I taught you nothing?"

"I told her it was a shitty idea," Allison defends.

He glances her way, and just like all women at the other end of

Steven Kellis's glare, she all but melts into a puddle at his feet. "Who are you?"

Allison thrusts her manicured hand his way. "Allison Summerhill. I'm friends with your sister."

She leaves out the part that she's a gossip columnist. I don't blame her. I rarely admit to being a beat reporter for dumb shit like food cart wars. Well, before it turned to murder, anyway. Not so dumb now.

He accepts her hand then releases her and turns back to me. "Body?"

"This way." After turning, I move carefully through the bushes, stopping a few feet away from Candie's body.

Grunting, Steven kneels beside her and shoves the bushes aside as carefully as I did earlier.

"I fucking hate nature." A feminine voice carries into the small clearing, and we all turn as my brother's partner, Chelsea, pushes through the brush with a handful of uniformed officers behind her.

"You knew her?" Steven asks, ignoring the entrance of his partner.

Chelsea smiles and offers me a wave before she starts telling the officers what she needs them to do. Chelsea's the nicest person I've ever met, but you'd never know it by watching her work a crime scene. Then, she gets bossy as hell. Especially now that she's seven months pregnant.

"Not well," I admit. "To be honest, she pretty much despised me."

"How could anyone not like you?" Chelsea asks as she stops at my side and wraps an arm around my shoulders.

I grin at her. "You'd be surprised. I can be quite nosy."

"Not surprising, at all." Steven straightens. "Any idea who'd want to hurt her?"

"I can do one better. I think I know who killed her."

It's a rare moment when I can surprise my brother. Eyebrow raised, he turns toward me and crosses his arms. "And who might that be?"

"There's a piece of red fabric next to the body."

"I saw that."

"Fabric that—I believe—came from a hoodie that belongs to Mallse."

"Who the fuck is Mallse?"

"Mallse Adams, Cajun food truck owner. He was wearing a sweatshirt that exact same color when I arrived at the scene."

Steven glances back at the body then back to me. Lips pursed, he nods and retrieves a plastic bag from his pocket. Then, after carefully lifting the fabric with his pen, he places it inside, seals the bag, and moves across the small clearing to me. "Let's go have a chat with Mallse, shall we?"

ANTONIO'S IS PACKED, BUT JUST LIKE I EXPECTED, ROSCOE IS already at the best table in the house. He doesn't see me, thanks to the phone screen his eyes are glued to, but that's Roscoe. Business first—always. I inhale deeply, and the aroma of fresh stone-fired pizza calls to me, making my already fast-paced day even better.

I'd hoped to get an inside scoop on a lame prank war between middle-aged meat vendors, and instead, I'd been the first reporter on the scene of an actual crime. I don't think it's too far-fetched to think the cards of destiny are dealt in my favor today. Serenity Kellis: homicide reporter.

Has a nice damn ring to it, that's for sure.

As I approach the table, Roscoe stands, and I lean in for a kiss. "Sorry I'm late. You won't believe the day I've had."

"It's no problem," he replies. "I ordered you a water."

"Perfect, thanks."

He clears his throat but doesn't say anything as he studies the menu. Roscoe's dark hair is perfectly styled, his suit crisply pressed, as it always is. The man never looks even a little relaxed. Even his pajamas are silk, pressed, and perfectly laid out.

When we first met, it was a running joke that I was going to wreck his perfectly planned life. Instead, I did my best to fit right into it, and here we are.

Ready to be married.

"How was your morning?" he asks, setting his menu aside to focus on me.

That's the other thing about Roscoe. Maybe it's because he's so busy he's rarely able to step away from work, but when I have his attention, I feel like the most important person in the world. "It was insane. I went to the food truck park because my contact said he had something wild to show me."

"Food truck park?" His brows wrinkle in complete confusion, and I do my best to ignore my frustration.

"The story I've been working on for about a month, now? The insane food war?" He continues staring at me as though this is the first time he's hearing about it. I remind myself he's knee-deep in an important case right now, but in the back of my mind, I can't help but think how I'm able to keep up with his work stories just fine. "It started out as super small revenge plots—missing condiments, stuff like that—and it ended in murder."

This piques his interest. Eyebrow arched, he leans into the table. "Murder?"

"Oh yeah, the gumbo guy murdered the hamburger lady because she was sleeping with the taco truck guy who was playing them both."

"The taco guy was engaged in a relationship with both of them?"

I nod. "And the gumbo guy apparently saw them getting after it in the woods last night and was so angry he murdered the hamburger truck lady on her way home."

"Damn."

"And what's even crazier is that he was at the scene this morning. When Steven went to talk to him—"

"Your brother was there?"

"Well, yeah, he's a homicide detective; there was a homicide."

"Huh." Roscoe doesn't further elaborate, but he doesn't need to. He and Steven do not see eye to eye on *anything*. In fact, Steven hates him, and Roscoe has always had a bit of a weird reaction when I go see my family.

"I wasn't sure who else to call."

"Of course, not." Roscoe smiles, but it's forced. "Go on. What happened when he questioned this gumbo man?"

I stare at him a moment before shaking my head. "He just claimed to have thought it was a dream."

"Ahh, going for the insanity angle. I see that all the time."

"Yeah, it looked that way."

"Hello, you two need a few minutes, or do you already know what you want?"

Roscoe beams up at the waitress. "Give us a few minutes, will you?"

"Of course." She turns and sashays away, but Roscoe doesn't pay her any more attention.

"How was your day?" I ask, reaching forward for a breadstick in the basket between us.

"Good." He hisses through his teeth then folds his hands together and rests them on the table. "Listen, Serenity, we need to talk."

My stomach plummets, so I set the breadstick down. His tone, it's all wrong. My mind instantly travels to worst-case scenarios despite my attempt to remain calm. He had a physical last week; did a terrible diagnosis come back? Are his parents okay? I know they've been traveling; did something happen?

Before I can fully spiral, I sit up straighter in my seat and ask, "What is it?"

His gaze flickers away then back to me. "I've been trying to find a way to tell you this, but I..." He trails off and shuts his eyes tightly. After a moment, he opens them again and smiles. "You're a great person, you know that?"

"What the hell are you getting at, Roscoe?" My words carry a bite, I know that much, but the way he's looking at me, the way he's acting, is making me incapable of sounding calm anymore—

"The thing is, I've been working a lot of late nights."

"Yes, I know."

"But I haven't been at the office."

My throat dries, and I clench my hands into fists as my pulse quickens to a roar in my ears. All the while, he keeps talking.

Talking and talking.

"See, I started spending time with Maggie. You know Maggie."

"Your paralegal?" I demand, voice shaky. "The one you swore was just a friend? That Maggie? The same fucking Maggie who you insisted I invite to my bridal shower?" I growl the words, a lump forming in my throat. He can't be serious; this *cannot* be happening.

"Yeah, that's her." His wistful smile has bile rising in my throat. It burns, and I seriously wish it would come up just so I can hurl all over the jerk. "Anyway, Maggie and I really hit it off, and I want to see where things can go with her."

"Hold the fucking phone." I stand up with enough force to knock my chair back; my head spinning as I try to formulate something even mildly adult-like to save the little dignity I have remaining. "You're dumping me for your co-worker?" I all but shout it, and based on his flushed face and the way his eyes travel around the room, he's pissed. Which only throws gasoline on my fire. "A month before our wedding!"

He smiles at a neighboring table then glares back at me, wearing the same fake grin on his face. "Can you please just sit down so we can talk about this?"

"What is there to talk about? You've pretty fucking much said it all!"

His anxious gaze darts right and left as he says, "Language, Serenity, people are watching."

"Good." I lift my glass of water, and before I fully comprehend what I'm doing, he's sputtering and jumping to his feet as liquid drenches his perfectly pressed suit. I spin on my heel, but he reaches forward to wrap a hand around my arm, stopping me before I can get the hell out of here and cry my eyes out. I whirl, my free hand tightened into a fist.

"You're going to want to let me go before I leave you with something a bit more permanent than a wet suit," I warn.

The look in his eyes says he knows I mean it, too. I've been in Brazilian jiu-jitsu since I was thirteen, thanks to my brothers. I've never used it on another person before—not in a situation where I meant to harm—but Roscoe is seriously tempting a girl right now. I could kick his ass all over this restaurant, and we both know it.

He drops his hand, his eyes conveying some attempt at contrition. "I really am sorry things turned out this way."

"No. You're not. Because if you were, you wouldn't have dumped me in a fucking restaurant."

"I am," he repeats. "I also need the…" he trails off, his gaze dropping to my hand and the diamond engagement ring glinting beneath the lights above.

It might as well have been a slap against my cheek. I rip the ring off and throw it at him then rush outside onto the busy street before I have a chance to completely lose it. My heart hammers, my throat so tight I can barely breathe, but somehow, I manage to make it inside a cab.

"You okay, sweetheart?" the driver asks, eyes flicking toward me in the rearview.

"Get me out of here."

Falls Gazette

Chapter Three

A shrill alarm rips me from my drunken sleep. "Motherfuc—" I groan and fumble for my phone as the loudest damn noise in the world pushes my hangover headache into a full-on stabbing migraine. The room spins, and instead of silencing the alarm, I accidentally shove my phone off the nightstand. It clatters to the floor, and I reach for it, not realizing how close I am to the edge of the bed.

"Dammit!" I follow it down, hitting the floor with a heavy thump as I land on the carpet right beside my annoying cell.

Groaning, I silence the beeping then roll over onto my back and squint at the screen. *Dammit.* Somehow, I've already slept through the first four alarms, and if the list of missed calls, text messages, and email alerts are any indication—I've missed more than that.

The sight of so many calls and texts sends reality crashing down around me. Roscoe. The breakup. My drunken after-party to drown my sorrows. The pain has me tossing the phone aside without reading the messages. Eyes still swollen from crying, I reach up and rub the palms of my hands against them.

Words my mother used to say to me pop into my mind, so I take a minute to repeat them. *"You can get upset, Serenity Kellis, and you can get knocked down, but don't you dare stay there. You don't belong on the ground."* With a deep breath, I force myself to sit up. "Okay, Mom," I mutter to my empty apartment.

Time to get my ass up and face the truth. Reaching for the glass of water near the bed, I take a gulp. It burns; I choke and gag.

Not water.

Vodka.

I should have known.

Last night is a blur of shots and rants that I'm pretty sure ended in me sob-singing the lyrics to every Adele song ever until my neighbors showed up, threatening to call the cops. That last part is kind of blurry, so I do what every self-respecting adult would: I pretend it didn't happen.

File deleted.

A stumbling trip to the medicine cabinet yields my last two painkillers, which I down with two gulps of orange juice because, you know, health matters. Then I somehow make it through a shower without throwing up.

My phone rings as I'm getting ready to leave, so I reach over and grab it, cringing at the name that pops onto the screen accompanying a photo of Roscoe and me. "What the hell do you want?" I demand, putting the phone on speaker as I finish pouring hot coffee into a travel mug.

"What happened to you last night?"

"You don't get to ask me those questions anymore," I remind him. "Remember? My favorite pizza place. Glass of water. Ringing any bells?"

He sighs into the phone as tears scald the back of my throat. "Listen, Serenity, I—"

"Did you need something? I'm busy."

"I wanted to check on you. Your brother called me."

Fuck. "Which one?"

"Steven."

"I'm surprised you're still breathing," I retort, tightening the lid.

"I didn't tell him what happened, figured you'd want to handle that."

Coward. "Yeah. Sure. Whatever. That all?"

"I just want to make sure you're okay, I never meant to hu—"

"Goodbye, Roscoe." I end the call before he can finish that placating sentence. Then I grab my keys and head out the door.

Time to face the music. I guess it's a good thing I love to dance.

THE OFFICE IS ALREADY BUSTLING WHEN I STEP OFF THE ELEVATOR. *Why the crap is everyone so loud today?* The constant noise threatens to undo the work of the painkillers, so I pop in my headphones, which serve as a mild barrier. Emphasis on *mild.*

What was I thinking, getting drunk on a work night? Oh yeah, that my fiancé and boyfriend of three years cheated on me with his paralegal and then told me about it in what used to be my favorite restaurant. Can't go back there ever again.

After all that, who can blame me for playing a solo game of "Who sang it better: Sober Adele or Drunk Serenity?"

And then that damned phone call—as if he gets to wonder how I'm doing.

Ugh.

I weave my way through the maze of cubicles and then stop short in front of my own when I see there's already someone waiting inside. My stomach drops to my knees, which actually brings me the closest to vomiting I've been all morning. I swallow —hard—as the person in my space turns to face me.

"Morning, Serenity."

Quincy, my boss and the editor of the paper, smiles at me, but it doesn't quite reach his eyes. Shoving his glasses back up onto his nose, he studies me.

My nausea turns to dread.

Quincy rarely seeks me out directly. Usually, if he needs something, he calls down with a request that I make the trip one floor up to his office. For him to be down here with us, it means something serious is about to go down. And based on the way he's looking at me? I am willing to bet that something is me.

"Quincy," I manage, despite my nerves—and nausea. "What's up?"

"I was going to ask you the same thing," he says. "I heard from a friend on the force there was a homicide yesterday involving the food truck vendors you were assigned to last month. But I didn't see a story come across my desk for this morning's issue."

"Shit," I mutter. Heat rushes to my cheeks as I realize I just cussed—in front of my boss. Lips pursed, he looks none too happy at my slip-up. "I mean, um, yes, I am working on it."

Crossing his arms, he tilts his head to the side. "I'm not sure I understand. We're in the business of printing news as it happens. Or is there some reason you couldn't do that?"

"I had, uh, some new information come to light, and I, uh, needed to verify my source." The lie is pathetic, at best.

His dark gaze hardens. "Well, feel free to send me what you have, and we'll see if we can use it."

He's calling my bluff. I open my mouth to respond then realize he used the word *see*. We'll *see* if we can use it. "Wait, what do you mean 'see?'" I stare at him like maybe I can read between the lines if I look hard enough. "This is a big story. Bigger than prank wars. It's murder. Of course, you'll want to use it."

"Serenity." His placating tone skyrockets my pulse. Ugh. Quincy's not overly nice, but he's reasonable. And it's that reasonable tone that's pushing my buttons right now. "You know as well as I that I can't print breaking news two days late and expect to keep my job. I had to run with what I had. But you're welcome to submit for a follow-up on the accused's charges and trial if you like."

"You had to run… Wait, who got the story?" I ask, my voice rising despite my attempts to keep cool.

"Allison."

He says it like it's the most logical thing in the world. Maybe it is. And hell, Allison's my friend. If it had to go to anyone else, I'm glad it's her, but—

Fuck that. I'm the one who's had her nose to the ground for *years*. I'm the one who's spent all that time building relationships; establishing a source. Me.

"Allison?" I repeat, my voice rising enough to earn a few sidelong looks. "Quincy, this is my damn story. You can't just give it away. Not even to Allison."

"Look, I didn't want to—"

"Oh, I'm sure you didn't," I say. "You could have given me the chance. You could have tried to let me know before sliding the story out from under me."

"I called you five times last night," he says, quietly.

I'm ready to blast him for the lie, but then I remember all the missed calls. The text messages. The ones I assumed were Roscoe—or at least, Roscoe-related—so I ignored them. Under Quincy's expectant gaze, I pull out my phone and check the log. Sure enough, there they are—his five missed calls combined with Allison's dozen. Even a few from Steven. I don't have the dignity left in me to pull up the voice mails he left, but there's one for every call he made.

Motherfucker.

"Listen, Serenity." Quincy's voice drops low, and the change in his tone is enough to make me look up from my phone, a new set of nerves churning in my gut. "Allison told me what happened…at your lunch date yesterday."

My eyes widen in horror as I realize he means my very public, very humiliating breakup. How the hell did she find out about it?

"Your personal life is none of my business, of course, but I want you to know that I don't intend to hold this misstep against you. Your track record here is spotless, and this doesn't have to change that. You're free to continue your current role, but if you need some time off before getting back to work, you're welcome to—"

"My current role?" I repeat, voice shrill as his words finally break the last shred of control I had. "My current role? Are you fucking kidding me? My current role is a joke. Last month, I covered corruption within a homeowners association. And before that, an ordinance blocking a retirement community's rights to construct a she-shed. I was first on the scene of a homicide yesterday. A *homicide*. And I solved it myself. I think that warrants something better than she-sheds."

Quincy doesn't answer right away, and it's at that moment that I realize the entire office has fallen silent around us. Horrified doesn't even begin to describe my disgust as I realize every single person is staring over the tops of their cubicles. Allison stands a few feet away from us, her eyes wide.

"Miss Kellis." The reasonable tone has been replaced by something else. Something very businessy and final. With what little dignity I have left, I redirect my gaze back to Quincy's. "I think it might be best if you take some time."

No emotion.

No temper.

Just a flat order to leave.

Fuck.

"And if I don't?" I ask, defiantly.

Quincy's mouth flattens. "I wish you all the best during your convalescence." He steps aside and stands like a sentry at the opening to my cubicle, his message clear: Get your shit and go.

My gaze flicks around the room one last time, my cheeks heating when I see two tall security guards already headed our way. I have no idea which asshole called them, but it doesn't matter. In no way, shape, or form am I going to allow them to forcibly remove me. I've been mortified enough for three lifetimes already.

I cast a final sweeping glance around my workspace, and my gaze lands on the framed photo of Roscoe and me.

Seeing it there brings a fresh wave of rage over me. He caused all of this. Every miserable moment over the past twenty-four hours. And then had the balls to call and "check up" on me. Tears fill my eyes, but I reach up and wipe them away before they can fall.

With an angry glare, I turn deliberately away from the photograph, leaving my past behind as I march for the door. There's nothing left for me here that I want to take. Before I step out, though, I turn toward my boss. "You're making a mistake, and I'm going to prove it."

Quincy doesn't even bother contradicting me—which I try to pretend is a win—as I head out, flanked by two security guards. But, by the time I'm standing alone on the sidewalk, bathed in the mid-morning sunshine, I realize that I'm lying to myself.

Quincy isn't the one who made the mistake—I am.

I lost it. My career, my fiancé, my pride. All of it.

Falls Gazette

Chapter Four

The scent of roast and potatoes greets me at the door of my parents' two-story Cape Cod. Once a week, rain or shine, devastating breakup or not, I drive out to Connecticut for a family dinner. Basically, it's the only reason I even bother with owning a car anymore—which is still a pain in the ass, considering how much I pay in storage fees.

But my mother would literally write me out of the will and then probably die of heartbreak if I tried to bail. Even the shitshow that is my life right now won't fly as a valid reason to miss it. So, ten hours after getting kicked out of my office, and thirty hours after the worst break-up of my life, I'm here to subject myself to the mind-numbing torture of sibling rivalry and "caring" family interrogation.

As if on cue, the moment I close the door behind me, a scream sounds, and tiny footsteps thunder toward me. A sandy-haired five-year-old wielding a plastic shield rounds the corner. On his heels, a girl a year older brandishes a matching plastic sword.

"Surrender or die, fiend," she yells at her fleeing brother.

"Aunt Ren!" The boy spots me and veers closer.

"Hey, Samuel." I bend down and scoop him into my arms just before his sister can make good on her threat.

"No fair. You can't let the grown-ups save you," she pouts when she reaches us.

"Trust me, I'm the least grown-up grown-up in this house," I tell her.

"Sarah," a familiar baritone calls from the other room.

A second later, my brother Stuart appears. He grins at me then scowls at his kids. "Your mother said no more swords until *after* dinner."

He plucks the sword and the shield from their hands.

"Ugh," Sarah groans. "No fair."

She stalks from the room, and Samuel wiggles out of my arms to follow her.

"Why does he follow her when he knows she's just going to terrorize him again?" Stuart shakes his head as he watches them go.

"Glutton for punishment, I guess."

My tone is slightly too bitter, and Stuart gives me a quizzical look.

"Something you want to tell me about, sis?"

"Nothing," I say innocently.

"Uh-huh. And how is Roscoe tonight?"

Steven. Damned detective brother probably figured it out already.

Before I can answer, another booming male voice calls out, "Serenity's here."

Sawyer rounds the corner with Steven close on his heels. I get hugged and then hugged again as I'm passed from Stuart to Sawyer, and then to Steven. The only one missing is Stone. Apparently, military service is a good enough reason to miss family dinner, although my mom has insisted he Skype in on more than one occasion.

"Is Stone joining us tonight?" I ask, but Steven shakes his head.

"He's on duty and unable to video chat."

"Damn." Sure, I miss the asshole, but mostly, I just wanted the attention off me for tonight.

Steven, way too sharp for his own good, lifts a brow. "You okay?"

"Fine," I say, a little too brightly. "Where are Mom and Dad?"

"Dad's out back with the hellions," Sawyer says, grinning at Stuart, who doesn't bother to contradict the reference to his children. "Mom's finishing up. Come on. I'll make you a drink." He swings an arm around my neck, half-guiding me, half-wrestling me into compliance.

The moment we step into the kitchen, the chaos amps up. More noise, more questions, more people. Just more *everything*. I'm used to it. My family has always been bigger and louder than most. But tonight, thanks to, well, everything, it's a challenge to field the questions being volleyed at warp speed.

"Ser, you look pale. Are you sleeping okay?"

My mother stops stirring the pot on the stove and comes to stir the pot that is my life.

"I'm okay, Mom. Just up late for work," I tell her. It's not technically a lie. After all, I *am* up late most nights for work. Just not last night. Or any night from here on out, it seems.

She hugs me, running a soft hand over my long hair. Then, she lets me go and cups my cheeks before peering closely at my face, "A hot meal with family will help," she says because, in this house, that's the cure for pretty much everything.

"Thanks, Mom." With a smile, I pull away and she returns to the task of prepping dinner for a family as large as ours.

"Here you go, sis." Sawyer hands me a frosted mug with something pink inside, and it only takes one whiff of the vodka-infused cranberry juice to send my stomach into a fit of 'don't you dare give me any more of that shit.'

"Thanks." I force a smile and pretend to take a sip. My brother falls into easy conversation with my mom, so I use his distraction to sneak away toward the hall bathroom where I relieve myself of the drink.

After rinsing the pink liquid down the sink, I slip back out and into my father's office. The moment the door is shut behind me, I breathe in the scent of old books, their pages perfectly cared for despite the decades of use.

But those aren't even my favorite part. No, whenever I'm in this room, I'm always drawn to the walls of old maps—some famous, some nostalgic.

So many places in the world; so many different civilizations. Wanting to travel and tell their stories is what drew me to journalism in the first place.

"I knew I'd find you here."

Steven startles me, but I'm not stupid enough to let myself get cornered, either. After a quick recovery, I lunge for the door.

Unfortunately, he's faster than me and grabs my wrist before I can dart back into the hall. He yanks me back into the room and kicks the door mostly closed.

"What?" I demand at the same time he shushes me.

Satisfied we haven't been heard, he turns back and pins me with a look I know all too well.

"Something's up, Ser. You can tell the rest of them you're tired or fine or whatever, but I know you. Spill it."

I pull my arm out of his grasp, feeling thirteen all over again.

"Ugh. This is stupid, Steven. Mom's going to come looking for us any second. You know she hates when we're late to dinner."

"The sooner you tell me, the sooner we can eat roast and rum cake."

He's positioned himself between me and the only exit in the room. Okay, not true. I could make a run for the window, but I have a feeling he'd catch me before I could make that particular plan work out. Without a hangover, I might stand a chance. But not with my limbs still feeling like lead.

I sigh. Heavily. That way he'll know he's being a nosy jerk.

"Fine. But you can't tell the others."

"Circle of trust," he says, using the phrase we used as kids.

"If you must know, Roscoe and I broke up."

His eyes register just the barest hint of pleasure. "I see. And is there any particular reason?"

"He cheated on me," I blurt—mostly because ripping off the Band-Aid now will keep him from cornering me a second time.

At my words, Steven's masked expression slips toward something more sinister. "You're fucking joking." His voice drops to a baritone I've only ever heard him use to threaten criminals. "Tell me you're fucking joking, Ser, because I will hunt that fucker down right now and—"

"Be my guest," I say, darkly. "You'll probably find him at Maggie's house doing a sex position I like to call 'she's only my paralegal, you're being paranoid.'"

Steven's gaze sharpens as he studies me. "You're being sarcastic. You're only sarcastic when things are really bad. What else happened?"

"What do you mean 'what else?' Isn't being cheated on by my fiancé enough?"

"Sure it is, but I know you. What else?" he repeats.

Steven has an uncanny way of seeing the shit I try to hide. Normally, I appreciate how well he understands me, but right now, it's pissing me off. This is what I get for role-playing as a criminal and letting him interrogate me all through high school.

"I might have had a…situation at work this morning."

His eyes narrow even further. At this point, they're barely even open. "'A situation.'"

I roll my eyes. "You're doing that repeating thing, again."

"What kind of situation?"

"The kind where I lost my shit and went off on my boss and then was escorted from the building."

His eyes widen, and his mouth falls open.

"Why do you look more surprised about that than about Roscoe?" I hold up my hand. "No, you know what? Don't answer that. You've always hated him."

"True, but now I am vindicated in my hate." He flashes a grin before turning serious again. "Ser, you never go off on people. It's hard to imagine, honestly."

I glare at him, feeling strangely defensive. "I go off," I say haughtily. His skeptical expression only makes it worse. "Fine, maybe I've been holding some stuff in."

"What is she holding in?"

The door creaks open, and my mom sticks her head in.

"Serenity went off on her boss," Steven says.

I groan. "What happened to the 'circle of trust?'"

He shrugs. "At least, I didn't tell her about the other thing."

My mom pushes inside. "What other thing?" she asks, instant concern transforming her soft features.

I throw my hands up. "Invite the whole family, why don't we?"

"What about the family?"

Stuart pushes in behind my mom, and my dad is close at his heels. They all shove forward until I'm forced to move back and give them space to enter. Sawyer hovers in the doorway with a serving of rum cake on a small plate in his hand.

"What's wrong with Serenity, now?" he asks.

My mother whirls on him. "Sawyer David, you had better put that back. No dessert before dinner."

He pauses and sets his fork down until she turns back to me;

then the bastard sneaks the bite into his mouth anyway and offers me a grin. His way of thanking me for keeping the heat off him.

"Oh, we're not bringing the little ones, too?" I ask, sarcasm dripping.

Stuart shrugs. "They're eating already," he says, as if that's the only valid reason for not inviting them to join us.

I glare at them all. Freaking traitors.

"What's the other thing?" my mother repeats into the silence.

She looks at Steven. Then me.

Steven hesitates, but I'm over it. "I went off on my boss this morning because he gave my front-page story to someone else."

"Well, that wasn't very nice of him." My mother frowns.

"Why'd Quincy do that?" Stuart asks. He met my boss one time at a Christmas party last year and has been on a first-name basis with him ever since. "You said he was a decent guy."

"Because I got drunk last night and didn't turn it in on time."

Steven shakes his head.

"Sweetheart," my dad begins in his lecture voice.

Oh, hell no, I am not here for that.

"Roscoe cheated on me with his paralegal," I announce. "There. It's all out in the open. I'm single, stupid, and jobless."

"They fired you?" Sawyer sounds heated, now. He's always ready to fight, though I can't help but notice he's way more pissed over me losing a job than a fiancé. "Over one damn story?"

"I'm on a leave of absence," I say. "Indefinitely."

No one speaks for a long moment.

I can feel them all staring at me, and while being the baby of the family—and the only girl—has always come with a certain amount of extra attention, this is torture.

My mother takes a step forward, and I know instinctively she's going to hug me. I also know if she does that, I'll definitely lose it.

Growing up with four brothers, you get very prickly about crying in front of them.

My stomach rolls, and I press my hand to it, swallowing hard.

"I think I'm going to be sick."

This time, when I flee the room, Steven moves aside and lets me go. I race to the bathroom, fling myself inside, and slam the door. I take deep breaths, dragging the air into my lungs slowly as I lean over the sink. Shutting my eyes doesn't help. Behind closed lids, all I see is my failure of a life. Instead, I open them again and stare into the mirror. The red-faced girl with bloodshot eyes who stares back at me is a stranger. A sad shadow of the woman I know I am. Or would have been, if Roscoe hadn't decided to dip his wick into another…ugh, how does that metaphor go again?

There's a soft knock on the door, and the knob turns. I back up as my mother cracks the door. "Sweetie, you all right?"

She looks worried.

And I hate that.

"I'm okay," I say, wiping the stray tears on my cheeks.

She slips into the room then holds out her arms, and I let her hug me. A few more tears are shed. Maybe on both sides. My mom's a crier. She keeps tissues beside the couch for pet commercials.

"You know what you need?" she says, and she so clearly wants to help, I don't cut her off like I would if Steven tried to say those words.

"What?" I ask.

"A vacation." I frown, ready to argue. She grips my shoulders. "I'm serious, Ser. You never do anything for yourself. Maybe now's the time. Get away for a while. Recharge." She leans in and says, "Maybe even have a fling. Forget Roscoe. He's a fool."

"Mom," I protest, but she continues to insist.

"I think that sounds like a great idea!" Stuart calls from the hall.

"Second!" Sawyer hollers.

"Stone and I agree!" Steven adds. When my mother opens the door all the way, my eldest brother holds up his phone and shows me a text thread full of expletives.

It honestly makes my heart swell. They may be assholes, but they're my assholes. And having them at my back is all I need right now to start feeling mildly human again.

"A vacation," I say with conviction. "I could probably manage that."

"Great. Now, Ser is on the mend, my stomach is not. Can we eat?"

Steven clasps Sawyer on the back. "What, that piece of rum cake didn't fill you up?" Stuart snickers and falls into step behind Steven as they move toward the kitchen, my mother following as she fusses about dessert before dinner.

Sawyer falls into step beside me. "Listen, if you want a wingman, I'm always up for some vacation."

"No, thanks. I don't think a girl should use her own brother as a wingman for a rebound fling."

He feigns sadness, but the moment he's in sight of the food, he claps his hands together, and suddenly Serenity's heartbroken, drunken outburst is forgotten over the great flavors of roast, potatoes, and conversation.

THE DRIVE BACK TO THE CITY IS SHORT AND FAMILIAR ENOUGH IT sends my thoughts wandering back to the idea of a vacation. I've never actually taken one alone, but the idea of getting away, of not having to talk to another person unless I want to—it's far more appealing than it should be. Normally, I'd ask Allison to join me. We spent last Memorial Day in the Bahamas, and it was such a blast. But after what happened with my story, I can't bring myself to forgive her just yet. Even if it was my dumb-ass fault in the first place.

I pull into my spot and am just reaching for the Tupperware full of leftovers my mother sent me home with when my phone rings.

Groaning, I honestly debate answering it, especially after I pull it from my purse and see Allison's name flashing on the front. But since I know, deep down, this is just as much on me as it is her, begrudgingly, I answer. "Hello?"

"I am so sorry, please don't hate me."

Her words make me smile. "I don't hate you, Allison."

She lets out a heavy breath. "I'm so sorry," she repeats. "I drove to your apartment last night and used my key, but you were passed clean out. You mentioned something about Roscoe, so I called him."

Which explains how she could tell Quincy. "I'm sure he had a lot to say."

"Not much. Just that you two were over. He didn't give me details, and I wouldn't have told Quincy except he thought you were slacking. I was trying to save your job. Ser, you're my best friend."

Guilt crashes down on me for how angry I've been. "I appreciate it, Allison. Truly. I'm sorry I put you in that position, to begin with."

"You didn't put me anywhere."

"I did, and while I hate that my one chance at a front-page story got tanked by a drunken night, I'm glad you got it."

"That makes one of us," she grumbles. "What happened with Roscoe?"

"He slept with his paralegal," I tell her.

"Mother-fucking-son-of-an-ass-face-bitch. Want me to kill him? I'll do it, and they'll *never* find the body."

Chuckling, I pull the Tupperware container into my lap. "It really is okay…probably for the better."

"Want me to go with you to Quincy's office? We can get your job back. I'll threaten to quit, too. We can run away together, head to Mexico."

I can't help the sniffle that slips out at her words. "I love you, bitch."

"Not as much as I love you. Seriously, Ser, anything you need."

"Actually, maybe you can swing by and water my plants once a week for a while? I'm going to take a vacation."

"A vacation?" She sounds way too happy, which means she's been more worried about me than she let on. "Where are you going? Seriously? Can I come?"

"As much as I'd love that, I just need time," I tell her. "A break. I'm not sure where yet, but I'll let you know as soon as I figure it out. Probably won't be far."

"Better not be Mexico," she says. "That's for us."

I laugh. "It won't be Mexico, promise. Anyway, I'm home now, and Steven made me promise not to talk on the phone in a parking garage, so I need to let you go."

"Okay, but call me if you need anything. Drinks? Co-murderer? Anything, Ser."

"I've had enough drinks for a lifetime, and as of now, I don't need a co-murderer. But you'll be the first I call if I do."

"You better. Night."

"Night." I end the call and shove the phone into my purse before climbing out and heading for the elevator that will carry me up.

At the door to my apartment, I stop. A manila envelope sticks out from the door-jam where someone's wedged it in tight. It has no stamp. No return address. Just *Serenity Kellis* written in black Sharpie across the front.

I glance up and down the hall, but it's empty and silent.

What the hell?

Curious, I let myself into my apartment and rip into the envelope. Half-expecting a note from Mallse threatening to off me for pointing the finger at him, I pull out the contents and frown in confusion.

Newspaper clippings flutter into my hands. A couple fall to the floor, and I bend down, scanning them for some kind of context. Several obituaries are piled in with articles boasting "Unsolved Murder" headlines. Some of them date back years. Intrigued, I scan them more closely. None of the names are familiar to me. But there's a strange link between them all, I notice. Every one of them was killed on the same day, in the same town. According to what I can piece together, once a year, a body shows up. No one knows why.

My journalist adrenaline kicks in, and I check the envelope for a note or some clue as to who sent this. And why the hell they chose me to send it to. But there's nothing. Just the clippings. And a string of mysterious murders all committed in some town I've never heard of.

Midnight Falls, Virginia.

If that doesn't sound like the cutest, most murdery town ever, I don't know what is.

And the fact that some anonymous person left me these very unsolved, very intriguing murder write-ups should maybe creep me out.

But after another scan of the articles, I don't even second-guess myself; I just decide.

This is where I'll go.

Forget some boring resort on a beach somewhere. This town has everything I need to decompress and do something just crazy enough that will get me my job back—and not just the job I had, but the one I actually want. It checks both boxes. Satisfies my family and my need to redeem myself with Quincy.

I'll drive down, solve these murders, and restore my career to heights that Quincy won't be able to refute. No more back corner cubicle. Or back page columnist.

Front and center. Serenity Kellis: homicide reporter. Investigative journalist. Confident. Capable. Way too badass to ever be cheated on again.

Roscoe who?

Falls Gazette

Chapter Five

Peering over the steering wheel like I'm sixteen and just learning to drive, I make a right onto the main street that, according to my GPS, slices right through downtown Midnight Falls, Virginia. Brick storefronts line both sides of the narrow, two-lane thoroughfare, and I have to admit, when you look past the historical "creepy" aesthetic, they're adorable. I'm half tempted to stop and browse through a few shops, but then I notice nearly all of them boast *Closed* signs in their dust-covered windows.

I check the clock and note that it's barely five in the afternoon. Weird for New York, for sure, but I guess it's not so strange when you consider that the town is situated in literally the middle of nowhere and is surrounded on all sides by dense forest. I can't imagine business would be that busy on a weeknight all the way out here.

I drive farther, and yep, the place definitely has a weird, horror movie vibe, but I'm pretty damn sure a good portion of that is due to the reason I'm here in the first place. After all, a small town chock full of unsolved murders sure doesn't lead to a feel-good moment upon arrival, even if those murders are my ticket to the good life.

"In four-hundred feet, turn left. Then, your destination is on your right." I do as the bossy GPS instructs, turning right beside what appears to be an old church. Just outside the church doors, at least half a dozen people turn and stare at me, their interested expressions quickly morphing into something akin to nervousness when I make eye contact. Services on a Thursday evening?

More weirdness...great. "It's all in your head, Ser," I remind myself.

My phone rings, and I jump then curse myself as I use one hand to put my earbud in. "Hello?"

"You there yet?"

"Almost."

Steven grunts. "Then why the hell are you answering your phone? I know that dinosaur you drive doesn't have Bluetooth."

"Okay, first of all, you shouldn't have called me if you didn't want me to answer. Second, using headphones. And third, don't you dare insult Diamond. She's taken me a hell of a lot more places in the last ten years than your half a dozen or so new cars in that same timeframe have."

"That's because I trade them in before they can fail me. It's called leasing."

"Yeah, okay. Whatever you need to tell yourself. But I don't have to lease or trade anything in once every couple of years."

"And you have hand-crank windows and an AC unit that barely works." The car argument is nothing new between us. Steven is always pointing out that the one time it breaks down is going to be the time I'm captured by a murderer on the side of the road, and then the next thing we know, he's having to fish my body out of a lake.

Being a detective has definitely made him dramatic.

"Did you need something? Or is this a 'let's shit on Serenity while she's down' phone call?"

"Neither. Just calling to let you know my captain gave you credit in the press conference today."

"What?" My stomach churns with nerves as I realize what that could mean for my career. Of course, less than a heartbeat later, I'm remembering that I don't currently *have* a career. "That was nice of him."

I can't bring myself to ask whether Quincy assigned Allison to the press conference or not.

"Quincy will take you back whenever you want; we'll see to it."

"I am fine, Steven. Soon, I'll have everything I need to claim that top spot, and not even the editor at the *New York Times* will be able to stop me."

He doesn't reply right away, but he doesn't need to. I know Steven Kellis well enough to know that he's choosing his next words very, very carefully.

"*In one-hundred and fifty feet, turn left. Then, your destination is on your right,*" the robotic voice announces through my earbud. I see my turn just ahead, so I flick on my blinker as Steven sighs.

"Just be careful, Serenity. I'm sure the local police there have done all they can to solve those cases. Don't get yourself in too deep."

He's the only one I told about my mission. Mainly because I needed his inside information on the victims, and the jerk refused to give it to me until I told him exactly why. Not that he'd had much to give me, anyway. The fact that almost no information exists on these victims only adds to the allure, if I'm honest.

"I promise, I will be fine." I pull up to an iron gate held open permanently by overgrown vines. As I pass through them, Steven's voice cuts out then back in. "I'm losing service."

"Ca– e– ater," is all that comes through before the line dies.

After tossing my headphones into the passenger-side seat, I gape up at the huge Victorian house situated in the middle of a grassy yard. Snow-white siding is complemented gorgeously with bright red shutters and a matching front door. Elegant filigree decorates the porch overhang, giving the place an old-world feel, even as the brightly colored garden gnomes situated in the sprawling flower beds modernize the place.

It's completely stunning, and I can't help but smile to myself in spite of it all. I shift my car back into *first* and start down the short drive, stopping just before the house in one of the labeled guest spots. The moment I'm parked, my engine safely turned off, I jump out of the car to take in the house and the grounds in all their glory. Moving quickly out of pure excitement, I make my way around the back of the house. *More trees.*

I note the perfectly manicured garden that flows out to meet the woods bordering the property. Benches, marble statues, and a fountain catch my eye, but it's nothing compared to the beautiful rose bushes and wisteria climbing over trellises in a bid to take over everything in its path.

It's secluded.

Quiet.

And absolutely perfect.

The crunching of leaves draws my attention to my left as a shiver of awareness washes over me. I find myself scanning the thick woods beyond the yard, though I don't know what I'm looking for. All the hairs on the back of my neck stand on end, and I'm suddenly very, *very* aware that someone is watching me. Or maybe some*thing*.

Goosebumps flare to life along my arms, and I instinctively reach out and rub them, trying to ease the heaviness settling in my gut.

Something moves just inside the tree line as I take a cautious step toward it. Even though I should know better than to move toward an unknown animal, I keep going. Like some force outside myself is pulling me in. Just inside the trees, I stop. My breath catches. A scent remains suspended in the air—unfamiliar and inherently dangerous. How do I know that? Who knows, but the hairs on the back of my neck stand on end, and I've never been one to ignore my gut.

A gut that is, in this moment, telling me I should be heading back toward the bed and breakfast behind me. As I'm about to do just that, movement catches my eye. A figure—too large to be anything but human—emerges from behind a tree.

Oh. My. Masculine. The man is nearly naked, his broad chest streaked with dirt and crimson. His face is obscured in shadow, except for impossibly bright eyes. I swallow hard, meeting a gaze that somehow appears more animal than man.

His eyes are so bright they're nearly yellow, and I'm helpless to look away. Slowly, his lips pull back to reveal teeth that glint even in the shaded light.

He looks ferocious. Animalistic. So why the hell am I not running?

Then he opens his mouth and lets loose a growl as piercing as if he'd fired a gun. I swallow hard, a shiver ripping through me, then slowly back away until there's enough space between us that I'm confident I can make it to safety.

As soon as he disappears back into the trees, I scramble back, nearly tripping over my own feet as I sprint for the yard behind me. It's stupid to think the open landscape will save me, but I can't help the thought that the man—or better yet, creature—behind won't follow me out into the sunshine.

Someone—or something—like that knows better than to venture into the light of day. Right?

Sure enough, when I make it back to the edge of the garden and turn around, he's gone.

Not a single trace remains.

In the normalcy of the silence, I wonder if I imagined the entire thing. This town is definitely creepy enough to have my imagination playing tricks on me. And an overactive imagination is certainly more explainable than a sexy man-beast lurking in the woods.

"Hello?"

"Shit!" I jump and spin, fists raised, knees bent. The woman behind me isn't even a little bothered by my clear fight response. She simply smiles, lines on either side of her dark eyes crinkling in response.

"Serenity Kellis?" she repeats.

"Yes. Sorry." I straighten, letting the fight drain out of me. "Thought I saw something."

Her gaze moves past my shoulder before returning to mine. "Ahh, yes, that happens quite often. We have a lot of wolves in these parts. Just don't go into the woods alone, and you'll be fine." She winks, and I realize just how screwed up I am, because despite her warning, I want—desperately—to go into the woods and see for myself.

Mainly because what I just saw was *not* a wolf. Although, the predator in that man was very, very real.

"Got it."

"I'm Yvette Abbett. You must be Serenity."

"Yes, hi."

"If you'll grab your bags, I'm more than happy to show you to your room."

"That would be great, thanks." Together, we move back toward my car, but my thoughts are still stuck on the way I felt staring at the nearly naked stranger. Clearing my throat, I open the back passenger door and retrieve the suitcase on the light-brown leather seat. "I'm so glad you guys had an opening."

Yvette is an imposing figure walking beside me. I always thought I was on the tall side for a woman, but this lady has me beat by at least six inches. And the dark hair on top of her head adds at least another two. "Oh, most definitely. We don't get many visitors here in Midnight Falls."

Can't imagine why. Unsolved murders, creepy townspeople, wolves and man-beasts in the woods. What's not to love? "It's beautiful here."

She smiles softly, as though her mind is a million miles away. "I honestly can't imagine anywhere I'd rather be."

I follow her up the steps and into the house. The walls are made of dark walnut shiplap, while the focal point behind the receptionist's desk is covered floor-to-ceiling in blood-red wallpaper. There are no pictures on the walls, just a few tapestries boasting wolves either howling or curled up asleep beneath a massive tree.

Whoever owns the place has a serious fascination. "Those are interesting."

She glances over at the tapestries then back to the guest book. "A local woman makes them. She runs the tailor shop in town. If you're ever in need of a dress, that's where you'll want to go."

Not really sure why I'd need a handmade dress out here in the middle of nowhere, but I smile and nod just the same.

"Oh, crud. The keys are in the back." She smiles up at me. "Give me just a second."

"No problem."

The moment she's out of the room, I hear loud chatter and heavy footsteps on the stairs.

"Lance, look! There's another guest here!"

Turning, I meet the wide smile of a woman who looks like she stepped straight out of a hiking catalog. A yellow puffy vest covers a black, long-sleeved turtleneck. Her dark leggings are complemented by thick socks sticking out of the top of a pair of new-looking mountain boots. The man is wearing almost the exact same thing, except he's wearing dark jeans. Both of them are perfectly groomed, and I can't help but get the feeling that while they're wearing all the right clothes, they've never actually hiked a day in their lives.

"Hi," I greet awkwardly.

"Oh my gosh! I love your shirt! Where did you get it? Isn't it adorable, Lance?" She all but jumps down the rest of the stairs, not even bothering to pause long enough for me to answer any of her questions. "How far did you drive? Are you here for the long weekend?"

"Victoria," the man chuckles. "Let's let her get checked in before you hit her with the interview."

She laughs and smiles at me. "When I get back, I'd love to sit and chat! Dinner's at seven. See you then."

The woman doesn't even bother waiting for me to respond before she's bounding out into the chilly air with the man right beside her. And here I'm left, trying to figure out exactly what the hell just happened and how I managed to get roped into a dinner date with two complete strangers.

"Here we go."

My eyes linger on the door a bit longer before turning back toward my hostess. "How many other guests are here?"

"Two. They're our regulars," she says, with a knowing grin. "Victoria is a lot at first, but you get used to her. Will we be charging the card on file?"

"Yes, please."

"If you'll just sign here, I can deliver a copy of your bill to your room when it's ready," she informs me.

My eyes catch on the title underneath Yvette's name on the bill she slides my way. "You're the owner, not just the manager?"

"Owner. Manager. Housekeeper. Chef…my list of titles goes on and on."

Heat rushes to my cheeks. "I'm sorry, back in the city, any of the B&B's I've been to are owned by someone else."

"We take pride in doing our own work here in Midnight Falls." She winks and slides a key across the countertop. "Will you need one key or two?"

"Oh," I say, startled at the suggestion. And my heart sinks. "Just one."

"If you take the steps straight up, then turn left, your room is the second door on the right."

My fingers close around the key, but before I can pull my hand away, her own lands on mine. "Remember what I said about the wolves, dear." Pupils dilated, she holds my gaze.

"I will. Thanks." It takes some effort, but I manage to get my hand away, and as quickly as I can without seeming suspicious, I rush up the stairs.

At the top, I pause to catch my breath and decide whether or not Yvette was being concerned or actually crazy-pants. I land on her being concerned because nothing else makes logical sense, and then I distract myself with a quick look around. Again, pictures of wolves line the wooden walls, and I see the wolf motif continues to be a decor staple around here.

My room is easy enough to find and decorated nearly as sparsely as the hallway. In here, there are no tapestries, no photographs, nothing. Just a large bed boasting a blood-red comforter, a dresser with a mirror, and a door that, after inspection, I discover leads to a connected bathroom with a clawfoot tub. No shower, no hairdryer, nothing so far as a soap dish to hold the wrapped bar of soap on the countertop.

"Clearly minimalists," I say to myself as I head back into the room to begin unpacking.

But before I can make it to the bed, my eyes are once again drawn to the tree line just outside. I move closer to the window, that feeling of being watched overtaking me again. Once I reach the window, I grip the bottom and slide the paned glass up. Fresh air fills my lungs as I watch the tree line, looking for anything out of the ordinary.

Any movement, shadows that shouldn't be there—anything that would allude to someone watching me.

But there's nothing.

My phone dings, drawing my attention to the inbox I haven't checked since Quincy tossed me out like rotten produce.

Allison.

SER, SINCE YOU REFUSED TO RUN AWAY TO MEXICO WITH ME AND insisted on some small-town B&B retreat, I wanted to tell you again how much I miss you.

Also, I may or may not have accidentally—allegedly—ran into and spilled my coffee all over para-whore for stealing Roscoe, even though I still maintain the stance that you came out on the better end of that deal.

Anyway, I love you. Here is a copy of the story just in case you want to read it. If you don't, I totally understand, but I wanted you to see it.

Love your face,
Allison.

. . .

Just below her name is the article she wrote, and while I honestly don't want to look at it, my gaze is already dropping down over the information before I can help it.

Well written, engaging, informative—exactly what all of Allison's pieces are, even though Quincy rarely gives her anything good. Not much you can do with who's screwing who in the celebrity world.

Spoiler: Most of them are screwing each other.

I continue reading, loving the way she set it up, and then, there, at the bottom, is a single line that I re-read three times over, my heart heavy with guilt that I was ever mad in the first place.

Written by Allison Marquee, story by Serenity Kellis.

Anger deflating like a popped balloon, I stare down at the byline. I know it's my fault that I lost out on the story. After all, I'm the one that went and got hammered. I'm the one who slept through my alarm. And, I'm the one who went off on her boss when confronted.

I plop down onto the bed and hit reply. The cursor blinks, taunting me as I try to decide what to say. We'd already worked things out on the phone call, but this was her way of reaching out a second time; of solidifying that we're okay.

So, I take a deep breath and reply.

First of all—allegedly—thank you. Second, that is a fantastic story, and I am really, really glad you got it. I just checked into the B&B, and there's limited service, so I'll be in touch. In the meantime, give 'em hell.

Love you,

Ser

. . .

It whooshes off, so I send another to Steven, something just to let him know I wasn't murdered and I'd be in touch soon.

Then, I push to my feet and stare down at my suitcase lying open on the bed.

With one final glance out the window, I decide unpacking will have to wait. After all, I smell a story, and I'm dying to get started.

Falls Gazette

Chapter Six

Midnight Falls is the kind of town you might put on a postcard. A very old, maybe haunted sort of postcard that is yellowed at the edges and probably never got sent in the first place. Its main street is roughly the length of two New York City blocks, and by the time I've done a lap down and back, I am certain that, in its day, this town was beautiful. Unfortunately, today is not that day, and what I'm left with—some one hundred and seventy-five years later—is a crumbling, withering, in-desperate-need-of-new-paint facade that is both charming and spooky. Every shop I pass is clearly locally owned, and I'm sort of taken by the fact that there isn't a Walmart in sight. Then again, there's no Starbucks, either.

Luckily, Bean There Coffee has a killer latte, and I decide that alone deserves an extra point for this place. Coffee in hand, I do a second lap, browsing more slowly now that I have the lay of the land. Pedestrians give me a wide berth, and I don't miss the strange, startled looks I get from more than one of the residents I pass.

Apparently, Yvette was right, and this place doesn't get many visitors. Could be the fact that nothing in this small town has been updated since the invention of the computer—but hey, what do I know?

Earning yet another nosy stare—this one from a woman who doesn't bother to lower her voice when she points to me and asks her friend, "Who is that?"—I increase my pace and duck into the next shop. The scent of lemon and vanilla immediately pulls me in. The combination brisk yet inviting.

Scanning the shop's interior, I see rows of clothing. Nondescript fabric in all colors and prints. Wandering closer, I realize it's not clothing at all, but uncut fabric. The counter at the back runs half the width of the store. In the other corner is a tri-fold mirror with a raised platform that looks like a fitting area.

Before I can figure out which century I've stumbled into, a woman emerges from the narrow doorway behind the register in the kind of dress I've only ever seen in cosplay and costume-wear. A full skirt swishes around her ankles, and the bodice is—well, the fact that I can only describe it as a bodice tells you everything you need to know. Her black hair is pinned into a functional bun at the nape of her neck, and her milky skin shines like she's shooting a beauty cream commercial. Her slender, petite frame is at odds with the forwardness of her stare, but a second later, she smiles, and it transforms her expression from guarded to welcoming.

"Hello," she says, her soft tone yet another contrast to my original impression. "You must be Serenity."

I blink. "I… How did you know?"

She chuckles. "You'll find word travels fast in a town like ours."

"Ahh, yes, I can see from the looks I've been getting," I say, wryly.

"Forgive them. We don't get many visitors. And we tend to be very tight-knit. Folks mean no harm. I'm Audrey. Welcome to A Stitch in Time. Are you finding everything okay?"

"Audrey," I say, as realization dawns. "Yvette mentioned you. Said I should check out your shop."

Her expression brightens further. "Are you in need of something special?"

"Oh, no," I say quickly. "I'm just browsing. Getting to know my way around. The town is very unique."

Audrey arches an eyebrow in response, and her expression tells me she knows exactly what her town is. And isn't. "Midnight Falls has a rich history," she says, simply.

Bingo. Exactly the opening I'm hoping for.

"Yes, I wonder if you can tell me about that history," I say. "I heard about the unfortunate death last year. A Mr. Kincaid, I believe. Was he a friend of yours?"

Something flickers in Audrey's dark eyes. It doesn't look welcoming or warm, but it's gone so fast that I can't be sure.

"Howard was a gentle man," she says, wistfully. "His death was a loss for us all."

"I wonder—I mean, the article I read doesn't say much about how he died. Only that the coroner ruled it a murder. Do you know anything about it?"

"No, I'm sorry," she says, and there's a flat note to her voice that suggests the conversation is over. "Can I interest you in something specific?" She gestures to the fabrics around us. "Maybe something to match those gorgeous blue eyes?"

Her eyes have hardened, her jaw tight—both shifts that tell me I came on way too strong. *Shit.* "No, thank you," I say.

She takes a step toward me, and a chill runs up my spine. There's something about her, something almost unwelcoming now. "Are you sure, Serenity? A woman's wardrobe is an expression of her true self."

"I'm sure, thank you." Forcing a smile, I back toward the door. "If that changes, this is the first place I'll come." I turn quickly and push open the door, one foot on the street, one in the shop. "Thanks again!"

"Enjoy your time here," she calls out. "It's like nowhere else you've been."

"That was awkward, at best," I mutter to myself as I physically shake the unease from my body.

As soon as my nerves are calm again, I begin walking as I try to decipher Audrey's reaction to my questions. It's clear she didn't like me poking into the murder last year, but then no one I've encountered seems overtly friendly toward an outsider. Plus, she'd seemed like she'd known the man, so it's entirely possible—plausible, even—that talking about him was painful.

Then, a lightbulb goes off, and I realize there's one place I can go where the mission is to ask and answer questions.

My phone's GPS signal is weak as hell, but after a few toe-tapping minutes of more strange looks from passersby, I manage to locate what I'm looking for. The *Midnight Falls Gazette* sits on a corner where the main thoroughfare intersects with a residential side street.

Just past the non-descript entry, Victorian townhomes line a narrow street with leaves scraping and dancing along the empty asphalt. Beyond that, woods press in upon the town's limits. Even though my investigative nature has me longing to know what's beyond those trees, I don't let my eyes linger there. Not after the strange encounter I had earlier. Right now, I need to focus on what I came to do.

Pushing my way inside, I'm greeted by a blast of warm air and a well-lit lobby with a few chairs lining the far wall and a large desk taking up nearly the entire right side of the room. It's piled high with stacks of papers that all look one light breeze away from toppling over. Well, all except the tallest stack, which has a dusty laptop holding it down.

"Can I help you?"

I turn toward the throaty voice and spot a woman not much older than me striding through a doorway leading from the back offices. Her silver hair is cut and spiked in an adorable pixie style that frames hardened brown eyes. Her dark jeans are paired perfectly with a crimson leather jacket and boots that nearly reach her knees. What the hell is someone with such a New York vibe doing in a place like this?

"Hi," I say, feeling immediately more at ease than anywhere else I've been. "I'm Serenity Kellis."

"Ah, so you're the famous columnist from the big city. Cara Anderson, Editor-in-chief."

She offers her hand in a firm shake.

I take it, tilting my head. "Is there anyone in this town who hasn't already heard my life story?"

She laughs. "Not likely. News travels fast around here."

"I keep hearing that phrase, and it sounds worse every time."

"It's not as bad as you'd think. The truth is, Yvette has been talking about your arrival since the moment your reservation came through. Oh, did I say 'talking?' I meant bragging." She grins at my expression, adding, "It's not often we get a noteworthy journalist passing through."

"I don't know about 'noteworthy,'" I say, doing my best to hide my grimace. If only she knew.

But Cara just shrugs. "You have *New York Times* on your resume. That makes you noteworthy around here." She gestures to a coffeepot. "Want any?"

"No, thanks." I hold up my nearly empty latte, mostly to avoid the coffee that, even from here, smells like burnt rubber.

Cara shrugs. "Don't mind if I do."

As she pours herself a cup, I try to figure out how to ask my questions without scaring her off like I did Audrey. It'll do me no good to piss off the entire town before I have a chance to get to the bottom of why I'm here.

"So," she says, turning around and taking a sip of the foul-smelling liquid—black. Ugh. She's definitely tougher than me. "What brings a seasoned reporter to our neck of the woods, anyway? Is it business or pleasure?"

"A little of both," I say, uncertainly.

Cara's eyes light up as she senses a story. "Oh? Do tell."

My eyes widen. "Oh, wait, no. It's not that kind of pleasure," I say.

"Too bad." She slumps back against the desk. "I could use a good sexcapade, even if it came second-hand." She sighs. "This town is dried up, if you know what I mean. The only good sweat I work up is from running down to the falls and back."

I find myself fighting a smile. Cara's fun. And likable. Here's hoping I don't drive her away with my nosy questions.

"Actually, I came here as part of a personal interest," I say. "I came across some articles you published." I take out a couple of the news clippings I brought, and Cara's eyes zero in on them. "I read about the Howard Kincaid murder last fall. Do you know anything else about it besides what you printed at the time?"

Her eyes narrow, her brows knitting together, but it's not irritation so much as concern.

"Where did you say you found those?" she asks.

"Uh, just sort of stumbled on them."

She sighs. "Listen, I get it. That story is probably an investigative journalist's wet dream. But take it from me, it's not a rabbit hole you want to dive into."

My brow lifts. "You realize that kind of warning only makes it sound juicier, right?"

"Okay, how about this warning: Others have come before you, and none of them are around to tell you about what they found."

"Nope. Still juicy," I say, and Cara shakes her head. "What do you mean they aren't around?" I ask, her words slowly registering. "Like, they left town or…"

"Who knows," she says—but there's an edge in her voice now. Like she does know. And she also knows telling me about it will only make me dig in more. "The truth is, I did everything I could with that case, but I couldn't find a single thread to pull on. So, I printed what I knew—which is a sad sack of nothing, as you can see —and moved on."

"But, the other murders… Didn't you wonder if they're connected? And how?"

"Sure, I wondered. And, like I said, I looked, too. But I can't pay bills on wild goose chases." She cocked her head at me. "Can you?"

Falls Gazette

Chapter Seven

As I retrace my steps through town, Cara's words ring in my head, triggering a mental replay of the moment Quincy tossed me out. My last words to him echo in my ears. *You're making a mistake.* Yeah, right. Or maybe I'm the one making a mistake by coming here or even thinking I could solve cold cases like it's nothing. This isn't some food truck war gone wrong. And Quincy made it clear the best news is always what's breaking in the moment, anyway. Not some stale, small-town murder gone cold. Ugh. I shove the memory out again, determined to stop replaying that moment no matter what it takes.

Back at the inn, I manage to bypass Yvette and any other guests by creeping up to my room like some kind of burglar. Tossing my clothes out of my suitcase, I slip into a sports bra and a pair of shorts then take a seat on the edge of the bed to tie the laces of my running shoes.

In the city, running was the one thing that could always clear my head. Well, that and a good fight with one of my brothers. But since they aren't exactly available as a punching bag, I slink back down the stairs and slip out the back door. According to the map I bought, the falls are just on the other side of these spooky as hell woods behind Yvette's. And if Cara can do it, so can I. Besides, I'm pretty sure what I saw was nothing more than a hiker in serious need of a shower.

I've faced way worse on the streets of New York.

After some quick stretching, I shove my earbuds in and crank my girl Bishop Briggs for courage. Then, I head into the trees.

The trail is easy to find, and once my eyes adjust to the shadowy light, it's surprisingly calm and peaceful. What had felt dim and haunted earlier is replaced by something quiet and relaxing. Above me is a thick overhead canopy that is only just beginning to turn colors for the quickly approaching fall. The air smells like pine and wet dirt, and after a lifetime of running the clogged streets of New York, I have never felt safer, honestly.

After a while, the path winds down and around until the smell of water reaches me. I slow my pace, careful not to slip as the trail becomes rougher. Tree roots and loose rocks litter the way, and I have zero interest in rolling an ankle way out here—peaceful or not.

I'm so caught up in the music—Shut Your Mouth And Run Me Like A River—that I don't see the shadowy figure moving swiftly toward me until it's too late.

Something slams into me, and I'm lifted clear off my feet. My breath whooshes out—more from panic than pain—and I become weightless. Airborne. Tensing for the inevitable fall, it takes me a long moment to realize I've come to a stop—gently. With no broken bones and without slamming against the hard ground. Strong hands grip my arms, and I hear a muffled voice; a deep baritone coming from someone whose words are drowned out by Bishop's killer beat.

Shit.

My earbuds.

I rip them out at the same time my gaze flies upward. And for the second time today, I look into the most gorgeous, most dangerous eyes I've ever seen.

It's him.

And he has me pinned with hands stronger than my jiu-jitsu-trained ass can possibly shake.

My heart still thundering, it takes me quite a few moments to realize that he is not dressed like a man who should be in the woods. Gone is the shirtless wild look from earlier. Now, he wears a white cotton shirt partially unbuttoned and tucked into gray slacks. Instead of hiking boots, his massive feet are covered in black, shiny shoes.

The kind Roscoe used to wear into the office.

Which means I'm standing in the middle of the woods with a man who, for all intents and purposes, should *not* be here. And he's looking down at me like I've just stumbled into a dark and twisted fairytale where he's about to eat me for dinner.

My heart thunders against my chest.

Out of fear and—even though it's absolutely insane—desire.

"What the hell are you doing?" he demands in a voice that requires an answer.

His eyes narrow on my face, but I can barely tear my gaze from the muscle ticking in his sharp jaw. *Damn, that thing could cut glass.* His dark hair has a silver stripe right up the front, and the ends are just long enough to fall into his angry eyes.

Okay, Serenity, maybe don't check out the man who might be about to murder you. Finding my backbone and shoving my hormones down for another day, I clear my throat. "I'm out for a run. And I just so happen to be an excellent fighter, so I'd think twice before attacking me."

His nostrils flare, and heat blossoms in my belly. *Damn hormones. Haven't you had enough of handsome men who show up in places they shouldn't?* "You'll find I'm not easily intimidated," he growls back. "Why are you here? How are you here?"

"I've already told you the why," I snap back. Hot or not, I don't tolerate men acting like they can order me around. "As for the how, it's simple: I put one foot in front of the other and ran my happy ass in here like everyone else."

His smirk is quick to come—just as quick to leave. "No one comes into these woods."

"You're here."

He crosses his arms, muscles bulging beneath the white cotton of his shirt. *Damn thirst trap.* "Don't you realize how dangerous it is to be out walking around all by yourself? You're pretty far from town. It would be impossible for anyone to hear if you were to find yourself in some kind of trouble."

I can't help myself; I swallow hard, my nerves momentarily obliterating the lust. This man is a giant compared to me. Hell, he'd even put Steven to shame in the height department. While I know my capabilities, he could easily overpower me should he choose to do so.

And it's that thought that has me taking a step back. "As I told you, I can take care of myself."

He chuckles, the deep sound warming my body like a damned fire. "I get that impression of you. Still…" He steps forward. I move back. Two pieces on a chessboard.

If only I was good at the game.

"You shouldn't be in the woods, Miss..."

Do not tell him your name. "Kellis." *Fuck.* "Serenity Kellis." *Double fuck.*

"And what brings you to Midnight Falls, Serenity Kellis?"

"None of your damn business."

His grin spreads, and I know it sounds crazy, but I swear the guy's eyes brighten momentarily before returning to their light honey brown. Just like the first time I saw him, there's a wildness to the way he looks at me. An edge that makes my heart race and my palms clammy. I can't decide if I want to jump his bones or break them in self-defense. "You should leave these woods, this town, Serenity Kellis, because sooner or later, whatever you're looking for is going to find you."

That does it.

I may be dumb, but I'm not too stupid to live. I spin on my heel and race through the woods, pumping my arms faster as fear courses through my veins. My head spins, and sweat beads on my collarbone as I race between massive trunks and duck from overhanging branches.

One whips me across the arm, but I pay it no attention because it won't be what kills me.

No, I have a sneaking suspicion I just left that back in the trees.

The clearing behind the B&B comes into view just ahead, and I burst through the trees just in time to collapse to the ground, my lungs burning with their need for oxygen. I'm pretty damn sure my heart is getting ready to beat out of my chest, so for good measure, I somehow manage to lift my lead-like arm to look at the BMP reflected on my watch. *One-hundred-seventy-two.*

Fantastic.

As I lie there on the grass, I close my eyes against the breeze. And then I realize I should probably get my ass into a public place before too-sexy-for-an-axe-murderer catches up to me.

Scrambling to my feet, I head for the B&B's back door. My legs are so heavy I can barely lift each one to put it in front of the other, but somehow, I manage to make it inside and toward the staircase.

I whimper as I take in the looming challenge. But one whiff of my sweat, and I know it's more than necessary. So, like the champion I am, I grab the balustrade and pull myself up, one step at a time.

Falls Gazette

Chapter Eight

Jet lag is real—even when you're driving and remaining in the same time zone. Because either I'm suffering from the worst case of local jet lag ever, or I was so damned tired, I slept for nearly eighteen hours. Which could honestly be due to having the shit scared out of me yesterday.

Or maybe it's the breakup and everything else finally catching up to me. As I step out of the coffee shop, though, a fresh, steamy brew in hand, I'm rejuvenated and ready to officially get started.

Even if I am battling with embarrassment over the fact that I was so damned stupid on my run yesterday. I mean, what kind of idiot goes deep into the woods alone and weaponless? As a New Yorker, I should know better. Still, out of self-preservation for my own dignity, I'm not allowing myself to focus on the latter. So I went into the woods? Cara said she runs in there all the time.

How the hell was I supposed to know some crazed—and far too sexy for his own good—lunatic was roaming through the forest? I take a sip and nearly groan with delight. Seriously, this place could run circles around New York's best cup of coffee.

For whatever reason, the scene from *Elf* jumps into my head, and I snort. *World's best cup of coffee*. I hold my cup up. "Congratulations."

"Do you often speak to your beverages?"

I turn and lock eyes with an older gentleman. He's sitting at a concrete picnic table with a chessboard in front of him. The seat across from his is empty.

"Only when they are delicious."

He smiles, and I'm immediately comfortable. Suddenly, the danger from the woods is a distant memory that no longer threatens to send me running for the hills. "Glad I'm not the only one who plays with their food. Care to join me?" He gestures to the chessboard.

"I have no clue how to play," I admit, my mind briefly drifting back to my thoughts while in the woods. How funny I'd be invited to play this game hours after comparing myself to a piece. No, not any piece. A pawn.

"Then it seems you're the perfect opponent for a man who hates to lose." He winks a second time, and I grin. Maybe it's because I've yet to meet a single person—Cara aside—who doesn't give me the creeps, or because I'm still licking my wounds over being a dumbass scaredy-cat earlier, but I find myself completely charmed.

"Very well. But you should know, I'm a sore loser." I take off my messenger bag and set it on the bench beside me, then set my coffee beside the board. The concrete is cold beneath my ass, but I ignore it for good company.

"Don't let you lose horribly—noted."

"Perfect."

"Tell me what you know of chess…?"

"Serenity."

He beams at me. "Serenity."

"I know that the pieces move differently, but that's all I've got. My dad has been trying to get me to learn nearly my entire life."

Something shifts in his dark gaze; a sadness that flickers across his expression. "Well then, let's teach you the basics so you can show off." He clears his throat and gestures to the front row of black pieces set up on his side. "These are pawns. When you set up the board, you fill them in first, then follow with the rooks." He points to two castle-tower looking pieces in the corners. "Once you get those in, you put the knights beside them then the bishops beside them, and finally..." He trails off and presses the tip of his finger to the crown in between two pieces that look like flames. "The queen sits in the center of them all."

Gesturing to my own board, I repeat what he mentioned. "Pawns, rooks, knights, bishops, queen."

"Fast learner."

"I try… I'm sorry, I didn't get your name."

"Phineas."

"Nice to meet you. You may find this shocking, but you're only the second person to be nice to me."

He snorts. "Not surprising. This town is not a fan of strangers."

"I've noticed. Any idea why?"

He ignores my question. "As you mentioned, each piece moves differently. They cannot move through other pieces, and two pieces cannot share the same square. However, you can move them to the same square as an opponent to capture that piece."

I listen intently to his description, determined not to embarrass myself.

"So your king is your most important piece," Phineas notes.

"The weakest, too, right?" When he looks up at me, amused, heat rushes to my cheeks. "That was a life analogy my dad uses. 'The king may appear the most powerful, but he's only as strong as the pieces around him. Never let yourself be fooled by the appearance of power, Serenity. It rarely lasts.'" I repeat the words I've heard more times than I can count.

"Your father sounds like a brilliant man."

"He is. If my memory serves, the king can only move one square at a time, right?"

"That is correct. When your king is attacked, that is called a 'check.' And when the king cannot escape, that is—"

"Checkmate."

He snorts. "That's nearly all anyone ever knows about chess these days."

"My father calls it a lost art."

"Yet, more wisdom."

"You two would likely get along."

"I would say the same." The man smiles softly, then gestures to the queen. "The queen is your most powerful piece." He meets my gaze, and I get the strange impression his words have a double meaning, though I cannot even begin to imagine why. Maybe because of my father's king wisdom? "She can move in any direction of her choosing and as far as she wants as long as she doesn't push past one of her own pieces."

"Got it. What about these?" I reach out and touch the top of one of the castle towers—the rooks.

"Rooks can move as far as they want, but only in four directions." In demonstration, he lifts one of the midnight pieces and moves it left, right, forward, and backward.

"And this flame-looking one?"

He chuckles and takes the piece from my hand. "The bishop can move as far as it wants, as well, but only in a diagonal direction. It also is contained to the spot it started on. Light squares or dark squares." He sets it down and retrieves the knight piece. "These pieces—the knights—can move three spaces each turn. Two squares in one direction, but then they can only move at a ninety-degree angle in the third."

"So they can move in an 'L' shape," I clarify.

"Precisely. Would you like me to cover the pawn, as well? Or learn by playing?"

"Definitely learn by playing. I do better hands-on."

"All right, then." He holds out his hands in the direction of my pieces.

"I go first?"

"You do."

"Okay." I rub my hands together and study the board with the scrutiny of someone who hates losing, but is at a massive disadvantage since I'm guessing Phineas' days are mainly spent behind the checkered board.

"Your pawns can move forward one square at a time, and you capture by moving diagonally."

"So this one I just move forward one square?" I touch the top of the pawn and gently push it forward onto the board.

"If you so choose." He touches one of his pawns and moves it forward as well, so they're facing off on the board. And just like that, as Sherlock Holmes would say, the game is afoot.

As we play, I allow myself to become completely immersed in the strategy—if you can call it that—and by the time we're done and Phineas has absolutely wiped the floor with me, I am already giddy to go home and apologize to my dad for not letting him teach me how to play years ago.

"That was invigorating," I tell him with a wide smile.

Phineas chuckles, the corners of his dark eyes crinkling with delight. "I would love to see how happy you are when you win."

"I'm glad you didn't let me win."

"Oh, dear, I never let anyone win. If they beat me, it's because they were truly better." He slides the board into a canvas bag then gets to his feet.

I follow, my coffee now cold. "Can I buy you a cup of coffee?" I ask, not ready for this outing to end. It's honestly the most fun I've had in…well…longer than I care to admit.

"I would love to take a rain check," he says with a smile that doesn't quite reach his eyes. "There's somewhere I need to be."

Something haunted has stretched into his expression—something darker than an afternoon spent playing chess in a beautiful park deserves. It makes me sad, makes me want to reach out and hug him, but I don't. Mainly because we just met.

After that, all bets are off because I'm a hugger. "Okay, well I will definitely be cashing in that rain check. Thank you for a wonderful and informative morning."

"You are welcome. Thank you for entertaining an old man."

"My dad claims that age is nothing but a number."

He chuckles. "See you later, Serenity."

"Bye, Phineas." I wave him off, and my gaze lands on a building in the distance. *Hargrave Library* is scrawled across the front of the building in elegant lettering, and my interest is piqued once more.

If I'm going to get the answers I need, it's time I get to work. What better place to end my day than a library that should have an archive chock full of all news reports from the last half-century—maybe longer.

With renewed energy, I head off toward the massive stone building.

Cara may have tried to warn me off, the creeper in the woods may have nearly scared me half to death, and the town may be treating me like a leper, but I'm a journalist. A New Yorker, dammit. And there's no way I'm leaving without getting all the answers I need.

After all, what else do I have to lose?

Falls Gazette

Chapter Nine

Hargrave Library is old and musty and smells like you hope a mysterious old library from the movies might smell. Basically, it smells full of stories and hidden alcoves, and maybe even a ghost or two. I know, the minute I walk through the main doors, there are secrets hidden in a place like this. The journalist-slash-detective in me is giddy with the possibilities.

Fresh coffee in hand—yes, I might have a problem—I inhale deeply and wander toward the main desk on my right. It's made of dark mahogany and stretches all the way to the far wall. Behind it sit stacks upon stacks of books just waiting to be reshelved—most of them older than me, by the looks of the worn bindings. But some are newer. I recognize the newest JR Ward novel and smile to myself. Whoever stocks these shelves has good taste. No one seems to be manning the desk, though, and I change directions, opting to wander the stacks myself.

Halfway down the romance aisle, the hairs on the back of my

neck stand on end. Suddenly, it hits me: I haven't seen a single soul inside this place, employee or customer.

My breath catches as I remember my encounter with the stranger in the woods. This empty library is feeling a bit like that. Deserted. Too quiet. Until… Boom! A psycho-killer appears.

"Oh, hello. May I help you?"

I shriek.

My coffee slips out of my hand, and I dive for it, determined not to spill in a place as sacred as this—not even if I'm about to get axe murdered. Some things are sacrosanct, and protecting books is absolutely top of the list.

I manage to grab the cardboard cup again just before it nearly hits the floor. Straightening, I look up into the face of a silver-haired librarian with green eyes. She looks around mid-sixties and all of five foot zero.

Definitely a serial killer.

I roll my eyes at myself because my true-crime-loving ass knows for damn sure that little old ladies make the perfect murderer. No one ever suspects.

"Nice catch," she says, cheerily.

"Thanks. I…you scared me."

"My apologies." She clucks her tongue. "We get so few visitors these days, and I wasn't expecting an unfamiliar face. Can I help you find something, Miss…?"

"Serenity," I say.

Her features light up bright enough to power the entire mystery section. "Serenity Kellis, big-city reporter. Welcome!"

"Word travels fast," I say, not even surprised at this point.

"We're so lucky to have such an accomplished journalist in town. I'm a big fan," she gushes.

And even though it's ridiculous, and I'm technically not a reporter at this moment in life, I can't help but smile at her affectionate enthusiasm. Her friendliness is obviously authentic, which reminds me of Phineas. Maybe the best way to make friends in this town is to seek out its elder residents.

"Thanks," I tell her.

"Now, then." Her green eyes sparkle. "I'm Mable, head librarian. Well, actually, I'm the *only* librarian if we're being technical." She chuckles at herself. "What brings you in today?"

"I was hoping to dig up some past *Gazette* issues. Anything you have on local spotlights. Unsolved crime, people of interest, that sort of thing."

"Oh, goodness." She leans in, and despite being otherwise alone in here, she whispers, "Is Midnight Falls going to be your next big story?"

My lips twitch. "I guess we'll see."

She clasps her hands together as if it's truly an honor to be investigated and then motions for me to follow her. "Come on. This way."

We do a quick march through the aisles that spits us out in a section with—I shit you not-—an actual honest-to-God microfilm set up at a desk along the wall. Mable motions to it proudly.

"Here we are," she announces.

I blink.

"Where is *here*, exactly?" I wonder. "Nineteen-fifty?"

Mable chuckles. "Oh, you're a funny one. Come on and sit."

She pats the seatback. I slide into the chair and wait while Mable powers the machine on. When it actually comes to life, I decide I'm impressed more than anything else. From what I've read, New York City Library still uses these things behind the scenes, but they aren't available to customers. I've never actually touched one before.

Still, it doesn't take long for me to figure out how to slide the date scanner up or down (past or present). In no time, I'm perusing old *Gazette* issues from ten then twenty and even thirty years ago—and am shocked to find these yearly murders go back even farther than I ever realized. Like, way too long for this killer to possibly be the same person each time. It doesn't make sense.

Mable comes and goes while I work.

She is a wealth of inserted comments that have nothing to do with the actual cases—"Oh, that's Bunny Hopkins. She donated her millions to the Free Britney movement when she died."—and has a never-ending supply of corny puns that she laughs at much harder than is deserved. But I like her. She has a clear love of books, and especially of history. We even bond over a shared obsession with Bridgerton.

"I had Lady Whistledown pegged in episode four, you know," she tells me.

Mable kind of reminds me of an aging socialite—someone the next generation has forgotten but still holds all the best gossip.

When I ask her about the murders, though, she is notably reticent. A reaction that doesn't seem very "Mable" and raises more questions than answers. Then again, her reluctance to talk about them is on par with everyone else I've encountered.

Another couple of hours go by as I dig deeper into each of the murder victims' lives. Who were they before they were killed? How long had they lived in this town, and why weren't any of their cases solved?

The whole thing is shady as hell and makes me wonder why no one else has ever tried investigating this. My Favorite Murder—one of my all-time favorite true crime podcasts—would have enough content for multiple seasons from this town, alone.

"How's it going, dear?" Mable asks, and I startle at the sudden sound of her voice after so many minutes of silence.

I look up, blinking to clear my head of the digitized newspaper scans.

“Did I startle you again?” she asks, apologetically.

“No,” I say. “Well, maybe. But I was just zoned out. There’s so much here.”

“Yes, you’ve been at it for two hours straight.”

Two hours?

Damn.

I really had lost track of time. No wonder she’d startled me.

“Well, listen, I know you’re mainly set on those news articles, dear, but I brought some books about some of the local legends and such. Not sure if it helps, but they’re all set up for you on the table around the corner.”

“Thank you.”

“Anytime.” She smiles and walks off, singing to herself.

I almost don’t bother with the books. The articles I found tell a dark story of a serial killer who obviously has a thing for murder-versaries. I’ve read through a decade’s worth of killings—all of which are unsolved and all of which happen on October 31. Every. Single. Year.

Not to mention, all of them are almost completely drained of blood.

It’s haunting and creepy as hell, but also fascinating. Same M.O. Same lack of suspects. I’m on to something, but I can’t even find any breadcrumbs to follow. Cara was right. Everything is a dead end.

Ugh.

Exhausted and tired of scanning, I stand to stretch my legs and end up at the table where Mable has piled a few stacks of dusty volumes. The volume on the top of the pile has a beautifully illustrated cover that looks like the dark and haunted Grimm fairy tale the rest of the world forgot. It’s called “Midnight Falls Local Lore,” and doesn’t even list an author or contributor.

I turn the cover, and the book falls open to a beautiful illustration of a dead body. A man lying prone on the ground in the middle of a grassy lawn. His skin is shriveled—wrinkled in a way that suggests a cause more sinister than simple aging.

Just like all of the actual murder victims I just read about.

What the hell?

I stare down at the picture, not sure I should believe what I'm seeing.

But I can't deny this illustration looks a hell of a lot like the grainy photo of one of the murder victims. Racing back to the microfilm, I scan through the dates again.

Bingo.

Ten years ago. October 31.

George McAdams.

The man in the news photo and the illustration in the book are nearly identical.

The fuck does that even mean?

I hurry back to the table and pore over the story that accompanies the drawing.

Once Upon A Time, it reads in scripted font, *there was a witch who came to live in Midnight Falls. On the night of Samhain, she found her beloved daughter murdered by her lover. In a fit of rage and bent on vengeance, the witch cursed the murderer, exiling him to the woods. Even now, the murderer walks the woods, unable to leave, yet cut off from everyone he's ever loved. Every year on this night, the curse lifts, and the murderer, in his rage, chooses another victim.*

Slowly, trying to wrap my head around the way fiction and reality have just mashed themselves together, I turn the page. My eyes land on the accompanying illustration of the supposed murderer, and this time, I leap out of my chair. From several feet back, I stare down at the photo of the handsome man in the woods looking back at me from the open book.

There's no way.

It can't be.

Flipping back again, I check the book's publication date. Sixty years ago.

The fuck?

I flip forward and look at the face again.

It's a dead ringer for the stranger I met in the woods.

Unlike with George McAdams, I'm too shaken to actually compare them side by side. Besides, I haven't seen a single news article with his photo, anyway. All I have to go on is my own memory. And that hormonal bitch is pretty sure she'd know his jawline anywhere.

The other impossibility?

This illustration was rendered sixty years ago. And he hasn't aged a day.

My heart pounds.

I have no idea how long I stand there, trying to rationalize my way into some sort of explanation that makes sense. Finally, the silence is broken by Mable.

"Dear, it's near closing time. I hate to rush you, but—oh my, are you all right?"

I force my eyes to Mable's and wipe my sweaty palms on my jeans.

"Yeah." I relax my shoulders. "I'm fine."

Lie.

Mable looks unconvinced, but I guess she doesn't want to beat a dead horse, considering how many times she's startled me now. It's honestly getting ridiculous.

Instead, she wrings her hands and looks at me sympathetically. "We're about to close up for the night, but you're welcome to come back tomorrow and continue where you left off."

"Right. Sure. Okay."

Turning my back on the book that's going to haunt me forever, I hurry back to the microfilm machine and grab my bag from the floor nearby.

"If there are any books you'd like to take home—"

"No, thanks," I say quickly. I may not know much about curses —or even believe they're real, to begin with—but there is no way in hell I'm letting that book anywhere near where I'm sleeping tonight. "I'm good."

She frowns like she's about to say more, but I whisk past her, trying not to give away how very much I do not want that book sleeping in my room with me tonight—or any night. I've had enough freakouts for one day—or one lifetime, thank you very much. All I can picture is some weird-ass monster crawling out from between those pages and murdering me in my sleep. Like some literary Chucky scenario. Yeah, your girl has an active imagination.

"See you tomorrow," Mable calls out hopefully to my retreating back.

I don't bother to confirm or deny.

Falls Gazette

Chapter Ten

Dusk settles over this town like a damned blanket determined to smother out all light. A bit dramatic, sure, but as I clutch the front of my jacket tightly around me and walk as quickly as possible toward the B&B, barely clinging to any rational thought, dramatic is all I've got.

He was there.

In that book of fairy tales and murderers.

Impossible. Right?

I swallow hard and cross the street. Ahead, the B&B is coming up fast, and I breathe a sigh of relief. Not that walls can stop an immortal killer. It's that thought that halts me in my tracks. Immortal?

The idea is laughable because it's *impossible*. Immortality is something you read about in sexy paranormal romance novels or when you binge-watch *The Vampire Diaries* for the hundredth time. Not in real life. That man in those woods is a living, breathing person. Is he creepy? Absolutely. Sexy as hell? Begrudgingly, I can admit that, too. But not immortal. That's just crazy.

The thing about growing up in New York is that, somewhere along the way, crazy stops scaring you. In fact, crazy starts to become normal. Once, when I was a kid, there was a guy on the subway wearing a penguin costume and rattling off the number for pi that went on longer than should have been humanly possible, even if his memorization skills were genius level. I had been terrified, but Steven had struck up a conversation and found out the guy was off the charts smart, had attended Harvard, and was only doing the whole penguin thing on a drunken dare from a classmate.

In the end, he'd been harmless—but only to those willing to look hard enough.

And I don't even feel like mentioning the guy who thought he'd been a hippo in a past life. He'd waded into a fountain naked and was still there at the "watering hole" when Steven responded to the complaints from his neighbors. I'd ridden along that day and got an eyeful. Ugh. There are some things you cannot unsee.

But with those thoughts, my fear shifts to a furious sort of determination.

Logic. Reason. There is always an explanation. I just have to find it.

The trees sway with the light breeze, and I stare blankly at them for a moment then glance up at the steadily setting sun. I have maybe an hour before it goes down for good. One hour to find my mystery man and prove to myself that he's as real as I am.

Weapon. I need a weapon. He may be real, but he could still be dangerous. Reaching into my pocket, I dig around until I find the closest thing I have to a deadly weapon. Attached to my keyring is a Tiffany Blue case containing the pepper spray Steven bought me last year for Christmas.

I'm crazy, right? I must be crazy because the longer I consider it, the better this idea sounds. Armed, I veer off course and head straight for the woods. Placing one foot in front of the other, I convince myself this isn't a horrible decision. The canopy shields me further from the setting sun as I break off in a run, damned grateful I chose to wear tennis shoes.

Leaves crunch in my pursuit, and it's only when I'm far enough in for the last rays of daylight to no longer penetrate that I realize I have literally no clue where this guy lives.

Or if he'll even be in—

"Back so soon?"

That deep baritone resonates in my body like a damned aphrodisiac. I stiffen. *Hormones, shut the fuck up.* Turning, I keep the pepper spray firmly in hand and face off with my own, personal axe murderer—probably.

"I have questions."

"It's dark, and you're in the woods."

His voice is accusatory. Almost lecturey. Almost like he's worried about my safety.

"I'm armed." I hold up the canister, and he smirks, melting my panties right there. *Traitorous body.* "I know how to use this."

"You think that will keep you safe if someone decides to make a meal out of you?"

"Someone? Are there cannibals in these woods?"

"There are wolves," he replies. "And you came armed with pepper spray."

"Left my gun in another pair of jeans," I snap back. "Who *are* you?"

He crosses his arms, muscles bulging from inside the white cotton shirt he wears. "I apologize for my bad manners." The bastard reaches up and runs a hand through thick hair, the muscles of his arms flexing as he does. *Delicious.* "My name is Sutton Hargrave."

"Hargrave." I narrow my eyes on him. "As in the library?"

"My family owns the town."

I snort and nearly lower my weapon. "You're kidding me."

"I am not."

He looks away, giving me a front-row seat to a profile view of that damned jawline. I know it was him in that book; more so now than ever. What I don't understand is how the hell it's possible.

Penguin suit, I remind myself. *Hippo man*, I add for good measure.

"You're telling me that your family owns the town and you hide in the woods?"

"Things are complicated."

"As complicated as your picture ending up in a book detailing fairy tale-esque murders as far back as The Brothers Grimm?"

Sutton's—if that is his real name—eyes harden. "That book is why I'm stuck out here. They've blamed my family for the killings inside it."

"That book was written sixty years ago."

"My family and I all share quite a resemblance," he replies. "Likely you saw my grandfather."

"You honestly expect me to believe that?" I demand, even as the possibility settles into my mind.

"A resemblance to my grandfather is less believable than me being over sixty years old?"

I narrow my eyes at the challenging tone—like he's daring me to agree to the idea of him actually being that old. "Fine."

"Can you lower your weapon now? I fear we simply got off on the wrong foot."

Warily, I do, though I keep my finger ready to press the button.

Sutton flashes a smile.

"Serenity," he adds; the way my name rolls off his tongue sends my already raging hormones into overdrive. At least, he's not a murderer. Probably.

"Yes."

"What brings you to Midnight Falls?"

"I'm here investigating the unsolved murders."

"Oh? Are you a detective?"

"No. Reporter."

I brace myself for judgment or distaste, but instead, his eyes gleam.

"Interesting."

The way he watches me, his near-golden eyes following my every move, is eerie enough. Add to that his predatory stance, and you might as well hold up a massive sign that reads: *"Here lies Serenity Kellis. She went into the woods at dusk with only pepper spray to protect her."*

"What do you know about them?" I ask him.

"Less than I want to know."

"What does that mean?"

Was this guy always so cryptic?

"As I mentioned, things are complicated, and I am unable to go into town to look into them myself."

"Your family is under suspicion, then."

Anger flashes in his eyes. "We were framed."

"You're saying that your grandfather was blamed for the murders, but someone else committed them?"

"Yes."

"Is he still alive—your grandfather? Maybe he knows who—"

"No." His eyes harden, and he leans back against a tree. The casual, suited woodsman look is so damn good on him. I just hope that doesn't make me the woman about to have her heart carved out.

"Then how can they still blame him? I've done the research. Another murder happens every single year, and I doubt your grandfather is in well enough shape to be capable of what I've seen."

"You've done your homework."

"It's my job," I remind him.

Our gazes hold for a moment, the air filling with unexplainable tension. Why the hell I'm so drawn to believe him, I doubt I'll ever know—but something about him, something about the way he holds himself, pulls me in. *Here for business, Ser. Not pleasure.* Though as I stand here, taking in the sight of his muscled body so casually dressed, I can't deny how damned good pleasure sounds.

Slow the hell down. I was engaged less than a week ago. Slowing my roll is *exactly* what needs to happen.

Still, it's Sutton who looks away first. "My grandfather passed away."

"Well, that settles it, then."

He shakes his head. "They don't believe he's dead. I'm the only one who saw him die. I'm the one who buried him."

An ache blooms in my chest. The pain he must have— Wait a damned minute. "You're telling me that you didn't bother to call a coroner?"

Creepy.

"Why should I? My family estate has their own plots."

"What was the cause of death?"

"He died shortly after his wife. Heartbreak would be my guess."

That startles me. *Heartbreak.*

The story in the book said the killer's first victim was his lover—the daughter of the witch who cursed him. Could that be the woman Sutton's talking about now?

But just as quickly as I entertain the idea, I dismiss it with a scoff. "That can't be true."

"You don't believe in love so powerful one literally cannot survive without the other?" He tilts his head to the side and studies me.

Heat rushes to my cheeks. "No. Your heart can't literally break."

"Pity." He's quiet a moment, then pushes off the tree. "It happened; I have a gravestone to prove it. The town was notified of his passing, but no one showed up to check. They all believe me to be covering for him as he continues to carry out these heinous crimes."

"So you live out here alone? Where are your parents?"

Another shadow passes over his face. This man has secrets; secrets I long to uncover. "My mother is dead, my father is no longer around."

"He took off?"

"Something like that."

"Sorry to hear that."

"I appreciate that, Serenity."

The way he says my name sends a chill up my spine. "And your wife? Girlfriend?"

My voice comes out weirdly high-pitched, and my cheeks heat, but he says, quietly, "I am not attached."

And I can't help the relief that washes through me at knowing he's single. Then again, there are probably not many women willing to live in the woods cut off from the rest of the world—even if the man looks like this one.

I clear my throat, forcing away images of just how fun things could get with this level of privacy and isolation. "Do you have any suspects? Anyone you know who would want to set your family up?"

"None. Never been able to get close enough to figure it out." He snaps his fingers and takes a step toward me. "I have an idea."

"What?"

"You can help me. We can work together."

"Excuse me?"

"You can move in and out of the town; I can't."

"And why do I need you? If I can get the answers, it seems you're the deadweight in this relationship."

He chuckles, and heat pools in my belly in response. Especially when he takes yet another step closer, so now I can smell the pine and leather of whatever aftershave he uses. "I am never deadweight," he says. "You need me to put the pieces together, to give you the history of our little town and its residents."

"The library has a lot of books—"

"So you've mentioned. Books that paint my grandfather as the murderer I know he's not. They're flawed, Serenity."

"And you're not? How do I know you're not just trying to kill me the moment I get too close?" My thoughts briefly linger on Cara's warning. Others have tried and failed. Is Sutton the reason why?

"There is no safer place for you, Serenity Kellis, than with me."

I want to believe him. Really, I do. Likely because of my love for fairy tales—the happy kind. They've apparently given me an unhealthy obsession with handsome men I find in the woods. Hello, Flynn Rider. Kristoff. Prince Phillip. All men the heroine met in the woods.

And hello, Sutton Hargrave.

Not to mention that he's right. His insight could prove to be the link between what I can dig up and what's actually been going on in this town. It could mean breaking this case wide open, and if I can manage that, I'll have Quincy eating out of the palm of my hand. I'll have my pick of stories. And a corner office instead of a cubicle. Sutton's help could be the thing I need to get my life back.

"Fine. I'll help you. But that doesn't mean I trust you. And next time, I'm coming with something a lot more powerful than pepper spray."

Falls Gazette

Chapter Eleven

I wake with a start, breathless and sweaty from a nightmare. Running a hand through my tangled hair, I look around to get my bearings. Outside my window, the day is gray with rain, and from my place underneath the layers of cozy covers, it looks cold.

But it's real, and I need to ground myself against the monsters and murder lingering from the nightmare. The mental image of a strange and haunting house still lingers, leaving me unsettled.

Determined to clear my head, I get up and head for a hot shower.

Today is about more than just chasing off a bad dream. Hell, it's about more than investigating cold case murders, too. Being in this town, refusing to run home when things get hard…this is about finding out what I'm really made of.

Roscoe broke my heart. What comes next will *not* break my spirit.

Twenty minutes later, I'm dressed and ready to tackle the day. First priority: coffee. After that, I have a few ideas about where to go for some answers. Sutton said he'll provide background on anyone in town, but I need a starting point. A list of suspects. People of interest. Anything that can point me in a specific direction. I can practically hear Steven's voice in my head telling me to go straight to the experts.

Okay, that's a lie.

If he were here, he'd be telling me to stop wandering in the woods with possible murderers. And to carry my ass straight home.

Good thing he's not here. I hate arguing with him.

I'm halfway down the main stairs when I hear voices drifting toward me from below. They're close, which means there's no way I'm getting out the door without being spotted. But after surviving my encounter with the possibly-murdery—but definitely delicious—Sutton Hargrave last night, I'm feeling friendly. Rounding the banister, I see Yvette chatting it up with the same couple I met on my first day here. They're wearing the same clothes as before, which makes no sense since the fabrics still look as impeccably off the rack as they did the first time, not a wrinkle to be seen.

The woman spots me and smiles, her face lighting up. "Oh, hello. I'm Victoria. It's so nice to meet you. I love your shirt! Where did you get it? Isn't it adorable, Lance?"

"Um…thanks." I look between her and Yvette in confusion. "We met, though. Before. I'm Serenity. You mentioned dinner…?"

"Dinner, what a lovely idea. But we're leaving this afternoon." She doesn't mention the fact that I was a no-show last night, so I don't bring it up. "Anyway, enjoy your stay. Maybe we'll see each other again another time. Bye."

I watch as her husband leads her by the arm up the grand staircase. Then I turn to Yvette. "That was…interesting."

"Oh, yes, Victoria and Lance are quite entertaining." She lowers her voice before adding, "A little eccentric. Cute couple, though.

I've never met anyone more in love than those two. Brings a whole new meaning to eternal passion."

My heart aches at her words because, once upon a time, I was just as in love. Or so I thought. Roscoe's face flashes in my mind, but before I can shove it away, it's replaced by another. Taller. Darker. And much more mysterious. A guy with a sort of woodsman-axe murderer vibe that shouldn't be a turn-on but totally is.

Yvette catches my eye and pulls me back to the moment.

"And where were you last night?" she asks, her brow arching in a way that says whatever I tell her will be all over town within the hour. "Already taking in the nightlife?"

"I was at the library," I say, going with a half-truth. Besides, what nightlife? "I met Mable, the librarian."

"Oh, yes, Mable Sabina. What a sweetheart." She lowers her voice and says, "Attention span of a mouse, but sweet, you know."

I nod. "Right. Hey, what do you know about the Hargrave family?"

Her happy mood is instantly extinguished. A clouded, almost angry look darkens her normally bright features. "That family is nothing but trouble. And that name is a curse upon this town. Don't mention it near me again."

She marches off, leaving me standing alone in the foyer and seriously wondering if I'm alone in my sanity in this crazy-ass little town.

On my way out the door, my phone dings with a text.

I glance at the screen.

Steven: Are you alive or what?

I type a quick response.

Me: You're being dramatic.

Then I head for my car.

Another text comes in.

Steven: You better be staying out of trouble.

I shake my head. If only he knew.

Before I can reply, he adds: *When are you coming home?*

Me: I'm onto a pretty big story here. Could be a while. STOP WORRYING.

Steven: Can't. It's what I do. You won't let me arrest Roscoe, so what's left?

I shake my head and shove my phone into my pocket as I head for town. On the short drive, my gloomy mood only intensifies given the dark weather above. No sunshine here, nope. Not today.

After parking close by, I duck into the coffee shop and am greeted with yet another tight smile. "What can I get for you?" the woman at the counter asks with a yawn.

"Coffee. Large. Black." Like my damned mood, I almost add.

"Coming right up." She turns away and retrieves a paper cup then begins to fill it. Something about the way she's side-eyeing me when she doesn't think I'm looking pisses me off.

"So, the Hargraves," I say, "You know them?"

The coffee cup slips and falls. I should feel bad that it splashes on her and she hisses, but in my shit mood, it takes everything in me to *not* laugh. "Are you okay?" I manage as I bite down on the insides of my cheeks to keep from smiling. *Serves you right for being an ass to me.*

She glares up at me. "Fine. I'll get you another." As soon as it's full, she hands it over to me and snatches the five I tossed on the counter. "Little advice for you. Leave the Hargraves alone, and get the hell out of our town. No one wants you here."

Her words serve as the fuel I needed to kick my ass into gear this morning. "Appreciate the advice—" I glance down at her nametag with a frosty smile frozen in place "—Jolene, but I'm not going anywhere. Keep the change."

Stepping out onto the street, I take my first sip of coffee before mentally adding the barista to the top of my 'could be part of a multi-generational murder plot' list. After all, if the food truck beat taught me anything at all, it's that it is almost always the ones you would least suspect.

THE POLICE STATION IS IN WHAT IS EASILY THE MOST MODERN building on the entire street, with fancy signage to match. It's clear where tax dollars go around here, which makes no sense to me, considering how low the crime rate is. Other than these mysterious murders—which are as yet, unsolved—there's practically nothing else to report from the research I've done so far. Inside, a petite middle-aged woman greets me at a large front desk that separates the lobby from anything important. "Can I help you?" she asks.

"My name's Serenity Kellis."

Her mouth flattens, and her tone changes to mild disapproval. "Ah. You're Yvette's guest, then."

"That's me." Why am I still surprised at how much everyone knows about everyone else here? And how much they already hate me.

She frowns. "Is everything all right? You're not having any trouble out there?"

"Oh, yes, everything's fine. I was wondering if I could speak with the lead investigator for the Murphy case."

She hesitates. "I see. Well, that'd be Sheriff Rhodes."

"May I speak with him?"

Her tone is less friendly now. A feat, given the shade she's already throwing. "I'll see if he's available."

She picks up the phone and dials an extension. After a few whispered words to someone on the other end, she sets the phone down and smiles tightly back at me.

"He'll be right with you," she tells me.

"Thanks."

While I wait, I wander toward the far wall and study photographs of various officers receiving awards and commendations. It's a history of the town's police force efforts, though none of these awards are for cracking any case larger than a missing cat. Most of them involve crisis management of natural disasters. Hurricane clean-up. Flood rescue. And a community 5k where a rookie officer took first place. It's much different from Steven's precinct where the recognition is all about who broke up the biggest smuggling operation or which task force solved a high-profile murder case.

I want to believe the charm Midnight Falls is trying to project, but the journalist in me is too suspicious. Especially given everyone's mistrust of outsiders. It's getting difficult to believe anyone is innocent.

Behind me, a throat clears, and I turn to find a man dressed in a sheriff's uniform. He's tall with an impressive amount of muscle for what looks like late forties or early fifties. And his brown eyes are sharp as he gives me a quick once over.

"Hi, you're Sheriff Rhodes?"

"That's me." He sticks out his hand for a shake. "And you are?"

"Serenity Kellis. Is there somewhere we can talk? Privately?"

A muscle in his jaw twitches. Aggravation, maybe? Mistrust? "This way."

He leads me around the large front desk and down a short hall. Up ahead, I can see where the hallway opens into a larger space. But he doesn't let me get that far and, instead, ushers me into a small conference room furnished only with a table and two chairs. On the far wall, a window lets in gray light through closed blinds. The whole vibe of the room is cold, detached.

He gestures to one of the chairs, and we both sit.

"Thank you for seeing me," I say.

He sits back in his chair, still assessing me. "And what is it I can do for you, Miss Kellis?"

The way he's already sized me up and shoved me inside a room reserved for social workers and grieving widows annoys me, so I get right to it.

"I'm a journalist doing a story on the unsolved murder in this town."

"And which murder is that?"

"All of them."

His eyes narrow, but he says nothing, so I add, "There's been a new one each year for a century, now. Maybe you can tell me why there's never been any arrests or even suspects named?"

His expression tightens.

"Miss Kellis, any information I have on an ongoing investigation is confidential. I can't share those details with a civilian, and especially not a member of the media."

"But you can make a public statement."

"Excuse me?"

I pull out my notebook and a pen. "As a member of the media, I have the right to request a public statement on the status of these investigations and whether anything is being done. Do you have a comment on this?"

"No."

"I see." I make a few notes and then flip back to where I've already begun making a list of the victims' names. Not that the page is big enough for all of them.

When I look up again, his expression is weighted with exhaustion and, underneath that, fear.

"Look, Miss Keller—"

"Kellis."

"You don't understand the depth of what you've waded into here, so let me be the one to explain. These cases aren't fodder for some attempt at professional recognition. There are darker forces at work here. People who will do anything to keep the truth from coming out."

"People like who?"

"It doesn't matter." He pinches the bridge of his nose then releases it and stares back at me. "Look, I'm trying to warn you. This is much bigger than you think. It's not safe for you to dig into this."

"I appreciate the warning, but I've covered murder stories before. In fact, I recently solved one myself." I gesture to the impersonal room. "And I'm a bit harder to scare off than this."

I give him what I hope is a disarming smile.

He pushes to his feet. "That may be, but I won't help you attract trouble by poking around. Leave the investigating to the professionals."

Knowing I've lost this round, I get to my feet. "I'm not going anywhere, Sheriff, and the sooner this town realizes it, the better." For some reason, I get the urge to name-drop, so I glance over my shoulder as we step into the lobby. "I'll be sure and pass on your message to Sutton Hargrave."

His eyes widen, and the receptionist pales. *Leave while you're ahead, Serenity.* With that thought in mind, I step out into the morning drizzle. My eyes land on the building across the street with renewed purpose. If the police station is the most modern, the library is the most authentic.

An antique whose insides are just as old and full of history as the outside.

That, I decide, is where I'll find my answers.

Hell, it's been a wealth of information so far.

I make my way over, ignoring the stares and whispers that are quickly becoming a staple of my Midnight Falls experience. Mable's at the front desk when I walk in and smiles when she sees me. But her smile is different today. More strained.

"Serenity, what a pleasant surprise."

Her expression doesn't match her words.

"Good morning, Mable."

She looks away then back at me, like she can't quite look me in the eye. "I didn't expect you back so soon. Everything all right?"

"Everything's fine. I wondered if I could take another look at that book you showed me last night. In fact, I'd love any more you have with similar stories."

"Of course. I'm a bit swamped." She gestures to the stacks of books as proof—the same ones that were here when I arrived yesterday. "But the book should still be on the table. And you're welcome to help yourself. You know the way."

"Yes, thanks, I'll do that."

She doesn't wait for me to leave before turning away and concentrating on whatever organization method she's attempting.

I walk off, not sure what caused the sudden change, but when I arrive at the stacks from yesterday, Mable is forgotten.

The table is empty, and the chair I sat in last night has been knocked over. I walk slowly, glancing around for some sign of another customer. But the silence has a stillness behind it that lets me know I'm alone back here.

Still, I stalk slowly through the aisles, keeping an eye out for any sign of the missing books.

When I get to the section where the fairy tale book should be shelved, I stop and stare at the space. It's empty. In fact, the whole section is missing. Not a single book left on the shelf.

Heart pounding, I double back to the non-fiction aisle where a placard labeled "Local History" marks the spot for anything based in actual fact.

That section is empty, too.

I retrace my steps, past the table, and to the far wall where the microfiche machine sits. It's powered down. I hit the button to bring it to life.

Nothing.

I check the plug.

It's still plugged into the outlet.

I do another once-over. Nothing looks out of place, but the damn thing won't turn on, even after multiple attempts to revive it.

Mable is still at the front desk, methodically moving books from one pile to another. There doesn't seem to be any real system, but when she sees me, she frowns and redoubles her efforts.

"Mable, has anyone else been in today?" I ask.

"Not that I'm aware of. Dear, are you all right? You look like you've seen a ghost."

"It's the book," I say. "The one from yesterday that you pulled for me. I checked the table. There's nothing there."

Her brows draw together in confusion. "Well, that doesn't make any sense. I just checked on it last night. Did you check the shelves?"

"Yes. The local history section and the folklore—they're all gone. Are you sure no one has come in and checked them out?"

"I've been here since I opened up this morning and haven't seen another soul."

I stare at her, completely at a loss. Something strange passes over her features. Now, she's the one who looks like she's seen a ghost.

"What is it? Did you remember something?" I ask.

"What? I…no, dear. Just an old woman's scattered thoughts." She forces a smile. Just like the one she gave me when I arrived. Something's wrong. I just don't know what. And Mable has clearly decided not to trust me enough to tell me.

I try to ignore how much that stings. Especially since she was pretty much my only lead in this town. And one of a whopping three friendly faces.

"Is there something else I can help you find?" she asks.

"No, I…thanks."

I turn and head back to the table where I left my bag, my thoughts stumbling over one another. From the moment I arrived, all I've done is take one step forward and two steps back. This town is full of secrets—secrets that, apparently, someone else doesn't want me to find.

I get out my notebook and start brain-dumping everything I can possibly think of that I've learned so far.

A century of murders.

A fairy tale using modern-day men as victims—and killers.

A mysterious man who lives in the woods and buries his own dead.

None of it makes any damn sense, and by the time I'm done, I don't know whether to write this up as an investigative exposé or a fiction novel about immortals and book thieves. But it's that last part that makes my heart race with renewed determination. Two full sections of library books—gone. Mere hours after I discovered the truths they held. Whoever took those books knows what I'm doing and doesn't want me doing it. Warning me off this story is one thing. Sabotaging my investigation is another. Unfortunately for them, they just did the one thing guaranteed to make me dig in my heels. Stubborn, meet Serenity Kellis.

Besides, if this town won't help me, I know someone who will.

Falls Gazette

Chapter Twelve

I'm just leaving the library when I hear someone call my name. Curious, I glance down the sidewalk and lock gazes with a smiling Phineas seated at the same table, likely in front of the same chessboard as yesterday. He raises his hand and waves me over.

I know I should take a rain check, but his hopeful smile crushes that. Besides, I am partially here for a vacation, right? And while pumping him for information didn't go quite as planned during our last meet, who's to say it won't go better this time around? He is, after all, the only resident not currently treating me like the plague.

"Hey," I greet half-heartedly as I slide onto the concrete bench across from him.

"You look disgruntled. Anything I can help with?"

"Someone else checked out some books I was looking for."

His expression falters, and he looks genuinely displeased on my behalf. "I am sorry to hear that; there's not much to do in this town but read. Believe it or not, the library is frequented."

"Really? There never seems to be anyone in there."

“Early morning, late nights, that’s when people typically come and go.” He smiles and gestures to the board. “You up for entertaining an old man with another game?”

“You just want to beat me again.”

“As I said, I hate losing.” He grins, and I’m completely helpless to deny him.

I move my first pawn, then wait for him to move his, and the game takes off.

“So, what books were you reading?” he questions as we play.

“Some old lore about the town. This place has quite the colorful history.”

He chuckles. “That it does.”

“You know why I’m here, right? I’m assuming you do since word in this town seems to be the only thing traveling faster than the speed of light.”

His mouth flattens as he moves a pawn again, but I don’t see the same coldness the others had. “I hear you’re here to look into the murders.”

“You’ve heard correctly.” When he doesn’t say anything, I continue, “You’re not going to warn me off? Tell me I’m in over my head and should run the other way?”

“I’m assuming you’ve already heard all of those. And you’re still here.” He meets my gaze, his hazel eyes haunted. “Seems like I would be wasting my breath.”

“Smart man.”

He chuckles. “I don’t know much about that, but I do know that strong women rarely follow orders.”

I sit up straighter in my seat and make my next move. “If I ask you questions, will you answer them?”

“To the best of my abilities, though I don’t know much about the murders. Knew a few of the victims, though.”

"Can you tell me anything about them?" I move my knight, capturing one of his pawns.

He sighs. "Just likely what you already know. The murders seem to happen every year, near Halloween, and they don't know who is carrying them out."

"I thought you all suspected the Hargraves," I say.

He coughs and bumps over his queen as he's reaching across the board. "Who told you of the Hargraves?"

"Read about them in one of the books I found."

"Interesting."

"Though I heard from a source that the man they believed to be murdering everyone is already dead."

A muscle in his jaw twitches, and I wonder if I've gone too far this time. I hate it because Phineas is charming and the only one who's treated me like a real person since I arrived. I'm just opening my mouth to respond when he shakes his head.

"I think there is more to it than anyone realizes."

"You mean the girl," I say, and to my complete shock, he glances up at me sharply. My jaw drops. "You mean that part is true?"

"There was a girl," Phineas says, quietly, "but not in the way the stories say."

I lean forward, completely drawn in despite my better judgment. I mean, this is a fairy tale. A witch. A curse. Her murdered daughter. But Phineas has me reeled in like it's Dateline's latest headline.

"Was she involved with the Hargrave guy?" I ask.

Phineas opens his mouth, then closes it again. Finally, he shakes his head. "The Hargraves were an easy target at the time. And they've sure suffered for it." He moves his bishop and captures my king. Then, he looks up at me and smiles. "Thank you for another entertaining game."

I gape down at the board then back up at him. "You have got to teach me to win so I can beat my dad."

He chuckles. "Keep playing against me, and maybe one of these days, I'll walk you through a strategy that will take anyone down." Phineas stands, signaling what I already know: this conversation is over. He won't be answering any more of my prying questions today. "While I won't warn you off, I do ask that you be careful, Serenity. No one has been able to figure this out yet, and those who poke around—well—you've heard what happens to them, I assume."

"I promise to be careful." Following suit, I get to my feet. "Another rain check for coffee?"

"Sounds good." With a smile and a wave, he tucks his hands into his pockets and heads off down the street.

Feeling better than I did before I sat down, I head toward Bean There.

Penguin suit, I remind myself as I step over the threshold and into the woods; this time armed with two coffees. *Not everything is as creepy as it seems.*

Besides, in this case, the worst possible scenario is that I'm somehow already dead and trapped in some twisted groundhog day, reliving the same crazy case over and over again until I manage to solve the unsolvable.

Snorting, I duck under a tree branch. "Because that's a possibility," I mutter.

"What's a possibility?"

I jump—my heart rate increasing exponentially in the span of a second—and whirl on the newcomer.

Looking as delicious as ever in a cream-colored sweatshirt and dark jeans, Sutton leans up against a tree as he slices pieces of a bright red apple off using a massive knife.

Not foreboding at all, right?

"Using coffee as a weapon. Definitely didn't expect that, though I guess if it's hot enough, it would do the trick."

I scowl at him. "Why the hell do you insist on doing that? One of these damned days, I'm going to knock you on your ass."

He smirks. "I'll take my chances." Pushing off of the tree, he uses the knife to scoop a piece of apple into his mouth. His complete disregard of my capabilities for ass-kicking pisses me off even more. "That for me?" he asks, shoving the knife into the apple then gesturing to one of the cups.

I offer it to him. "I was going for myself and figured it would be rude not to bring you one, too—but now I'm not sure you deserve it."

"Thank you." He tips up the cup and drinks deeply then lowers it. "How's the investigation coming along?"

"I—"

"Wait." Sutton pauses, his gaze traveling around the tree line behind me. I turn, trying to see what it is he's looking at, but it's empty. Just the two of us. Way out here in the woods. Where no one can hear me scream…

I'm just shifting my attention back to him when he stabs the apple and balances it on top of his coffee cup, freeing up a hand he then uses to grab mine. Beneath his touch, my skin sizzles, warmth spreading through me as though this very moment is the exact reason I'm here at all.

"Come on."

"Wait." I stop, digging my heels in and forcing him to cease his efforts to yank me deeper into the trees. "Where the hell are we going?"

"Somewhere private. There's no telling who might be listening. I'd rather our conversations be private."

"Didn't you tell me no one ever comes into these woods?"

A bird calls overhead and Sutton's shifty expression is back. "Please, just trust me." He tugs on me again, and I narrow my eyes.

"If you're planning to try to murder me—"

"You're a certified badass who will put me down. I remember your threats from our last encounter. Now, can we go?"

"If I say no?"

"This conversation is over." He releases me and begins moving through the woods with the grace of a man who knows exactly where he's going.

And as I'm sure he knew I would, I fall into step right behind him. "Where are we going?"

"Somewhere safe," he replies as he continues moving.

We walk for what feels like nearly an hour, and as the sun disappears behind gathering clouds, I grow even more nervous. "Listen, it looks like rain—"

"We're here."

I open my mouth to reply, but all the air is sucked from my lungs as I find myself staring up at a house I should not recognize. The architecture is a cross between Victorian and Gothic, and almost none of it seems to have been updated in at least fifty years.

Large, brooding, and ominous, the looming house is not something I will likely ever forget, mainly because of its uniqueness.

Well, that and because it's the same house I saw last night in my nightmare.

"Impossible," I whisper.

"Impossible? What's impossible?"

"I saw this place." I move closer, stepping through an iron gateway covered in thick, leafy vines.

"When?" he asks. I barely notice how concerned his tone is, not that I give it much care, anyway. I'm far too damned overwhelmed.

"In a nightmare." Whirling on him, I place my free hand on my hip. "How could I have seen it? It doesn't make any—" Then it hits me, and I snap my fingers. "The fairy tale book. I bet it was in there, probably with that image of your grandfather. Did he live here?" My mind settles on that rational explanation as it refuses to acknowledge any other possibilities.

I'm rooted in non-fiction.

Reality.

Not fictional fairy tales featuring sexy men who live in houses that might as well be castles.

"He did." Sutton moves around me and steps onto the porch. It creaks with his movement but remains sturdy, so I follow. When he pushes the door open and steps inside, though, I hesitate.

This could absolutely be where I get murdered.

"You coming in?" he asks, taking a bite out of the half-eaten red fruit just below where the knife still sticks from the side.

I've never wanted to be an apple more in my life.

Until he swallows it down with a drink of coffee. Then my aspirations are to become something—anything Sutton Hargrave will put his mouth on.

You were just dumped. Fantasizing is normal, but you still need to keep it in your pants, I remind myself. Then, I clear my throat. "That depends. Will you leave the front door open?"

He smirks. "Easy escape?"

"Something like that."

With a chuckle, he removes the knife from the apple before tossing it up in the air and catching it by the blade. Then, he offers it to me, hilt first. "I'll raise you one lethal blade."

I take it. Mainly because it would be stupid not to accept a weapon from a potential murderer…and also because I really, really want to see the inside of this house. Despite its creepiness, there's an allure I can't deny. A pull to this place. Like I'm meant to be here.

The floor creaks underneath my feet as I step inside. The scent hits me first—heavy pine mixed with plush leather, and the mixture has warmth swirling in my belly. *Damn.* Sutton's house would smell freaking delectable.

But to be honest, that's where the good vibe ends. Tapestries hang from aged walls, the floral and gold paper that once adorned them peeling away. Sconces hang crookedly from rusty hinges, and a tarnished chandelier dangles overhead, the combination casting the room in soft yellow. They're the only form of light in the entire place—at least, from what I can see because the windows are either boarded up or painted black.

Honestly? If the town gives off a murdery vibe, this is *definitely* where they do the killing.

I turn on my heel. "On second thought—"

"Wait. Please."

Something in his tone has me stopping. Which means I've clearly gone straight off my rocker. "This is a little much," I say, facing him.

"I know." He nods, sadly. "But since I can't go into town and no one comes here, there's no repairing anything that falls apart."

My heart aches for his loneliness; something I see clearly now. How must it feel to be ostracized by an entire town? "That definitely sucks. Okay. I won't leave, but I'm also not moving from this spot."

"It's a bit more presentable farther back," he says, but I plant my feet. No way am I falling for that trick.

"No, thanks. And don't even think about trying to drag me off, or you'll be sorry."

He swallows hard and nods, the ghost of a smile playing at the edge of his lips. "Let me guess. Older brothers?"

"How do you know that? Did you Google me?"

He snorts. "I most certainly did not. You just have that 'I have older brothers and they will kick your ass' vibe."

"Oh." I grin. Steven would love that. "I do, actually. Four. One is a homicide detective with the NYPD, too, so if I go missing, they'll come looking."

"Noted." He clears his throat and gestures to my notebook. "What have you found out?"

Why do I hate that I'm about to have to tell him that I've gotten nowhere? I sigh. "That everyone in town is either lying or they're too afraid to say anything."

A darkness passes over his features. "My guess is it's the latter."

Afraid. That makes sense.

"You think they're worried they're next?"

"Possibly." He begins to pace back and forth, feet echoing softly over splintered hardwood. "Who did you talk to?"

I count them off on my fingers. "Yvette, who runs the B&B, Mable, the librarian, a coffee barista who hates me—"

"That must be Jolene," he says with a chuckle. "Don't take it personally, she hates everyone."

I stop and narrow my gaze. "I thought you didn't go to town."

"Not anymore, but we—uh—we grew up together."

A green-eyed monster who has no business being anywhere near this conversation growls. I shake it off. I'm here investigating murders. Homicides. Everyone—including tall, mysterious, and handsome—is a suspect. What do I care what HO-lene and Sutton did together when they were younger? "Okay. I also talked to the sheriff."

At that, he stops moving and arches an eyebrow. "You talked to Rhodes? I'm assuming that went nowhere."

"You'd be assuming correctly. He gave me the runaround, claiming it was because he can't talk to members of the media—but I got the impression he was scared to say more. Who the hell could they all be covering up for? Who has the power to hurt everyone in town?"

"If I knew that, I wouldn't need you."

"Fair enough. There's more, too. Someone cleaned out all the books I was looking at. Anything pertaining to the town, to the legends, fiction, non-fiction—all of it. Mable has no idea who did it or how it happened, but they're all gone."

"Fuck." He turns away, and I try not to be royally turned on by his foul language. Roscoe wouldn't even use the word dammit because, to him, cursing isn't civilized. I have a sneaking suspicion Sutton is an animal caged beneath civility.

And there I go, sexualizing a murder suspect again. I seriously need to lay off the true-crime podcasts.

"What are you going to do now?" he asks.

"Well, we still need to come up with a list of suspects. Somewhere to begin in all this. So far, all I have to go on is your deceased grandfather."

"My family didn't do this," he says, eyes flashing at my words.

I hold up a hand. "Listen, I'm not accusing. But I need to know everything you know if I'm going to crack this. Is there anyone you can think of that I should investigate? Anyone at all you think could be capable of something like this? I mean, the killings go back a century, so obviously, we're looking at multiple perpetrators, but—"

"There's only one person responsible for those people's deaths."

His voice is hard—and certain.

"Um, listen, I don't mean to ruin your theory with facts, but there's just no way a hundred-plus-year-old person is running around, offing the nice people in this town. There's just no way someone that old could be capable of something like this."

"Your facts are rooted in a reality that isn't real," he says.

"I don't even know what that means."

He growls in frustration, and my mouth goes dry. In this moment, I am the desert, and he is the rain down in Africa. Holy shit, I'm turned on.

"Wait here."

He stalks out of the room before I can respond.

Blinking rapidly, I clear my head of all lustful thoughts and refocus on the task at hand. By the time Sutton returns, I'm mostly breathing normally again.

"Here."

He shoves a stack of envelopes at me, grabbing my empty coffee cup to help free my hands.

"What are these?" I ask, studying the elegant but faded scrawl on the front. The date puts these letters at just under a century old. That fact, alone, makes my heart pound. I know instinctively that whatever I find in these pages will have something to do with the murders.

"Read them and see."

He stands back, clearly waiting for me to discover for myself what this is all about. I slide the first letter out and scan the words.

My Dearest,

I waited all night for you to meet me, but you never came. Your family undoubtedly kept you away again, but I have a plan. We will be together, and no one can stop us, not even my mother. She thinks her threats will stop me, but nothing and no one can keep me from you, my true love. We are fated, you and I. No one else understands. But I do. I know that's why you pretend to ignore me. Pretend not to care when I'm nearby. But I know your heart. And I will find a way to be with you—even if it kills me.

Love with all my heart,
Tabitha

I LOOK UP AT SUTTON, THE WORDS SINKING IN SLOWLY. OR MAYBE it's my own belief finally starting to seep into my heart. Belief in a story that should be nothing more than a fairy tale—but is looking more and more real by the minute.

"This is a love letter," I say.

He grimaces. "Something like that."

"Who is Tabitha?"

"She was the daughter of a very powerful woman," he says, quietly. "And she was killed."

"By your grandfather."

"No." His eyes blaze with sudden fury. "Tabitha was in love."

"With your grandfather?"

He nods.

"But he didn't return her feelings."

The rage cools in exchange for surprise. "How do you know that?"

"This letter reads a little like the ones I wrote my crushes in middle school." I snort as his brows knit in confusion.

"I don't know what you mean."

"It means I never sent them, and thank goodness because they were borderline crazy and one hundred percent obsessed."

Sutton nods. "Obsessed is an apt description."

I cock my head. "You sound like you know from experience. Something tells me you've had your own unrequited crushes."

"Maybe."

I shake my head and look back down at the letter. "Okay, so Tabitha was in love with your grandfather, but he wanted someone else. And what? Tabitha killed herself?"

"No." His voice is hoarse.

There's grief in his eyes now. And pain.

"It was an accident. Her mother learned of her feelings and confronted them both. Words were exchanged. The mother produced a weapon and fired a shot. Tabitha put herself in between them."

My eyes widen. "Tabitha was killed by her own mother." He nods, but I barely notice it, too busy following my racing thoughts. "And then blamed your grandfather so she wouldn't have to face what she'd done. Wow. Crazy mother, crazy daughter, huh?"

Sutton's expression is unreadable.

I glance at the letters again and realize, for the first time since meeting him, there's nothing left in me that believes he's guilty. The letters might have given me proof, but it's my gut that allows me to accept it.

"Thank you," I tell him. "For showing me these."

"Take them with you," he says.

"Are you sure?"

"I've only kept them as proof of my grandfather's innocence. You stand more of a chance of doing that than I do. Keep them, read them, maybe you'll notice something I didn't."

"You think Tabitha's murder is connected to the rest?"

"Yes."

His voice carries a tone of finality that makes me think he still knows something else. Before I can grill him for more, he runs a hand through his hair and exhales.

"What happens next?" he asks.

"Well, um… As soon as I get back to the B&B I'm going to start looking online, combing through anything I can to see if there is anything even mildly helpful on there. My hopes are not high, though. But maybe there's something in these letters. Something you missed."

Like a mother with a grudge against a whole town who's decided to live forever in order to exact her revenge. Yeah...not likely.

"This is the most hopeful I've ever been about finding out the truth," he says, softly. "Thank you for helping me, Serenity."

I could bathe in the way he says my name. "It's my job," I say before clearing my throat.

Our gazes hold, his hazel eyes locked on me. The air between us shifts, filling with an entirely new tension that I'm not even sure I understand.

A cracking sound suddenly echoes through the empty room.

His gaze flickers upward, and his eyes widen. He rushes toward me, body slamming into mine with the force of a sledgehammer.

Before I can even utter a single word, my back hits the wall, and the chandelier crashes down from where it's ripped free of the ceiling, landing precisely where I'd been standing a second ago.

My breathing is ragged, and I wish I could say it was because of the adrenaline. However, when my gaze meets Sutton's once more, our bodies pressed together as he pins me to the wall, I know it's something far more primal that has my blood pumping.

His chest rises and falls rapidly as his hot breath warms my skin.

Dammit.

Dammit.

Dammit.

"Are you all right?"

"I—" What are words, again? "I'm fine, thank you."

Too damned soon, he's pulling away from me, and I hate that I feel a chill where his body touched mine. He bends down and retrieves the knife he gave me. The one I didn't realize I'd dropped at the first sign of danger. Wow. Obviously, I can take care of myself. Sutton doesn't even offer it back to me. He merely closes it and tucks it into his pocket—which is probably better for us both. It's not like I'm going to use it, apparently. Shit, we're lucky I didn't stab one of us when he crashed into me.

Besides, I think it's clear I don't suspect him of trying to kill me anymore. Between the letters and the fact that he just saved me from death-by-chandelier, my level of trust has gone past the point of needing a knife on hand.

"I've been meaning to repair that loose hardware for months. I'm so sorry."

Sutton sounds gutted by what just happened. I want to comfort him. Or even myself. But instead, my horrible dark humor kicks in as a coping mechanism.

"I guess the townspeople's warnings were warranted." I chuckle nervously. "Only it's not a person who's going to kill me but a house."

"Warnings?" he asks, crossing both arms. "What warnings?"

Shaking my head, I do my best to think un-sexy thoughts to curb my libido. "It's nothing. They're just trying to keep me from finding out the truth."

"Are you in danger? Has anyone threatened you directly?" He takes a step toward me.

The air between us heats, and my nipples threaten to announce themselves by just showing up. *Down, girls.*

"No. Not directly. Cara—the editor at the newspaper—told me that anyone who looks into these cases ends up missing—whether that's because they run or someone incapacitates them—she didn't know. Then there's the sheriff, who told me I'd be attracting trouble. Just minor warnings, that's all."

Why doesn't he look convinced? Brows drawn together, he stares at me a moment before retreating two steps. "If you feel like you're unsafe, you need to stop. This is not worth your life."

"Are you serious? This *is* your life."

My chest pangs when I think about how long this has gone on. His being shut out from town. Losing friends. A chance at a normal life. All because of a crazy-ass woman from a hundred years ago. And now, I want to help him—not because it's my job or because I need the story, but because he deserves to have his name cleared.

"Yes. And I've managed to survive this long in it. Unearthing the truth is not worth your life, Serenity. Promise me that if you are in danger, you will leave."

"I can't promise that, Sutton. This is about more than this town; it's about my life, too."

He tilts his head to the side and studies me. "How so?"

Swallowing hard, I purse my lips. What can the truth hurt? "My fiancé cheated on me back in New York. He dumped me—publicly—which sent me spiraling, and I ended up losing my job. This story, solving this mystery, and telling the truth to the world is my way of getting back on top. Without it…well, I have pretty much nothing left."

Sutton is silent for a few moments. Have I said too much? Is he pissed because I'm using his tragedy to get my life back? I take a step toward him, feeling far more vulnerable than I care for, but finally, he nods.

"I can understand your drive, Serenity, but getting your job back is not worth risking yourself."

"I don't have a life without it."

"Not true." He moves toward the door and steps out onto the porch. "And for the record: Your fiancé is clearly a fool. You're better off."

I take a deep breath and try to convince myself it's the near-death experience that has my pulse hammering.

"Come on. I'll walk you back to the edge of the tree line."

When I step outside, I realize with stomach-churning unease that night has fallen.

"Stick close," he says, and I hurry to do just that. As we begin our walk through the dark, I can't help but wonder if Sutton is everything he seems to be. Either he's the nicest, unluckiest man in this town, or he's exactly what they say he is.

A murderer.

If it's the former, I'm more determined now than ever to solve this and bring him closure.

And if it's the latter, well, I've not exactly behaved overly intelligently by venturing into situations where we're alone together, and I'm still standing. He's had plenty of chances to get rid of me, so if he really is part of a family who murders people, why is he keeping me alive? And why am I starting to believe he'd give up his life for my own?

Falls Gazette

Chapter Thirteen

I sleep like shit that night, my nightmares full of chandeliers that morph into wild beasts and lunge at me with snapping teeth. The temptation to pop an Ambien is strong, but I refuse to lower my defenses and leave myself vulnerable. Not a soul in this town is my friend. Except for Sutton. And the more time I spend with him, the more my ovaries are not interested in friendship. Unless you count friends with benefits. All the benefits.

Sure, there's Phineas, but I get the impression even he is hiding something from me. Outside my window, the sun peeks over the horizon in streaks of pink. It's beautiful after all the rain and clouds yesterday, and I stare at it sleepily until my eyelids begin to droop. I'm just about to nod off again when I hear the sound of something chafing against my floor.

I sit up quickly—just in time to see a manilla envelope slide into view beneath my bedroom door. Then footsteps sound from the hall, and I toss the covers aside and leap across the space. By the time I fling open the door, the hallway is empty.

Son of a bitch.

I close the door again and lock it.

Then I bend down and pick up the envelope. It's blank but identical to the one I received back in the city when this all began. Sliding the flap open, I reach in and pull out the single slip of paper inside.

I stare down at the news article, scanning the text. It's been cut, though, so I don't get the full story. And then my eyes land on—and register—the photo. It's grainy. Black and white, but also clearly taken with a camera not from this decade. Or maybe even this century.

Still, there's no mistaking the man in the picture.

Sutton. Or his grandfather, I guess.

But then my eyes land on the caption below it.

A date: June 7, 1912.

And a name: Sutton Hargrave.

No fucking way.

His words echo in my mind. Grandfather. Well, unless his grandfather and he were twins, I'm starting to think that story is bullshit. Determined to cut through the bullshit once and for all, I grab my phone. It takes three tries for the call to go through, thanks to shitty reception, but finally, it rings, and Allison answers.

"Hey," she says, sounding relieved and a hundred other things.

"Hey." Guilt pricks at me for not calling sooner.

"How's it going? Everything okay?"

"Yeah, what about for you?"

She hesitates, and I realize there's something she's holding back. My stomach knots.

"I didn't want to tell you," she admits.

"Just say it."

She sighs. "Quincy's been conducting interviews."

"Interviews?"

"For a job opening."

My jaw drops, and dread turns to shock and then white-hot anger.

"That asshole," I say.

"I'm sorry, Ser. You don't deserve this."

"Hell no, I don't. The bastard said he'd hold my job. What a crock of lies."

"I know. I wish I could do something to fix this."

"No," I tell her. "You've been awesome," I say, and I mean it, too. "If anything, he should give my column to you." She starts to protest, but I don't let her. "You're an amazing reporter, Al. The best. And you deserve the best."

"Well, I don't know if your column was the best but okay."

There's a beat of silence, and then we both crack up laughing.

"Fair point," I say.

"Please tell me you've met a pool boy or something," she says. "A hot one that doesn't speak English so you don't have to waste time talking. You deserve the best, too."

I snort. If only she knew—talking here is wasted anyway since no one in town will speak to me. But I don't say that.

"Actually, I'm on to a big story. But I ran into a snag."

"What kind of snag? Maybe I can help." There's no surprise in her tone; no shock at my admission. No, Allison knows me too well for that, and right now, I'm more than grateful. The last thing I want to do is have to argue my reasoning.

"Well, I need to verify someone's birth year, for starters."

"Done."

"Really?"

"Ser, I dig up gossip for a living," she says, as if this is all child's play to her. "Text me the full name and city of birth, and stay near your phone."

"Thank you," I say.

"No need to thank me, Ser."

“Yes,” I say, “there is.”

We hang up, still arguing about that last part, but twenty minutes later, my phone pings with an email. I open the attachment and stare down at the birth certificate Allison just produced like it was nothing more than a Google search away.

I guess for her, it was.

The name is Sutton Benjamin Hargrave.

Born July second.

One hundred and twenty years ago.

My knees buckle, and I slide to the floor, the door at my back. I force my eyes back to the document then, after a long beat of complete shock, I grab for the news clipping again and stare at the words underneath the photo. Sutton Hargrave. 1912. Holy shit. This isn’t his grandfather like he said. It can’t be. My mind drifts back to the letters he showed me; to the pain on his face.

Add that to the clippings and this birth certificate, and you have—one crazy fucking situation.

Allison is the best of the best. This birth certificate is real.

Which means this is also real.

The room spins. No, not just the room. My entire fucking world. All of it has tilted at this moment. Everything I thought I knew is wrong. The rules of mortality are at the top of that list. Sutton’s words from yesterday ring in my ears: *Your facts are rooted in a reality that isn’t real.*

Now his words make sense.

Or maybe I’m crazy, too. Maybe whatever insanity has infected him is spreading to me. Maybe it's in the water or something. Because, either I’m batshit…or the hottie in the haunted mansion is older than the invention of the automobile.

My mind puts pieces together against my will. It doesn’t take me long to realize a chilling truth. The reason why Sutton is so convinced the same person murdered every one of those people—

for a century straight. Because if he's this old, that means others have lived this long, too. Probably others in this very town. And one of them kills someone every year on Halloween.

After a few deep breaths and a couple of minutes of shoving my head between my knees, I'm fairly certain I'm not going to pass out. Still, I focus on my breathing as I stand and dress. With the article in hand and enough piss and vinegar to keep me upright, I make a beeline for the one place I probably shouldn't ever go again. But as much as I'm tempted to get into my car and head for the city, I have to know the truth.

Who knows? Maybe there is some logical explanation for all of this. A lynchpin of information that, once put in place, will force everything else to make sense. Though, even as I consider that, I don't believe a word of it. Something is off here; something has been off since the moment I crossed the boundary between normalcy and this damned town.

The lobby is empty and quiet. No Yvette. No Lance and Victoria. Then I remember they left. And it's quite possible Yvette is avoiding me after our strange interaction before.

I halt, suddenly wondering if Yvette knows something about this. Maybe she's even the one who slid the article underneath my door. But a quick search yields absolutely nothing. The place is empty from what I can tell. And beginning to feel creepy for it, too. Or maybe it's just my new awareness that this town might not be completely human. Not the kind who live and die like the rest of us, anyway. Obviously, my mind plays out the entire scene from Twilight where she figures out what he is. But that doesn't fit Sutton. He's warm. Hot, even. And not just because he's the most attractive thing on two legs I've ever seen. But even if I believed in vampires, I don't peg him for one. He's something else entirely.

And I'm going to find out what.

Forgetting about Yvette for now, I slip out the back door and head for the woods.

The forest is more alive than usual today. Sunshine warms the air, and birdsong echoes in the canopy above my head. Dead leaves crinkle beneath my feet, and I know I'm doing nothing to mask my arrival. However, after twenty minutes, I realize none of that matters because I am completely and hopelessly lost.

The Hargrave house is nowhere in sight.

Even Sutton, the creepy asshole, hasn't snuck up on me yet.

In a small clearing, I stop and do a full circle, trying to pick a direction, but it all looks the same to me. Trees. Leaves. More trees. *Ugh.* I should have been a Girl Scout.

Left. It's as good a direction as any.

I stop walking as a branch cracks behind me.

"Ha. I heard you coming this time," I call out.

Nothing.

Leaves rustle, and I roll my eyes, turning toward the sound. "You sound like a herd of elephants—"

My words are cut short, and I stare across the small clearing at the enormous bear that has emerged from the brush. It wanders a bit closer, and I do my best to remain perfectly still—terrified trembling, notwithstanding. Heart hammering against my ribs, it's all I can do to remain standing as I study the larger-than-it-should-be black bear. I try to remember if bears are normal for this part of the world, but it's not like I did any wildlife research before coming here. My entire focus has been on *people* who murder. Not bears who commit homicide.

When it spots me, I suck in a breath, and my bladder squeezes until I'm pretty sure a little pee comes out. Something that likely won't matter in a few moments.

The bear raises his snout into the air and sniffs.

I hold my breath and pray to baby Jesus himself that this bear is blind and dumb. But apparently, the Lord loves all His creatures because, in the next moment, the bear looks right at me and begins making a grunting-growling sound that I think is the bear version of "you look delicious."

I whimper, and apparently that seals the deal.

The bear opens his mouth and bellows at me, a jawline of canines on full display.

I pee a little more.

The bear advances.

Every fiber of my being wants to run, but I force myself to remain rooted where I stand. I've seen National Geographic. And Jurassic Park. If I don't move, he won't consider me a threat.

I think.

Then my phone rings.

The bear stands up and bellows again.

I know what I have to do.

Spreading my feet apart, I raise my hands high in the air and bellow right back.

The bear drops to all fours again and charges.

Shit.

I should have gone with the "remain still" thing.

I scream and take off running.

My lungs burn, and my arms pump, and still, I know there's no possibility of me being faster than a bear.

Brush crashes behind me as the bear closes the distance.

My eyes blur with hot tears as I think of my parents and my brothers. Steven. He's going to kill me for getting killed this way.

Out of the corner of my eye, something moves.

I blink, still furiously sprinting as I try to focus through my tears.

Then I see it.

On my left, an enormous gray wolf leaps from a tree. It hits the ground on paws larger than I've ever seen, and I falter, suddenly confronted with two predators. I mean, what are the fucking odds, right? I have clearly pissed off the Big Guy. This is overkill—no pun intended.

But the wolf runs right past me and throws himself at the bear.

The two go crashing to the ground in an angry pile of fur and teeth.

I use the distraction to grab onto a low branch and shimmy my ass straight up a tree. Thank you, martial arts training. I manage to get onto a branch thick with leaves. Praying it's enough to keep me out of sight for whoever survives this Nat-Geo special, I hunker down and wait.

Below me, the two animals wrestle one another for the right to eat me.

I sort of expect the bear to put the wolf down because, well… bear. But in the end, the wolf sinks its teeth into the bear's throat and rips. My stomach churns, thanks to the disturbing sound of tearing flesh, and blood sprays the ground. The killing blow drops the bear to the ground, though, and he falls still.

The wolf releases him and takes a step back, giving me a front-row seat to the blood-soaked wound in the bear's throat. Normally, I can't even bring myself to watch documentaries about predators because I hate seeing animals hurt. However, this time I can't quite bring myself to feel too badly for him. He was going to eat me, after all.

The wolf, apparently satisfied he's neutralized his enemy, turns and looks straight up at me. I duck behind the cover of leaves, startled at the clarity and directness of its stare. Something about those golden-brown eyes seems to reach right into my soul. I can't help but feel…recognition.

I am definitely losing it.

After a beat, I lean out again and find the wolf hasn't moved, which means I am seriously stuck.

"Great. So I've traded one predator for another."

As if my words have actually affected it, the wolf backs away and lowers his head.

"What the…"

Then, right before my eyes, the wolf begins to tremble and shake and—change. The heavy thumping of blood in my ears is drowned out by the sickening cracks of bones breaking. Something I can't even begin to process because, in a matter of seconds, the wolf is gone.

In its place is Sutton Hargrave, naked as the day is long.

Falls Gazette

Chapter Fourteen

Oh balls. Literally. I mean, I know that logically I should be processing the fact that a wolf just turned into a human, but when that human is very, *very* naked, and very, *very* hot, one can't help but let their gaze drift.

"What? How? I—" Leaning down from the branch, I blink rapidly. Surely I didn't see that. Or did I? When I lean forward again, I realize my mistake—too late. The bark beneath my fingers moves, and I slip, a guttural scream ripping from me as I tumble out of the tree.

But do I hit the ground? No, of course, not…because, apparently, this is not freaking reality. Strong arms come around me, and I'm cradled against a warm, hard body. My uterus literally trembles with glee, and I swear my nipples could cut glass. I crack open one eye.

Sutton is studying me with the same expression one might use while attempting to lull a wild animal into soft compliance. "Are you all right?" he questions, voice deep, raw, and too fucking sexy.

Hormones, take a vacation. Dude literally just went from animal to man, he might be older than your grandpa, and oh, yeah—he can apparently kill a bear like it's nothing more than a squirrel. "Fine. Put me down, please."

With a nod, he sets me carefully on my feet. I take three cautious steps back before I nearly trip over the bear corpse. My center of gravity shifts and I reach out to grab the trunk of the tree before I make yet another ass of myself.

The bear's entrails catch my eye. Uh-oh. Spots invade my vision as the world spins far too quickly around me. Adrenaline surging through my veins, I take a few careful, deep, steadying breaths then lift my gaze to the man before me.

Not a vampire, at all. No, apparently, he's a damned werewolf!

"Serenity?" he questions. "Serenity?"

I don't respond. What the hell is there to say? Especially when I let my gaze drop down his muscled body. *Damn.* Tanned skin stretches over taut muscle with more ridges than a *Ruffles* potato chip. A stomach you could wash clothes on trails down to a trim waist—which is where I force my perusal to end.

I've already seen the goods, and trust me, they are *not* anything I will be forgetting any time soon. But if I start salivating, I can't imagine he'll be too keen on answering my questions. "You're naked," I finally say.

"Shredded my clothes when I had to shift to save you." His brows draw together in frustration, and he crosses his arms. Like I'm the one who should be on trial here. "Why the hell are you out here, Serenity?"

"You shredded your clothes when you had to shift? What the hell does that even mean? What *are* you?"

"Isn't it obvious?" he asks, holding his arms out to the sides as though this is the most normal thing in the world.

"You just changed from a wolf into a man!" I scream.

Birds take flight overhead, obviously not wanting to remain here out of fear that my crazy is contagious. Who knows? Maybe it is.

Would be the least of my problems, at the moment.

"Keep your voice down," he scolds.

"Or what? I'll attract another bear? Seems like you can handle those just fine."

His expression darkens, and he takes a step toward me. "There are worse things than bears in these woods."

"Like men who change into wolves? How many of you are out here? Is that what's been happening? You're—"

"Come with me," he interrupts as he reaches for me.

I shake my head. "Not a damned chance."

"I'm not going to hurt you, Serenity," he says, tone exasperated. "Please, there's no telling what that commotion has attracted."

"Why would I go with you? So you can eat me?"

His wicked grin is so potent it makes my already weak knees feel like jelly. "If I put my mouth on you, it will be because you've asked for it."

My mouth goes dry as all the moisture in my body rushes straight between my legs. *What the fuck is wrong with me!?* "That's never happening," I say, with very, very little conviction.

He inhales deeply, his grin spreading. "If that's what you need to tell yourself." Hazel eyes flicker behind me then back to my face. "Either way, we need to get somewhere safe."

This is ridiculous. Even if I'm not already dead—which, I have my suspicions—going somewhere with this man will likely result in me going from "probably dead" to *"Here lies Serenity."* But then I remember my call with Allison.

I remind myself of everything that's on the line. I'm about to lose my job at the freaking *New York Times*. There's no going up from there. My entire life is already at risk, my future on the line, and even as all signs point to Sutton being a dangerous beast—my gut tells me there's more to it. More to him.

And if Steven has taught me anything, it's that the gut is rarely wrong. Though I doubt he'd appreciate me risking my life for a job. But what he doesn't understand is that my job has been my entire life.

However screwed up that is, it's how I feel. So, I take a step forward. Then another and another, until I'm in front of Sutton.

"You don't know where you're going," he calls out from behind me.

This is either the dumbest or the bravest thing I've ever done. Probably both. Either way, I clear my throat and call back, "Then give me directions because I refuse to stare at your naked ass."

Apparently, I'd been nearly at his house when the bear attacked because the walk takes us less than twenty minutes. The entire time, Sutton walks behind me, and his soft footsteps are my only proof he's still back there as I refuse to steal a look.

I've already seen too much to keep my own, personal feelings out of this, and yet even as I know that to be the truth—I'm already craving another peek.

Have I mentioned that something is seriously, seriously wrong with me?

I blame my true crime obsession for making me legit attracted to shady-ass men. Scratch that. Shady-ass *wolf*-men.

I step up onto the porch then turn to face the wall as Sutton moves around me and pushes his way through the front door. Keeping my gaze carefully cast to the floor, I step into the foyer.

"Wait here," he says over his shoulder.

"Yeah, sure." As soon as I know he's gone, I glance up to the ceiling. No damned way I'm letting myself get taken out by another chandelier. And as much as I loved having Sutton come to my rescue, the last thing I need are my hormones raging in response to his body pressed against mine.

Faded wallpaper surrounds me, but I peek around the corner. For what? Who knows. But a massive neon sign saying "Sutton is innocent and you are not a foolish moron about to die" would be helpful. *Gut don't fail me now.*

"Better?"

I glance to my right as Sutton comes down a massive staircase wearing jeans and a t-shirt. But the fucker is still barefoot, and somehow that casualness makes him even more alluring.

No, I don't have a foot fetish. Apparently, I have a Sutton fetish, though.

"Much," I lie. Truthfully, Sutton Hargrave looks delicious whether he's naked or fully clothed. I have a sneaking suspicion he'd look damned good wearing a prison jumpsuit. Which is exactly what he'll be wearing—wolf or not—should I discover he's the killer.

My heart sinks. Why does the thought of him being locked away make me so damned sad?

Awkward silence stretches between us. Where do I even begin asking questions? None of this should have happened; none of it should be real. And yet, I've never turned my back on something just because it seems far-fetched.

Especially not when I literally saw it with my own eyes.

"How long have you been able to…" I trail off and gesture to him.

"Shift? Since I turned nineteen and was able to access my abilities."

"Which are?"

"Shifting from man to wolf and vice versa."

"Which are you? A man or a wolf?"

"Both," he replies, easily. "Want some coffee?"

"How the hell can you say it like that? Like it's the most natural thing in the world!"

"For me, it is." He walks past me and down a long hallway. I follow, too intrigued to remember to watch for falling light fixtures.

More faded, peeling wallpaper lines these walls, and soon we're standing in an aged kitchen. Wooden countertops line three of the four walls with two large windows looking out at the trees. An old gas stove is centered on the far wall, its white exterior painted with faded violet flowers. The design is intricate—clearly hand-painted. A metal pipe extends from the top of the stove, disappearing into the wall behind it. Despite the design's clear ties to the previous century, everything in this room has been lovingly maintained, especially compared to the rest of the house. As if there is a personal connection to the space here that doesn't exist elsewhere.

Sutton reaches for a lighter then turns the knob on the stove and lights the lighter. Yellow flames spark to life, turning blue after a heartbeat. He sets a kettle over the top of the flame before moving to a cabinet directly to his left.

After pulling out a container with coffee beans, he turns and sets them and a small stone bowl on the island directly in front of me.

I watch, fascinated as he grinds the beans up by hand before depositing them into a mesh filter seated on top of a glass carafe.

It's only then that he bothers to look up at me. "You look pale."

His comment yanks me out of my reverie, and the comfort of watching him perform the mundane dries up.

"Gee, thanks," I retort. "You'll excuse me if I'm a little uncomfortable when I realize you're the big bad wolf and I've just wandered into your house."

The dark expression that flickers over his face has me regretting my choice of words—even if a part of me genuinely worries they're the truth.

The kettle begins to whistle, so he turns away and retrieves it then begins to pour the water into the hourglass-shaped container on the counter.

Dark liquid pools at the bottom moments before the aroma of fresh coffee reaches my lungs.

"Hold on. How do you get groceries and stuff if you're not allowed in town?"

"I receive monthly care packages from the town. Basically, they stand at the tree line and throw things inside."

"But you said everyone in town hates you. Why would they bring you supplies?"

"Not everyone," he replies, coolly, as he replaces the kettle and turns to face me. "There are a couple who know me for who I am. In actuality, they are unable to cross into the woods just as I am incapable of going into town."

I stare at him, processing what he's telling me. "You lied to me."

"You weren't ready for the truth."

Shutting my eyes momentarily, I pinch the bridge of my nose in an attempt to beat back the budding headache. When I open them again, he's pouring dark coffee into two mugs. "Listen, asshole, this is not A Few Good Men, and you are not Jack Nicholson, so don't hit me with that bullshit line."

"I'm not entirely sure what you mean, nor do I know this Jack Nicholson, but had I told you the truth, you would have run. I needed you to become so invested in solving the mystery that nothing would force you away until you helped me figure this out."

"You sure as hell weren't feeling that way yesterday when you told me to leave if I felt my life was in danger."

His expression grows unreadable. "Something you still must do should that happen."

I don't accept the offered coffee. Instead, grinding my teeth together, I take a step forward. “Listen, a murder takes place in this town every single year on Halloween. In case you don’t have a calendar out here, that’s in three days. Which means we have exactly that much time to solve this and save someone’s life. And I can’t do that if you’re lying.”

Sutton sets his mug down and places both palms on the countertop. “I know all too well what happens on All Hallows Eve, Serenity Kellis. I’ve been forced to suffer through the aftermath of it—of not knowing who in my town has died—until the next year, when I get to begin worrying all over again. A century of this suffering, ever since that damned curse was placed on us.”

I step back, the rage in his hazel gaze knocking the air from my lungs. “Curse?”

“Yes.” The muscles in his jaw flex. “A curse.”

“As in magic?” Unable to stop myself, I bark out a laugh. “This is outrageous.” Turning away, I stare out the window at the trees as the branches sway in a light breeze. I refuse to let him see it in my eyes—that I’m actually entertaining this. My memory recalls the fairy tale. About the witch who cursed them all.

“So you can believe in men who can shift into wolves, but a curse is where you draw the line?”

“Believe?” I whirl on him. “Believe?” I repeat as I move around the island and jab my finger into his muscled chest. “I don’t even know that I believe in you standing in this kitchen! Maybe I died. Maybe I’m lying in that forest, bleeding to death because I was mauled by a fucking bear! Or, maybe this entire town is fake and I died in the car on my way here! And if that’s the case, this is definitely The Bad Place.”

His gaze darkens so rapidly I try to back away. An action that is stalled when he wraps his fingers around my wrist and holds me firmly in front of him. “Your death is not something I wish to discuss." His tone is calculated, and even in my angered state, I can sense he's choosing every word carefully. "You are no coward. Therefore, I can surmise that as soon as you are through the shock of it all, you will begin to see the truth for what it is, regardless of how *outrageous* your new reality might appear."

"Let. Me. Go." I try not to inhale as he leans in.

Serenity, get your shit together, I scold myself.

Back to the facts. Facts I can do.

Fact number one. This town is sketchy as fuck. People don't want to talk to me; they avoid me at all costs.

Fact number two. The murders go back a hundred years. Which means, logically, it's either a copycat serial killer I'm dealing with —or the same person, no matter how unlikely that should be. (Unlikely except for a birth certificate that's impossibly real.)

Fact number three. I literally watched Sutton change from a wolf to the impossibly sexy man before me.

All of that, added to the feeling in my gut, leads me to believe what he's saying, even if it does seem impossible. After all, I'm sure electricity seemed fiction at one point.

Modern medicine.

Cell phones. Britney free of her conservatorship. All of those things *seemed* impossible, and now they're reality.

Yes, this too seems crazy. But the facts are there. And they are irrefutable. The only thing I don't know yet is whether or not Sutton is innocent. Is he a victim? Or the murderer? Or something in between? I do know he saved me from a bear earlier, and that counts for something.

Crossing my arms, I attempt to approach this as I would any other case. And for that, I need more truths. "Tell me about the curse."

"A hexerei placed it on our town as punishment for her daughter's death."

"Hexerei?"

"I believe they are also known to humans as witches."

My mouth falls slack. "So now broom-riding, cackling old women are real, too?"

He does not even crack a grin at my joke. "I assure you, hexerei are no laughing matter."

"Fine. So she placed a curse, what, locking you in the woods? What is this, Rapunzel? Snow White? Because if seven tiny men show up, I'm going to lose my shit."

He doesn't react.

"Tough crowd," I mutter. "Fine. Why you?"

Sutton leans back against the wooden countertop. "Because she blames me for the death of her daughter."

The guilt radiating off of him is suffocating, and even without him saying the words, I know there's no way in hell he was responsible for whatever happened to that girl. And before I can ask the question, I realize I already know the answer. "The letters. They were about you."

His gaze shifts again, eyes darkening, and I can see he's somewhere in the past, his memories taking over. "Yes. The hexerei have never been friends of our kind, and for most of our history, we steered clear of each other. When Tabitha's mother brought her family here, we gave them space. No one wanted war. They stayed out of our town, and we didn't bother them." A muscle in his strong jaw flexes, and he looks away from me. "I met her by accident, or so I thought. Tabitha made sure to be where I'd find her; I realized later that she'd orchestrated it. She became obsessed with me—believed she was my mate despite me consistently telling her it was not true. I didn't set out to hurt her, but she became angered by my refusal. The letters ceased, and some time passed. I thought she'd forgotten all about me. But then our paths crossed in the woods. She'd changed—grown harder—and when she began uttering a spell, I tried to run, to get away, but her mother found us before I could escape. She believed I was harming her daughter—that I'd lured her out into the woods when, in reality, it had been the opposite. She tried to kill me, and Tabitha jumped in the way. The magic the hexerei used…it was fatal."

I cover my mouth with my hand to smother a gasp. "She killed her own daughter? With magic?"

"Yes."

"So this curse is her revenge?"

"Yes," he repeats. "Every year, she returns to this blasted town and kills another to reinforce the curse binding us all." He closes his eyes, and when he opens them again, they're darker. "My mother was her first," he chokes out. "It was her blood that sealed me in these woods and the rest of my pack in town."

My stomach drops, my heart shattering for the man in front of me. "Have you ever followed her? Tried to find out where she—"

"I cannot leave this place," he interrupts, reminding me what I already know. "And I've no clue where the witch goes when she is not here."

"Which is why you asked for my help," I say, fitting the jagged pieces of this insane reality together. "Because I can leave."

"Yes." He pushes off the counter. "I have a duty to my pack, Serenity. Stopping the hexerei is my top priority, and I will stop at nothing to put her down. There is only so much I can do from this side, though."

I sigh. "You do realize how insane this all sounds, right?"

"I do." His expression is so broken, so defeated, I know that no matter how crazy this all sounds, Sutton is innocent.

It's that fact alone that makes my decision easy. There's no walking away from this for me. No leaving until I've brought him peace. I'm no longer doing it just for the story. Hell, I'm going to have to spin my own lies to cover this crazy-ass truth just so Quincy won't laugh in my face—or have me locked away. Which reminds me. "How old are you?"

He smirks now, though it doesn't reach his eyes. "One-hundred and twenty years."

Swallowing hard, I cement this entire story into my brain as fact then reach for the still-steaming cup of coffee and take a sip. "Well, let me be the first to say you look good for your age."

His smile spreads—a full-on morphing of his broken expression. "I appreciate that." He lifts his own mug and presses it to his lips. "It feels good to speak the truth. It's been a long while since I was able to have an honest conversation."

"What about the townspeople? You said they throw stuff over the boundary line?"

"I cannot hear what they say," he says. "The only time I can speak to them is on All Hallows Eve when the veil holding the curse in place is at its thinnest."

"So you can see and talk to everyone one night a year? On the same day the murders have taken place?" My eyes narrow. "You realize that gives you the opposite of an alibi for this curse-killing thing, right?"

"They're my people, Serenity. I could never hurt them."

I don't answer. He's given me a hell of a lot to think about, and right now, I'm not sure my brain can keep up.

He rests both hands on the island between us and drops his head. "Do you know what it's like to see your own father standing before you but not be able to touch or speak to him? To spend over a hundred years a few miles from the people you love most in the world, yet they're still out of your reach?"

His voice is anguished now, and my heart squeezes at the pain in his eyes. "I can't imagine," I say, quietly. "I'm so sorry."

Sutton shakes his head. "It's my own fault."

The guilt in his tone pains me more than anything else.

"The girl's death was not your fault," I tell him. "While her actions brought her to that situation, it's her mother who is the true killer. The hex-whatever she is. And she's the one we need to bring to justice."

He looks at me now, hazel eyes full of pent-up anger, frustration, and—if I'm not mistaken—fear. "What justice is there for a woman more powerful than any human law enforcement in the world? Prison cannot hold her, Serenity."

"I think my brother would beg to differ." Just thinking about Steven brings a smile to my face.

"I almost forgot you have brothers," Sutton says. "Are you close with them?"

"I am. And Steven is a homicide detective with the NYPD. He's a pain in the ass—they all are—but I love them, and Steven will be able to help us. I'm sure of it."

Sutton looks less than convinced. "Then you understand my need to protect my family."

"I do." Pulling out my cell, I open the note app on my phone. "Tell me her name. We still have seventy-two hours until Halloween. We can stop her."

"A hundred years ago, her name was Myrtle Augustus."

"Okay. Give me time to search her out. I can make a few calls—"

"That's not her name anymore."

"What do you mean?"

"She wears a different face. A new name. It's why we haven't caught her yet."

"She can change her face? Wow, I bet the makers of Botox would love to know her secret."

"Myrtle is powerful, Serenity. You have to promise me you'll be careful. If she finds out what you're doing, she's not going to stop until you're—" He stops for a moment. "Disposed of."

"I can be discreet," I promise.

"You must," he says. "Out there, I can't protect you."

"You don't have to."

He gives me a long look I can't interpret, and my heart beats a little faster. "Yes," he says, "I do."

Falls Gazette

Chapter Fifteen

The sun has long set by the time Sutton walks me back to the edge of the woods. My emotions feel beat to hell, and my body is exhausted. It's been quite a day, and turns out, a bear trying to kill me was the least harrowing part. Who knew?

"This is as far as I go," he says, coming to a stop well inside the cover of the trees.

Through the branches, I can just barely make out the gardens at the back of the B&B. The outside lights are on, casting it all in a pretty yellow glow.

"I wish you could come inside with me," I tell him.

"So do I."

I hesitate, strangely lonely at the thought of walking away from Sutton now. But he makes the decision for me and melts into the shadows before I can say another word.

Shaking off my ridiculous urge to turn and chase after him, I step out of the woods and onto the stone walkway leading up to the back door.

It opens before I reach it. Yvette takes one look at me and lets out a squeal.

"She's here!" Yvette's eyes are wide as she takes me in. "Dear, I have been so worried. Are you all right? Do you need a doctor?"

"What?" I glance in confusion from her to the figure coming up behind her, his footfalls heavy and purposeful. "Sheriff Rhodes? What are you doing here?"

"Miss Kellis, I received a call that you were unaccounted for. Are you all right?"

"I'm fine." I look back and forth between them. Unaccounted for? The hell? "What is going on? Who called you?"

"Your brother, Steven Kellis, reported you missing this afternoon."

At the mention of the name, my jaw drops, and disbelief turns to a rage that only sibling-on-sibling violence can solve.

"Steven called me in as a missing person? Don't I have to be gone more than twenty-four hours for that?"

"Normally, yes. But Yvette confirmed you'd been gone all day." The sheriff looks less than thrilled as he adds, "I came as a favor to a fellow officer."

Unofficial, then. A cop-to-cop favor. I guess that's something. At least, there'd be no report filed. I bet my mother would have loved that. Ugh. "You could have just called."

"I tried calling the number he gave me, but your phone went straight to voicemail."

I pull my phone out of my pocket and frown down at the blank screen. Shit.

"Dead battery," I mutter.

"Dear, you had us so worried," Yvette says. "And now here you are with your arms full of scratches. Are you sure you don't want a doctor?"

"I'm fine." I tuck my arms behind my back. I hadn't even

noticed the scratches earlier. By the looks of them, I'm pretty sure they're from shimmying up a tree, and no part of me wants to relive that story right now. "Well, I'm here. Safe and sound. If that's all, I'm going to head upstairs—"

"Miss Kellis, if I may have a word?" Sheriff Rhodes looks nervously between me and Yvette.

"Sure," I say, wary now. "We'll just…"

"Oh, I'll give you some privacy." Yvette waits until we're both out the door and then shuts it with a click behind us.

I wander down the steps and into the garden then turn and look up at the sheriff.

"Is there something else I can help you with?" I ask.

"Miss Kellis," he begins.

"Serenity," I offer.

"Serenity." He glances back at the house nervously. "I hadn't realized you were staying here when you came to me before." He frowns. "You should seek other housing while you're in town."

"I'm not sure I understand."

He starts walking away from the house, and I follow, my patience thinning. All I want is a hot shower and enough energy to yell at my brother for bringing me this bullshit. But one look at the sheriff's face, and I know there's something else going on here. This isn't about Steven reporting me MIA.

He doesn't stop until we reach the tree line, and then it's like an invisible wall has smacked him in the chest. He yanks to an abrupt halt and turns to me with fear in his eyes.

"Are you okay?" I ask.

"This town isn't what you think, Serenity."

My heart pounds at what he's just implied. Sure, he hasn't come out and said "Sutton Hargrave is a werewolf," but I think we both know what his words truly mean here. And it's the closest thing to honesty I've gotten from anyone I've met here, so I run with it.

"I've recently become aware of this town's more unique aspects," I say, carefully.

His eyes flash with surprise. "Then you know how much is at stake. How dangerous it is to be here during this time of year."

This time of year. Halloween.

Wow. He's really laying his cards on the table.

"I do," I say. "What I don't know is exactly who makes it so dangerous. But something tells me you do."

He hesitates. "It's not safe," he whispers.

"Give me a name," I press. "Just one name."

He shakes his head. "She's listening. Always. You can't begin to understand how powerful she truly is."

"But not so powerful she evaded you. I mean, if you know who she is—"

He shakes his head. "I didn't discover her. She came to me. Made sure I used my position to keep the truth from getting out."

I pause, remembering the obvious show of money I noted at the station. And the accolades, all for non-serious crime-solving. Like someone was making sure nothing too serious drew attention from the outside.

"Like blackmail?"

He doesn't answer, so I try a different tactic.

"She's using you to keep the truth about the curse hidden? About her role in those murders?"

"How did you…?"

"Sutton told me everything," I say. "Everything except her name."

He takes a step back as if the mere mention of Sutton's name has spooked him. I watch as he glances wildly into the woods and then back at the house. When he looks at me again, his eyes are unfocused, his expression stricken.

"You spoke to Sutton?"

"Yes."

"If Sutton is involved, there's no going back," he says, almost to himself.

I take a step toward him, trying to regain his attention. "Tell me her name, Sheriff."

He hesitates, his expression pinched in anguish. "I guess it doesn't matter, now. She'll come for me either way. Her name is—"

Whatever he says is drowned out by an ear-splitting crack.

"The hell?" I look up and spot the enormous oak towering over our heads. Except, it's now tilting sideways. Another crack and the trunk detaches, the entire tree falling straight for where I stand.

Sheriff Rhodes tackles me to the ground, pushing me out of the way just in time. A few branches scrape my skin as the tree crashes and settles. I gasp, trying to catch my breath against the panic of what just happened.

I look over at the sheriff and catch his eye.

He doesn't even have to say it; I already know this was no accident.

I stand, wobbly but unharmed—and newly determined to get that name. But I never get a chance to ask. In the next second, footsteps thunder toward us, the sound of my name drowning out anything else, including my scattered thoughts. Yvette rushes at me, pulling me into a crushing hug and talking a mile a minute about that "close call" and whether I need a doctor. On her heels are Victoria and Lance.

"Oh, darling, are you all right?" Victoria fusses over me. "Look at her, Lance, so pale. Let's get you inside."

"I'm fine," I assure her. "Hey, I thought you were leaving," I add, dazed.

"Yes, exactly, we're leaving tomorrow. Otherwise, we'd love to have dinner with you, wouldn't we, Lance? And have I told you that I love your hair?"

She strokes my hair adoringly, but I stop and stare at her.

"Why do you wear the same outfit every day?"

"What?" Victoria's expression turns from blank to confused. "I don't—"

"And your hair is always perfect. Your make-up, too. And you're so damn cheerful." I shake my head. "This can't be real."

"Of course, I'm real," she says brightly. Then her face falls, and she looks at Lance with a quivering lip. "I am real, right, sweetie?"

"Are you a witch?" I blurt.

Victoria's eyes widen in horror, and her voice drops to a stage whisper. "Witches are real?"

"Sweetheart, we're specters," Lance tells her. "I don't think we can be surprised to hear we're not the only impossible creatures in the universe."

"You're right," she says, nodding while still looking stricken. "Specters. I always forget about that part."

Lance takes her by the shoulders. "Come on, let's get you inside. We have an early departure in the morning."

Lance puts his arm around her and leads Victoria inside. I stare after them and then let out a shriek as a hand lands on my arm. Yvette blinks at me, taken aback.

"Dear?"

"I…" I struggle to get my bearings and redouble my efforts to shake information from the sheriff, but another glance around reveals we're alone.

The sheriff is gone.

The beautiful couple with a bad memory have just proclaimed themselves as ghosts.

And Yvette is looking at me like *I'm* the crazy one.

Shit just got real, and try as I might, I cannot get my brain to form a sane response.

"Serenity," Yvette presses when I don't answer. "Darling, come inside and let me get you a drink."

"Victoria and Lance are…ghosts."

"Yes, I'll explain everything. Come."

She steers me toward the house, but I pull free, wrenching my arm from her grip and backing away. "I can't go in there," I say.

"Of course, you can. It's perfectly safe, I assure you—"

"Safe? Your tree just tried to take me out."

"Darling, you're in shock," she begins, but I'm so done.

"Maybe," I say, "but that tree didn't fall by accident, and I'm rooming beside a pair of ghosts—"

"Specters."

My eyes widen as I realize she already knows and is clearly more than okay with putting up a pair of dead lovers in her spare room.

"Those two have been here since before me," she says, as if that somehow eases the shocking truth. "They're harmless."

"Yeah, I think I'll take my chances elsewhere."

My heart thuds as I realize Yvette might be more than just a bed and breakfast hostess for dead people. She might very well also be a witch. The same witch who drains people's bodies of their blood so she can curse an entire town for eternity.

But whatever Yvette Abbett may be, I've learned a few things about myself since coming to Midnight Falls. Like how not to be an idiot. So, instead of sticking around to question a woman who may or may not be dropping trees on people's heads—I run. Straight into the woods because, at least in there, the only threats to my safety are non-magical, woodsy predators. And I'll take a bear over a bitch with a curse any day.

Falls Gazette

Chapter Sixteen

I'm halfway in the trees before I realize that I just left everything I own behind in a B&B that is likely owned by a murderer. A witchy, face-changing, blood-lusting murderer, at that.

What. The. Fuck.

There's no going back. That's for damn sure. My lungs burn as I run faster, hoping this time I remember the way to Sutton's. But, aside from having actual breadcrumbs in my possession as Sutton walked me home earlier, I can only rely on my memory. Thankfully, I have a good one. Even in the steadily darkening sky above. I can barely see my own hands, but thanks to the moonlight shining through the trees, I manage to dodge a massive tree trunk looming ahead just in time.

Not wanting to call out to him in case anything—or anyone—else is nearby, I remain silent aside from my own heavy breathing. Holy shit, I nearly got crushed by a tree.

A *tree*.

First a bear, then a tree. Maybe coming to this town truly was a bad idea. But then, Sutton's massive house comes into view, and I realize that, if I'd never come here, I never would have met him, and I wouldn't have the chance to bring him at least some sense of closure.

The murders would have simply continued, and people would have suffered. So even with the bear and tree in mind, I'm glad I'm here.

In a Lewis & Clark moment, I spot the house dead ahead. *Bingo*. I rush through the iron gates and head toward the porch. Before I reach the bottom though, the door flies open, and Sutton rushes out. Eyes wide, he stares at me. "What happened? Are you okay?"

The sight of him in this moment, of his touching concern, snakes its way right past my defenses and into my heart.

Unsure as to when it happened, I simply accept the fact that, for whatever reason, he is my safety net in this crazy new reality. Not breaking stride, I slam into him. Muscled arms come around, and he crushes me to his body.

We stand there, embracing on his porch for what is probably far longer than is accepted as far as platonic friends go, but I can't be bothered to care. Not to be dramatic, but I nearly died—twice—in the last twenty-four hours.

A few moments later, he releases me and, gripping both of my arms, pushes me back to look at my face. "What happened?"

I inhale deeply, lungs still burning from the run. "A tree fell on me."

"What?"

"Well, not *on* me, but almost. The sheriff pushed me out of the way in time, but it almost killed me!"

"Arden?" Sutton frowns. "What was he doing there?"

I turn away and start pacing. "Ugh, that's a shitshow-and-a-half. Apparently, my brother reported me missing because he couldn't get a hold of me, so Sheriff Rhodes was there, then Yvette was there, panicked, and she hugged me, and Victoria was wearing the same shirt again and—" I whirl on him. "Did you know *specters* are real?" Without waiting for him to answer, I continue, "Of course, you did. You're a fucking wolf for shit's sake."

"Serenity." He moves in front of me and stops me in my tracks. "Breathe."

"What? I am."

"Then slow the hell down because I can hardly follow what you're saying."

Taking a deep breath, I gesture toward his front door. "Can we go inside?"

He holds out his arm and nods but doesn't speak. Taking it as a formal invitation, I haul ass into his house, stopping just inside the foyer. And yes, I absolutely check above me just to make sure nothing overhead can fall. Well, except maybe the building itself, in which case, that would suck and I doubt very much even Sutton's wolf strength can help us.

Sutton shuts the door and leans back against it. "What happened when you arrived back at the B&B? You said your brother called Arden?"

"Yes. He was worried about me, so he reported me missing. Sheriff Rhodes was there when I got back, and Yvette was freaking out. She rushed forward and hugged me; asked if I needed to see a doctor. Then, she said she'd give the sheriff and me some privacy—but I think that was just a ruse—"

"A ruse?"

"I'm getting ahead of myself, again." I take a deep breath. "The sheriff pulled me aside. Privately. He told me that I needed to seek different housing and that the town wasn't what I thought it was, except I already knew that; he just didn't know I knew that."

"He warned you."

"Yes. When I told him that I knew about the curse, he said I should realize how dangerous it is this time of year. He also told me that he knows who she is." Excitement building, I take a step toward Sutton. We're so close, *so close* to figuring out who she is. "The witch, Sutton. He knows her name and her face!"

Sutton's mouth falls open, his eyes widening. If this were a comedy and not a life-or-death situation, I might have laughed at his shock. But this isn't a comedy. It's reality, and real lives are at stake. "Did he tell you who it is?" he demands, crossing the floor toward me.

I shake my head. "He started to, but that's when the tree fell. It cracked and fell down right where I was standing. He knocked me out of the way then left before I could ask any more. Of course, by then Yvette and her ghost buddies were out and about. I think she's going to try and hurt him, Sutton. Why the hell did I come here instead of warning him that Yvette is on to him?"

"Yvette?"

"She's the witch," I say. "She has to be." I shake my head and start to head for the door.

Sutton blocks me. "Stop, Serenity. For one damned second; let me wrap my head around this whole thing."

"I have to get to him. He knows who she is. She's been blackmailing him!"

"If the tree falling was no accident—which I'm guessing it wasn't—she already knows he told you too much. Being near him will endanger you both."

"You can't be serious. What if she comes for him?"

"Rhodes is good at protecting himself. If he thinks he's in danger, he'll find a way to stay safe."

"Sutton—"

"No." His curt tone and the sharp gaze he's currently pinning me with leaves no room for argument, but I'll be damned if I let him stop me from potentially saving someone's life. "Serenity," he finally says, softer this time. "It's possible she doesn't know what he was about to tell you. Or that she does and the tree was a scare tactic. She needs him, right? Otherwise, why blackmail him?"

"True," I say, half-heartedly.

"You going back to find him could be more dangerous than you staying away. If she sees you two together, she might choose to eliminate you both to save herself trouble later."

The words he's saying make sense, but the thought that I might have in some way put the sheriff in more danger is eating at me. Why the hell hadn't I been more careful? I know better!

Defeated, I nod and let out a breath. "Fine."

"Good." He crosses both arms. "Now, why do you think Yvette is the witch?"

"Because the sheriff told me to leave the B&B. That I should find safer housing. He specifically wanted me away from her place, Sutton. What if it's been her this entire time? I've been sleeping there! Right where she could get to me!"

"Calm down." He reaches out and runs his hands over my arms. The contact heats me from the inside, and suddenly, the butterflies in my stomach have little to do with nerves. *Damn hormones.* "Even if it is her, you're safe now."

"I left everything at the B&B. I didn't even go up to my room. The tree and ghosts really threw me for a loop."

"Ghosts. You said they're staying with her?"

"Yes. I thought they were just spontaneous people who kept changing their plans, but they told me themselves that they were ghosts…or rather specters."

"They're likely trapped here by the same curse we all are."

My heart cracks at the thought of them not being able to move on. “You think they died here?”

“Possibly. Or they were killed in one of the witch’s rituals and are trapped inside the town.”

“That’s so sad.”

“It is,” he agrees. “Come on, let’s have a drink. I sure as hell could use one.”

As I follow him into the kitchen, I mentally go through my checklist of the items I left behind. My laptop—which, unless she can crack my password, is safe—my cell phone charger, keys, clothes—all of which can be replaced if need be.

My main concern is Steven. Shit, I should have called him. Wait. Called him. The sheriff! If I can call and warn— Reaching into my back pocket, I check my phone. And remember that the battery is dead and I have no charger.

“Here.” Sutton hands me a glass of whiskey I didn’t even see him pour then takes a deep drink of his own. “It’s been a day, hasn't it?”

I snort. “Understatement. I don’t suppose you have a cell phone charger, do you?”

“No. No service out here, anyway.”

“Figures. I need to get a call out to my brother.”

“It’ll have to wait. The sheriff will likely have called him to let him know you’re accounted for.”

“You don’t know Steven. A phone call from the sheriff is exactly what would bring him here.”

“The woods aren’t safe at night,” he replies. “But I can walk you to town tomorrow, and you can get a charger from the store. There’s one close enough that I can still keep an eye on you from the trees.”

“Lot of good that will do since you can’t actually come to my rescue.”

His expression falls, and I want to kick myself. “I can still watch your back.”

“I’m sorry, Sutton. I didn't mean to insult you. It’s just…” Trailing off, I set the whiskey glass on the counter and pinch the bridge of my nose. “It’s been a day. And I’m hangry.”

“Hangry?”

“Oh, it means angry and hungry.”

“Ah.” His eyes light up. “I think I can help with that. Hang on."

He turns back for the fridge, which was probably called an icebox a hundred years ago when it was brand new. After a moment of rummaging, he comes away with eggs and bacon.

“It’s simple, but—”

“It sounds perfect.”

He goes to work on the food, and I lean against the counter, content to sip my drink and watch him work. Sutton in the kitchen is a strangely intoxicating sight. I’ve never felt like the kind of girl who needed to be cared for, but having Sutton cook for me is endearing. I feel myself falling in a way I never expected to fall. And for a wolf-man, no less.

“That stove is something else,” I say—mostly because I have to think about something besides the man’s forearms.

“It was my mother’s,” he says, and I realize I was right. This space—these things—are special to him.

“Did she paint the flowers?”

“My father had it custom made from a family friend,” he says. “Hydrangeas were her favorite.”

“Sounds like your parents loved each other very much.”

“We were a happy family,” he says, wistfully. “And yes, there was love.”

His voice cracks, which threatens to rip my heart right in half.

“Do you have siblings?” I ask.

He shakes his head. “No, thankfully. I wouldn’t have been able to bear... Losing my mother was hard enough.”

My throat closes with emotion. I can’t even imagine losing my mom in that way. And my brothers... Tears threaten, but before they can fall, I blink at the sight of a steaming plate of scrambled eggs and crispy bacon.

“Here,” he says, holding out a fork in his other hand. “Sit. Eat.”

I slide gingerly onto one of two barstools, waiting to be sure it’ll hold. When it does, I waste no time digging into the food. If there was a time for polite, demure manners, today is not it.

But Sutton doesn’t seem to mind my enthusiasm. If anything, he takes it as the compliment it is. A moment later, he joins me, and together, we wolf down our breakfast-for-dinner—pun intended.

When we’re finished, I get to my feet and begin washing dishes. Sutton tries to stop me, but I wave him off. “In my house, if you don’t cook, you clean up. That’s the rule.”

“Your house sounds happy, too.”

I smile. “It is. Loud and annoying, and with everyone tripping over everyone else. So yes, happy.”

“I would love to meet them sometime.”

I turn to him just in time to see the uncertainty flash. Like he hadn’t meant to say the words. I nod, feeling awkward. “That would be great.”

If this were any other date or any other guy, I’d probably be full of anxiety over that comment. Meeting a girl’s family was a big step. Usually one that suggested feelings. But Sutton’s trapped here. He probably only means that he’d love to go anywhere. Visit anyone.

Right?

The idea of deciphering it is too much for my tired brain, and as the last dish is washed and dried, I yawn.

“Coffee?” Sutton asks, amused.

"No, thanks. Maybe I can just get some sleep? Do you have a spare room?"

"Not one that's suitable, but you can have mine. I'll take the couch." He grips my hand and pulls me toward the stairs. When we reach the bottom, I eye them warily. Something he notices with a tight smile. "If you fall through, I'll catch you."

"Uh-huh." But the thrill of having his arms around me has me stepping up despite my reservations. Is it bad that I almost hope to trip?

We reach the top, and he leads me down a narrow hall with more peeling wallpaper. At the end, a door is half-ajar, and I know without him saying, it's his room. A theory that is confirmed when we step inside and my lungs fill with the combined scents of pine and leather.

His bed is massive—a huge four-poster that is at least a king-size, but the blankets adorning it are worn, having been patched many times by someone who could use a sewing lesson or two—and now I feel like an ass.

"It's not much," he says, his tone betraying a bit of self-consciousness.

"It's perfect," I reply, turning to smile at him. "Thank you."

"I have some shirts in the drawer. You're welcome to one if you need to get more comfortable."

"Thank you."

He turns to leave, but I grip his hand, not wanting to be alone. It's silly, but being attacked by a bear and nearly crushed by a tree puts one's mortality into consideration. Not to mention discovering wolf shifters, witches, and ghosts exist—all in the same day. "Everything all right?"

Sucking my bottom lip into my mouth, I chew on it for a moment as I ponder how to even ask what I want to ask. Will he think I'm trying to seduce him? Trap him?

Sutton's growl pulls me back, and I glance up only to find him staring intently at my mouth, pupils dilated. "Please stop that."

"What?"

"Chewing on your lip."

"Why?"

He doesn't respond.

"Listen, I don't want to be alone. We can put a mountain of pillows or something between us, but can you please stay in here tonight?"

I wait for his response, practically holding my breath until, finally, he nods. "I'll leave you for a few moments so you can dress if you'd like."

"Yes, please."

"Top drawer."

"Got it, thanks."

With a tight smile, he closes the door behind him, and I cross the room, stopping in front of the dresser. Honestly, if I were to give too much thought to what I'm about to do, I'd likely not do it.

I've always been logical. A planner. And sharing a bed with someone I barely know, who I also thought was a murderer until this morning, is less than logical and definitely not planned. Pulling open the top drawer to his dresser, I run my fingers over worn black t-shirts. The cotton is strained from being worn over and over again.

For a moment, I'm struck by how truly solitary Sutton's life is out here. I'm not overly social, but even I need my time amongst people. Family. Friends. To be completely isolated, cut off from everyone except for one night a year—it must be torture.

Not for much longer, I remind myself. By November first, Sutton Hargrave will be free of this place and its curse.

Selecting the shirt on top, I undress quickly, leaving only my thin bralette and underwear on before I slip into the soft fabric. It caresses my skin, sending my already anxious nerves ablaze, and for once, I'm grateful for my OCD nature of needing to shave my legs every single day.

Ready for bed, I cross the room and fold back the blankets. They are soft, smooth, and smell exactly like him.

I climb into the giant bed, slipping beneath the fabric and pulling the comforter up to my chin. The mattress is beyond comfortable, the pillow plush, and exhaustion hits me like a ton of bricks.

"May I come in?" Sutton asks, after a soft knock.

"Yes," I call out, making sure I'm completely covered. Not that it matters—I'll likely kick everything off in the night.

He pushes open the door, hesitating only a moment before moving inside. He's changed from dark jeans and a t-shirt to nothing but low-hanging shorts.

My mouth goes dry.

All liquid surges to another area—one that has *no* business being anything but neutral around this man—or any man, for that matter. I mean, I was nearly killed. You'd think my brain would be focused on that fact, but here we are, wondering if near-death experiences normally induce lust or if it's just my weird-ass. Because right now, I can't even be bothered to remind myself that, until less than a week ago, I was engaged to someone else.

"I, uh, sleep hot," he explains, running a hand over his hair. The white stripe up the front moves with his fingers as he combs them through, somehow making him look even more attractive.

Maybe coming here was a bad idea. Or a great one, depending on which body part you ask.

"It's fine," I say, far more eager than I should have been. "As it happens, I do too, so I apologize in advance if I throw the covers off of both of us."

He grunts and moves to the opposite side of the bed.

"Is this where you normally sleep? I can move—"

"No. You stay there." His interruption saves me the embarrassment of trying to scoot over while attempting to keep his shirt covering my ass, so I nod appreciatively as he climbs beneath the covers and settles.

The mattress dips on the left side, his weight pressing it down. Within moments, though, he has pulled the covers up to his chest, tucked an arm behind his head, and fallen silent. As we lie here, I briefly entertain the idea of what it must be like to fall asleep next to him every single night.

"Thank you for letting me stay."

"Of course. I want nothing but your safety, Serenity."

"Why?"

"I need a reason?" He turns his head to the side, so I roll over to face him. There's little more than a foot between us, and my pulse trips over itself at the awareness of how close his half-naked body is to mine.

"You don't know me, so why aren't you more concerned with getting your answers than you are with keeping me safe?"

"Because I'm not willing to risk your life for a fight that's not yours, to begin with."

His answer is so heartbreakingly heroic that, if I weren't already lying down, I might have swooned—if I was the swooning type, that is.

"Well, while I appreciate that, I do plan on solving these murders. You deserve a life. And this," I say, waving my hand around a room that's aged where he has not, "is no life at all."

"Promise me something," he says, turning his head to the ceiling.

"What?"

"If we haven't solved them by October thirty-first, you'll leave."

I lift onto my elbows. "You want me to go?"

"Yes."

"Why? Can't I just stay out here with you and ride it out?"

He shakes his head. "Nowhere in Midnight Falls is safe on All Hallows Eve, and especially not this house. The entire town comes out here. It's the one day they're allowed to cross the threshold. They come for a ball, food, festivities, but by the time it's over—someone doesn't walk away."

"That's how she's choosing her victims? At a ball? Here? Wait. That means she comes, too."

"Yes. I've suspected it for quite some time, but figuring out who she is among the faces of my pack has been impossible."

"Pack? That's the second time you've used that word. Does that mean—"

"The entire town are wolves?" He chuckles darkly. "Yes, though they cannot shift. Part of the curse."

"So they're trapped in their human forms?"

"Yes."

I fall back again. "How freaking sad. To exist as half of what you are." When he doesn't immediately respond, I glance over to see him watching me. "What?"

"You are truly an enigma, Serenity."

"How so?"

"You're strong, brave, heroic, and empathetic. It's a potent combination."

Before I can stop it, I snort. My cheeks flush. "I'm a journalist. Empathetic is not something I ever would have used to describe me."

"You are a human who is sad because the town cannot shift."

"You told me that you were both a man and a wolf. That means they're all living as half of themselves. No wonder they're all grumpy."

"I can imagine they are also wary of you. Everyone knows the same as we do. The witch shows up, chooses her victim, then leaves after the ball."

I sit straight up. "You mean they think I'm her?"

"It's a possibility."

"Shit. I hadn't considered that." All the times they treated me coolly—was it out of fear?

"Serenity."

"Hmm?" I look over at Sutton, his yellow-brown gaze boring straight through to my heart. I want to bury my hands in his thick hair, run my hands over his body. I wet my lips, knowing it's a poor idea. And still unable to help myself.

In the dim light cast by the moon outside, I can see his pupils dilate.

"I can't risk you being here."

"But that could be exactly what we need." I shake my head and turn my attention away from the sexy, argumentative man beside me. "We can corner her, get her to talk! If it's

Yvette—"

"Serenity," he interrupts. I meet his gaze in the dark room. "Please promise me." His voice cracks, concern weighing it down.

I can't leave town, now. I know we're too close to just give up, and I'm sure, on some level, he knows it, too.

So, I do what any good reporter does when they're trying to reach the truth: I lie. For both our sakes. And for the sake of her next victim—whoever he or she may be. "Okay. I'll go if we haven't solved the murders by then."

Sutton visibly relaxes. "Thank you. Goodnight, Serenity."

"Night, Sutton."

A MASSIVE FORM PRESSING AGAINST MY BACK ROUSES ME FROM sleep. I come to slowly, my senses flaring to life, one by one. First, there's the feeling. Heat at my back, a solid body curled around me. Next, Sutton's scent fills my lungs. I want to hold my breath for eternity so I never lose the way it makes me feel.

My eyes can only make out shadows in the dark room, and before I am fully awake, I'm pressing back against his hard body out of pure lust-filled reflex.

Sutton groans, his arm tightening around my waist. As he tucks me in against him, his erection presses against my ass, pulling me from sleep completely. *Balls, he's huge.* My entire body flares to life, nerves firing at ten thousand percent.

Moisture and heat pool between my legs, and I squeeze my thighs together in an attempt to curb the throbbing. A useless effort since I imagine the only thing that will fix this type of ache is the erection pressing into my back.

Or his hands.

His mouth.

To be honest, I don't even care at this point.

His hot breath fans over my ear, and goosebumps erupt along my skin. I tilt my head up, giving him access to my throat. Access he greedily takes. A hot tongue runs along my jaw, his fingers tightening on my belly.

I moan.

He flips me over and climbs on top of me, settling his heavy weight between my legs. Then, he stares down at me, pupils dilated. My gaze drops to his full mouth, and I suck my bottom lip in.

"I told you to stop doing that."

"Or what?" I ask, voice barely above a whisper.

"It fucking undoes me." He drops his head lower, right to the base of my neck, and inhales. "Fuck. Tell me to stop, Serenity. Please fucking tell me to go to hell."

I should.

But why?

Reaching up, I thread my fingers through his hair and yank his mouth down to mine. The moment our lips meet, the entire world shifts on its axis. Birds sing; butterflies take to the sky—all that ridiculous earth-shattering shit. I open beneath him, and he slips his tongue into my mouth, expertly fucking me without so much as his mouth on mine.

Whatever I think I've felt before, it's nothing compared to what Sutton does to me.

I arch up into him, desperate to feel any release at all taking over me, and in this moment—this incredibly hot, perfect moment—Sutton's not the only animal in the room.

He growls against my mouth, and I cling to him as though he's the only thing keeping me grounded. Who the hell knows these days, maybe he is.

Strong hands slide down my body until one cups my breast, his thumb running over the taut nipple beneath the thin fabric.

Another moan leaves my lips as I arch up into his touch. He drops his other hand down to my hip, then pauses a moment before cupping me.

Fire slams through me; an inferno that devours everything in its path.

"Fuck me, you're wet." He slips a finger beneath the thin layer of my underwear, sliding it over my clit.

I'm so close, already. The mother of all orgasms just out of reach.

Sutton leans up and takes my mouth again, only this time, the connection is electric—literally.

Something zaps us both, and he flies off of me, breathing ragged, fingers touched to his lips. He stands at the foot of the bed, looking dazed and yet, still obviously aroused.

"I didn't know sparks flying was a literal expression." I laugh nervously. When he doesn't respond, I sit up and touch my own mouth. It sizzles, the sting not completely abated. "What was that?"

"I don't know," he says, softly. His bare chest heaves with every breath he takes. When his gaze levels on mine, someone might as well have thrown a bucket of cold water on us both. "But before we do that again, we should probably find out."

Falls Gazette

Chapter Seventeen

Sutton doesn't come back to bed. That, more than anything, tells me our strange little spark is a big deal. But even as I'd love nothing more than to dwell on the best make-out session of my life, I have problems much larger than static electricity. In the light of day, even murder and magic take a backseat to the fact that if I don't get into contact with Steven soon, the National Guard will be called, and I'll never hear the end of it.

After a quick shower, I dress and do what I can with my hair considering I have zero belongings to help me tame it. Downstairs, the scent of coffee lures me to the kitchen where I find Sutton with a freshly brewed pot. He's already dressed in dark jeans and a tight black t-shirt as he pours a fresh mug and offers it to me.

"You know the way to my heart," I say, and he smiles, but it doesn't reach his eyes.

There's a distance between us that wasn't there before.

Stupid spark.

I have no idea what that was, but something tells me Sutton

knows. Or, at least, has a theory. Judging from the very serious look in his eyes, I don't know if I can handle hearing it. Not with so many other problems pressing in around us.

One thing at a time, Serenity. Stop trying to chomp on the elephant.

"How did you sleep?" he asks.

"Pretty great, considering," I reply. "You?"

He doesn't answer, and I cringe. Why the hell are things so awkward now? It was one kiss, right? One mind-blowing, toe-curling kiss. We're both consenting adults. Now, though, it feels as though whatever we'd built between us is gone. Or too far out of reach for me to grab it again.

"You still up for that walk to town?" I ask. "If I don't call Steven soon, we will have a national emergency on our hands, and I'm not so sure either of us can handle anything else on our plates."

"I'll walk you as far as I can," he says. "But I need you to promise not to wander. Just the store. Nowhere else."

"How am I supposed to investigate for you if I can't go into town?"

He shakes his head. "We're done investigating. It's not safe anymore."

"Look, we know who the witch is. At least, let me check on Sheriff Rhodes. See if he can help us take her down."

His expression darkens to instant fury. "There is no 'us' when it comes to taking her down."

His words are a blow I didn't expect. "What does that mean? Our partnership is over?"

"It's not—" He huffs out a breath. "Fine. The store is across from the station. You can go in and make sure he's all right. But that's it. Then you come right back to where I can protect you."

I hate everything about his overprotective plan, but I nod, choosing my battles. "Deal. Let's go."

He sets his coffee aside—resigned to this errand—and we head out.

Sutton takes me on a different route, veering west instead of south to the B&B, and we end up at the edge of a thick stand of trees. Beyond where we stand is the relative bustle of downtown and a clear view of the drugstore that sits adjacent to the police station.

"I'll wait here," Sutton all but growls, frustration that he can't come with me clearly in his tone.

"What happens—" I ask "—if you try to go any farther?"

"Pain," he says simply, and I don't have the heart to ask him to elaborate.

"I'm sorry that this is happening to you."

He meets my gaze, hazel eyes full of pain that has nothing to do with the boundary line. "So am I."

I look back at the drugstore, pondering the idea of just forgetting this errand. But, with my dead phone burning a hole in my pocket and an overprotective brother I don't want to piss off, I know there's no choice.

"Here," Sutton says, and hands me a twenty.

"I can pay for my own things," I say, but Sutton rolls his eyes.

"With what?" he asks.

I groan, remembering I actually can't. Not without my credit cards and cash, which are all back at Yvette's fun house of specter horrors.

"Right." I take the twenty and stuff it into my pocket. "Be right back," I say and hurry out of the trees toward the store. The moment I hit the sidewalk, I become uncomfortably aware of just how vulnerable I am. For the first time since coming to town, I don't want to be noticed. The side-eye I get from the few pedestrians reminds me of what they think I am—and what all of them are, too. Wolves. Even if they can't shift as Sutton says, these people are animals. Shifters capable of things no human could ever dream of. Knowing what I do, I see them in a whole new light.

Striding past the empty table where I played chess with Phineas, shock ripples through me all over again. If everyone here is—was—a wolf, that means Phineas, too. I can't help but try to picture him shifting and morphing as Sutton did. An old man turned wolf is a hard thing to imagine, but it helps calm me. Even as a deadly predator, I know instinctively, Phineas would never hurt me.

And the idea of letting him be hurt because I couldn't stop Yvette in time only fuels my resolve. If I'm their only hope for freedom, I can't walk away. Not now, not ever.

A little bell dings as I shove open the glass door boasting *Midnight Falls Drugstore* along with the operating hours.

Inside, it smells like day-old hotdogs, which makes sense when I spot them still roasting on the counter. A man sits on a stool behind the cash register, and he glares at me as I walk in.

Friendly.

Then, I remember—he thinks I'm a witch. I force a smile. "Phone chargers? I lost mine."

He doesn't speak, just points to the left.

"Thanks." I move through the small store and down an aisle packed with individual bags of chips and packages of candy. There, at the end, is a tower with both chargers and cheap sunglasses.

It doesn't take me long to locate a charger that fits my phone, so I grab it and head to the counter.

As the man rings it up, I locate his name badge. "So, George, how long have you lived here?"

"Feels like forever," he replies. "That will be ten-eighty-one."

Handing him the twenty, I grab the charger and remove it from its packaging.

"Here's your change. Have a great day." His tone tells me he doesn't give two shits whether or not I actually do, though.

"Thanks, you too," I reply sweetly. "Can I plug this in somewhere?"

He stares at me.

"Please?"

With an eye roll, he gestures to the wall closest to the door, so I flash a smile. "Thanks." Heading over to the tiny cafe table in front of a large bay window, I lean down and plug in the charger, stick the other side into the bottom of my phone, and set it on the table, screen side up.

Minutes tick by. I stare down at it as though my frustration alone will bring the bastard to life.

A symbol illuminates on the screen. *Finally.* It finishes booting up, so I tap Steven's name in my favorites list.

Before I put it to my ear, I glance at the screen. *Fantastic.* 1% battery.

I call Steven, praying there's enough power for this call and the phone won't die mid-charge.

"Serenity?"

Steven's voice is full of actual worry and guilt stabs through me.

"It's me," I say. "I'm fine. Safe. Alive. Whatever. You can stop worrying."

When George, who seems to hate me, clears his throat and points to the door, I roll my eyes and unplug the charger then resist the urge to flip my middle finger up at him as I step onto the sidewalk.

Murdery witch or not, I don't deserve this kind of pre-judgment.

"Where have you been?" Steven demands, his panic quickly turning pissy now that he knows I'm okay. Not that I expected anything less.

"I went for a hike yesterday, and my phone died, and then I lost my charger." Close enough. "Sorry."

"Sorry?" he repeats, incredulously. "You went MIA for over twenty-four hours, and I get 'sorry?'"

"Steven," I begin, but he's not having it.

"What is going on down there, Serenity?"

I glance around to make sure no one is close enough to hear me and lower my voice. "Something happened yesterday and I figured out who the killer is."

"You what?"

"It's the old lady who owns the bed and breakfast, if you can believe it."

He mutters a curse and then, after a beat of silence, says, "Have you gone to the police?"

The fact that he doesn't even question my statement warms my heart.

"I tried. The sheriff already knows who it is, and he hasn't done anything. I think he's being blackmailed."

"What—"

"I think I need outside help on this one."

"Okay. Shit. Wow. Yeah, I can make some calls. See if someone from the Richmond precinct can come over. What evidence can you send me?"

"Evidence?" I bite my lip.

"Yeah, you know, the stuff that supports the claims you're making. Proof irrefutable enough that a judge will issue a warrant."

"About that…"

"Fucking-A, Serenity. You don't have evidence? You can't just go around accusing people of murder without any proof. I've taught you better than that, dammit."

"I know, I know. Okay, look, I'm working on getting it."

"Why do I have a feeling you're planning on doing something stupid?"

My phone beeps, reminding me of its low battery.

“What was that?” Steven asks, sharply.

“Low battery. Listen, I’m going to get the evidence. Soon. And when I do, I’ll send it to you so you can get a warrant.”

“This is way outside my jurisdiction, Ser. You’re out of your league here.”

“I’m not. And I’m not alone, either, so don’t worry. I’ll call you soon, I swear. Just…stop calling the police on me, okay?”

“Call me every twenty-four hours, or I’m going straight to the FBI,” he warns. “And I’m not bluffing. I have a friend—”

“Okay, okay. I’ll call you tomorrow.”

He starts to reply, but the call ends. I look at the screen. Dead.

Dammit.

Hopefully, he’ll actually wait the full twenty-four hours before calling said friend.

I move past the building and stare into the tree line. It takes me no time at all to find Sutton standing just inside the trees like some kind of sexy lumberjack stalker. My heart does a weird flutter thing that my inner middle-schooler actually finds adorable.

Ugh.

Ignoring my fluttering heart, I hold up the charger as if it's some sort of trophy and then raise one finger in the air to signal I’ll be right there. Without waiting for his reaction—which I already know is moving toward an unhappy one—I dart across the street and into the police station.

The receptionist’s desk is empty, and I use the opportunity to plug the charger into a wall outlet beside the computer monitor. Then I plug in my phone and will the thing to juice up as quickly as possible.

I’ve just tucked the phone out of sight when the receptionist returns. She takes one look at me and loses the cheerful expression she wears. Wow. So, the sourness is reserved just for me. How nice.

“Do you need something?” she asks.

"I'm looking for Sheriff Rhodes."

"He's not here."

"Well, do you know when he'll be in?"

"He's been called away. You can leave a message."

Not really an answer—but then, I have a feeling she is making it her mission not to give me anything helpful.

"Do you have a direct phone number for him?" I ask. "It's important that I speak with him. Today."

"No," she says, simply.

I roll my eyes. "Fine. Can you just tell him to call me?"

"I'll do my best."

She doesn't bother asking for my number, so we both know how that's going to go.

"Thanks, you've been super helpful." I yank my phone and charger from her outlet, and her eyes widen.

"You can't—"

"Bye," I call, and march out before she can finish her lecture. Or arrest me.

Outside, I step into full view of Sutton again so he can see I haven't been murdered by person or tree—in this town, you can't be too sure.

Stuffing the phone back into my pocket, I start for the trees. A shadow falls in front of me as a figure crosses my path. I look up and lock eyes with a familiar woman.

"Audrey."

The tailor offers me an austere smile. "Serenity. How are you today?"

"I'm good." I spare a glance at the trees. Sutton has moved out of sight, but I can still feel him there, watching, waiting. Dropping my voice, I take a step closer to her. "Hey, listen, I have a question."

"What can I do for you?" she asks.

I hesitate, hoping Sutton wasn't lying about not being able to hear anything past the tree line.

"The annual ball," I say. "The one held every year at Hargrave Manor. It's the day after tomorrow, right?"

Audrey registers surprise then quickly masks it. "Yes, how did you know?"

"Oh, people have mentioned it here and there," I say, waving a hand. "I know you're probably slammed with orders, but I was wondering if it's too late or if you might have something left I could buy from you. I would love to come, but I have nothing to wear."

I pause, wondering if she'll warn me off. Tell me it's too dangerous, or even to mention the curse or Yvette. But her expression remains smooth and polite as she says, "What exactly are you looking for?"

Good. That makes this easier.

"I'm not picky," I say. "Anything you have lying around would be great."

"I may have something," she says, "but you should know the ball is very private. Only locals are invited. And pardon me for saying, but I don't think it's an event an outsider would appreciate."

It's not a warning, per se. But it's close. And while I appreciate her concern, I am determined to get the evidence I promised Steven.

"Thank you for the information," I tell her. "But I'd like to attend if it's all the same. Can you help me?"

She looks like she might refuse, but in the end, she nods. "Come by my shop tomorrow morning. I'll have something for you."

"Thank you," I tell her. "You're a lifesaver."

With a wave, I hurry back to the woods and Sutton.

He meets me with an anxious look. "What the hell was that?"

"What? I got the charger like we talked about."

I hold it up for emphasis, but he shakes his head like he's willing himself to calm down.

"Inside the drugstore— You took longer than I expected."

"I had to charge my phone long enough to get it to make a call," I say.

"And your brother knows you're safe?"

I snort. Safe is a relative term. But one look at Sutton, and I realize he isn't going to appreciate that particular irony.

"Yes," I say. "I promised to check in again tomorrow, so we're good."

He nods. "What did the sheriff say?"

"Nothing, he wasn't there."

Why does Sutton not look surprised? "Let's go."

He starts for the house, and I hurry to catch up, wondering why he didn't ask me about Audrey or what our conversation was about. But I'm not stupid enough to bring it up either, so instead, we walk in silence for a moment.

When we reach the house, Sutton goes inside and disappears upstairs. I plug my phone into an outlet near the table then fumble around the kitchen until I find the makings for more coffee. A mission that proves successful. After starting the gas stove, I place a full kettle over the flame and wait.

I'm just turning around to check my phone when Sutton reappears, holding a wad of cash in his hands.

"What's this for?" I ask as he offers it to me.

"A bus ticket. Or a rental car. Your choice." He shrugs.

Narrowing my gaze, I stare at the cash a moment longer then look back up at him. "I don't understand."

"I had a feeling you wouldn't want to risk going back to your car just yet," he says. "This will help you get out of town before the ball."

"Wait. We said if we can find a way to stop Yvette, I don't have to go."

"Yes, and unfortunately, we're out of time."

"What if I can get her to admit to the curse and the murders?" I ask.

He frowns.

But I refuse to let his overprotectiveness ruin my determination. "Steven says if we can get evidence, he can call the state police in Richmond and get them to send people down with a warrant. We can have her arrested before she can do this to anyone else."

"Serenity."

"No, listen, it can work. I just need to fully charge my phone—I mean, obviously—and then I can use it to record her—"

"Serenity." He grabs my arms, and I fall silent.

That look in his eyes is back again. The distant brooding one that holds a secret.

"What aren't you telling me?" I ask—a mixture of betrayal, anger, and helplessness taking over. I thought we were past this; past lies and half-truths.

"Yvette is powerful. She'll never let herself be taken like that. And human police don't stand a chance against her."

"But…they have guns," I say, hopefully.

"I'm an immortal predator with the strength of a hundred men," he says. "And even I couldn't take her down before she locked me inside these woods. What makes you think a human with a handgun can do it?"

I scowl.

He's poking holes in the only plan I have.

Out of sheer stubbornness, I refuse to admit he might be right. Otherwise, why the hell am I here? What is my purpose in this creepy-ass town if not to help him?

"We have to try," I say.

"I plan to," he says in a resolute voice that makes me instantly suspicious.

"What is that supposed to mean?"

"It means, in the morning, you're going to buy a bus ticket and get out of this town. And two nights from now, when the moon is high and the witch is here, I am going to kill her like I should have done a hundred years ago."

Falls Gazette

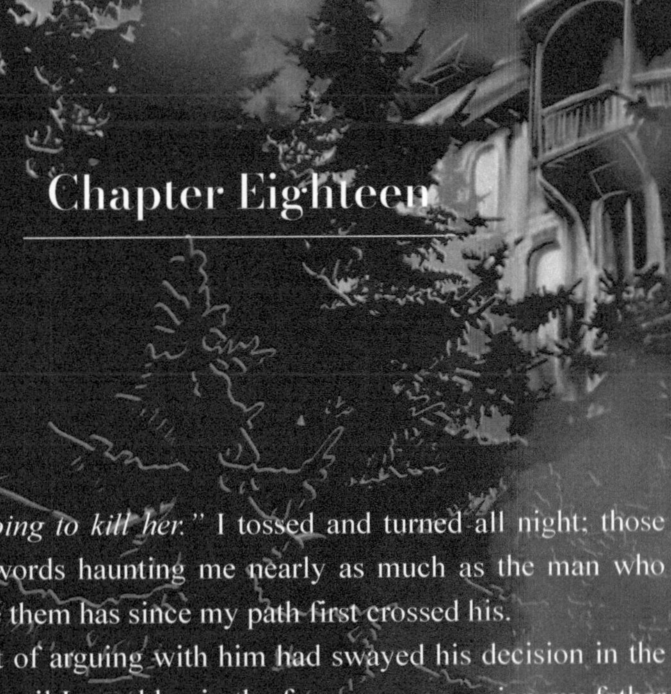

Chapter Eighteen

"I'm going to kill her." I tossed and turned all night; those five words haunting me nearly as much as the man who spoke them has since my path first crossed his.

No amount of arguing with him had swayed his decision in the least. I talked until I was blue in the face—an expression my father once used with me and I didn't understand. Well, Dad, I sure as hell get it now.

He'd ignored everything I said, insisting I was foolish not to see what must happen. And he'd broken my damn heart in the process. The entire night had been pure torture with Sutton sleeping downstairs on the sagging couch and me trying to will my body to rest. Clenching my hands into fists at my sides, I glare up at the ceiling. He may think this is over, but for me? This is just the beginning.

There's no way in hell I'm letting Sutton become a murderer. Not when I might stand a chance at saving him. Throwing the covers off of my body, I stand and pull up the jeans that I've now worn three days in a row—fun.

Reaching down, I finger the hem of Sutton's shirt. Tears fill my eyes, and my stomach burns with regret. I should have seen the signs sooner; should have solved things sooner. Then, maybe— Swallowing hard, I shut my eyes and shake my head.

Serenity Kellis does *not* have regrets.

Instead of removing the shirt, I tuck it partially into the top of my jeans so it doesn't hang down to my knees, finally pulling on my sweater.

As soon as I'm dressed, I grab my now fully charged phone and check the bars. *No service.* Perfect. Figures. Shoving it into my pocket, I take one final look at Sutton's bedroom, letting myself relive that moment between the sheets where the entire world fell away and his lips on mine were all that mattered.

Before the stupid, cock-blocking spark. Granted, it's probably a good thing we didn't sleep together, considering his ability to push me to the side like we were nothing more than acquaintances. Were we, though? Anything more? A tear slips down my cheek so I reach up and brush it aside quickly. To me, it sure as hell felt like we'd started something.

"Are you ready?"

His voice washes over me like warm fingertips caressing my skin. I turn to see him standing in the doorway, wearing jeans and a faded blue t-shirt. Hair still mussed from sleep, he looks so casual, so easy-going that it pisses me off.

"Don't act like you care." I shove past him, trying to ignore the lump in my throat.

"Serenity."

"Not interested, Sutton." I march down the stairs, each step killing me just a little.

He beats me to the front door, moving in front of it before I can stop.

"Move."

"Please, don't leave like this."

"Like what? This is what you wanted, isn't it? Because you can't trust me to help. To find a way that doesn't end with you being a monster just like she is."

"I'm begging you to see it from my side. You've only ever known human justice, but human justice does not work for my kind. We must police our own, or the risk is far too great."

"You're wrong."

He straightens. "So your brother can shoot and kill her? He can take a life and be a murderer, but I cannot?"

I grind my teeth together. "He wouldn't kill her unless he had to."

"Which he will," he replies. "And that's only if he survives."

The very mention of my brother dying—of losing Steven to this town—sends hot rage burning through my body. Almost as much as the idea of losing Sutton. I drop the phone charger into my hand and stab him in the chest with my finger. "You are the one endangering innocent people, Sutton. You are the one who used me to get information, only to toss me to the damned curb the moment I no longer was of service to you." Tears burn my eyes, slipping down my cheeks despite me willing them to remain. "As soon as you think I'm getting in the way."

"I'm trying to keep you safe!" he bellows.

"By sending me into the very town where the crazy witch is. Great freaking move, Sutton Hargrave." I try to shove past him, but he's on me before I can take even a single step. We spin, and he presses me back against the door, his body hard against mine. My pulse hammers, drowning out the sound of my own breathing.

I can't fight it. The way he makes me feel, so how the hell can he?

"You have no idea what I'm going through right now. What the idea of you leaving—of you being somewhere I cannot protect you—is doing to me."

I snort, trying to feign disinterest even as fire blazes through my veins. "You are the one throwing *me* out."

He drops his head, hot breath fanning over my neck. "I cannot risk you. I will not risk you. Even if it causes you to hate me for it."

"Good. Because I do."

The moment the words are out of my mouth, Sutton releases me. It's cold, this distance between us. "I—"

"Don't bother with a goodbye, asshole. Your words mean nothing to me." I grip the handle and rip the door open then rush outside into the chilly air. Each step carries me farther and farther from the only man who's ever truly managed to consume me.

For him, this is goodbye.

But little does he know, I'll be back, and I'll end this damned curse if it's the last thing I do.

THE TOWN IS EERILY EMPTY, WHETHER THAT'S DUE TO THE HEAVY fog settling over it like a thick blanket or the impending arrival of the ball tomorrow night, I'm not sure. But it's creepier than normal. I head to the station first, but the lights are all off. A sign on the door reading "*Be back soon*" is the only sign of life.

Perfect.

I try not to let my nerves overwhelm me as I think of all the reasons the sheriff would be gone. Especially with the coincidental near-death experience.

Across the way, Audrey steps out onto the sidewalk and sets out an Open sign. Then, she turns and sees me. She smiles and waves me over, so I force myself to put my broken heart and wounded pride aside. There will be plenty of time to drown myself in ice cream later.

Right now, I have a murderer to pin.

"Good morning, dear."

"Morning." Offering her my cheeriest smile, I shove my hands into my pockets.

"I worked nearly all night, but I have the perfect dress. Just needs some final alterations."

Shit. "Oh, I don't have any money on me."

Audrey smiles. "Not to worry. Consider this a freebie for a newbie." With a wink, she completely disarms my nerves.

"Are you sure?"

"Absolutely. It would be a crime for you to not wear this dress." She ushers me inside and straight over to a fitting room. "It's hanging just inside. Slip it on, and come out here so I can make any final alterations."

"Okay." I move into the small room. A white garment bag hangs on the wall, giving me a slight boost of excitement. Even as I want to peek now, I make myself wait as I undress. As soon as my clothes are tossed haphazardly on the cushioned seat, I unzip the bag.

The gasp leaves my lips before I can stop it.

The gown is strapless and utterly beautiful. A navy-blue, low-cut bodice covered in bright sequins makes way for a huge tulle skirt in the same dark color. I run my fingers over the sparkles, enjoying the way the color shifts with each movement.

"Do you like it?"

"It's gorgeous," I call out as I pull it off the hanger and unzip the back.

"Well, then hurry up. I'm dying to see you in it."

I do as she asks and quickly step into the gown. After sliding it up, I hold it over my breasts then open the door.

Audrey's eyes widen with delight. "Turn around; I'll zip it up."

Her fingers are cold against my skin as she draws the zipper up, but it goes smoothly, and soon, she's guiding me toward a circular platform in front of three full-length mirrors.

"I knew this color would look stunning on you." She reaches up and pushes my long blonde hair back over my shoulders.

"I look like a princess." I run both hands down the skirt, and Audrey smiles.

"That you do. It needs a bit of taking in on the waist, though. Let me grab my pins." She hurries away, leaving me staring at my own reflection. It's been days since I actually took time to study myself in the mirror, so I do so now, noting the dark circles beneath my eyes.

Exhaustion does not become me.

And thinking of that somehow brings Sutton's face back into view. I close my eyes against the emotional bashing his memory brings me and take a deep breath. When I open them again, Audrey is studying me curiously.

"Are you all right?"

"Yes. Sorry. Haven't been sleeping well."

She kneels. "And it's no wonder. The whole town heard what happened at the B&B. We've all been concerned about you."

"I'm fine. Went home for a couple of nights."

"Without your car?"

I hesitate. Audrey is nice enough. Hell, she's kinder than anyone else, giving me a free dress. But that doesn't mean I can trust her with what I'm really doing.

"Took an Uber," I lie.

"Ahh, yes. Well, I am glad you returned for the ball; there is no way you won't be allowed in looking like this." She pinches some fabric and inserts a pin. Then, she moves to the other side and repeats the gesture, only this time, pain pinches my side.

"Ow!"

"Darn it, I'm so sorry." Audrey withdraws the pin and looks up at me. "Are you all right?"

"I'm okay."

"I truly am sorry." She goes back to work and, for whatever reason, I'm hit with another memory from when I was being fitted for my wedding dress. In reality, the breakup wasn't that long ago, but it feels like little more than a distant memory.

Sutton drove Roscoe straight from my mind. Should I feel bad about that? Not for Roscoe, of course—screw him—but for how quickly I let someone else in?

In fact, thinking of Roscoe no longer makes me want to hurl. That's a victory, right?

Sutton, on the other hand... Dammit.

"Okay, you can slip it off now, dear. Just hang it back up and let me know if you need a bandage for the stick."

"Will do." Gathering the skirts, I cross the room and shut myself in the fitting room. After hanging the dress back up, I pull my own clothes and shoes on then head back out into the main room.

"Everything okay?"

"Yes. It already stopped bleeding." To demonstrate, I pull up my shirt and show her the tiny pinprick.

Her expression falters, guilt taking over. "I truly am sorry. It's been quite a while since I've accidentally stuck anyone."

I smile, hoping to put her at ease. "Completely fine, I promise. When I was being fitted for my wedding dress, I must have gotten needled at least a dozen times."

That gets her attention. "You're married?"

"What? Oh, no. Long story short, he found someone else he'd

rather spend forever with, and I got dumped in one of my favorite restaurants a month before our wedding."

"I'm so sorry to hear that. Sounds like he was quite a fool."

"He was. Are you sure I can't pay you for the dress?"

"Positive."

"I can go get my cards—"

"Don't you fret about it, dear. I will take care of it. You can come pick the dress up tomorrow morning. I open at nine and will close by eleven to get ready for tomorrow night's event."

"Got it, I'll be here by then. Thank you so much."

"It's my pleasure, I assure you." She waves me out the door where I stand for a moment, taking in the near-empty street with a heavy heart.

Twenty-four hours. That's how long I have to solve this before someone else dies. And if I don't, who will be next? The sheriff? Audrey? Mable? George from the drugstore? I swallow hard, trying not to focus too intently on the what-ifs. What I do have is the now. And now, my next step is the library.

At least, this time, I have a place to start, a person to investigate. Who knows? I might manage to discover the lynchpin I need to link Yvette to the murders. I'm reaching for the handle on the library door when my phone rings.

One glance at the screen tells me it's Steven, and since an all-out manhunt for me isn't off the table, I go ahead and answer it. "Hey."

"'Bout damn time."

"I'm sorry, I was hiking."

"For a woman who hates peeing outside, you're sure hiking a lot," he retorts.

"I'm a convert. What's up?"

"What's wrong?"

"Why would something be wrong?"

"You sound off."

"I'm fine, Steven. Promise. Just tired."

"Then stop being stubborn, and come home. We can look into things together from here."

If I do that, someone will die. "I have a few more leads to tug on, and if they don't lead somewhere, I may do just that."

He sighs into the phone. "I'm worried about you, Ser."

"I know, but I'm being safe. Besides, after your last call, the sheriff has been shadowing me."

"Good. You're trouble."

"I'm about to walk into the library, so I need to let you go. I love you, assface."

"Love you, too. Check in with me later so I know you're okay."

"Will do." I end the call and shove the phone into my pocket before pulling open the library door. "Here goes nothing," I murmur.

Mable is sitting at the desk and looks up at me through thick-rimmed glasses. She, at least, offers me a smile—even if I can tell it's fake. "Serenity, good to see you. I heard what happened at the B&B. Are you okay?"

"Fine. Just tired."

"Everyone thought you'd run back to New York."

Oh, did they? "I'm not scared off that easily. Not even ghosts can do the trick."

Her eyes widen. "Ghosts?"

"Oh, I'm sorry, specters," I reply. "This is all new to me."

She has the grace to look guilty. "So you've uncovered some of our more peculiar secrets."

"I'd say secrets is a pretty bold term for a town full of werewolves who are trapped in their human form by a curse placed on them by a witch."

Obviously appalled by my callousness, Mable stands quickly. “You mustn’t speak that loudly of these things.”

“I’m done with half-ass answers, Mable.”

Her eyes shift back and forth from the entrance to the emergency exit at the back. “Come with me.” She moves around the counter and ushers me into a back room where she seals the door behind us.

“You planning on finally telling me what I want to know?” I ask.

She shakes her head. “That’s just it, I *don’t* know. No one does.”

“The sheriff does,” I correct her.

Her eyes widen again. “Arden knows the witch?”

“She’s been blackmailing him to keep him quiet.”

“Of course, she has!” Mable says, her shock turning to outrage as her cheeks redden. “Otherwise, the murders would have drawn much broader coverage.”

I soften. “Why didn’t you just tell me?”

“Would you have believed me?”

I sigh. “No, probably not.”

She reaches forward and grips my arms. “You were brought here to solve these murders and break this curse.”

Her words are a jolt I wasn’t expecting. “How do you know?”

Releasing me, she pushes the glasses up further on her nose. “I just do. Please don’t let us down, Serenity. We’re counting on you.” Eyes misty, her shoulders slump in defeat. Am I really their only hope?

Why in the hell would anyone put their faith or hope in *me*, of all people?

I’m opening my mouth to ask just that when a bell dings. The security camera on the counter shows a man and woman walking into the library with a stack of books in their hands. They head for the “return” bin. “I need to go. Use whatever you need; stay as long as you like. I'm locking up early, but you can simply leave out the back when you're done." Before I can reply, she's already out the door.

I turn my attention to the security camera as she greets the newcomers.

We're counting on you.

No pressure there.

Falls Gazette

Chapter Nineteen

With Mable gone, I turn to the only helpful item in the tiny room—an aged desktop computer with a questionable internet connection. *Time to get to work.* I start with researching Yvette Abbett and her bed and breakfast. I find scant details about either one, so I move on to the other townspeople I know—the sheriff, Audrey, Cara, even Mable herself—and then begin cross-referencing every single murder victim with Yvette. It's tedious as hell and yields a whole lot of nothing, but somehow, when I look up again, the clock shows that nearly the entire day has gone by.

My stiff muscles prove it.

Standing slowly, I stretch and pat my grumbling belly.

As usual, when I'm down a rabbit hole of research, all sense of self disappears. Now that I've come to, I have some seriously pressing needs like food and a bathroom—and not in that particular order.

I emerge cautiously from my little hideaway and pause, listening. But the library is silent, and only a few lights near the front remain on. Behind the front desk, I find a note with my name on it along with a bronze key.

Serenity, make yourself at home. Lock up when you're done. We're rooting for you. —

Mable

Wow.

Rooting for me.

No pressure.

I make a beeline for the bathroom and then do a quick round to make sure all the doors are, in fact, locked. Outside, twilight has fallen, and the creep factor seems to be rising right along with the nearly full moon.

I'm not sure when I started feeling safer inside a crumbling mansion in the middle of the woods than I do in a public library, but here we are. Worse, the idea of venturing out into town after dark makes staying in here look like a cakewalk.

For reasons I'd prefer not to think on, Sutton's face pops into my mind. I miss him. How stupid is that? A guy I've known all of a few days has a stronger hold on my heart than anyone I've known my whole life. And to top it off, what he wants most in the world is to see me leave and never come back.

Maybe *my* curse is picking men who never pick me.

Get it together, Serenity. Shaking my head to clear it, I head for the tiny kitchenette in the back. It's near bare, the fridge holding a single yogurt cup that, upon further inspection, I realize expired over two months ago. Fun.

After opening every cabinet, I manage to find a single, very-ripe banana and a bag of Doritos.

It'll do.

Taking my findings, which includes a bottle of water, I return to my little internet cave and get back to work. This time, I try searching for information about the curse itself. Witchcraft is a hot mess of a topic online, and I realize, unlike earlier, there's *too much* information for me to sift through for a lead. The sheer number of blogs, websites, and books out there on the topic overwhelms me, and most of them are nothing more than info-dumps about the uses of crystals and herbs to ward off colds and allergies. Anything resembling what's happening in Midnight Falls ends up veering too far into science fiction for me to take seriously.

My phone dings. Glancing down, I open my texts to one from Allison.

Allison: You okay? Steven about called in the Marines for you earlier.

Me: How does he have your number??

Allison: he strikes me as the type to get whatever he wants.

Me: I can't believe this. What did he say?

Allison: Asked if I'd heard from you. I told him you were likely folded up like a pretzel with some local hottie.

I snort and shake my head. I bet Steven loved that.

Me: All good; went hiking, and my phone died.

Allison: Ewww. Nature. Pass. Anything come up on that birth certificate?

Me: It was just what I needed. Thanks.

Allison: No problem. Let me know if I can assist.

With a smile, I toss my phone down. Part of me wants to ask about Quincy and whether or not he's filled my position, but my heart can't handle that kind of disappointment right now. Besides, if I pull this off, it won't matter. He'll take me back even if it means dismissing my replacement. "Here goes round two."

There are few to no articles about wolves in the area, but if Sutton's right and no one else can shift, that doesn't surprise me. Next, I search how to stop a witch. The results are...interesting. One blog suggests casting stones at the accused witch. Pebbles, in fact—which doesn't strike me as particularly threatening. Another says "Why bother? Witchcraft is good." I immediately click away from that one. The third offers step-by-step instructions for an incantation that ends with punching the witch in the face. Obviously. Ugh.

More hours pass as I scroll and scan. But nothing I find offers a more logical solution than simply arresting the woman and carting her off to a cell. I can practically hear Sutton's response in my head, though. *Kill her. It's the only way to be free.*

When my vision will no longer cooperate, I push back from the desk and yawn so hard my eyes close. I need sleep if I'm going to be ready for tomorrow.

Hmm.

Mable said to lock up when I left. She didn't say when that had to be.

A quick search of my options yields a thick coat in the lost and found that'll serve well enough as a blanket.

Balling up my own jacket, I use it as a pillow and stretch out inside the tiny room. Truthfully, I've spent much fewer comfortable evenings sleeping at my desk back in New York. You know…when I still had a job.

My eyes grow even heavier, so I snuggle down and begin to drift. Slowly, steadily, until all of my current life-or-death problems are little more than background noise.

Blood. Death. I twirl in a circle, desperation to find him taking over as I scan the bodies covering the marble floor. "Sutton!" I scream, gripping the skirt of my blood-stained gown and rushing toward the stairs.

He has to be here somewhere. My throat is raw from screaming, my head pounding, but none of that matters right now, because the one thing I'd set out to do—the one thing I'd needed to fix—I was too late.

They'd counted on me.

I failed them.

And now someone is dead.

I SHOOT UP, MY SKIN SLICK WITH SWEAT, MY HEART BEATING A million miles a minute. *What the hell?* The throbbing in my temples only grows as I throw the makeshift blanket off of me and take a deep breath.

So much blood.

So much death.

Is that what's waiting for me at that party?

As soon as I get ahold of my breathless disorientation, I remind myself that I'm safe in the tiny computer room of Mable's library. I'm not too late; I still have a few hours to get all the information I need so Steven can make the arrest.

Then, I can free Sutton and this town for good.

One final deep breath and I reach for my phone to check the time. *Shit!*

I scramble up and shrug into my jacket. I have almost zero personal effects to grab on my way out, which is a sucky reminder of the state of my life, but I shove that thought away and hurry to the doors. I lock them behind me and set out for Audrey's.

She's just about to lock up when she sees me.

"Serenity. I was starting to worry," she says, brows drawn together.

"Sorry. I overslept."

"Come in." She motions for me to enter and points at the white garment bag hanging behind the counter. "There it is. All ready for you."

“Thank you,” I tell her.

“Oh, and I stashed a pair of heels with it,” she adds, with a glance at my boots. “Thought you might need footwear to match.”

I stop just short of kissing the woman. “Audrey, I owe you for this, seriously.”

She beams at me. “Nonsense. You can repay me by letting me see you in it tonight.”

“You got it,” I say with a smile.

Despite the danger that awaits, the idea of getting all dressed up is a fun one. I haven’t had a fancy night out in way too long. Shit, the last time would have been New Year's Eve with Roscoe. You know, before I discovered what a miserable fucking ass he was.

“Oh, you’ll want to wait until seven to broach the woods,” Audrey warns, her tone sharper than it was before.

“Okay.” I wait, but she doesn’t elaborate. I may know that the curse prevents everyone from entering the woods, but she doesn’t need that shred of information. With a shrug, I add, “See you, then.”

We part ways, and I make a pit stop at the coffee shop, stocking up on double of everything. Coffee. Water. Muffins. It looks like another long day in the library for me. Especially considering the unfriendly stares and pointed whispers I get from the few people out and about.

Careful to avoid any streets that give view to the woods, I carry my loot back to the library, more than ready to put my nose back to the grindstone.

I’m just reaching the steps when a woman grips my arm. Silvery hair braided down her back, she stares at me through haunted crystal-blue eyes.

“Can I help you?” I try to pull my arm out of her grasp, but she clings to it.

“Leave,” she whispers, her raspy voice pleading. “Before it’s too late.”

"I…"

"Leave," she warns one final time before releasing me and power walking back down the street.

I stare after her, too stunned by her blatant warning to respond. Mainly because I find myself wondering what the hell is wrong with me for going against all the warnings.

She wants me to leave.

Sutton wants me to leave.

Leaving *would* be safer.

But apparently, safety is not one of my core values because, even as I give the idea brief consideration, I'm shutting it back down.

Idiocy. Recklessness. Disregard for common sense. Those I have in spades. And I know leaving would condemn these people to yet another year of this nightmarish loop they're trapped in.

I continue to stare after the woman until she turns the corner, disappearing from view. Then, I turn and face the town. People move down the street, hushed whispers I can't quite make out between them.

But there is one thing I see clearly: the warning in their gazes. Are they looking at me and wondering what the hell is wrong with me, too?

MABLE NEVER MAKES AN APPEARANCE, AND THE DAY PASSES exactly like the one before. Internet searches. Bathroom breaks. I prowl the stacks to stretch my legs and see if I can spot anything that can help me piece this mystery together, but whoever stole those books when I first arrived cleaned out anything helpful.

I end up eating my last banana muffin for dinner and chasing it with stale coffee leftover from this morning.

After tonight, I promise myself a proper meal.

If I'm still alive.

The thought echoes like an uninvited guest in my mind, and I immediately shove it away again. It's not *my* life on the line. It's the residents of Midnight Falls who are in danger.

The only one I'm actually worried about killing me is Sutton when he finds out I never left. Hopefully, by the time he discovers me tonight, I'll have already gotten the proof needed to nail Yvette. The legal way. Not the murdery way.

I dress carefully, smoothing out the navy-blue tulle skirt until it's wrinkle-free and absolutely perfect. Another check of the garment bag reveals the shoes Audrey promised. They're blue velvet and match the dress perfectly. Lastly, I find a small blue clutch that Audrey apparently added to the bag. The woman is a saint. I make a mental note to buy her a drink when this is all over.

Maybe two—or three. I have a feeling, by the time this is all said and done, we will have earned all the drinks.

With a deep breath, I study myself in the library's bathroom mirror. Without any pins or clips in my possession, there's little I can do about my hair. Running my fingers through the pale strands, I manage to at least somewhat tame my day-old waves.

Then, I get to study the awesome reflection staring back at me. I don't have even a drop of concealer, so it looks like they're getting Serenity Kellis, au naturel.

I pull my phone off the charger, verifying that it's sitting at a hundred percent battery life, then open up my voice memos and stare down at the tiny red record button. Since the cell service is spotty at best, I'll need to make sure and record everything without raising suspicions.

As soon as I have what I need, I'll slip away, find service, and send it all to Steven. After tapping the button, I shove it into my clutch and clear my throat.

"Serenity Kellis: investigative journalist." Speaking the words aloud, I pause then open the clutch, shut off the recording, and hit playback.

The words come through crystal clear. *Perfect.* I shove the phone into my clutch again and take one last look in the mirror.

Even without makeup, I look pretty damn good—thanks to this epic dress. Once this is over, I may be making trips here on the regular to have Audrey stock my closet. Woman has epic talent.

Okay, Serenity. It's now or never.

As ready as I'll ever be, I lock the library behind me and step out onto the sidewalk. The sun has already dipped behind the rooftops, casting shadows along the pavement. And the fog from last night is back, rolling in thicker than before because…of course. What magical ball doesn't come with a dense blanket of fog?

I cross my arms to ward off the chill and head for the edge of downtown. There are others all going in the same direction, but no one seems to notice me through the haze. Rounding a corner, I jump back again to avoid colliding with someone.

"Sorry," a female voice says.

"Cara?" She's stunning in a sexy silver slip dress that brings out the silver flecks in her eyes. Her pixie cut has been spiked and styled to look edgy and chic. Crystal earrings dangle from her ears. "Girl, do not apologize for a damn thing. You look hot."

"Thanks," she says, smiling. "You look beautiful as well." Her friendliness turns to wariness. "Where are you headed?"

"The ball. Same as you."

"Serenity…" Her expression tightens. "I don't know if that's a good idea."

Her concern is touching, but there's absolutely nothing she can say that will change my mind now. So, I decide to save us both the back and forth.

"Listen, I know all about the curse and what could happen at that ball tonight." Her eyes widen.

She lowers her voice to a whisper as she says, "Not what *could* happen. What *will* happen."

I don't bother arguing semantics. "I am fully aware of the risks and don't make this decision lightly, okay?"

"I see. Someone's done her homework." She bites her lip. "Mind if I ask where you got your information?"

"I have my sources."

She hesitates, clearly debating with herself. "Okay," she finally says. "But you stick with me—especially until we arrive. And once we're inside, you don't go anywhere alone, got it?"

"Got it," I say, grinning.

"Come on," she says, not nearly as enthusiastic about this. "We're going to be late."

I let her lead the way, careful not to let on that I've been to Hargrave Manor before. In the darkness, no one else seems to notice me, and for once, I avoid the whispers and stares that I'm used to. More townspeople converge around us, and by the time we reach the end of the sidewalk, a crowd has formed. In the front, a line of people stand shoulder to shoulder, facing the thick woods just beyond. No one speaks, and the silence adds to the fog to create an eerie stillness.

It's as if everyone is waiting for something. Or someone.

I use the close-up to scan for Yvette or the sheriff, but I don't see either one.

"What happens now?" I whisper to Cara, drawing several looks from the people around me.

Cara holds a finger to her lips and points at the trees.

"Watch," she mouths.

The fog thickens, the damp droplets clinging to my skin in a way that feels like another presence. It snakes along the ground, and when I look down, I realize I can no longer see my feet.

The haze crawls forward until it reaches the edge of the woods and then stops as it hits an invisible barrier. From there, it crawls upward, scaling whatever wall it's found until a cloudy, murky curtain hangs between us and the forest.

Still, no one speaks, and I shift nervously as the creep-factor level skyrockets.

Then, as if on cue, the curtain drops, and the air warms until the fog is completely chased away. When it clears, the line of people up front takes a unified step forward. One, then another. The row behind them does the same. And then a third wave behind them. Until we're all moving forward into the woods like some kind of choreographed interpretive movement routine. Like puppets; all of us at the mercy of whatever evil magic holds this place and its people hostage.

Eventually, the rows break out into smaller groups and single units, and for some reason, that makes me feel better. While we walk, Cara lectures me again about being careful and staying with the crowd. I let her lead, feigning confusion over where we're headed. Finally, the house comes into view, and I have to steel my nerves at the sight of it.

The dilapidated façade against a glowing moon is the stuff of horror movies.

Cara hesitates, too, and studies me with concern.

"You can still turn back," she offers, quietly.

I look at her then the house and square my shoulders. "No," I say, "I can't."

I can feel Sutton. I don't know how, but awareness climbs up my spine, warming my body in a way that only he could have caused.

I'm coming, I will silently. *Coming to free you.*

Cara leads the way, and I have to concentrate on my breathing to keep calm. This is it. My last chance to save the life of someone here tonight. And to save Sutton from becoming a killer.

Failure isn't even remotely an option.

With a final steadying breath, I follow Cara through the doors and then immediately come to an abrupt halt as shock and confusion ripple through me. Someone bumps me from behind, and Cara tugs my arm. I'm shuffled sideways from where I've blocked the entrance.

"Serenity?"

Cara's concern deepens, but it's not fear that has me rooted to the spot.

I stare at the walls surrounding me, totally in awe.

The house has been completely reborn. The crumbling plaster and rotting drywall have been replaced with ornate molding, framing patterned wallpaper done in golds and whites that gleam underneath chandeliers polished to shine. The floor is solid marble patterned in a way that swirls along, practically sweeping me from the grand foyer toward the open doors on the other side.

"Holy shit, it's like *Titanic*," I breathe.

"What?" Cara asks.

"In the movie," I say, "You know. When they flashback from what it looks like now to what it must have looked like brand new and everything's restored…?" Her expression is baffled, and I wave my hand. "You know what, never mind."

She arches a brow. "Are you sure you're up for this?"

"Totally," I assure her.

She looks unconvinced, but I run out of things to say to reassure her as I note a grand staircase off to one side that winds up and around to a second level. My thoughts wander to Sutton and his bedroom. What does it look like now that it's been made over?

Probably a lot nicer than before. Although, it was never the room itself that drew me in. Rather, the occupant.

I wander across the foyer, my heels clicking against the fine marble until I reach the open doors that reveal a large ballroom beyond. Again, my steps falter. It's beautiful. Lavish spreads of food line tables set up against the wall. On one side are round banquet tables set with red satin cloths and gold chinaware. In the center of the room, a chandelier hangs overhead, dripping with diamonds. The fixture looks large enough to fill my entire New York apartment—and, thankfully, much sturdier than the one that fell on me before. An orchestra plays soft music from a far corner, and in between, stunningly dressed couples sway to the melody.

I'm so distracted by the lavish setup that it takes me a while to realize everyone else has noticed me, too. Soon, the whispers start, and heads begin to turn until, one by one, everyone stares at me.

"Do I have something on my face?" I joke to Cara, but when she doesn't answer, I turn to find I'm alone.

Wow. So much for being my wing-woman.

Instead, Audrey appears in a simple velvet gown that matches her eyes. She smiles and says, "Don't pay them any mind. You're beautiful, and they're simply stunned."

"Uh, yeah, not sure that's it, but thank you for the compliment." I raise my hand in an awkward wave, and everyone goes back to the party as I breathe a sigh of relief. I'll never corner Yvette alone with so many eyes on me. If this is going to work, I have to blend.

I glance behind me toward the front door, hoping to spot my target, but instead, movement from above catches my eye. I look up, and my breath catches. Standing at the top of the stairs is the one person I was hoping to avoid. At least, until I'd completed my mission.

Sutton wears a black tuxedo that accentuates rather than hides his muscled arms and toned body. His hair has been combed back, but he's kept the stubble. Stubble I've already felt against my skin.

Seeing him standing there—it does weird things to my ovaries. Like melting them. He is breathtaking.

When our eyes meet, the rage he exudes is strong enough to taste. Even with the anger rolling off his tense body, I am completely drawn in by him. At this moment, I know I have never felt such a connection with another person the way I feel it with Sutton Hargrave. Like a thread tying us together, pulling it tighter and tighter until we end up inevitably sewn together again, no matter how many times we tear ourselves apart.

"Someone has their eye on you."

Audrey's voice in my ear is playful, but I can't bring myself to answer her. I can hardly breathe as Sutton descends the stairs, slowly, his movements calculated like a predator stalking its prey. Shit, I don't even care if he devours me.

He stops in front of me, so close his scent envelopes me. Lust burns in my belly. I want to tell him I'm sorry for our fight. For leaving the way I did. For ever saying a single thing that might have hurt him.

But he speaks first, and when he does, my apology dies on my lips, and my entire body turns cold.

"You shouldn't have come."

Falls Gazette

Chapter Twenty

Sutton's massive hand closes around my arm, and he pulls me closer, all but dragging me through the crowd. "What the hell are you doing?" I hiss through clenched teeth.

The people close in around us, trapping us on the dance floor. Sutton turns, likely scanning for an escape, but it's wall-to-wall people dancing, moving around the floor in perfect sync.

"Dance, you two."

I glance over and catch Audrey's twinkling eye as she moves with a man I've never met before.

Sutton's hand snakes around my back, his other raising mine.

"Not on your life," I growl, and try to yank back.

Sutton's hold is firm, though, and he leans in and whispers, "We have to dance."

"Like hell—"

"Your life depends on it," he interrupts.

His words are a jolt to my system. Not only because of their severity but because I realize, for the first time, there's still a lot I don't know about tonight's rules. The curse. These people. I've stepped into something I still don't yet fully understand.

Falling silent, I let him hold me against his hard body, and we begin to move. One step to the right, one forward, then to the left. The waltz carries us around the room, his hand on my lower back.

I mean, if I am going to die tonight, there are worse ways to go.

Sutton remains silent as we dance, moving around the room. I try to search for Yvette—to make eye contact with anyone—but they're all looking down. And then I take careful notice of the strained expressions each and every person here is wearing.

None of them—and I mean *none* of them—actually look like they're enjoying themselves.

Cara dances with a man who looks like he's one breeze away from snapping in half, he's so stiff, and she looks no better.

One woman I've never seen before has silent tears streaming down her cheeks.

"Sutton—"

"Quiet," he scolds.

"Let me go."

Instead of doing as I ask, his grip on me tightens. "You should have left when you had the chance." His stubble scrapes over my cheek as he growls the words into my ear. I know he's trying to scare me, to make me regret my defiance, but the blood hammering in my veins is having the exact opposite effect.

No matter what anyone says, I know I'm exactly where I'm supposed to be. Here, helping him, helping the town. Roscoe, the breakup, my getting fired—all of those events were mere dominos falling into place.

"Where is—"

"Not here." He spins me out, and I come right back into his arms. When the music comes to an end, everyone steps away from their partners and claps, the joyous sound so out of place in a room full of such pain.

Sutton grips my hand and pulls me toward the edge of the dance floor. We pass through a small opening then head for a narrow hall. He doesn't speak, doesn't look back at me, just all but drags me through a house that was near falling down the last time I saw it. Now, it's beautiful, and that beauty is haunting.

At the end of the hall, he stops in front of a plain door only long enough to shove it open.

"We don't have time for a lecture," I snap as he yanks me inside and slams the door shut behind us. A soft glow from a single lamp casts shadows along the walls, but even as angry as I am, I can't help but gape at the floor-to-ceiling bookshelves making up three of the four walls. A massive mahogany desk gleams in the center, though there's nothing on top of it.

I would have been more enamored, maybe taking some time to look at the books lining the shelves—much in the same way Belle does when she's introduced to the Beast's library—but I'm far too pissed. Especially when my Beast is glaring at me like he wants to forego finding Yvette and kill me, instead.

"You damned well better make time," he growls as he takes a step toward me.

I move back. "I won't let you condemn yourself."

"You have no idea what the hell you're getting into." Eyes dark, he closes the distance between us until my ass is pressed against the desk, giving me nowhere else to run. "You shouldn't be here," he whispers. "It's too dangerous, Serenity."

"It would have been worse if I'd stayed away."

"Why? Why couldn't you just listen?"

"Because, for some reason, I care about you, asshole." Reaching out, I jab a finger into his chest. "All I need is a confession, and I can have cops here before this ball is over. No one else has to die."

He leans down and cages me against the desk, his hands splaying across the dark wood. Stubble scrapes my cheek as he drops his head to the crook of my neck and inhales deeply. “Serenity.” My name is a plea; a sharp growl. The emotion behind it makes me waver despite my steely resolve. I want Sutton. Almost as much as I want to save him.

“Please don’t do this,” I beg, goosebumps flaring to life along my skin. My blood hammers in my ears, the deafening drumline blocking out all sounds of the party taking place just outside the door.

“Do what?” he asks as he moves one hand and grips my hip. Fingers dig into my side. It’s all I can do to not beg for him to touch more of me.

To touch all of me.

“Push me away.”

“Do I look like I possess the power to push you away? Every fucking time I close my eyes, there you are, an assault on my mind. You ripped all shreds of willpower I possessed until you completely consumed me.”

His words are a punch to the chest. “Oh,” is all I manage. I tilt my head, giving him access to my throat. He traces my jaw with his lips.

“I can smell your arousal,” he whispers. “Your want. Your need.” He growls again then presses a kiss to the hollow of my throat. “I want to fucking devour you.”

Holy shit balls.

The throbbing between my legs consumes me. I clench my thighs together, trying desperately to ease the ache. An ache I *know* won’t go away unless Sutton releases it.

“I—”

“That dress should be a crime.” He releases my hip, his other hand leaving the desk, and he trails them both down, gripping my ass through the tulle and depositing me on the desk. His hands knead the muscles of my thighs as he spreads my legs and moves between them, pressing his hard length against me.

All rational thought vanishes.

Right now, it's only him and me. In this library. So fucking turned on I would let him do things to me you only read about in romance novels—and not the sweet ones, either.

"Don't make a sound," he whispers, as he presses his lips to my jawline.

I hold my breath as he leans down and traces his fingertips up the inside of my leg. Even if he hadn't ordered my silence, words fail me. Especially when he locks eyes with me and drops down to his knees.

My mouth falls slack as his fingers find the edge of the lace between my legs moments before slipping beneath them. He toys with me, gently sliding his fingers over me. My blood turns molten, every nerve in my body firing at a thousand percent—is that possible? Is this how people spontaneously combust?

Because I believe it to be a possibility now.

Just before I don't think I can take anymore, he disappears beneath the skirts, and his mouth covers me.

"Sutton," I whisper, as a shock jolts through my body, I lean back, barely managing to remain sitting as his tongue slips inside of me.

The orgasm tears through me at lightning speed, and every muscle in my body turns to little more than jelly beneath sensitive skin.

He continues devouring me, breaking down every wall I've ever built around myself, and completely obliterating any idea I had of ever walking away from him.

One way or another, after tonight, I belong to Sutton Hargrave.

And I'll be damned if anyone takes him from me.

Slowly, he retreats, moving back from me and standing. Hooded eyes shine so brightly, the hazel might as well be gold as he stares up at me. “You taste like salvation, Serenity Kellis.”

“You don’t need salvation,” I tell him, breathless.

Then again, after what he’s just done, he’s anything but innocent.

“I wish you were right.” He steps closer to me and leans down to touch his lips to mine. It’s gentle and, thankfully, lightning-free this time.

“I’m sorry about our fight.”

“I was such a fool,” he whispers as he pulls back and turns his back to me. “I never should have made you leave.”

“Yeah, you’re a real dumbass,” I shoot back, attempting to lighten the mood and shove the rest of my already building arousal back down.

“Where did you go? Not back to the bed and breakfast, right?”

“Of course, not. I went to the library,” I reply. “No matter how much you pissed me off, there is no way I could leave you—not when you’re trapped.”

He’s across the room so fast I barely see him move. “You’re not leaving me. Ever,” he growls, then grips my hands and pulls me from the desk. “Stay by my side tonight, Serenity. Every moment you’re here, you’re a target.”

Cara had warned something similar. “You do the same. No killing anyone, Sutton.”

“I can’t promise that,” he replies. “If you’re in danger, if there’s no chance of stopping her your way—”

I press the palm of my hand to his chest. “Everything will go as planned.”

“How do you know that?”

“Because it has to,” I tell him. Then, I smooth my hands over my skirts. "Now, do I look okay? Or do I look like someone who just had her world rocked in a library?"

Sutton laughs, darkly. "That was only the appetizer," he says, leaning in. "Just wait until tonight is over."

Even though I just had the most intense orgasm of my life, warmth spreads through my belly at the anticipation. Shit, if that was the— My gaze lands on a stack of books placed neatly on an end table beside a high-backed leather chair. My lust winks out, replaced by shock, then anger. "What the hell are those?" I demand, marching across the room and lifting the hardbound topping the pile.

Sutton shoves his hands into his pockets. "Books."

"Obviously," I reply, dryly. "You stole those from the town library."

"I can't go into town."

"Fine." Rolling my eyes, I put the book back and turn to face him. "You had someone else steal them, but why? You said you wanted my help."

"I did."

"Then why take the things I was using to research!"

He looks away from me for a moment then returns his gaze to mine. "Because I wanted you to come looking for me, instead."

I narrow my gaze on his face. "You manipulated me into coming back out here?"

"Yes."

"Why?"

He removes his hands and crosses the room toward me. "I've been lingering in this place between life and death for longer than I care to dwell on, but the moment you crossed into the woods, you changed that. Serenity, you changed everything, and having you near me…" He trails off and runs a hand through his hair. "It was the first time I felt alive since this blasted curse first started."

His words break my heart. I know I should still be angry, but it's just not there. "Don't ever manipulate me again, Sutton. You want something? Just ask. I do not appreciate being pulled around like a puppet."

"I promise."

With a deep breath, I reach into my clutch for my cell so I can hit record. But my fingers find nothing but smooth velvet. "What the hell?" I open it further, but it's empty.

Completely empty.

"What is it?"

"My phone. It's gone." Then, I realize the only person who would have been close enough to take it is standing in front of me. Crossing my arms, I glare up at him. One minute, he's throwing out promises, the next, robbing me.

Figures.

"Give it back, Sutton."

He stares down at me, confused. "I didn't take your phone."

"Sure you didn't. You promised we could try it my way first."

"Serenity, I swear—"

The door opens, and we both turn. The sound of a swishing skirt puts me on edge. Part of me expects Yvette, the cold-blooded murdery witch herself. But it's not her, so I relax. Until my gaze drops to the familiar cell phone clutched in the woman's raised hand and my blood ices.

I've managed to completely overlook one huge piece of this puzzle because I was blinded by what I thought I knew.

And now, that mistake is staring me straight in the face.

"Hello, dear."

Falls Gazette

Chapter Twenty One

"That's mine," I say, clenching my hands into fists.

"Not anymore." Audrey snaps her fingers, and my phone disappears.

I stare at her now-empty hand in confusion. "What...?"

She smiles, and I watch as her previously friendly grin turns to something much colder and more twisted than I ever could have imagined. "Come, Serenity. You've gotten this far. Don't tell me you don't believe in magic."

Sutton growls.

"It's you," I breathe, the reality of what she is knocking the air from me. "Not Yvette. You're the witch. The one who's holding these people hostage. Killing them..."

Beside me, Sutton trembles, and it's his reaction more than anything Audrey has said or done that sends a cold dread snaking down my spine.

"Hello, Sutton," she says to him, disdain dripping from every syllable.

"Serenity has nothing to do with this. Let her go." His glare is hot enough to melt anything human. Unfortunately, Audrey is not that.

Instead, she laughs at his words. “She isn't going anywhere. In fact, she’s exactly what I've been waiting for.”

I open my mouth to ask what the hell that could possibly mean —though part of me dreads finding out the answer. Before I can utter a word, another figure graces the doorway, and where I once thought the worst of her, now, hope surges.

“Yvette,” I say. “Get out. Get help. Audrey’s the witch, the one who cursed you all—”

The twisted expression she wears stops me cold. Sutton’s hand on my arm is more evidence that my suspicions are correct.

“Serenity,” Yvette says, stepping into the room and closing the door. “We’ve missed you at the house. But looks like all’s well that ends well.” She glances over, and her smile turns almost playful. “Hello, Sutton Hargrave. Happy Hallows Eve.”

“I trusted you,” Sutton growls at her.

“We all make mistakes.” She turns to Audrey. “Hello, sister.”

My jaw drops.

Sister?

“What the hell is going on?” I demand.

My voice pitches high, and I know I’ve let my fear show through, but who can fault me? I’ve been bamboozled by evil siblings who make Maleficent look like a saint.

“You’ve been behind it all,” Sutton says, “Both of you. All these years.”

“I’ve exacted my revenge, if that’s what you mean,” Audrey says.

“There is nothing to avenge,” he growls back. “What happened to Tabitha was your doing. As is this curse.”

“Do not dare speak her name,” Audrey snaps at him.

But Sutton is undeterred. “If you blame me so much, then let's end this. Once and for all. You and me. Leave the rest of my pack out of this."

"Ah, but what fun would that be?"

On the heels of her words, Yvette giggles, and Sutton loses it.

He takes a step forward, and my heart leaps as I realize he's going to skip right to the part where we do this his way. But then, Audrey snaps her finger, and Sutton abruptly halts. He struggles to move, but some invisible force holds him in place. Trapped.

My rage and fear blend until they're one emotion. One force.

"You'll pay for this," Sutton warns, in a voice deadlier than I've ever heard from him before.

"Oh, I think you're the one who's paying, Sutton Hargrave. As you will continue to do for a century more, at least." Audrey's smile turns to menacing, and Yvette practically jumps up and down with glee.

"Oh, I do love a good showdown," Yvette says.

"This is insane," I say. "You're both insane."

"I am powerful beyond measure," she says, a note of warning creeping into her tone. "You'd do well to respect that power."

"You're a murderer. You kill people, for what—some twisted idea of revenge? This has to stop."

Audrey's dark gaze gleams with challenge. "Let me guess. You think you're the one to stop me?"

"Someone has to."

She scoffs.

I try not to think about how obvious it is that I'm full of shit. But considering she has Sutton on some kind of invisible leash, leaving me outnumbered, I can't help but become very aware of how bad this is.

"Powerful or not, you're a bully," I tell her. "And a total bitch—but that's just me taking this personal."

Audrey's eyes narrow, her humor vanishing. "Pardon me if your insults don't quite land," she snaps. "You've stepped into something you know nothing about. And now, you're going to suffer the consequences."

She opens her hand, and in her palm, a tiny blue flame begins to dance.

Sutton roars and rages, struggling harder against the magic holding him down.

"Serenity, you need to get help," Sutton says in a low voice.

I don't answer. All I can do is stare.

I know that flame is beyond dangerous. That despite its small size, it could very well be strong enough to kill me where I stand. But for a fleeting moment, I am suspended. Entranced by the sight of the unassuming display of an otherworldly force. Something about that flame feels almost...familiar.

"Do you like what you see, Serenity?" Audrey's voice is silky smooth. Inviting me in. "It's beautiful, isn't it? The power."

I don't answer, but something inside me wants to. Some part of me I don't recognize wants to touch it.

I extend my hand, inching my fingers toward the flame.

"No, Serenity! Run!"

Sutton's roar is the thing I need to snap out of it.

I hurl myself past Audrey and Yvette, throwing the door wide. It swings easily open, and I register brief relief at finding it unlocked. Then I realize all that means is that bitch really thought she had me. The thought sobers me, and I grab my skirts and bolt for the exit.

The only hope I have left is getting back to town and finding a working phone.

Reaching Steven and sending out an S.O.S. is my last hope.

Even if it gets me killed, I make a silent promise to myself that I'll be the last.

That no one else will have to die because of Audrey's evil.

Especially Sutton.

Faces fly by me as I run.

The ballroom is full of somber-looking guests now. No one's dancing, which makes my escape that much easier. Apparently, they've abandoned whatever charade Audrey's little party has forced on them.

"Stop!" Audrey's urgent scream rings out, echoing around me.

Up ahead, I see a crowd of people gathered. They're talking in low voices. Some are crying. When they see me, someone screams.

I get all the way to the door when the crowd parts, and I finally catch sight of what drew them all here.

My feet stop of their own accord, and I stare down in horror at the body in the middle of the floor.

Sheriff Rhodes stares back at me, lifeless.

Dead.

A deep gash has been sliced into his throat. His blood has pooled around him, so thick and wide that I wonder if there's any at all left inside his veins. Before my eyes, the blood pooled around him vanishes—sucked away by some invisible force.

Or witch.

From deep in the house, a cackle echoes.

Audrey.

She's renewed her curse for another year—and I've failed.

Just like my nightmare foretold, I've failed them all.

Every hope I had of finding reason and purpose in this fucking mess of a night dies with the sheriff. I turn to the others, words tearing from my throat before I realize I'm the one saying them.

"Someone call an ambulance," I demand, knowing damn well it's much too late for that.

No one moves.

"Call nine-one-one," I tell them.

Still, only silence answers me.

Silence and sadness.

I look past the others and realize Audrey is gone. So is Yvette.

Footsteps thunder across the quiet room.

Hands grab my arms, shaking me.

“Serenity.”

Sutton’s voice seems far away.

“Serenity,” he says again, shaking me hard enough to rattle my teeth.

I blink, looking up into his wild eyes.

“He’s dead,” I choke out. “We lost.”

“No,” he says, firmly. “There’s still time to get you out of here. Come with me. We have to go, now.”

I don’t argue, and I don’t resist.

In fact, I pretty much let him carry me out the door and into the night.

For some reason, I expect him to take me back to town, but when we stop a while later, we’re still in the middle of the woods. Thick darkness surrounds us both so that Sutton is merely a shadow by my side.

“This is as far as I can go,” he says.

He’s breathless, and something tells me it has nothing to do with the physical exertion of practically carrying me here. Suddenly, I’m glad for the darkness. I don’t want to see his fear when I look into his eyes.

“Where are we?” I choke out.

“This is the line that separates Midnight Falls from the rest of the world. Walk north from here, and you’ll hit a highway. You’ll be safe.”

“You want me to walk through the woods? At night?”

“See this tree?”

When I don’t answer, he lifts my hand and presses my palm to a thick trunk on my right.

"Once you step past this tree, you're safe," he says. "Audrey won't follow."

Safe?

"What about the bears?" I ask.

"There's nothing in this world that can hurt you like she can," he whispers. "Go, Serenity. Please," he begs.

"Sutton, I...I'm sorry." My voice cracks, and Sutton wraps me in his arms, burying his face against my neck. But then just as quickly, he pulls away again.

"There's no time, Serenity. Go."

Somewhere behind him, a branch snaps, and I know he's right. We're out of time, and even with so much left to say, it's over.

We've failed.

"Go," he says again, as the sound of footsteps draws closer.

My throat closes, and hot tears burn my eyes as I ready myself to do as he says.

I take a step, and my foot hits the ground in front of the tree.

Then another. In line with the tree.

But when I try to move past it, I slam into something hard and stumble back.

"What the hell?" I mutter.

Behind me, there is a beat of deafening silence, and then Sutton roars. "Nooo!"

I try it again, determined to prove this isn't what I think it is.

But again, I hit a wall I can't see and am driven back inside the town's boundary line.

Sutton makes a guttural sound that nearly breaks me in two.

A sickening understanding begins to dawn, and I realize I've been worried about the wrong thing. All along, I worried I'd fall victim to the witch's killing spree if I got too close. I never actually considered she'd want to keep me even closer.

"Am I...trapped?" I ask, my throat raw.

From grief. From fear. From acceptance of a horrific new reality settling in.

Sutton refuses to meet my eyes. He stands before me, looking torn between rage and despair. His hair hangs in his eyes, and his shoulders are hunched.

Behind him, figures appear in the darkness. Silhouettes, one after another, as the townspeople converge on us. To either protect us or sell us out, I have no idea. My breath catches because I know Audrey can't be far behind. And now, I'm out of places to hide. Whatever it is she wants with me, she's going to get.

I turn back to Sutton.

"We need to keep moving," I hear myself say. "She could be anywhere."

"Why couldn't you have left when I told you to go?" he whispers. I hear the defeat plain in his voice now, and it breaks my heart. "I tried so hard to save you. And now, it's too late."

I want to reach for him, to comfort him, but my own emotions are a tempest I can't yet control. Rage, fear, desperation—it all wars for domination inside me. Until whatever dam I've been using to hold it all back breaks.

I scream.

It's blood-curdling and shrill, and so loud it hurts my own ears.

For a moment, I am swept up in the effort it takes to unleash my pain into sound.

It wracks my body until my knees buckle and I'm forced to the ground on shaky limbs.

Blue light flashes around me, illuminating the myriad faces that have crept silently forward.

In that instant flash, I see Cara and Mable, and even George staring back at me with shock and awe written across their faces. The blue light hovers above us all and then, like a force of its own, slams into the crowd. One by one, they are consumed by it.

If I had breath left at all, I’d scream again, terrified I’ve somehow hurt them.

Instead, the light seeps into their skin, and then, they transform. Every single one of them shifts. One second, they're human. And in the next, every last one is a wolf.

Leaving me staring at an entire town full of cursed creatures who’ve just renewed their stay for another year in this prison of a town.

And I’m trapped right along with them.

Midnight Hunted

Falls Gazette

Chapter One

Holy shit. I'm trapped. The realization hits me the moment I open my eyes. It's the first thing on my mind just as it was the last thought I had before finally drifting off sometime before dawn. Not that those hours of sleep were particularly restful. Hard to find rest when my sleep is riddled with nightmares about how horribly I failed—and how there's no running away from any of this. Not anymore.

Groaning, I roll over and bury my face in the pillow. Sutton's scent hits me like a ton of bricks. No surprise, considering I spent the night in his bedroom—again. He'd offered to stay with me, but I'd refused—too upset about the party to want company. Okay, not so much the party as the murder and witchcraft and werewolves at the end.

Hell of a finale.

Most human parties end with fireworks, but, apparently, that's not enough for these people. Ugh. Not *people*. Not when every one of Midnight Falls' residents can once again shift at will into a wolf.

It was maybe the craziest moment of my life watching them all turn into four-legged predators at once. When the shock wore off, though, I recognized it for the opportunity it was. And I wasn't the only one.

With their wolf senses restored, the pack had tried hunting down Audrey and Yvette so we could end this, once and for all—due process be damned. But a full search of the town had yielded nothing. They'd simply … vanished. My only hope is that they're trapped just like I am. Hiding out somewhere nearby. Otherwise—I don't even want to consider what it means if they've managed to sneak out, leaving us trapped in here with nothing but a magical curse to contend with until next year's renewal.

One thing is certain, though: Nowhere is safe until they are found.

Gripping Sutton's pillow with one hand, I breathe him in. Maybe having him here last night would have been a healthy distraction. A way to pass the time. I can't freak out about my nightmarish reality if I'm too busy orgasming...right?

Ugh. No.

It was my raging hormones that got me into this shitty predicament, and the last thing I need is to listen to them again. Who knows what'll happen if I slip again? Another murder? Refusing to let my hormones be the reason for another death, I force myself to get out of bed.

After crossing the room, I pause in front of the door. Shutting myself in here alone has cocooned me even just for a few hours. It let me pretend or try to forget the impossible reality of my life. When I leave this room, it all becomes horrifyingly real.

I'm trapped in Midnight Falls.

Being hunted by a woman—no, a witch—bent on revenge for a crime she, herself, committed.

And somehow, last night, I broke the part of her curse that was keeping the residents of this town trapped in their human forms. A flash of blue light and now they can shift at will again. Maybe that's good news for them, but for me, it only adds to the 'crazy.'

I double back to the mirror that hangs over the sagging dresser. A hairline crack runs across the top edge of the reflective glass.

Seven years bad luck, I can't help but think.

Kind of sums up the turn my life has taken.

My gaze flicks to my reflection. Dark circles under my eyes. Rumpled hair. Deep lines around my mouth where I'm frowning without even realizing it.

I smooth my hair and school my features as best I can. Nothing is going to get solved with me hiding in this room. *Get your shit together, Serenity.*

With a deep breath, I step out into the hall and make my way down the stairs. The wooden floorboards creak as I walk, the magic that restored the house to its prior beauty last night gone now that we're back to square one. And it *is* square one. With Sheriff Rhodes dead, his blood drained and gone, the curse has been renewed for another year.

I failed.

Honestly, the crumbling manor house is the least of my problems. But right now, it just adds to my pissed-off mood.

Muted male voices carry out of the kitchen, so I stop on the last step and listen.

"Things are different now." *Where have I heard that voice?*

"Maybe," Sutton replies. "But we're still no closer to breaking the curse." His voice wraps around me like an embrace, warming me from the inside. Guilt nags at me for pushing him away last night.

The familiar voice speaks again. "We are, though, don't you see? Serenity being here changes things."

Sutton doesn't immediately reply, so I wait, holding my breath for his response.

A response that comes in the form of him appearing around the corner and coming to a stop right in front of me. "Morning, beautiful."

His smile nearly knocks me on my ass, and I can't help but agree with the stranger. Some things *have* changed because Sutton Hargrave looks more relaxed than I've ever seen. And inner peace looks good as hell on this man's face. It's out of place amid such chaos but no less welcome. And it reminds me exactly where his face was last night in that library—before everything went to hell.

My heart flutters. "Morning. Am I interrupting?"

Another man comes around the corner from the kitchen, and I realize he's no stranger at all—at least, not entirely. "Good morning, Serenity," Phineas greets.

My eyes widen in surprise. As one of the few people to extend a friendly word to me in this town, Phineas is a more welcome sight than others. Still, I'm not sure what he's doing here, other than discussing me. And since neither man looks inclined to explain it, I let it go. For now. The journalist in me is all about strategic information gathering.

And I get the impression that badgering either of these men about anything will only result in more questions. "Morning. Coffee?" I ask, directing my attention to Sutton.

"Absolutely."

I step down, ignoring the way Sutton reaches for me. I know it's pathetic to try to pretend things are not as complex as they are between us, but honestly? I don't know how much more complicated I can take. Besides, he's the one keeping secrets and talking about me behind my back. Until I know why, I can't trust anyone. Not even Sutton. Letting my emotions cloud my judgment resulted in a man's death, and I won't repeat that mistake.

Phineas reaches for a paper cup still sitting in a drink carrier then hands it to me. "Jolene said this is your favorite."

"Jolene?" I eye it warily.

"It's not poison," Sutton says as if the bastard can read my mind.

"Are you sure about that? She doesn't like me."

"You'll find things have changed since last night," Phineas says softly.

Sutton clears his throat and glares at Phineas.

"What's up your ass?" I demand. Then, deciding that if the coffee kills me, it wouldn't exactly be the worst thing at the moment, I take a drink. The hot liquid slips down the back of my throat, and I decide it *definitely* wouldn't be the worst way to go. The current threat to my life notwithstanding.

Phineas answers for him. "My son believes things are going to get worse before they get better."

Coffee spews out of my mouth and burns my nose. It splatters Sutton's once-white shirt, and I cough, barely managing to cling to my cup in the process.

Phineas reaches across the kitchen counter and retrieves a towel, offering it to me. I don't take it. Instead, I stand there, coffee all over my face, glaring at the two men, who are both trying to feign innocence.

"Excuse the shitballs out of me," I say, snatching the towel from my chess buddy's still outstretched hand. "Did you just say *son?* As in you're his—"

"I am Sutton's father," Phineas replies easily as though it's not a huge brick of knowledge he just dropped on my head.

"You're related." I look to Sutton, who shoves both hands into his pockets and quickly glances down at his feet.

"Yes," he says.

"And no one thought to give me this very interesting piece of information before?"

Sutton withdraws his hands and shrugs. "It wasn't pertinent."

"Are you fucking kidding me?" I roar, slamming the coffee down and dropping the towel so I can cross both arms. *"Not pertinent?* I had coffee with you," I gesture to Phineas. "Played chess. Told you about my family. Why didn't you tell me who you are to each other?"

His gaze darts to Sutton, telling me all I need to know. "I didn't think it was necessary, and I didn't want to put you in more danger."

Lie. I don't even bother addressing Phineas. Instead, I turn to Sutton. He's the one who had his tongue in my mouth last week and his face between my legs last night. Therefore, he's the one who *should* have been honest. It's not like there weren't plenty of opportunities for him to say, 'Hey, Serenity, say hi to my dear old dad for me, will you? His name is Phineas.'

"You told him not to tell me, didn't you?"

"That information wouldn't have helped."

"How the hell do you figure that?"

"Tell me how your knowledge of my familial relations would have assisted in discovering the identity of a witch?"

I glare at him. "It would have helped me trust you sooner."

"I didn't want to earn your trust by process of elimination," he replies sternly. "I wanted you to trust me because it's what you felt."

I shake my head, so pissed off I can barely formulate words. "You are both assholes," I announce then turn to Phineas. "You, less so."

He offers me a half-smile that tells me he understands, and I turn away, abandoning my coffee and marching back to the stairs.

As I climb, my eyes fill with tears as my throat burns. Pushing into the room, I take a seat on the bed and rest my face in my hands. Tears flow freely down my cheeks as emotion burns my throat.

I came here wanting to solve these murders so no one else would die. And I failed. Miserably. The memory of Sheriff Rhodes lying in a pool of his own blood—what little was left of it anyway — surfaces.

Is this what Sutton feels like all the time? Useless and stuck?

The door creaks open, and I glare through angry tears at Sutton. He doesn't say anything, just crosses the room and takes a seat on the bed beside me. It dips with his weight, and I avert my gaze to the window.

"I should have told you," Sutton says calmly.

"Yeah, you should have. Any other family members you've left out?" I snap.

"Not living, no. My father is the only blood relative I have left."

The way he says it, the sad tone of his voice, *almost* makes me feel like an asshole for being pissed off. I look back at him. "I don't do secrets, Sutton. I get that you had them before you could trust me, but when it comes to this curse and the people involved, you'd damn well better be honest with me. I'm trapped here, too, which means this is also my fight. Do not keep me out of the loop again."

A muscle in his jaw ticks, but he nods.

I start to respond but am cut off when my ringtone fills the small room. "I thought I had no service—" I reach for it, more than surprised to see three bars and Steven's name illuminating the screen. Sniffling, I wipe a hand over my face before answering and do my best to clear the emotion from my voice. "Hello?"

"You're almost late."

I move an inch to the left, and the signal goes fuzzy. Jerking back again, I freeze in place where the call is clearest. "For what?"

"Calling me."

Shit. "I slept in. It was a long night."

"You have anything new for me?"

"No. I was wrong." The lie is bitter on my tongue. It tastes like deceit, and I fucking hate it. "Yvette is innocent, so we're back to square one over here."

"Serenity."

"Steven," I reply instantly. I know my brother. If I give him even the slightest hesitation, the smallest reservation, he will jump all over it. And the last thing I need is him bringing the National Guard into a town full of werewolves.

He sighs. "Why don't you just come home? It's not like you're relaxing anyway."

"Actually…" I pinch the bridge of my nose, hating myself for what I know I need to do. "I think I'm going to let the locals handle the case. I've started to enjoy hiking. And there are really beautiful waterfalls here."

More lies. My life seems to be built on them lately, something that makes me want to hurl myself off the nearest cliff. I'm no liar. Brutally honest? Sometimes. But I pride myself on always telling the truth.

"You're going to vacation in a town you traveled to in an attempt to investigate unsolved murders?"

"I'm perfectly safe."

"Then why do you sound like you've been crying?"

Damn. Steven's always been way too perceptive for his own freaking good. "Allergies, moron."

"Serenity," he warns.

I sigh. Might as well give him something good. "They gave my job away."

"What?"

"Allison called to let me know," I say. "Quincy is interviewing for my position at the paper."

It's not a lie that helps. It's also not exactly numero uno on my priority list, what with this magical curse and a witch trying to kill me. Still, letting my dream job slip through my fingers stings like a bitch.

"Damn, Ser. That sucks. I'm sorry."

"Yeah, so let's just say I'm running out of reasons to rush right back to the city."

"Look, I know it's hard, what you're going through, but this is a time for family. You need to come home." Clearly, I have not convinced him.

"No," I snap, a little ruder than I mean to be. "I'm not a little girl anymore, Steven, and I want to stay. This place is really great, and as far as I know, no new dead bodies have popped up."

I'm going to hell for that one, for sure.

Steven is silent for a few moments, something not unusual for him, but it still makes my skin crawl. I've never been good at tricking him, and if he senses anything is off— "Fine," he finally says. "But if anything happens, you need to come home, or I'll drive my ass out there to get you."

The very idea of him getting caught in this web makes my stomach roll. "I'll be fine, and I promise to check in. I'll send you lots of hiking pictures," I add.

"I love you, Ser. You're a massive pain in my ass, but life would suck without you. Don't tell the others, but if I had to pick, you'd be my favorite."

Tears spring to my eyes, and my chest tightens. "Love you, too, assface." I end the call and toss my cell to the bed before burying my face in both hands. Steven doesn't typically do feelings. He's straightforward, logical—so for him to be that soft on me… I choke on a sob. He's worried, and this time, he has every reason to be.

What if I never make it home?

"You lied to him."

"What the hell else was I supposed to say?" I whip my head toward Sutton, glaring through the tears. "I'm trapped in a town full of wolf people as I try to break a curse placed on the sexiest one of them, all by a witch who murdered her own daughter?" I snort and get to my feet, turning to face him. “Yeah, he would have taken to that really well.”

Sutton grins at me and stands. He eats up the distance between us in two strides then reaches forward and cups my cheek. “I’m the sexiest one, huh?”

Rolling my eyes, I pull away. “That would be the only part you heard.”

I start to head for the door, but he grips my arm and spins me back toward him. “My father is right. You gave me part of my life back. I’m not sure how, but you being here changes things, Serenity.”

The pad of his thumb strokes my lip, and despite my guilt over lying to Steven, lust pools in my belly. Unable to help myself, I reach out and wrap my arms around Sutton, leaning into him and breathing deeply. “I’m trapped.”

“We’ll find a way to free you.”

“There’s no world in which I can stay here for a year without my family showing up, Sutton. And if they come here—”

“They will stay safe,” he assures me.

I pull back and turn my face up to his. “They have to.”

Sutton nods. The way he watches me, the smoldering heat in his gaze as it momentarily drops to my mouth and then back up, burns me.

But, just when I think he might lean in to kiss me, Sutton lets me go. “I need to go into town and meet with my pack.”

Surprise spears through me, shoving past the disappointment. “You can do that? But I thought you were confined here.”

“I was. Until last night. Whatever you did... it opened the barrier between the woods and the town.”

“That’s how Phineas is able to be here right now,” I realized. How the hell did I miss that little nugget of information? Oh, yeah, Daddy Phineas.

He nodded. "It's been a very long time since I've stepped foot in that town. I honestly cannot wait." Hope shines brightly on his handsome face. "We're going to organize patrols and search parties so we can look for Audrey and Yvette. Do you want to come?"

The excitement in his eyes is unmistakable. He doesn't just have to go. He wants to. But I can't. Not if it means facing everyone. Guilt crushes down on me, eliminating the rest of whatever lust his touch stirred. "No."

"Ser—"

"I am the reason the Sheriff is dead," I tell him. "And they already hated me before."

He shakes his head and reaches forward to take my hands. The pads of his thumbs run along the tops, but I can barely feel it, far too focused on the realization that, not only am I trapped, but I'm stuck in a town where the majority of the population despises me. "They don't hate you. Especially not now," he insists.

Even if that's true, fear and defeat keep me rooted. Besides, what the hell would I wear? My clothes are all still in the B&B, and the dress I wore last night is a no-go, mainly because I plan to burn it at the first convenient moment. Nothing Audrey made will touch my body again. I highly doubt they would take kindly to me showing up in Sutton's shorts and baggy t-shirt.

Nothing. "I don't want to go, Sutton."

His expression falters, disappointment passing over his handsome features, but he nods and releases my hands. "I'll be back as soon as I can."

I don't answer.

He turns to leave, and I take a deep breath before plopping back onto the mattress. Minutes pass as I stare at the ceiling above me, contemplating all the positives.

One: things could be worse than being trapped with Sutton.

Two: nope. There's pretty much just the one.

This town never felt suffocating before, but right now, knowing I can't leave, that there's no way out—it's more confining than I've ever felt. So, getting to my feet, I head back downstairs to retrieve my abandoned coffee so I can get started making a list of everything I know.

Research. Logic. Working through the facts. It's what I do best. And with Sutton's library catalog, I should be able to come up with something I didn't know before. Some piece to this curse-riddled puzzle that's now mine to solve whether I want it or not.

I'm just rounding the corner into the kitchen when I realize I'm not alone.

Phineas smiles at me and gestures to a chess board he's set out on the dinette. He looks nervous, almost, uncomfortable, and it makes me feel a little guilty for my earlier outburst even as warranted as it was.

"Care to join me?" he asks.

"I—"

"I'm very sorry for my deceit," he says quickly, interrupting me.

"No apology necessary," I reply, my anger toward him deflating like a week-old balloon. "He's your son. I get it." Grabbing my coffee, I take a seat at the table, and he sits across from me. "I wish he would have told me, though."

"Sutton is..." Phineas trails off as he moves his pawn forward. "Complicated."

"Understatement."

He chuckles, but the amusement fades quickly, a shadow passing over his usually open expression. "Myrtle—the witch who cursed us—hated my family for what happened to her daughter. She killed Vivian first, knowing how much it would hurt. And it does, of course, but out of all three of us, Sutton was punished the greatest. Being trapped out here, surrounded by memories—" The man's eyes mist, and I know he's recalling his late wife.

Reaching over, I cover his hand with mine. "Sutton told me what happened to her. I'm so sorry."

Swallowing hard, he nods. "She was my life. My everything. Losing Sutton on top of it, even in the way I did, it nearly killed me."

"I can't even imagine."

Phineas pulls his hand from beneath mine and swipes his fingertips under both eyes. "Knowing he was out here and not being able to touch him, to talk to him—" He shakes his head angrily. "I have carried so much rage and grief all these years. And knowing Yvette and Audrey were right under my nose—"

"You couldn't have known," I assure him. "No one did."

He takes a deep breath and nods. "You did. You suspected Yvette."

"Outsiders perspective," I tell him. "Easier to see when you don't have any kind of attachment."

"Maybe." He reaches across and takes one of my hands, his gaze meeting mine. "You gave me my son back, Serenity. I am forever in your debt."

"Help me figure out how to get the hell out of here, and we'll call it even."

Falls Gazette

Chapter Two

Phineas and I spend two hours scouring the downstairs library for any books that might offer a clue about the details of this curse and how to break it. I start with the books Sutton stole out from under me when I first began researching. The thief, I now know, was Phineas himself. They'd wanted to ensure I came to Sutton for help rather than going up against Audrey on my own. But in the end, there's nothing useful inside their pages, making his theft by proxy a moot effort.

Empty-handed, we return to the kitchen where Phineas proceeds to kick my ass at chess, not once but twice. I go with it, mostly because I need a bit of normalcy after the crazy twenty-four hours I've had, not to mention the complete dead-end we just hit in the library. Something about the black and white rules of chess are a comfort amidst the real-life chaos going on now.

By the time Phineas has set up the board for a third game, my stomach is growling with a serious and sudden need for food. Phineas lifts a brow, letting me know he heard it too.

"Sounds like someone missed breakfast," he says.

I'm surprised then delighted as Phineas jumps up and begins making sandwiches for us both. He moves about the kitchen, clearly comfortable. And why wouldn't he be? Before Audrey ruined his life, this *was* his home.

"How does it feel?" I ask cautiously. "Being back here after everything?"

Phineas sighs and continues spreading mayonnaise on a piece of white bread. "It feels natural," he replies. "And a bit empty. My Vivian brought sunshine into every room she walked into. Sutton is a bit like her in that sense, I suppose."

I snort, and he grins at me, arching a dark eyebrow. "You don't agree?"

"He's been quite broody since we met."

Chuckling, Phineas reaches into the refrigerator and pulls out some cheese. "I imagine being trapped here alone has changed him. My hope is that you will help bring that side of him back."

He says it so easily, so casually, it catches me off guard. "How will I bring it back?"

After adding some sliced turkey to the top of the cheese, he squeezes a bit of mustard on top and closes the sandwich. Then, he slides it across the counter to me. "I'm no fool," he says. "I can see the way the two of you look at each other. A look I recognize because I had the very same one with my wife."

My stomach twists, a vice closing around my heart at the same time. "Sutton and I are— Things are complicated."

He finishes prepping the second sandwich then puts everything in the fridge and moves around to join me. "Sutton has this selfless side that I can't help but admire. It's why he makes a much better leader than I ever was. But I always wondered if one day he'd meet the woman who would make him yearn to be a bit selfish."

"And you think that woman is me?" Not one to beat around the bush, I don't see the point in pretending we're talking about someone else.

"I do," he says easily before taking a bite of his sandwich. "Though I imagine you're considering all the ways I'm wrong," he adds as soon as he swallows.

"There are quite a few."

He shrugs and grins. "Then I suppose only time will tell."

I take a bite of my sandwich and nearly groan in response to the food. Shit, I don't even know when the last time I ate was. I guess at the library yesterday? "This is delicious, thank you."

"Anytime."

"Are wolves usually this nurturing?" I ask after another bite.

"Excuse me?"

"Sutton cooks for me, always has fresh coffee brewed, and now you're making me lunch."

"Ah." He relaxes and wipes his hands on his napkin. "My wife taught us both how to cook and care for our own needs—beat us over the head with it, actually."

I suppress a smile. "Hopefully not literally."

"If that's what it took."

"She sounds like a very fascinating woman."

"My Vivian was one of a kind," he says wistfully and takes a drink of water.

"I wish I could have met her."

"She would have loved you."

For several minutes, we eat in silence, and I'm struck by how easy the quiet is between us. Phineas isn't a replacement for my own father, but he's definitely the next best thing. A source of comfort in the middle of a terrifying situation.

"Can I ask you a question?"

Phineas sits back, his expression genuine. "Anything."

"That blue spark last night," I say and watch as his open expression immediately shuts down again, but I press on. “The one that flashed just before everyone became wolves... that came from me, didn’t it?”

“What do you think?” he asks, and I scowl.

“I asked you first.”

His lips twitch. “Fair enough.” Then he rubs at the stubble along his chin. “Yes, I think it’s safe to say that blue spark came from you.”

His honesty has me leaning forward in earnest. “How?”

He shakes his head. “That's not something I can answer.”

My eyes narrow. “What about Sutton?” I ask. “Can he answer it?”

Phineas tries to bite back a smile. “My son has his own ideas about you and what he thinks is best.”

“Keeping secrets, you mean. And lies.”

His brow lifts. “He doesn’t lie, and neither do I.” When I open my mouth to argue, he adds, “We leave out details at times, but we won’t lie. Not to you, Serenity. I swear it.”

I want to believe him. But the last twenty-four hours have left me reeling. And that blue spark feels important. Like there’s something about me I don’t know. Add that to their private pow-wow this morning, and the questions are piling up way faster than the answers.

“At the party, Audrey said she'd been waiting for me.”

“Did she now?”

He rubs at his beard again, and I swallow back the impatience that rises. My need for answers is overwhelming. Almost as consuming as the guilt of my failure.

I want to ask him the real question: about what I am and what I did last night to help free the wolves from whatever Audrey had done to bind them. But then I remember the blue flame Audrey conjured... How familiar it felt. How drawn to its power I was. And

I'm suddenly afraid of what Phineas might tell me. Maybe there's a reason for his half-answers. I've always sought the truth—no matter how twisted or painful it might be. But maybe, just maybe, this time I should wait. Because I can't help but wonder if the answer won't reveal me to be less of the hero and more of the villain.

After all, magic is what cast this curse in the first place.

"I take it the sandwich was terrible," he quips, giving me a change of subject I didn't realize I needed.

I look down at my empty plate and snort. "Oh, yeah. Terrible."

He chuckles, and I release a heavy breath—and my frustration with it. Phineas is not the enemy here. In fact, he's been nothing but kind to me.

"You know, being fed by two caring, handsome men could make a girl forget she can't leave town," I tease.

"That's the idea." Phineas winks.

I laugh, surprised to find I can still find any humor in it all. But then a figure moves in the doorway, and my smile vanishes.

Sutton's gaze collides with mine, and there's a shift in the air that I feel straight to my core. His presence fills the space more than his physical form ever could, but it's more than that. It's his mood. He looks way too serious for the lighthearted moment Phineas and I were having. And the way he's watching me? The hardened gaze trained directly on me? It's way too damn hot for my liking.

He shares a look with Phineas that honestly makes me wonder if they can communicate telepathically. To prove my point, Phineas rises from his seat. He sets his empty plate beside the sink and says, "Well, that's my cue." He looks at me. "I'll be back in the morning, and we'll see if we have better luck, deal?"

"Deal," I tell him.

He squeezes my shoulder on his way out.

Sutton doesn't say a word. Even when we're alone, the silence stretches, and without Phineas as a buffer, it feels awkward. Or maybe I'm afraid I'm going to respond to whatever subliminal message he's trying to send me and strip naked right here to finish what we started in that library of his last night.

It's tempting.

And that's exactly why I can't let myself do it.

"How'd it go with the pack?" I ask, feeling strange about using that word.

But he nods and crosses to the sink where he fills a glass full of water. "Good. The teams are set up, and we have a schedule worked out so no one's on shift alone. Hopefully, something will turn up soon."

By "something" he means Audrey. Or Yvette. Preferably both.

My stomach clenches at the image of their faces burned into my memory. The idea of facing them again both boils my blood and terrifies me, all at the same time. Two contrasting forces, both with the power to send me into a full-on spiral.

Sutton lifts the water glass and empties the contents in one long swig. When he lowers it again, his gaze is steady and trained on me. I recognize the look he wears now. It's the same one he gave me in that library last night just before he buried his face between my legs. My insides curl in anticipation at the same time my heart shutters closed against the prospect of letting him get that close to me again.

"Well, I should get started on that research," I say, pushing to my feet and heading for the door.

Sutton rounds the counter and plants his feet, blocking my escape. "Serenity." My name is rough in his throat, and it sends a shiver down my spine. "We should talk."

"Sutton," I begin, ready to shut him down, but he doesn't give me a chance to finish.

He takes a step forward, and I retreat, repeating the actions until I am trapped between his hard body and the wall. Slowly, as if I'm breakable, he lifts his hand to my cheek and trails his fingertips gently down my face. Hunger reflects back at me from the depths of his eyes. I blink away a sudden rush of hot tears, desperate to give him what he wants. Most of me wants it too.

"Last night, we—"

"Last night we were stupid," I snap before he can say something dirty or romantic. Either one will completely shatter my control.

His brows knit in confusion. "How can you say that?"

"C'mon, Sutton. You know it's true. If we hadn't been so distracted, we might have actually found a way to stop Audrey before she killed Rhodes. We might even have broken the curse completely. Instead, I let myself forget my real reason for being here, and now someone is dead because of my carelessness."

"This isn't your fault," he says quietly.

"Isn't it?" I shoot back. "What was that blue spark last night, Sutton? I know you saw it, and we both know it came from me. Whatever it was, it gave everyone their ability to shift again, didn't it?"

He grimaces. "We don't have to talk about this right now."

"No? But we can have sex, right? We can sleep together, but telling me the truth is where you draw the line." He doesn't respond, though the harshness in his gaze tells me I'm getting to him. *Good.* "What are you hiding from me?" I demand.

Pulling back, he crosses his arms. "I'm not hiding anything."

"Bull shit. Did I do magic? Am I a witch like Audrey? Tell me the truth. No more secrets, remember?"

His sigh holds the weight of the world in it. "Yes, it was magic. And yes, it gave everyone their shifting ability back."

"How?" I ask in a small voice.

"I don't know," he admits. "I spent all day trying to find out. I wanted answers before I came to you."

"And did you find any?"

"Not yet."

"You shouldn't have kept it from me. Especially after our conversation."

"I wanted answers, Serenity. Answers that, for once, wouldn't lead to more questions since we both have enough of those."

He's right, but that doesn't mean I can give myself over to my feelings. In fact, it only strengthens my decision not to. "Well, I intend to figure all of this out. And that's exactly why I can't take things any further with you. Not while the curse has us both trapped."

He cocks his head, studying me intently. "You think I want to be with you because we're trapped together?"

"No, of course not." I say the words with much more confidence than I feel. "Look, you've lived this reality for a century. And, well, it's probably been a while, hasn't it?"

I expect him to get angry. Defensive. Instead, he arches an eyebrow and cocks his head to the side. "So you believe I want to sleep with you because—what—it's been a while and you're the closest opportunity?"

Swallowing hard, I stand my ground even when he takes a step closer. "You will never be a convenience for me," he replies. "And I've done just fine on my own the past century. Believe it or not, I want more than sex from you."

Even as I fight it, the image of Sutton pleasuring himself slams into me. I blink rapidly, trying to shut it out, but not before it pushes my own libido into overdrive.

"Fine. Good for you. You know how to play with yourself. But, as I said before you de-railed us, you've known this reality for a long time. I've known it for less than a day. I just... I can't think about my own feelings when lives are on the line. Not after last night."

"First of all, Serenity, I don't 'play'. In *anything* I do. Second, I've already told you that this isn't your fault."

"You're their alpha," I say, completely ignoring yet another wave of heat. "You can't tell me you don't feel responsible for what happens to the people in this town."

Something flashes in his eyes. Anger, maybe. But he doesn't contradict me.

"What I feel for you is more than a mere distraction," he replies, his voice cracking with emotion.

My heart aches because, two days ago, I would have given my right tit to hear him say that to me. But now, it only strengthens my resolve. "That's exactly my point," I say, heartbreak softening my words. "These people are counting on me. On us. If someone else dies because I lost focus—again—I wouldn't be able to live with myself."

I can barely live with myself now.

I don't say that part out loud, but I know he sees it in my eyes because he takes a step back. It's a small step, but it's a retreat nonetheless. And I know it means he's giving up. For some reason, that makes me want to cry.

"I have to find a way to free them," I add softly. "And you." *And me*. "Until I do that, I can't let myself feel things for you."

"You can't stop feeling," he says. "It doesn't work that way."

I shake my head, willing him to be wrong even though I know he isn't. "It has to."

Falls Gazette

Chapter Three

Just outside the bedroom window, the sun crests over the mountains. I've already been awake for hours, though. Mostly texting with Allison, which can only be done if I sit in a very specific position with one leg higher than the other and my phone tilted to the left. It's ridiculous, but I needed girl talk too badly not to deal with the horrible signal I get out here. After our confrontation yesterday, Sutton left, and I haven't seen him since. I can feel him though, his presence, yet another oddity I cannot explain.

One more damned question that lacks an answer.

But it's how I know he was merely avoiding me and hadn't actually left.

It's also how I know he's already gone this morning. The warmth I feel when he's near, the tingling of awareness, is no longer there. In its place is an absence that feels oddly lonely.

Still, it's another day. A chance to find out how to break this damned curse so I can leave this town and forget all about it and its ridiculously sexy, broody leader. Or take him to bed with me. I can't let myself choose either until the curse is done.

Judging by her last text, Allison is clearly on Team Sutton, which doesn't help matters.

Whoever this "S" mystery man is—I'm calling it: S stands for SEX, girl! Get you some!

I didn't tell her about the magical curse or town full of werewolves, obviously. Only that I'm trying to resist feelings for a guy because I don't want to let him be nothing more than a convenient rebound from Roscoe. She doesn't seem to follow my logic.

Tossing my phone aside, I force my ass up and out of bed for another riveting day in Midnight Falls. Dressed in a pair of baggy shorts and a sweatshirt I pilfered from Sutton's closet, I pull open the bedroom door and step out into the hall—only to nearly trip over something blocking my exit. With a hand on the wall, I barely manage to keep my feet under me. The culprit, a black duffel, sits on the floor with a note boasting my name.

Curious, I reach down and lift both then head back into the bedroom and set the bag on the bed before opening the note.

Serenity,

I thought this might help with your lack of supplies. I'll be out most of the day but will be back at four to get you for the funeral.

-S

Funeral. My stomach rolls, and I toss the note to the side. As much as I want to skip it, I know I can't. Regardless of how shitty I feel, not paying respects to the man who tried to warn me would be far worse. Sheriff Rhodes deserves at least that.

Swallowing hard, I unzip the bag and nearly weep with joy when I see an assortment of women's clothing and toiletries inside. All of my emotional turmoil momentarily pushed aside, I reach in and start pulling the items out.

Lavender scented body wash, actual shampoo—my hormones

lean hard toward Allison's way of thinking as I picture Sutton picking all this out for me. I waste no time stripping out of Sutton's clothes and redressing in a pair of black leggings and an oversized baby blue sweatshirt before stashing the shampoo, conditioner, and soap in Sutton's shower for later.

All dressed up with nowhere to go, I head downstairs and smile at Phineas as he pours a steaming mug of coffee. But then my gaze shifts to the pile of groceries on the island and the gift baskets sitting beside it.

"Go shopping?" I ask.

He chuckles and offers me a mug. "Hardly. Those are gifts. For you."

I narrow my gaze at him then turn back toward the stack. "What do you mean for me?"

"The town is very grateful for what you've done. This is how they show it. Be glad it's not dead animals."

I blanch, my stomach churning. "Why the hell would it be—" And then it dawns on me. "You're wolves."

He smiles widely. "Wolves who have been unable to access half of ourselves for a hundred years. We owe you a lot, Serenity."

"I don't want gifts. I sure as hell don't deserve them. It's my fault someone is dead."

His gaze darkens. "It's not your fault. The blame lies solely with the witch."

"I—" My explanation dies on my lips. How do you tell a man you let a murder happen because you were too busy letting his son devour you like you were the last macaroon in the box? "I was distracted the night she killed him. If I'd been focused—"

"Then you might have been the one killed." He reaches over and gently touches my shoulder. "Do not underestimate what you granted us. Let them be grateful. Not accepting the gifts will offend them."

Unease swirls in my belly. I've never been good at receiving gifts—but this? This is way too damned much. And it's completely undeserved. The mistakes I've made since coming here have been many, and ignoring that won't change it.

I thought I'd been brave. Determined. But really, I'd been stupid. How the hell could I have thought I had what it would take to solve these murders? To stop them? Granted, I'd had no idea just what I was getting into. At least, not until Sutton had warned me.

He'd begged me to leave, to get myself out and come back when it was safe, and I'd ignored him. Arrogance, determination, stubbornness, whatever you want to call it, the fact still remains that this curse is more than any human can handle. Magic is not something to trifle with. And I did it anyway.

Now, I'm paying the price.

We all are.

If I had just listened, I could have come back the next morning and not been trapped. And maybe if I could leave, I could head back to New York and try to pull some strings to bring in real help. The idea of trying to explain any of this to Steven tells me that's not exactly a solid plan, either.

"Get out of your head, girl," Phineas says softly. "Regrets will get you nowhere."

"I wish I could," I reply. "Thanks for the coffee."

He smiles softly. "Anytime. What can I do to help today?"

"We need to finish going through the books in Sutton's library—or I guess it's yours."

Shaking his head, he beams at me. "That is Sutton's. This house, all of it. I'm merely here for you."

"Thank you," I say again, my heart warming. "I really appreciate it."

"No need to thank me." He claps his hands together. "Let's go get some reading done."

"THIS IS USELESS." GROANING, I TOSS THE BOOK DOWN ONTO Sutton's desk and run both hands over my face.

"It has definitely been a fruitless venture, hasn't it?"

I glance up at Phineas, who is pacing the room with a leather-bound book in his hand. Between the tweed vest and his glasses, he looks incredibly studious, and it makes me smile. He and my dad would totally get along. Not to mention the original hand-drawn map of the Falls I found and the amount of history in these volumes we've uncovered. Dad would be a kid in a candy store right about now.

And that thought brings a wave of pain down onto me. My parents are going to be heartbroken if I can't get out of here. If I miss a year's worth of dinners... Hell, they'll probably come here—I jump up from the chair, panic racing through my veins.

"We have got to figure this out."

Phineas turns toward me. "Are you all right?"

"No. Yes. I don't freaking know. But I just realized that if I don't solve this, I'm likely going to have all of the Kellis family members descending on this town to try to drag me out. And then—what if she finds them? What if she hurts them to get to me?"

All the horrific worse-case scenarios begin to pile on top of one another. Yvette knows my name. They know where I lived before here. They could easily track my family down. And since they're damned witches—

"They will not harm your family, Serenity."

I look up into Phineas' kind eyes. He's abandoned the book and managed to move directly in front of me without me even knowing. "You don't know my family."

"Yvette and Audrey didn't harm you, right? Both had ample

opportunity, yet neither made a move. Their issue is not with you or your family."

I know he's placating me, trying to ease my anxiety, but it's not going to work. Not when we just discussed his late wife—and what Audrey did to her all those years ago. I'd known coming to investigate homicides could potentially put me in harm's way, but I never, not for a second, considered the effect it could have on my loved ones.

"I need to go call my mom."

"You can't tell her about this place."

"Don't you think I know that?" The words come out harsher than I meant, but Phineas' calm expression doesn't change. "I haven't had a chance to really talk to her since I came here. I need to go call her."

"I'll keep looking." He nods at the door, encouraging me to go.

I turn and head for the stairs, fighting tears the entire way up to my room. As soon as I'm safely inside, I take a deep, steadying breath, and wipe my face with the sleeve of my sweatshirt.

Then, I reach for my phone, praying my signal is strong enough to make this call, and tap Mom's contact information.

Holding the phone out, I wait for her to answer. Finally, after two rings, her flushed face comes into view on the screen. "Serenity," she greets, a broad smile on her face. "How are you, honey?"

"Hey, Mom." I smile at her, and if she notices it's not real, she doesn't comment. "I'm doing good. Just got up a little bit ago."

"Is that Serenity?" I hear Dad ask in the background, and my chest tightens.

"It is. Come say hi." Mom waves him over.

Dad's face pops into view, and he smiles, the lines at the corners of his eyes deepening. "Hey there, sweetie. How is that little town?"

"It's good," I lie. "Relaxing." Double lie.

"If you're sleeping in, you must be truly relaxing," Mom comments. "Good for you."

"I am getting plenty of sleep. I even learned a bit of chess so I can give Dad a run for his money when I get home."

Dad beams at me so warmly, and the ice in my veins thaws just enough that I can offer a genuine smile back. "I can't wait to see."

"How in the world did you learn chess all the way down there?" Mom asks.

"They have a really neat town center here," I tell them. "I met a guy who talked me into a game."

"Oh, really?" Mom grins and glances at Dad.

"Not that kind of guy." I snort.

"Have you met that kind of guy?" Mom questions, and my dad pales.

"Not here for this conversation. Love you, Ser, see you soon?"

"Maybe. I think I'm going to extend my time here a bit longer. I really love it here."

"We miss you at family dinners," my mom says softly. "Though, I am so proud you're taking a break. I imagine after the whole Roscoe thing—"

"I really do not want to talk about Roscoe," I interrupt.

Mom smiles. "Understood. How is everything else? You eating okay?"

"I am. Everything is fine, promise."

"Good." She glances off-screen then looks back. "I need to get to my spin class. Can you call me later? I've missed our chats, but I didn't want to bother you."

"You're never a bother," I say quickly. "I'll give you a call when I get a chance. I love you Mom, love you, Dad."

"We love you, too, sweet pea. Talk soon."

The call ends, and I stare at my phone screen as a tear slips free from my eye. My heart aches with emptiness. I never realized just how much I counted on the routine of family dinners until I was unable to attend. Isn't that the bittersweet truth of it all, though?

You never realize what you have until it's gone.

Life is short. Sometimes way too short. And now, who the hell knows when I'll get to see my family again? When I'll get to hug my mother or see my nieces and nephews?

I toss the phone to the side and take a deep breath.

"Are you all right?"

Sutton's voice slams into me, and in my emotional state, I very nearly rush over to where he stands across the room and throw myself into his arms. Instead, I sit up, swiping at the tears staining my cheeks.

With a cup of coffee clutched in his hand, Sutton remains in the doorway, watching me. My gaze drifts to the dark suit he's wearing, much like the one I first saw him in. His jaw is freshly shaven, his eyes boring into me as though they can see straight through to my soul. I could tell him the truth. That I feel broken, lost, aimless, hopeless—but I know that if I let my walls down with Sutton now, I'll never leave him. Hell, I might even stop caring that I'm trapped at all. Somehow, that feels worse than fighting and losing. Giving up is not something I'm programmed for.

Despite my sadness, my heart flutters at the way he watches me. He doesn't make a move toward me, doesn't say another word. And I honestly can't tell if he's treating me like I'm fragile for my sake or his. But I hate it. Just once, I long to be reckless, stupid. And damn, I wish the weight of this little slice of the world wasn't resting on our shoulders.

"Fine. I just miss my family."

Sutton nods, but he doesn't press me for more. I know my rejection has hurt him, but I can't take it back.

"I wanted to let you know it's nearly time." He reaches behind him and retrieves a garment bag he must have draped on the balustrade when he'd walked up.

"Is that for me?"

"A gift. From Cara. She knew you didn't have anything besides—"

He doesn't finish.

We both know he means the dress I wore to the ball. And we both also know I'll never wear that thing again.

Silent, he crosses the room and sets the mug on the nightstand beside me. Then, he lays the bag down on the bed, though he doesn't move away. We're inches from one another, so close I can all but feel the body heat radiating from him.

"You're killing me," he growls.

"How?" I tilt my face up to look at him and lose my breath. Sutton closes his eyes and breathes deeply, the action sending my heart racing within my chest.

"I can sense your feelings," he whispers. "Even if you want to deny them. And knowing that you're just as aroused as I am, that you want me as badly as I want you, yet I cannot act on it, it's driving me mad."

"I..." Words fail me. Because I have no good argument other than we cannot allow ourselves to be distracted—something that I know Sutton does not agree with. So, I swallow hard and try to do what Allison said she's done in the past—I think about softball.

That does the trick, at least enough to break whatever hold we both had on each other—for now.

Sutton takes a step away from me. Then another. "I'll be downstairs. We need to leave in thirty minutes to make it in time."

Swallowing hard, I nod but continue to stare at the bag as he leaves. As soon as the door is shut softly behind him, I reach out and unzip the bag. The dress is simple. A black "V" neck with heavy lace that hits just below my knee. Simple—but elegant. Cara somehow nailed my style, and I make a mental note to thank her for the gesture.

I've only ever been to one funeral in my life. When my grandmother passed away, I was only ten, but I can recall every moment of that day. From my mother's swollen eyes as she helped my grief-stricken father to the car, to the pleats of my black dress and the casket's reflection in my shiny black shoes.

It had been sad and awkward all at the same time because I hadn't known how to act. Steven was there, though, holding my hand and telling me that it was okay to cry.

I'd barely known the woman, and still, I'd wept for her.

And I hadn't caused her death. Not like I caused the Sheriff's.

There's no Steven here. No one to hold my hand. And certainly no one to help me face the crowd of people who—despite the gifts they've sent over—likely blame me for his death.

Still, I've never been a coward. So, with a deep breath, I dress, slipping into the black fabric and throwing my hair in a low ponytail. I reach into the bag and withdraw a pair of black flats from the bottom along with a small, hand-written note.

Hope these fit. I had to guess your size.

-Cara

I put them on, pleased to find they're a perfect fit, then head down the stairs.

Phineas is gone, leaving Sutton standing at the front door like we're headed to some twisted, dark prom night. The daydream is so far from reality it makes me want to scream, but it's in my mind before I can filter it out. Hands sweaty, I rub them on the black lace of the skirt, but it itches my skin.

"I'm ready," I say, and Sutton nods.

"I know I shouldn't say it, but you look beautiful."

"Beautiful for a funeral," I deadpan.

As I'm passing by, Sutton gently grips my arm, stopping me in place. “What happened to him was not your fault, Serenity. You can either keep beating yourself up or move forward, but you can’t do both.” He releases me and steps aside as I move toward the door.

I don’t make it far, though, because I nearly trip over a bouquet of crimson roses someone has left on the top step. Sutton’s quick maneuvering helps to keep me from trampling the flowers. He bends down and lifts them up, offering them to me.

“What the hell are these for?” I snap, a hell of a lot ruder than I meant.

He presses them into my arms. “For you.”

"You got me flowers?”

Anger flits through me, setting my temper ablaze. I told him what I expected from him—friendship, nothing more. And today is absolutely not the day for romance, no matter what either of us wants. Especially when I can’t help but notice how the red roses remind me of blood against our black clothes.

He shakes his head. “Not me.”

“Then who...?”

I wait as he bends down again and picks up a small silver box. It’s dainty with an intricately carved design covering all four sides. He offers it to me, taking the flowers so I can hold the box.

I stare down at it, not sure how to feel about the fact that my name has been carved into the lid. Opening it carefully, I withdraw a small folded note.

Fate has favored us at last. Destiny is on your side, and so are we.

It isn’t signed, but the words themselves make my gut churn. I want to send it back. The note, the box, the flowers, the gifts from earlier. The sentiment. It’s all wrong. All of this is wrong.

“Who did this?” I ask, my stomach roiling. Hands shaking, I all but fling the box and note at Sutton.

He studies the writing, then meets my gaze. “I don’t know.”

I narrow my eyes. “This is your place. You mean you didn’t notice someone right outside? I thought your wolf senses—”

“There have been many people,” he tells me.

“What do you mean?”

“You’ve had several visitors these last few days.”

“What visitors?”

“Cara. She brought your dress. Jolene with the coffee. Then there was Mable. She brought dinner and a few other gifts from the others.”

The gifts from earlier. The baskets from town. But if I’d known it was Cara and Mable— “Why didn’t you tell me?”

He sighs. “Because I didn’t want to alarm you or make you uncomfortable. My father told me you weren’t overly thrilled by the gifts earlier, but”—he gestures to the box—“they want you to know they support you.”

My heart sinks. The presents, the visitors—it's all to woo me. So I’ll give them what they want. So I’ll break their curse. Except I don’t know how, and even if I did, I’m not sure why they think I’m strong enough when they clearly aren’t.

I turn away.

“We should go. I don’t want to be late.” My tone is emotionless, but I can’t be bothered to care. Mainly because I care too fucking much. Especially about the man I want nothing more than to lean into when I feel so broken inside.

Falls Gazette

Chapter Four

The funeral is being held at Midnight Falls Chapel, a quaint little building that sits on the edge of town. I can still recall my initial impression of the small church I'd passed when I first arrived in Midnight Falls. Shit, my arrival that day feels like it happened a lifetime ago now. That version of me would have never imagined I'd be attending the funeral of the town Sheriff. Yet, here I am, walking inside a building that I'd initially thought was a tad on the creepy side to honor a man who wasn't even my friend to begin with.

Today, the small building is packed with people. And unlike the day I arrived and walked the streets of downtown, they don't whisper and stare at the sight of me. Instead, when they see us coming, the crowd parts in reverent silence, giving us clear passage straight to the front.

Sutton doesn't seem to expect anything less. Our progress slows as he pauses to greet people. It's clear he knows every one of them by name. It's impressive and endearing, the affection and respect they offer him. The obvious relief—joy, even—at being reunited.

For the first time since the party, I allow myself to focus on what this town gained instead of what I lost that night. And I'm glad to have played a part in Sutton's freedom, such as it is.

Still, after two days shut inside Sutton's library, I'm no closer to understanding how Audrey has trapped me here. Or what I did to break the parts of the curse that let these people shift into their wolves again. I've been thrust into a new world, one I don't understand, and by an enemy I am not nearly strong enough or smart enough to contend with.

Arden's lifeless body is proof of that. He's been lain out in a dark walnut casket that's surrounded by piles of flower arrangements. The casket lid is open, offering mourners one last goodbye. From here, I can see the dark fabric of his suit contrasting starkly with his pasty skin. His body has been cared for and cleaned, but the powdery coating of makeup across his cheeks makes me cringe.

I can't bring myself to move any closer.

When Sutton leads me to a seat in the front row and gestures for me to sit, I hesitate, not sure I have a right to this space reserved for close friends and family. Then again, from the looks of it, Arden Rhodes had no family. The bench is nearly empty save for one face I recognize.

"Serenity." Mable, the town librarian, reaches over and takes my hand, gently pulling me down beside her on the bench. "How are you, dear?" she asks quietly. "Holding up all right?"

"I'm fine," I tell her as my insides tense with the lie.

"Did you get the fruit basket I sent over?"

"I did, yes. Thank you."

I feel suddenly guilty for resisting the gifts. Mable is sweet. She's never been anything but nice to me—even when others weren't. Still, it's hard to imagine little old Mable shifting into a deadly wolf. The image is a bit amusing, in fact. Granny as the Big Bad Wolf.

"You need anything else, you let me know, all right? The library is yours to use as you see fit. Oh, here." She presses a tissue into my hand. "Just in case."

I take the tissue and ball it up in my fist. My heart warms at Mable's kindness then squeezes as Phineas steps up to the podium. He clears his throat and looks out over the quieting room.

"Thank you all for coming."

Sutton sits down on my other side. The heat of his body is an awareness I can't ignore even at a somber event like this. We're magnets, him and I. Forever drawn to each other, no matter how many reasons we have to stay away. Reasons that are becoming more irrelevant by the minute if my hormones have any say in the matter.

Once, I held back because I thought he was a monster. Now, I hold back because I am. "We're gathered here today to honor the life of Sheriff Arden Rhodes," Phineas says, and my eyes blur with hot tears, my focus returning to the casket up front and the man inside it, put there by my failure. "Arden was a friend to many of us, but he was also a protector. He dedicated his life to law enforcement and service to the people. He made sacrifices for that role. And in the end, he made the ultimate sacrifice for every one of us who call this town home."

Phineas pauses to collect himself, and it's all I can do to stay where I am. My hands fist tightly with the urge to run from this room. To scream. To beat on something—or someone. Anything to make sense of what happened. But there's nothing sensible about murder.

As Phineas talks about the life of a man I barely knew, I take deep, measured breaths to keep from falling apart. The rest of the room is silent other than a few sniffles and coughs. Mable dabs her eyes with a crinkly tissue. Beside me, Sutton is rigidly stoic. Once, his hand twitches, and I wonder if he's about to reach for me. But he doesn't, and I don't know whether I'm disappointed or relieved.

At the podium, Phineas offers a final prayer, and then it's over. My gaze locks on the casket as two men move forward and close the lid, securing the recently departed inside.

It feels smothering even watching.

I swallow hard as six more men join the two—then again as they take their places on both sides of the casket. They reach down and lift, and I stand with the crowd as the Sheriff's body is carried down the aisle and out the door.

"Thank you all for coming." Sutton's voice pulls me back, and I realize he's moved up onto the stage.

I quickly sit down, not wanting to feel like an intruder on this moment.

"If any of you need anything, please feel free to come find me. My door is always open to the pack." His gaze drifts to mine briefly then back to the crowd. "I will do all I can to make sure Arden is the last pack member stolen from us by this wretched curse. We're going to find Myrtle and Yvette and put an end to this cruelty. You have my word."

Hushed voices whisper words I can't hear, but I remain focused on Sutton. On the way he carries himself, the hope in his gaze as he looks out over his people. Then, he steps down, and chaos surrounds me.

People block my view of the stage, a sea of faces I don't recognize. "Serenity, it is so good to meet you." An elderly woman grips my hand. I don't recognize her, but she clearly knows who I am. "How did you like the jam?"

"I knew you would be good for this town." Another woman with white hair grips my other hand and beams at me like she's been the president of the Serenity Kellis fan club all along.

A man pushes in between the two women. "Arden would be

happy to know you're still here with us."

"You helped us. Thank you."

"Thank you."

"Thank you so very much."

The words are repeated by dozens of voices. Sweat beads on my brow. It covers my palms while my heart races and spots invade my vision—all classic signs of a coming panic attack. I try to breathe, to suck in enough oxygen to calm my pulse, but the people just keep coming. I can't even hear them—not with the blood pounding in my ears.

"I need to find—"

Someone blocks my attempt to escape.

Until, finally, Sutton moves toward me, gaze hard. "Let's give Serenity some breathing room," he orders. The moment the words leave his lips, everyone backs off.

Hand on my elbow, he guides me smoothly through the crowd and outside. "Breathe," he orders as he leans me back against the side of the church.

I do, taking one deep breath after another. "They were everywhere."

"They don't know how to pace themselves," he says. "This is the first time we've ever had hope."

"I'm not the hero they think I am," I say, my voice cracking. "I'm a fucking journalist who lost her job because she got hammered when her fiancé cheated on her."

Sutton's gaze darkens. "You're a lot more than that, Serenity. And you'd damn well better figure that out sooner rather than later."

"What the hell do you think I'm trying to do?" I snap, regaining a bit of my composure. "I spent all day in your library, going through the books you pilfered from my stash. They hold nothing! Not a single fucking answer."

"Keep your voice down unless you want more company," he

warns, his sharp tone more like the man I first met in the woods. The man who had more walls than Fort Knox.

Good.

If he shuts me out, it'll only make it easier to do the same to him.

"We're all going to die in this fucking town because you guys are relying on someone who knows nothing about magic or how to fight it."

His cheeks redden, his golden eyes glowing brightly. "We are not going to die here. And we certainly aren't only relying on you. Every single person here knows what's at stake because we've lived this reality for a century already. Every single year, someone has died, cementing our fate. Then you show up and things changed."

"You all got your wolves back, you mean. That could have been anything. Maybe she decided to give you that—"

"You can't believe she'd show mercy now. No, things changed —because of you, Serenity, regardless of what you choose to believe. What the hell is wrong with us having hope that you being here will change even more?" He steps back. "If you ask me, you're the dangerous one here because you refuse to see what's right in front of you."

My eyes fill with hot, angry tears, and I sniffle. "I'm the reason he's dead."

"If you want to blame yourself, then blame me too." He moves in closer, his voice dropping low. "Because I'm the one who was so desperate to taste you that I couldn't wait another moment. I'm the one who had his mouth on you in that library. So, if you're to blame, then so am I."

Lust burns in my belly at the not-so-distant memory he's awoken, and I can't help but let my gaze flicker to his lips despite the fact that we're standing outside a damned funeral surrounded by a crowd of mourners.

Because, I know that even with how scared I am of failing, of what happens if we don't fix things, I want him.

I crave him.

And that wanting might very well get us both killed.

Clearing my throat, I push past him. "Fine, then we're both selfish assholes." Leaving him behind me, I push my way through the crowd, intent on heading for home. But when I see the woman standing on the steps, my thoughts of Sutton are forgotten for the moment.

Cara's expression is dark, her gaze hollow. She meets my eyes then looks away from me to someone over my shoulder.

"What is it?" Sutton questions from behind me.

"We found her."

I don't have to ask who she means. I know.

My breath catches.

"Where?" Sutton asks, moving to my side. I risk a glance at him, not at all surprised to see the change in his demeanor. He's tense, ready to spring, to fight.

"The eastern woods," Cara replies.

Sutton moves past her, taking my hand and pulling me along with him whether I want to go or not.

"Sutton," Cara says.

He spares her a glance. "What?"

She hesitates, her eyes on me again.

"If it's about Audrey, I want to know," I say.

"She should hear it," Sutton agrees.

Cara nods. "All right. Well, it's good news and bad news, I guess."

"Cara," Sutton warns.

He's running out of patience.

Cara's expression hardens. "Audrey's dead."

Falls Gazette

Chapter Five

I wouldn't exactly call my experience with death limited—I've seen my share of dead bodies—nor do I suffer from a weak stomach. But the sight of Audrey's decaying corpse nestled among layers of equally dead leaves is enough to make my gut churn threateningly. It isn't just the sagging, mushy skin draped over her bones like some kind of wet cloth. Nor is it the transparency of her flesh giving way to a clear view of the bone underneath. It's the fact that I can see nearly every inch of that skin—even the parts of her that really should have remained private.

I swallow hard against the urge to vomit right here where I stand in the middle of the woods.

"Serenity?" Sutton's voice is soft. Tentative. Like he's not sure if he'll spook me.

"What...happened?" I manage. "Why does she look like that?"

"This is what that bitch does," Cara says with distaste. "Every year, she outs herself at the ball, and then she chooses another unsuspecting victim to hide in. Audrey's not the first, and she won't be the last. I'd hoped to catch her before she did it again, but..." She frowns.

Sutton pats her on the shoulder. "We did our best, Cara."

Her words register with alarming clarity. Audrey's death is not a victory. It's only another loss.

"So, the witch used Audrey's body as a host," I say slowly.

Sutton nods. "The woman you met... That wasn't Audrey. Not really."

I shudder at the idea of it all. The witch is nothing more than a parasite taking over a host.

"I remember you mentioning this before, but I guess seeing it for myself is a different story."

"Audrey Fenrick has been dead for a year," he explains grimly. "The body was preserved because of the magic contained inside it. But when Myrtle left this body for the next, so did her magic. The decomposition reflects the time this host has been truly gone."

God. What a way to go. And now the witch, Myrtle, is walking around inside some other person, wearing their flesh like a twisted meat puppet.

But that still doesn't explain the nudity.

"What happened to her clothes?" I ask.

"Decomposed," Cara offers quietly.

Right.

Just like the rest of her.

I can't take it anymore; I look away.

"What should we do with her?" I hear Cara ask Sutton.

He gestures to the men we brought with us from the church. Pack members. He called them his security team, though I didn't catch their names before. Phineas is among them, and his gaze is hardened like the rest of them.

Instead of disgust, there is vengeance in their eyes.

I can't blame them.

Myrtle has taken so much from them.

I'd hate her too.

"We'll bury her," Sutton says quietly. "Here. I know it's not orthodox, but I don't think it's right to move her considering her condition. Put the word out. We'll do a small graveside service for anyone who wants to attend."

"I'll coordinate it," Phineas says. He pats his son's shoulder. "You have enough on your plate."

"Thanks," Sutton tells him.

Phineas motions to a couple of the security guys, and they all set to work clearing the brush so they can dig a grave.

I shudder.

Cara's head snaps up and she scans the trees.

"What is it?" Sutton asks.

"I don't know. I feel like something's out there," Cara murmurs.

Tensing, Sutton sweeps the forest, and I do the same, darting glances left and right. My heart thuds as I try not to think about who —or what—might be watching us.

"Check the perimeter," he says.

Cara nods and slips away, leaving us alone.

"Come on," he says, turning to me. "I should get you home. It'll be dark soon."

I grab Sutton's arm but hesitate to walk away, once again caught up in the nightmare that is Audrey's remains.

"What is it?" he asks.

"If she's not in there, where is she? Who is she?"

He hesitates, and I look up at him, only to realize it isn't uncertainty that gives him pause. He studies me like he's trying to decide if I can handle the answer. "She has always hidden among us," he says finally. "Taking the face and the body of one of our own. Audrey was only the most recent. And now, she has moved on."

Moved on.

My stomach tightens as I let his meaning settle over me. Audrey—Myrtle—is more than just a witch. She's a body stealer. A demon. A ghost.

No, not a ghost.

Something much worse than that. She's hiding in plain sight. She could literally be anyone.

As if he's thinking the same, Sutton glances at the security team, his worried gaze lingering on Phineas. "She could be any one of us now." His words so closely match my thoughts that I have to swallow the terror that rises. The knowledge that she is out there, wearing the skin of someone we trust, is far too terrifying a concept to be reality—but it is.

Real. All of this is real. A living nightmare, and we're all stuck inside it.

Cara doesn't find anything in the woods, but even so, Sutton insists on taking me home. I don't argue. Not when the alternative is to watch Phineas and the others bury a body that looks way overdue for being six feet under. He's quiet on the walk. So am I. All I can think of is Audrey Fenrick, the woman who became the face of a monster. She isn't Myrtle. I don't even know what Myrtle looks like. Not back then when she cast this horrible curse and not now that she's hiding inside another's body.

Yet, it's Audrey who will haunt my nightmares because she's the only face I can put on the monster we're up against. It's unfair to the kind woman she probably was before Myrtle sunk her claws into her. But I can't stop it.

The late afternoon sun slants in through the canopy overhead. It should have been a nice day. And it is as far as the weather. Somehow, the cheery sunshine makes my mood darker in contrast. Rain would be more appropriate. Or maybe a hurricane. I never knew sunshine to be so foreboding until I came to Midnight Falls, but it seems as if the sunnier it is, the deadlier things seem to get.

I stop suddenly, a horrifying thought suddenly hitting me.

"What is it?" Sutton asks.

He looks from me to the woods around us as if my senses somehow trump his. I look at him with wide eyes. His worry is sliced raw, and I can't blame him after the day we've both had. But I have to know.

"If Myrtle has stolen another body, that means whoever she's chosen is dead now too."

He sighs, his shoulders sagging. "Yes."

He doesn't say anything else. Neither do I. What is there to say? Someone we know is dead, and we can't even mourn them.

When he takes my hand, I let him, though I can barely feel it through the numbness that has descended like a coating over my skin. Death. That's what I've witnessed since coming to this town. The familiar guilt threatens to override my apathy, seeping in through the cracks in my armor.

Tears well in my tired eyes.

By the time we reach the house, the grief has settled on my shoulders, weighing me down until the world itself seems like it's resting on my back.

Sutton holds the door to let me pass and then shuts it behind us with a slam hard enough to knock some plaster loose.

The sound jars me, and I jerk toward it—and him. "What was that for?"

"Apologies," he says, though his tone is too snide to be genuine. "I'm losing my patience with this performance of yours."

My jaw hangs open until I can find the words. "You call reacting to three deaths in one day a *performance*?"

"Three deaths," he agrees, "And none of them were your own. Yet, you're acting like you're already gone."

"I'm not *acting*," I say through clenched teeth. "Or performing. I'm feeling. Pardon me if I'm processing in two days what you've had a century to accept."

He runs a hand through his hair, his eyes a bit wild now. "Maybe you're right. Maybe you deserve more time. But, dammit, we don't have that luxury. You might be willing to ignore what you feel for me, Serenity, but I care too damn much about you to watch you go down this path."

"And what path is that?" My voice rises.

This asshole has some nerve.

"The one where you give up without a fight."

We're both yelling now. I'm not sure when my temper eclipsed my sadness, but the fire in my veins is a welcome feeling after so much grief and guilt. It brings a clarity I lacked before. He's right, I realize. I had given up, or nearly, though I refuse to admit that now that he's being an ass about it.

"I'm doing my best, Sutton. The problem is—what I'm capable of and what this town thinks I can do for them are two wildly different things."

"You're wrong," he says quietly.

He might not be yelling, but his words still get under my skin.

"How can you be so damned sure?"

"Because I've known since before I met you that you're—"

He breaks off, clearly not willing to finish, but with a beginning like that, I'm just getting warmed up.

"Before you met me? What the hell does that mean?"

"Nothing. Look, it's been a long day. Get some sleep. Take some time."

"If you tell me to relax or calm down, I swear, Sutton, the next dead body in this town will be yours."

He sighs though it almost sounds like a growl. I've irritated him. Good. He's confused and infuriated me.

"What do you mean, 'before you met me'?" I repeat.

I don't expect him to answer me. Not with the argument we've just had. So when he starts telling me the story, I forget to be mad and instead get caught up in the tale. "Six months ago, I met a woman in the forest near this house. A witch named Rina. She's a bit of a gypsy, no coven, no family." He snorts at some memory. "I very nearly killed her, thanks to my own prejudices against her kind. But she eventually earned my trust, and we became friends for a time."

Despite it having no place here, jealousy stabs through me. What kind of friends, exactly, were they?

"How did she earn your trust?"

"She performed a blood augury."

"A blood what?"

"Augury. What you would call a spell, though it's more of a divination."

"I see."

Actually, I don't. Not really. The more I hear about it, the more complicated the idea of magic seems.

"And what did this augury show you that made you trust this Rina woman so much?"

Is it wrong to hate someone without ever meeting her? Because my hormones kind of want to stake a claim I have no right to make right now. Whoever she is, she's not good enough for Sutton, that's for damn sure.

"The point of an augury is to answer a question. You can ask anything you want." He hesitates and then adds, "I asked her to give me the name of the witch powerful enough to stop Myrtle and break this curse."

My mind empties. Jealousy is replaced by anxiety. My heart

pounds. I stare at Sutton, not sure I want to hear the rest, but I can't walk away now. I have to know.

"And?" I say on a whisper, my eyes searching his. The answer is clear in his gaze before it ever passes over his lips.

"The name she gave me was yours."

Shock, disbelief; a hundred arguments, and even more excuses land on my tongue. In my throat. Squeezing my chest until my heart constricts. "It can't be."

But I already know it is. Or that he's not lying, at least. Whatever he saw, this blood augury he witnessed ended with me. That much is clear from the way he stares at me now.

"I saw it for myself," he says quietly, and while he speaks, my memory takes me back to that first day in the woods. He'd been shocked to see me on his side of the boundary line, but that surprise had been short-lived. He'd known then who I was. Or what.

"Were you the one who sent the newspaper articles to my apartment?"

Hot anger works its way into my veins. The very idea that he's been lying to me this whole time is a wrong I can't imagine making right—

"What articles?"

His confusion is convincing enough alone, but the sharp worry that follows is undeniable.

"Serenity, did someone from this town contact you before you came here?"

"Yes. And they made sure I knew just enough to want to investigate. They knew me," I add, realizing with stark clarity how true that is. They knew I was a journalist, one with nothing left to lose. Why else would I have come in the first place?

They gave me just enough information to hook me. But not enough to know how dangerous it would be to even try.

Sutton's brows furrow, and I know from the look he wears—a

look that suggests he might just kill whoever it was—that it wasn't him.

"I believe you," I say. He doesn't answer, clearly waiting for me to decide how I feel about this information. After a beat of silence, I add, "And you're really sure your friend wasn't wrong about me?"

"A witch can lie, but blood cannot," he adds. "You are the key to breaking this curse, Serenity. And the sooner you accept that, the better we'll all be for it."

Falls Gazette

Chapter Six

Sutton insists on walking me upstairs. Inside the bedroom, I turn to face him, wanting only to be alone, and brace myself for an argument. But he's already heading out again. His shoulders are a bit hunched, but he doesn't push me, not about what he just admitted.

"Where are you going?" I ask, unwilling to admit a big part of me wants him to stay. More than that. I want him to strip this dress off my body and love me so completely there's no room left for the fear and uncertainty I feel now. But a love like that scares me almost as much as learning I'm a witch.

What I feel for Sutton Hargrave is beautiful and terrifying.

"I'm going to make some dinner."

I blink, surprised to hear his answer includes something so normal as preparing a meal. But I should have known. Sutton's always been good at taking care of me.

"Sutton," I call before he can disappear down the stairs.

When he turns back, stormy emotions swirl in his dark gaze. I clasp my hands together to keep from reaching out to him. To run my hands over the lapels of his jacket. To bury them in his hair.

"Thank you for being honest," I say, my voice barely above a whisper.

He studies me, the intensity in his eyes sucking all the air out of the room. My breaths are shallow, and my heart thuds so loudly I'm sure he can hear it. The silence stretches, and I can feel my control slipping. Any longer and I'll give in to the urge to let him comfort me.

I turn away, staring blindly out the window. "I'll be down soon."

I don't look up until the sound of his footsteps has faded down the stairs.

Alone, I hurry to the door and push it closed. My fingers fumble with the dress, and suddenly, I can't get it off fast enough. The lace is a reminder of everything that's happened today. I want it gone.

I'm just pulling a sweatshirt on over leggings when my phone rings. The shrill sound of it makes me jump. Allison's name flashes on the screen. I grab it off the bed, answering quickly to silence the sound.

"Hello?" I do my best to force cheer into my voice.

"How are things in Smallville?" Allison jokes into the line.

"Peachy. What's up?"

"You okay?"

I try harder to coat my words with false cheer. "Fine." Settling onto the bed, I lean back against Sutton's headboard and tuck my knees to my chest. "How are you?"

"Great. Had a date last night, was horrible. Dude talked about cats all night."

"Cats?"

"Yes. And we're not even talking about the animals. He's obsessed with the musical."

I snort out a genuine half-laugh, a sound that is alien to me in my current state. "Hey, I like it too. My grandmother and I used to watch it once a year."

"Okay, but did you have special bed sheets made with the faces of your favorite felines?"

"No, he didn't."

"Yes, yes he did."

I let myself be distracted by the easy conversation, a nice break from the dark reality that has descended on me like a truckload of bricks. "Wait, how do you know what kind of sheets he has?"

Allison groans. "Don't slut shame, Ser. It's been forever, and he was really, *really* hot, especially when he stopped talking."

I shake my head, in no way judging. Hell, I wish I could have a quick roll in the sheets. Might help me get my head right. The image of Sutton above me, of his hands on my body, assaults my mind and I shove it away. "No judgment here, trust me." Only jealousy. "Was the sex at least good?"

"Guy is bendy, I'll tell you that much. I might be seeing him again later."

"You get that kitty some catnip," I joke.

Allison falls silent, her lack of words telling me there's more to the reason she called than to discuss hot sex with cat-man.

"Out with it, already."

She sighs into the line. "Quincy hired someone for your position today."

Her words are yet another blow. And it's just not today either. One after the other, they've been coming since the day Roscoe dumped me in the middle of that stupid restaurant. My hand tightens on the phone. How many more hits am I supposed to take before I just stay the hell down?

And then it hits me. I've *been* down. Whether I realized it or not, I got knocked over the night of that ball, and I've been staying on the ground ever since. But that shit ends now. Myrtle may not be who called me here in the first place, but she's the one who has trapped me. Because of her, I can't go back and see my family. Can't return to the *Times* and demand my job back. Can't take that Mexico vacation with my best friend that I promised her I would.

Myrtle stole my life. And it's well past time I took it back.

"Serenity?"

"That really sucks," I reply.

"It does. But you'll get it back. You're still working on that story, right?"

"I am."

Am I? Is Midnight Falls a story I'll write? Something about the idea feels too much like crossing a boundary.

"It has to stay a secret though," I add. "Steven is insisting I come home, and I can't. Not yet."

"Always the stubborn-ass," she replies, and I can hear the smile in her tone.

"Always and forever," I retort. "Thanks for letting me know about the job. I'll find a way to get it back when I'm done here."

Even as I say the words, I'm not sure I believe them anymore. Or that I care. It unsettles me. Working for the Times was my dream. If that dream is gone, what do I have left?

"That's my girl," Allison says proudly.

"Now, go have crazy sex with cat-man," I tell her, and she laughs.

"Cat man? Really? That sounds like a superhero name. Though, given what he did to me last night, it's fitting—"

"Save the details for brunch when I get home. Love your face, bitch."

"You too."

With renewed purpose, I end the call and toss the phone to the bed beside me. I've never been one to give up or wallow in self-pity. And without realizing it, that's exactly what I've been doing since Roscoe dumped me.

Wallowing. Which is absolutely pathetic. I got hammered, let my responsibilities slip, blamed Quincy for giving my story away, and then ran away. I was chasing a story, yes, but running nonetheless. But no damn more. From this moment on, I'm going to stop running. Instead, I'm going to turn around and face my problems head-on. Starting with what I feel for Sutton Hargrave.

AN HOUR LATER, HAIR STILL WET FROM MY GET-YOUR-SHIT-together shower, I open the bedroom door and step into the hall. The moment I do, I'm hit with an absolutely mouthwatering aroma. Following it, I descend the stairs and head into the kitchen.

At the bottom of the steps, I round the corner—and halt.

My heart hammers as I take in the scene before me. Sutton has covered the table in a black cloth and placed two candlesticks on top. A flame flickers atop each one. It's romantic as hell, and when Sutton turns to me, I know I'm a goner. He's wearing a fucking apron, and for some reason, I'm instantly turned on. Who knew I liked my men domestic? Or maybe it's the fact that the wildness in him is only ever tamed for me. Either way, Sutton Hargrave in a white apron is pure sex.

"Figured you might be hungry." Using a spatula, he lifts a steak from the skillet and sets it on a plate. Then, he scoops some potatoes out of a large pot and puts them beside it.

My stomach growls, and Sutton grins. Apparently, the way to my heart is through food—and Sutton's already figured it out.

"What are we having?" I ask, working hard to keep my voice neutral.

"Garlic butter steaks and mashed potatoes."

Fuck it, that's it. I'm going to marry this former murder suspect. "That sounds amazing."

"Glad to hear it. Mable brought the groceries, and, well, it's been a while since I've been able to cook a steak. Usually, my meat consists of—" He stops and grimaces. "We don't need to get into that."

He sets my plate down and pulls out the chair.

Grateful he left out something that might have ruined my appetite, I move toward him and take a seat at the table. He helps me scoot my chair back in then heads back into the kitchen to retrieve his own dinner.

I study him as he comes back carrying his plate and a bottle of red wine. He takes a seat to my left, not across from me, and pours the crimson liquid into my glass.

"Were you able to rest?" he asks.

I eye him, knowing full well his werewolf hearing picked up on my conversation with Allison. But he gives nothing away, clearly intent on preserving my sense of privacy.

"A bit," I reply, watching him curiously. *What the hell caused this shift?* Less than an hour ago, he was pissed at me. Hell, I was pissed at him too.

When he's filled his own glass, I take a sip of the wine, savoring the heavy flavor as it dances on my tongue. "Actually, my friend Allison called me. Apparently, she had epic sex with a cat-man last night."

Sutton chokes on his wine, and I grin.

"I'm sorry, she what?" he asks.

"He is obsessed with the musical Cats." When Sutton continues to stare at me, I shake my head. "He's not an actual cat-man," I tell him. "Just wishes he was."

"That is … interesting."

"It is. The whole no-strings thing is something I miss." The words are out before I realize their implication.

Sutton doesn't miss it though. He stares at me, his hazel gaze locking on mine. "Oh?"

My cheeks heat, and I'm forced to backpedal. "Not that I've had a lot of no-strings relationships. Honestly, that's how things started with Roscoe. I guess I shouldn't have been surprised when he fucked his paralegal behind my back."

Sutton's mood shifts, the energy in the room shifting with him as he sets his wine glass down.

"I'm sorry. I shouldn't be rambling. Especially not when you made us such a great dinner." I lift my fork and knife and slice off a piece of steak. Slipping it into my mouth, I nearly groan as the explosion of flavor overtakes my senses. "Oh my gosh, this is delicious," I manage as soon as I've swallowed. I take another bite and then a third before I realize Sutton isn't eating. He's watching me. "Eat, Sutton. Please. You're missing out."

"I disagree. Watching you is not missing out on anything."

Heat rushes between my legs. Because I know what kind of pleasure he is capable of granting me, it's easy to imagine him throwing this entire table aside and doing it all over again right here. Right now. The idea of letting him have me for dessert hangs between us.

But he doesn't move toward me, and I can't decide if I'm relieved or disappointed.

"Please eat," I say with a half-hearted smile. "It's been a long time since you've had steak, remember? And you were so excited."

"It's been a long time since I've had a lot of things," he replies, "as you so generously pointed out just the other night." He retrieves his fork and knife and begins to cut himself a bite. With controlled movements, he spears the steak and puts it into his mouth.

Now, it's my turn to watch him, and I can't even be bothered to care that the way the man eats turns me on. The way he breathes. Takes a drink. Honestly, Sutton Hargrave breathing is a thing of beauty. And with that realization, I lift my glass and down my wine.

The buzz doesn't even touch my lust. Honestly, it makes it worse because the alcohol blurs the line drawn between us, making it damn near impossible to remember why it is such a bad idea.

Sutton sets his silverware down and grips the table. "Serenity." My name is a plea, though for what, I cannot be sure.

"What?"

"I can sense it," he says, tone strained as if he's barely leashing the animal inside.

Is it bad I want to let it free? We're trapped here. Why can't we have something casual? Something like Allison has? A bit of life when we're surrounded by so much death?

"Sense what?" I ask, my voice hoarse. I may already know the answer, and taunting him may be wrong, but I can't help it. I want to hear it.

He turns to me, his gaze brighter now, almost shimmering with gold. "The way I make you feel."

I swallow hard and clench my thighs together, trying like hell to ease the throbbing between them. "We—"

"We what?" he asks, slowly getting to his feet.

Uh-oh.

"We shouldn't..." I trail off as he drops to his knees and scoots my chair back. "I don't know if this is a good idea," I manage as he slips between my legs and braces his hands on either side of my chair.

Sutton leans in. "Then why do you smell like you want me to bury myself in you? Like you want my hands on your body? My mouth on your skin?"

Fuckballs. "Because I can't think straight when I'm around you."

"Why is that, I wonder?"

Umm, because you're fucking sexy? Because you brought me more pleasure in five minutes than Roscoe did in all the years we were together? Because my hormones want me to mount you right here, right now? "I can't think of anything," I lie.

Sutton grins because the truth is my body has already betrayed me. Since I didn't have any underwear, my leggings are soaked completely through, and given his ability to sense things—I know he knows it too.

"What would you do if I touched you right now?" he asks.

Come apart. "I don't know."

"No?" As if to test a theory, he reaches out and runs a finger along my jaw. I shiver, his finger lighting a fire along my skin. "You want me, Serenity, the same way I want you. Why are you holding back? It has to be more than wanting to focus."

"Why?"

"Because we have nothing to focus on now. So, tell me, what is it?"

I meet his gaze, and my honesty makes my voice raw. "I don't know."

That does it. Sutton snaps. In the span of a heartbeat, his hand snakes around my neck and he slams his mouth to mine. My hands go to his hair then his shoulders and I grip him, throwing myself out of the chair and onto his body. We tumble to the floor, landing with me on top of him as his tongue slips into my mouth.

His kiss is a claiming, and I've never wanted anything more.

Straddling him, my hands go to his waist, gripping his shirt and ripping it up so I can feel his warm flesh against my fingertips. I grind down against his hard length, moaning as it presses against me. He rolls us over and thrusts against me.

The clothes between us have never felt more like a prison.

Sutton is savage as he fucks my mouth with his tongue. Taking.

Tasting. And I'm just as damned wild. Because right now, in this moment, I want him inside of me more than I want to draw my next breath.

He reaches down and tears my shirt open then drops his mouth to my exposed breast. I arch up into him, crying out as he gently sucks and nips, his nimble fingers expertly toying with my other breast. I let my hands trail down to the fly of his jeans, and I undo the button, slip my hand inside, and grip the hard length of him.

He growls, the sound vibrating against my skin, and I squeeze gently before stroking him. He pumps into my hand, one thrust, two, before taking my mouth again with a hungry growl.

I was wrong before. Being with Sutton isn't something I need to deny myself. Not if I can do it on my terms. Nothing this good can be that bad. Right?

Something shifts inside of me, an energy I don't recognize, and before I can pull away, a flash of blue fills the room, and Sutton is thrown from my body. Chest rising and falling in heavy succession, he stares at me from where he's landed against the wall, eyes wild and knowing.

I don't speak.

Don't move.

"My magical gift is apparently a cock-block." My bleak attempt at a joke is not met with a smile from Sutton, though he does crawl back over to me so we're sitting a few feet from each other. "If that was magic," I add.

"It was," he replies.

"Why? Why does that happen whenever we... And why didn't it happen the night of the party?"

He shakes his head. "I don't know. But it had better kill me the next time it interrupts us."

I take a deep breath, trying to get control of myself now that the damned blue spark has thrown yet another cold bucket of water on the two of us.

Though, this time, it cemented my resolve. Solidified my purpose.

I am going to stop Myrtle.

Fix this town.

Free myself.

Get my job back.

And I'm *going* to get the chance to experience what Sutton and I can be together.

Because what I feel for him is far too potent to not try.

Falls Gazette

Chapter Seven

The following day, I agree to attend a pack meeting. Sutton does a terrible job at hiding his pleasure when I say yes. Even Phineas is exuberant. You'd think I already broke the curse, considering their light moods as we walk to town. More than once, I catch Sutton's gaze on me, and I can't help but wonder if he's still thinking about last night. Just the memory of how he felt against me heats my skin. I'm not sure whether to be ashamed of the fact that my determination to master my magic stems just as much from wanting Sutton as it does from wanting to stop Myrtle.

It's why I've agreed to come today.

So I can *come* tomorrow, so to speak. Even as I think it, the image of me looking down at Sutton comes to mind, only overpowered by the memory of him rolling us over and grinding into me like—

"Serenity?"

"Huh?" I glance at both Phineas and Sutton, who are watching me, concern reflected in their gazes. "Did you hear me?" Phineas asks.

Shit. "Sorry, I was distracted."

"You feeling all right?" Phineas asks.

Sutton's knowing grin makes me blush. Thankfully, though, he lets it go.

I force a smile, grateful Phineas doesn't seem to be picking up on the fact that I am in a constant state of 'turned the fuck on' whenever I'm near Sutton. "Fine. Just tired." *And imagining having sex with your son,* I add silently because doing so out loud would be awkward.

Besides, add that to my lack of sleep last night, and I figure I've got a pretty damn good reason for being distracted. After getting my shit together and resolving to not wallow in self-pity anymore, I laid awake half the night, trying to come up with some plan that doesn't involve me facing off with a witch whose ability and knowledge of magic surpasses mine by at least a century. But nothing else comes to mind. Not while I have no idea whose body she's hiding in, anyway.

She could literally be anyone at this point. Which makes priority number one to learn more about this magic I somehow unknowingly possess and figure out what it makes me capable of.

At some point, I'd even given up on sleeping and crept down to the library where I scoured the pages of books I'd already read. Anything with local legends or any mention of witches. Sutton found me there early this morning. He'd walked in carrying a croissant and coffee, wearing nothing but a pair of low-slung sweatpants.

It's a good thing Phineas walked in behind him. Otherwise, I might have tried for round two right there on the desk, magic sparks be damned.

That blue spark is giving me lady blue balls, and I don't appreciate it.

"We were just brainstorming ideas about where Yvette might be hiding," Phineas says.

"Are we sure she's not hiding in another body too?" I ask.

The moment the words are out, I regret them. Speculating on something like that only adds to our problems. Sutton and Hargrave exchange a glance.

"In a hundred years, Myrtle's been the only one to steal a host," Sutton says.

"Things are changing," Phineas says, clearly not as convinced as Sutton.

"True," he agrees reluctantly.

"I don't think Yvette is quite as powerful as her sister," I say, thinking back to the tree she uprooted the last time we were at the bed and breakfast together. If she were as powerful as Myrtle, she wouldn't have missed me.

"What does the pack say?" Phineas asks.

"A lot of them are angry with themselves," Sutton admits.

"For what?" I ask, surprised.

"For never figuring out Myrtle and Yvette are sisters," Sutton explains.

"That isn't their fault," I say. "Besides, what matters now is finding them."

"If she can't steal a host body, Yvette will be easier to find," Phineas says. He glances from me to Sutton. "She can't have gone far from her place of business, don't you think?"

"I'm not sure I'm the best person to ask," I say with a shrug. "You two know this town better than I do."

"Yes, but you lived under the same roof with her," Phineas points out just as we pass very nearby the Bed and Breakfast in question, and I shudder.

"Don't remind me," I say, refusing to look up at the imposing Victorian house I once thought was cute and cozy. Since the night of the ball, it's been under constant surveillance from the pack.

Yvette hasn't shown her face once, but anytime someone tries to enter, some sort of invisible barrier blocks their attempt.

The place is magically locked up tight. Either she's holed up inside or she hopes to return; no one knows which.

"We'll think of something," Sutton says, and I can see he doesn't like the idea of me being involved in any way where Yvette is concerned.

The feeling is mutual.

"What we should be discussing is how we're going to narrow down our list of suspects," I say. "If Myrtle could be anyone, that gives us an entire town's worth of people to investigate." I look at Phineas apologetically.

"I know, that includes me," he says.

"Dad, come on," Sutton says.

"He's right," I say. "Until we know for sure, everyone's a suspect. Myrtle's chosen men just as often as women over the years."

Sutton scowls. He doesn't argue, but I can tell he wants to. The truth is I've already been alone with Phineas twice since the night of the ball, which has already given him more than enough chances to make a move. But I have to look at this like a true investigator would. Without emotion or bias. Because there's no room for either when it's a matter of life or death.

"Fine," Sutton says begrudgingly. "We'll bring it up at the meeting."

"Talk to Mable. She's always been the one to head that up for us." Phineas gestures at the building just ahead, and I realize we've arrived.

The church is already crowded, and being back here so soon after the funeral turns my stomach. I can still visualize the casket up at the front, hear the muted sobs of the people in the pews. I doubt it's a memory I'll ever forget.

We pause in the vestibule while Sutton greets people. Through the open doors, I see pack members I recognize from the funeral, as well as some I don't, gathered inside the cramped sanctuary. The pews are packed full of bodies with the overflow crowding in against the walls on both sides.

I take a deep, steadying breath to calm my nerves and remind myself of my decision. No wallowing. No hiding. *Serenity Kellis doesn't run.*

Phineas goes in first, but before I can follow, Sutton grabs my wrist.

"What's wrong?" I ask quietly.

"Just... Stay close," he says.

"If there's a threat, just tell me—"

"She could be any of them," he says, and I stiffen, realizing he's right.

There's a very good chance one of the people inside these walls is Myrtle, and I'm not about to make myself an easy target. Not again.

"You too," I say and then head inside, heart in my throat.

I make it as far as the sanctuary doors before people begin to recognize me. They press in closer, shaking my hand, hugging me, patting my arms. Every one of them carries a familiar glint in their eye: hope. It's unnerving. And way too much even for my newfound determination.

I hesitate, unsure about continuing if it means enduring this kind of attention. But then Sutton is at my back, his warmth pushing me onward. At a single word from him, the crowd moves aside for us.

I make my way down the center aisle, eyes on Phineas, who waits at the front. In the front row, Mable gestures for me to sit beside her. I sink down, grateful for friendly faces.

Sutton watches to be sure I'm settled and then makes his way to the front. Rather than demand silence, he simply stands at the podium and waits for them to give it.

"Thanks for coming," he says when the room quiets. "I know many of you have already heard, but we found remains yesterday that belong to the late Audrey Fenrick."

The room fills with hushed conversations. When I turn to glance at the rows behind me, their uncertain gazes are sweeping the room. They're just as uneasy as I am about the implication.

Sutton holds up a hand. "I know we all understand what this means."

"If she isn't Audrey, she's one of us," someone says. He stands, and I recognize George, the grumpy cashier at the drug store where I bought my phone charger. He still looks just as salty as he did the day I met him, except now, I can't really fault him for it.

"You have every right to be concerned," Sutton says. "But this is something we go through every year—"

"That's where you're wrong," George snaps. "*We* go through this shit every year. Find a body. Clean it up. Wait for the next one. Meanwhile, you just sit up in your mansion and bide your time until the next party. And now you're here, trying to order us around like we haven't been already doin' this shit for a century."

I tense, waiting for Sutton's inevitable reaction. But he simply nods. "You're right, George. Thanks to the curse, I've been unable to help you all until now."

George scowls, and I wonder if he's disappointed he didn't get the reaction he wanted from his alpha. Honestly, it's for the best. I've no doubt Sutton could rip him apart before George could so much as howl.

Sutton's calm, quiet gaze sweeps the crowd. "The curse punished us all because Myrtle wanted to punish me. We've all paid the price, and maybe I've been away too long. In my absence, you've been forced to lead yourselves. To pick up the pieces of Myrtle's horrific actions every year."

"Yeah, and maybe that shouldn't change." George's tone is icy now. It pisses me off. I start to stand, but a voice in the crowd stops me.

"Bull shit." From across the aisle, Cara stands, glaring at George before turning back to Sutton. "Don't let George get in your head. He's grouchy from not getting laid last year because he was too afraid Myrtle was using the body of Fred Gordon's wife, which meant he couldn't use it for himself if you know what I mean."

A few gasps sounded.

"Uh-oh," Mable mutters under her breath.

"Now, you just wait a damn minute," George begins. "First of all, my personal life ain't none of your business."

Another man stands up, eyes narrowed at George. "Are you saying it's true?" he demands.

"That's Fred Gordon," Mable whispers. "And his wife Sylvia."

Obviously. My gaze shifts to the flushed brunette woman with her hands folded tightly in her lap. She doesn't look up, doesn't make eye contact with anyone.

George doesn't answer, which only seems to make Fred angrier.

Fred's hands ball into fists. "You were sleeping with my wife?" The woman beside him on the bench literally sinks a few inches in her seat, still refusing to meet anyone's eye.

"Well, not in the last year anyway," Cara says wryly, and I have to press my lips together to keep from laughing at her candor.

Beside me, Mable seems like she's trying to keep it together too. She takes my hand and squeezes, and I wonder if she's comparing this scandal to an episode of Bridgerton in her head.

"Look, all I'm saying is ever since that woman came to town, nothing's been safe." George looks at me, and my smile vanishes.

"After she got here, Myrtle stepped up her game, and now, supposedly Yvette is a damned witch too."

"*Supposedly*?" Cara echoes. "Are you saying you don't believe it?"

"I'm saying the only people whose word we have to go on is that outsider over there." George points a stabbing finger in my direction, and the entire room fixes me with their stares. "And the man she's fucking. Our supposed alpha."

I search for the right words, but it turns out I don't need to have any. In the silence that follows, a roar fills the room, so loud it shakes the rafters. The floor booms with the weight of Sutton's body as he leaps from the stage and strides down the aisle.

George doesn't have time to move before Sutton grabs him by the shirt and hauls him into the air, growling into the man's face. "Watch your mouth, asshole," Sutton snarls at him. "You want to challenge me for alpha, you go ahead. We'll take this outside and settle it here and now. Otherwise, you bite your tongue, and do not speak her name again unless it is with respect."

Sutton lets go of George and turns slowly, eyeing the crowded room. "I know you've all been left alone, cut off from the rest of the world, but I've been more alone than anyone in this town has a right to claim. And still, I come, and I fight for you. With you. I am your alpha, and if you want to change that, you will challenge me and take it." He looks over at George, who's climbing unsteadily to his feet from where Sutton unceremoniously dropped him on his ass. "Until then, we keep fighting the real enemy instead of each other."

George doesn't argue.

"Well, now that we've gotten that out of the way," Cara says dryly, "Can we talk about the actual bitch we're here to kill instead of acting like one ourselves?"

I bite my lip to keep from cracking up. The look on her face means business, and no one questions her. I can't blame them.

Sutton returns to the front where Cara waits impatiently.

"Well, alpha?" she says pointedly. "What are we doing to hunt these two psycho sisters down?"

Others murmur what sounds like their agreement to her question. I look at them then her and realize it's Cara who's been holding all this together while Sutton's been away. At some point in all this, she took the reins. And now she's just handed them right back over to him.

My respect for her grows immensely. It takes great strength to step up when the world is falling apart. And even greater strength to know when to return the power granted during chaos.

Sutton returns to the podium.

His eyes linger on mine a moment before he clears his throat and answers her question. "Now that we're able to shift again, we have senses and strengths we didn't have before. That means we have an advantage we didn't have before too. We've upped the patrols and are doing everything we can to scour every inch of this town for any sign of either one of them."

"How does that help if we don't know who she is?" someone calls. One of the guys from Sutton's security team yesterday. He's not arguing like George, but he looks worried. "She could literally be any one of us."

"You're right, Vaughn," Sutton says grimly. "But we have to be smart. That means not going anywhere alone. Groups of three are best, actually. More when you can."

Murmurs of agreement go around. They already have a pack mentality, I realize. For some reason, it makes the gifts they've sent me seem less crazy. More flattering. Neighbors who are also a wolf pack; you don't get more tightly-knit than that, and here they are, welcoming me in knowing I'm just as much a suspect as they are. I turn my head just enough to spot George glowering in the crowd. Well, *most* of them are welcoming.

"It's only a start, but we can't forget how far we've come already," Sutton goes on, gaining steam as his pep talk seems to gain traction. His confidence and determination are contagious. I can see it in the way they watch him, nodding at his words. "Getting our wolves back. Bringing down the wall between town and the manor house." His eyes flick to me, but he doesn't say my name, and I'm grateful for it. He looks back at the crowd. "We have Myrtle and Yvette on the run, and we have each other. Wherever Myrtle is, whoever she is, she knows we aren't going to wait another year to hunt her down. This ends now. And she knows it."

When he finishes, the crowd cheers.

Their energy pumps adrenaline through me until I can barely catch my breath just sitting here in the front pew. For a wild moment, I believe him. Just like they do. That we'll find her in time. That we'll uncover a way to beat her at this macabre game she's forced us to play. That we'll be free.

And it's exhilarating. Sutton himself is inspiring. I can see why they follow him.

When the room quiets again, Sutton talks about logistics and reminders about not being alone if possible. He calls Mable to the podium, and she rattles off something about initiating "suspect protocol," which, from what I can tell, is a process involving everyone registering at the library for some sort of interrogation process they've developed from past years of narrowing down suspect lists. I'm impressed, though I'm not sure whether I should be since it hasn't seemed to work before.

Still, at least, they're trying.

After that, Sutton calls for more volunteers for patrols as well as anyone interested in taking the Sheriff's position to please contact him, and the meeting begins to break up. Most people leave, and I find myself sitting alone on the bench while Sutton and Mable coordinate all of their plans.

"Hey." Cara sits down beside me. "How are you holding up?"

"I'm not sure," I admit.

She smirks. "Honesty, I like it."

"In that case, full honesty? Life is really fucking weird lately."

She snorts and spreads her arms wide. "Welcome to Midnight Falls."

I can't help but laugh at that. So accurate.

"Hey, listen," I say, the humor fading way too fast as reality sets in again. "Thanks for everything you said earlier. Standing up for Sutton—"

"No thanks necessary. He's a great alpha. Being trapped away from us hasn't changed that. I know he would have been here if he could have."

"Well, I appreciate it. And everything you're doing out there with the patrols and searches. You finding Audrey..."

"It's no big deal," she says. When she sees my face, she shakes her head, rueful. "Okay, it was a big deal. Disgusting, actually. But it's also nice to just be doing wolf things again. Shifting, running, tracking—I've missed it so damn much."

"I can't imagine," I say quietly.

She studies me. "Listen, I know everyone's pressuring you about all this." She glances around the room, now nearly empty, thankfully, and I look away. "But don't let them get in your head."

"Too late," I mutter, and when I look up, empathy is written all over her face.

"Oh, girlfriend, you're a mess, aren't you?" I don't have a chance to answer—not that she can't see it clearly written on my face—before she adds, "That's it. Girls' night out. You and me. Tonight."

"Wait, seriously?"

"Do I look like I joke about stuff like ladies' nights?"

"No, but... There's so much going on."

"If there's one thing I've learned about living in this damned cursed town, it's that our problems will still be there tomorrow."

I sigh. She's not wrong.

Sutton catches my eye, and even though Mable's still talking, he nods at me. I realize with a start that he can actually hear our conversation way over here. And he's telling me to say yes.

Maybe Cara's right.

And after what she did earlier, siding with Sutton as alpha, she's officially been crossed off my suspect list. No way would Myrtle argue for Sutton keeping his power. Besides, a night away from it all sounds too good to pass up.

"Okay," I say, smiling. "I'm in."

"Hell yeah, you are," she says. "And no talk of witches or wolves at all, deal?"

I smile gratefully. "Deal."

Falls Gazette

Chapter Eight

"You're going out like that?" Sutton all but chokes out when I make it downstairs. As uncomfortable as I was with the dress Cara dropped off for me earlier—which is short enough to qualify as a shirt, honestly—the look on Sutton's face makes every missing inch of fabric worth it.

A shimmering blue, it barely covers my ass, and to top it off, I've actually taken the time to style my hair and put some makeup on my face. I feel like a new woman. "I am. Is that a problem?" Turning, I bend over and slip into my shoes.

Sutton growls, the predatory sound shooting straight through me. Suddenly, the evening I was looking forward to doesn't seem so great because I know, without a doubt, Sutton and I would have far more fun staying in.

"You're going to kill me," he snarls.

I turn around. Eyes so bright they're practically glowing, he stands less than three feet from me now, both hands clenched into fists. "Considering you're immortal, I can't say I'm all that concerned," I reply.

He actually looks pained as he does his best to collect himself and say, "You look stunning."

"That's more of what I was looking for."

He takes a step toward me, and the doorbell rings. "I'm going to kill whoever is on the other side of that door."

"I'd really rather you didn't," Cara calls from outside.

Chuckling, I pull it open to see she's not wearing much more than I am. In fact, she's wearing less. A crop top bares her midsection while a skirt the length of mine sits low on her hips. She's styled her pixie-cut hair into short spikes, massively embracing the whole Tinkerbell look. "You look awesome."

"So do you." She winks then turns to Sutton. "I'll have her back by one."

He doesn't respond, gaze still on me.

"He's going to stand there all night if we don't leave," I joke.

"Then let's get going." Cara turns and heads down the porch steps, so I move toward the door. Before I can get there, though, Sutton snakes an arm around my waist and yanks me back against his body. The feel of him pressed against me—

"Waiting for you to get home is going to be torture." His breath fans over my neck as he speaks.

Home. His word slams into me with much more strength than I'm sure he intended. I hadn't even realized it, but Sutton's house *does* feel like home to me. Shit—we are living together. When the hell did that happen? I swallow hard. "I'll be back soon enough. Besides, you could probably use a break from me."

I pull away and turn to face him.

"Never."

I suck in a breath at the intensity of his stare and force myself to turn away and join Cara outside before I do something stupid and rip his clothes off. Then again, maybe that's not so stupid…

"You ready?" Cara asks, pulling me back to reality.

"I am."

"Great."

Minutes tick by in silence as we make our way to town, wearing shoes that should never be worn in the woods. But without a driveway, Sutton's house is not accessible any other way.

"You okay?" Cara questions as the town lights come into view ahead.

"I'm good."

"Thinking about Sutton?"

My stomach burns with need at just the mention of his name.

Cara laughs. "You can't hide it, and why should you? Guy's a snack. There's no way around that."

When I turn to her, she throws her hands up in defense. "Relax. I'm not interested. Rest assured I have no interest in hooking up with the alpha, nor him with me."

I hate it, but her calling out my jealousy actually eases it a bit. Sutton *isn't* a snack—he's an entire fucking buffet of bottled-up passion and the promise of an orgasm unlike any other. And if it weren't for the blue-balls-inducing sparks shooting from my fingertips every time things get hot, I would have absolutely already slept with him.

More than once.

"Things are complicated," I say honestly. While I won't full-on admit to this cock-blocking magic I possess, it's the truth. Things go far beyond that with him and me.

We're knee-deep in a murder mystery that might very well end with one or both of us dead.

"Complicated things are almost always the most rewarding," Cara replies as we cross the boundary line into town. It no longer bars entry, nor does it even ripple at our presence—another sign the magic separating Sutton from the others is completely destroyed. I should be happy about that, but instead, I'm left wondering how in the hell it happened in the first place.

"True. But I just got out of a relationship that was headed for the altar, so jumping into another one is probably not a great idea." The excuse is smooth, realistic, and just that—an excuse. Truth is I haven't thought of Roscoe much since I arrived here.

And our breakup feels like it took place in another timeline entirely.

"Oh? I didn't know that."

"Yeah. He was a lawyer who dipped his wick in his paralegal."

"Eww."

"Pretty much."

"I hope you nut-punched him," she says as we step up to a brick building with the words *The Old Fashioned* illuminated in bright yellow.

"The Old Fashioned?"

She grins at me. "Best and only bar in town."

I glance down at our clothes. "We're dressed for a nightclub."

"So? How often does a girl get to dress up these days?"

She doesn't bother waiting for a response before she pulls open the door and ushers me inside. A man with a guitar sits in the corner on a stool, singing an acoustical remix of Coldplay's hit *Yellow.* Patrons sit at the tables, some turned toward him, others wrapped up in their own conversation.

A long bar spans nearly the length of the place, and behind it, a man wearing a white apron serves drinks to the people crowding around.

"This is the most packed I've seen it in a while," Cara observes.

"People need to forget. Alcohol helps with that," I reply.

It doesn't take me long to spot an unfriendly face in the corner, though. George sits in a booth on the far side of the room, already glaring at me. Across from him, I can barely make out two more heads over the top of the high booth seat. They turn to look at me. Then all three men turn back to one another, falling into hushed conversation at their own table.

Fun. A little anti-Serenity and Sutton powwow.

"Mable," Cara exclaims as she crosses the room and slides onto a barstool next to the librarian. I do the same, just on her opposite side.

Mable smiles brightly at me. "You look lovely."

"Thanks. What are you drinking?"

She blushes. "An old fashioned."

"Is it any good?" I ask. "I've never been much of a bourbon drinker."

"Trust me, Ernie will change your mind," she says, not meeting my eyes. "He certainly changed mine."

With a grin, I look up at the bartender and raise my hand. A broad-shouldered man with graying hair and a fully gray mustache rushes over quickly, and Mable's cheeks turn crimson. *Interesting.* "What can I get you?" he asks.

"I'll have one of these," I say, gesturing to Mable's drink.

"Make that two," Cara corrects cheerfully.

He taps a hand on the bar and nods. "You got it, ladies. Mable, you want another?"

"Yes, please, Ernie, thanks."

He beams at her, and my heart warms. "You got it, beautiful."

Mable's crush is obvious and pretty much the most adorable thing I've ever seen. But since the wolves have incredible hearing, I keep my comments to myself. I don't want to embarrass her.

"So, what are you two doing out and about tonight?" Mable questions.

"I figured Serenity needed a girls' night out. Something to blow off some steam."

"I couldn't agree more. Thank you," she adds as Ernie sets three glasses down in front of us.

"Anytime, if you need anything else, let me know." Then, he winks and leaves.

"Oh shit, here comes Jolene," Cara shivers. "Not the friendliest, but I swear she puts crack in her coffee."

I stiffen. While she's been sending coffee out to the house for me, I haven't seen her one-on-one since before the ball, so when she actually approaches the area where I'm sitting, nerves unfurl in my belly.

"Serenity," she greets, sliding onto a stool one over from mine.

"Jolene. Thanks for the coffee you sent over. I appreciate it."

She purses her lips, and the vibe coming off her is as chilly as it's always been. "You're welcome. I didn't expect to see you out."

"Just trying to take a break from it all," I say with forced friendliness.

She glances past me, giving Cara a once-over. Then, she turns her attention to the bar. "Ernie, can I get a whiskey sour? And three shots of Jameson for my friends here."

"You got it." He grabs a glass and begins pouring.

"Shots?" I question, and Jolene side-eyes me.

"Consider it a welcome gift."

I would. Except she doesn't seem very welcoming.

"Thanks," I tell her, "But you don't have to do that—"

"You're right," she says and slaps some bills onto the counter in exchange for the drinks Ernie has set out. Grabbing her whiskey sour, she turns to me as she leaves and adds, "That's what makes it a gift."

I look at Cara, who shrugs.

"Thanks," I say as she walks away.

Ernie picks up the shots. Then, he hands one to Cara, one to me, and one to Mable, who tries to protest.

"Oh yes," Cara says. "Mable, you're doing one, too."

"I don't—"

"You can't argue because you are now officially a part of our girls' night," I tell her.

"Oh, all right." She picks up her shot.

"Here's to being the hottest bitches in the room." Cara winks and turns her glass up. Mable and I share a look before we do the same.

The whiskey burns the back of my throat, but I'm already wanting another. Maybe Cara's on to something with ladies' night. It's been way too long since I let myself chill out and unwind. Mable throws hers back with an expertise I honestly hadn't expected from the quiet librarian.

"Whoo!" Cara shakes her head a little and sets her glass aside. "Okay, Serenity, I now know you have an ex and you were a reporter. What else is there to know about you?" When I raise an eyebrow, she shrugs. "The journalist in me."

Chuckling, I take a drink of my old fashioned. Mable was right. It's good. "There's really not much else to tell. I have parents, who I'm close to, and four older brothers."

"Wow," Cara says. "That's a lot of testosterone in your house."

I snort. "You have no idea. My oldest brother, Steven, is a homicide detective in New York. I suppose he pushed me to be as curious as I am, though he'd kick my ass sideways if he knew what I was getting into while I'm here." Smiling, I try to ignore the pain in my chest. I miss my family far more than I was prepared to. Mainly because I hadn't planned on being gone this long.

"And the ex?" Cara prompts. "Or if that's too personal, how about the job at the Times?"

"Ugh. Roscoe's not really worth mentioning, though it is connected to my job—or lack thereof."

"Oh, no, what happened?" Mable asks, concern knitting her brow.

"The short version is that I got dumped in public, then proceeded to get hammered, and forgot to turn in a story featuring food truck murder."

"Food truck murder?" Cara's eyes widen. "Seriously?"

"Oh yeah. Burger lady was murdered by the gumbo guy because both of them were sleeping with the taco truck dude."

Cara snorts and tips her glass up. "That's—wow. And I thought we had drama."

Mable just continues to stare at me wide-eyed.

I snort. Back then it seemed like such a big deal, but now? When compared with a murdering witch who has managed to trap an entire town? It might as well be little more than a blip. "Anyway, I was kind of a mess, trying to figure out my next move when I came home and found newspaper clippings waiting for me in an envelope."

"Newspaper clippings?" Cara questions.

I down the rest of my drink, the alcohol numbing my senses just enough to have me relaxing. Damn, I haven't felt this good since I got here. "Not sure who sent them, but they were local edition articles documenting the unsolved murders. My plan was to come here, solve them, write a story that would knock my boss's socks off, and get my job back."

Both women are silent for a moment. "And instead, you got trapped in a town by two witches, all while trying to ignore your attraction for a certain wolf shifter," Cara comments. "What a lucky girl you are."

Snorting, I nod. Ernie replaces my empty drink without me having to ask, so I tip it up and down a good portion of it. "Yeah, I won the lotto."

"I'm so sorry you're trapped here with us." Mable touches my hand. "Do you regret it?"

I consider her question. "I did at first. But now? I'm starting to believe I'm supposed to be here. My mom always says everything happens for a reason."

Mable smiles. "You've done a lot for us."

"You have," Cara adds. "Breaking part of the curse—or, at least, that's what the rumor is."

I shake my head, noting the way my eyes blur a bit with the movement. A definite buzz has kicked in. "I don't know how I did that or even if it was me. Maybe something went wrong with the spell."

"Maybe," Cara says, though she doesn't look convinced.

Mable frowns. "I doubt it. This has been going on for over a hundred years. For Myrtle to make a mistake now... it doesn't make sense."

We fall into complete silence; a dark, dreary mood overtaking the laughter from minutes ago. It feels wrong, though, to celebrate when this place—these people—have lost so much.

"Wait a damned minute." Cara shoots up from her chair and points at me. "No. No. No! No more doom and gloom. We promised."

Mable cocks her head to the side. "Promised what?"

"No talk about witches, werewolves, or what-the-fuckery tonight. We are normal women out for a drink and a night of partying." She whirls. "Collin! Karaoke!"

Falls Gazette

Chapter Nine

The chill in the air feels refreshing against my flushed skin as Cara and I make our way home through the woods. My toe catches on something, and I stumble, nearly face-planting before Cara grabs me and pulls me upright. My heel comes off in the process, wedged into the soft dirt beneath my feet.

"Shit," I hiss, reaching down to scoop up what's left of my shoe. Then, I slip off the other shoe, opting to go barefoot. Seems safer. After two hours of karaoke with bottomless drinks to match, I'm drunker than I've been in a long time—well, aside from my Adele marathon post-breakup. I'm not sure I'll ever top that night, though. Hell, I'm not sure I want to.

Cara urges me onward from where I've halted. "Girl, we need to move our asses before Sutton comes looking and I'm in trouble."

"Hold on," I say then hiccup.

I'm readjusting my grip on my heels when my balance wobbles, and I nearly fall again, thanks to what looks like the same overgrown tree root. Damn thing has it out for me tonight. Cara yanks me up just in time, locking elbows, and we both dissolve into laughter at my clumsiness.

The sound echoes against the silence, but the stillness of the woods doesn't bother me. Not tonight. There's more than enough moonlight to see where I'm going, and I've had more than enough alcohol to fuel my sense of bravery.

In other words, liquid courage.

"You have to walk straight," Cara says as we weave left to right, narrowly avoiding a tree trunk. At least, this time, it belongs to a different tree.

"I am," I say. "You're crooked."

"I'm not crooked."

"Fine, the trees are crooked."

We both crack up again.

"You think Sutton's waiting up for you?" Cara asks.

"Ten bucks says he's standing on the damn porch."

"I'm surprised he hasn't come looking yet, honestly," Cara says with a snort. "The way he watches you... he's like a dog with his bone."

"I'd like to bone *him*," I say, and we both hoot with laughter. I hadn't realized how badly I needed the normalcy of tonight. It's been far too long since I enjoyed hanging out with a friend. Shit, even before I came here, it had been months since Allison and I went out. Roscoe looked down on party girls, and I'd changed myself to fit into his box.

Never again.

From now on, the dude will have to fit into my box. I snicker at the dirty undertone of my own thoughts. And then inevitably picture Sutton trying to fit into my box. Even the mental image is torture right now.

"Speaking of boning," Cara says, pulling me from my fantasies, "am I the only one who noticed the tension between Mable and Ernie back there?"

"Nope," I say, popping the "p" extra hard. "Those two are adorable. But how long do you think Mable's been harboring a crush? I mean, haven't they known each other for like a century now? It seems a little ridiculous at this point—like, just go for it already."

"I think we've all been living in a sort of holding pattern," she says with a shrug. "I mean, we've been trapped here for a hundred years. Our lives are sort of frozen. Until that changes, what's the point of anything else, you know?"

Her words penetrate my drunken state, reminding me once again what all these people have lost. And more, what they stand to gain if I can help them. It's sobering as hell.

"What about you?" She bumps my hip, which sends us veering left. "What's keeping you and Sutton from doing the dirty—"

A *crack* sounds from nearby, and I picture a branch snapping.

We both shut up and stare at each other wide-eyed.

"What was that?" I whisper.

Although, I'm pretty sure it comes out way too loud.

"Someone's out here," Cara says, looking worried.

Shit. If she's worried, I'm definitely worried. After all, she can go all wolf girl, and I'm just a measly human who supposedly has witch powers she can't actually use.

"Who?" I ask.

She shakes her head to indicate she doesn't know. "Don't move."

My ears strain to hear anything else, and all I can think is, if a bear shows up, I'm not sure Cara's current state will allow her to fight it off like Sutton once did. And I damn sure won't be fighting anything except gravity and a loose bladder in my current state either.

Snap.

Another branch. This time, it's closer.

If I strain, I can hear footsteps as they crunch over the dried brush covering the ground.

Cara tries to move but wobbles when her heel sticks in the ground.

Suddenly, having a drunken Cara as my escort home through the woods at midnight doesn't seem like the smartest plan. *Sutton is going to kill me. Unless whoever's out there does it first.*

Cara holds a finger to her lips, and I nod.

The footsteps are nearly upon us. Don't have to tell me twice.

Cara drags me behind a tree, which, even buzzed, I know is stupid since the trunk is only wide enough to cover maybe a hipbone each. We're completely exposed with nowhere to go. And I'm not dumb enough to think I can outrun a damn thing in this town. Even sober, I'd be nothing but prey to these people.

Illuminated by moonlight, a figure walks into view, and I gasp.

Yvette.

Her head whips toward me, and our eyes lock.

"Hello, Serenity." Her voice is scratchy as if she hasn't used it in a while. But otherwise, she looks fine. Freshly showered, clean clothes, combed hair. My eyes narrow as I try to figure out how she's here, looking like she hasn't been in hiding while we've hunted her nonstop for days.

"What do you want?" Cara asks.

She sounds just as shocked as I am to see the witch.

Yvette cocks her head at Cara. There's a moment of hesitation as she looks between Cara and me. In that split second, I can feel energy rising inside me, and I hold my breath as my fingertips zing with blue magic.

Yes.

If I can just—

"I came for her," Yvette says, nodding at me. "You're going to pay for the damage you've done."

"Damage?" I repeat. "Are you serious?"

"You've destroyed the hard work my sister has put in to avenge my niece." She raises her hands, and her expression twists into an angry snarl. "And now you'll pay."

Magic slams into me with the force of a train.

I'm thrown backward, knocked on my ass hard enough that I can barely pry my eyes open as I struggle to get up. Pain shoots up my back and then lances through my left arm when I roll to the side, my stomach rolling along with it.

"Serenity, run!" Cara screams.

But I can't even walk. Not with my head still spinning.

I prop myself on my elbow and look up in time to see Cara limping away. She doesn't get far before a blast of magic hits her squarely between the shoulders. She grunts and falls face-first into the dirt.

She doesn't get up again.

I'm too shocked to even scream. Cara, a werewolf with strength far beyond mine, is down. And I have no doubt I'll be next. Is this how I'm going to go out? Drunk in the woods and shot dead by a witch's magic bullets? Are you fucking kidding me?

Yvette turns back to me, stalking closer to where I'm still struggling to get on my feet again. Fear grips me as reality sinks in. I'm alone out here with a very angry, very powerful witch, who thinks I fucked with her sister and deserve to be punished for it. A sibling bent on protection is a dangerous thing even without magic involved—I would know.

"You don't have to do this, Yvette." I inch backward, for all the good that does. "You can still walk away. Have a life of your own."

"You ruined what my sister worked so hard to create," she says, striding toward me. "I must avenge that, or else what kind of sister would I be?"

She doesn't give me a chance to answer before she blasts me again. I roll sideways, taking the brunt of the hit against my hip. The fabric of my dress singes with the heat of its impact. My skin burns, and I grimace as I scramble to my feet.

Yvette stands before me, her twisted smile making it clear she's enjoying this little game. I have no doubt she could end this anytime, but she's toying with me. It pisses me off, and that anger has me running my mouth—the only weapon I have left.

"Your sister is a psychotic bitch," I tell her. "Wrecking lives all because her own daughter was apparently a chip off the old block. Looks like crazy runs in your entire family."

Yvette's eyes narrow.

Okay, maybe talking shit to the murdering old lady wasn't the smartest thing to do.

"You're going to regret your insults." Yvette raises her hand, and I brace myself, knowing full well this will be the killing strike—but it never comes.

On my right, a snarl sounds. Angry, rageful—and all too familiar.

Sutton's wolf emerges out of the darkness. He springs forward and launches himself at Yvette. Hope blooms inside my aching chest. We're safe. He'd never let anything happen to me.

He's come like I knew he would.

Yvette throws her hand up toward Sutton, and magic slices through him. He falls out of the air, a pained yelp escaping as he lands in the dirt several yards short of the woman he intended to attack.

I feel it like a punch in the gut.

Yvette turns slowly back to me, a batshit crazy self-satisfied smile on her lips.

This. Bitch.

"Now," she says, "Where were we?"

"You did not just attack my man." My energy spikes, my hardened voice unfamiliar to me as I climb to my feet.

Yvette does nothing. And why would she? She thinks she's already won, so why not let me stand up first? Ugh. Fear, anguish, desperation—it crashes together, and I don't think. I just act.

My hands shove at the air between us, and magic flies from my fingers. Blue sparks that grow stronger and hotter until it's a wall of flame aimed straight for Yvette. She screams as the magic hits her, and I watch as she goes down in a crumpled heap. Her clothes smoke, and her skin burns as the fire consumes her. The stench of charred skin fills my nose, but I'm far too angry to puke.

This bitch hurt Sutton. She's going to die for it.

Screams split the air, and she thrashes on the ground, rolling to try and put out the consuming blue fire. The gut-wrenching sound of her pain both disgusts and satisfies me until the moment her screams cease. The woods around us fall eerily silent.

I drop my hands and rush to Sutton. Resting a hand on his furry neck, I lean down. "Sutton?"

His eyes are closed. I can't even tell if he's breathing. Dread coils in my stomach, and tears burn the back of my throat. I run my palms along his fur, urging him to wake up. Something warm coats my fingers, and I pull them back. Beneath the light of the moon, I can see the dark crimson blood staining my skin.

Tremors take over my body. "Sutton!"

No answer.

A sob builds in my throat.

Fear threatens to tear me apart. More magic leaks from my hands, but I ignore it, gripping him tighter. It's an easy draw now, the power inside me. Whatever I just did to Yvette somehow broke whatever barrier had been keeping it from me. Now, I can barely stop it from flowing at all. None of it affects Sutton, though. Not like it did before. And that, more than anything, scares me.

Is it because he's—

"Sutton, wake the fuck up right now," I demand.

In the distance, a wolf howls.

Someone knows we're here. The pack will probably arrive soon enough.

My eyes blur with tears because, in this moment, there isn't a damn thing anyone else can do. The damage has already been done. It's too late.

"Sutton, I mean it. If you die, I will kill you," I threaten, barely holding back a sob. My fingers tighten on his fur.

A faint grumble sounds from his wolf's chest, and I straighten, afraid to hope. The noise comes again, and Sutton stirs. I concentrate on pulling my magic back. The last thing I want to do is injure him further.

His form trembles, and his massive claws twitch dangerously close to my exposed skin. I jump clear just as he shifts back to his human form and opens his eyes.

He looks up at me, blood coating most of his skin; a dark crimson so thick I can't even make out where it's coming from.

"You're alive," I say, choking on my relief.

He reaches for me, tensing with what I can only imagine is pain. I grab his hand, sinking down beside him once more. A single shard of magic sparks between us and then fades. I try to pull my hand away, but he holds tight.

"You're not going to get away from me that easily," he says, voice rough and strained.

Maybe it's the alcohol still flowing in my veins. Or the fact that I'm pretty sure I just killed a woman. But his words pull a dark and heady laugh from me. And once I start, I can't stop. It's something out of a Disney villain moment. My head tipped back, my tangled hair flowing down my back, the unhinged sound of my own laughter ringing in my ears. I cackle until tears run down my cheeks and my ribs ache from the effort.

Sutton looks at me like I've lost it. Maybe I have.

“What’s so funny?” he asks when I finally quiet enough for him to get a word in.

“Oh, nothing,” I tell him. “Just that I killed an old lady and figured out I’m in love with a werewolf all in the same night. And the only thing I’ll probably regret tomorrow is the karaoke.”

Falls Gazette

Chapter Ten

"Thank you, Jasper," Sutton says to the tall dark-haired man currently standing on the porch.

Soft moonlight frames both their faces, but over Jasper's shoulder, I can see where late-night shadows creep toward the house from the dark woods beyond. With a shudder, I turn away, reminding myself we're both alive and well—and Yvette is neither.

"No problem, alpha," Jasper says. "I'll have a guard posted outside for the rest of the night. And we'll see to it that Cara gets home safe."

"Great. I'll check in with you tomorrow." Sutton closes the door, making it just the two of us in the house for the first time since I left hours ago for a night out that turned into a freaking night*mare*.

Jasper was the first to show and the last to leave, which makes him my current favorite pack member as far as I'm concerned. But now that I'm home, I don't know what to do next. From where I stand near the stairs, I have a front-row seat to Sutton's blood-smeared back, and I can't make myself look away.

Tears blur my vision, the effects of the adrenaline and alcohol both gone, leaving me to deal with the events of what happened tonight completely sober. I almost lost him. And the thing that guts me most about that moment is that I never really had him to begin with.

He turns, and my gaze drops to the huge wound on his side. Thanks to his abilities, it's already started healing, but the center is raw, bloody, and looks like it hurts like hell. "First-aid kit?" I manage, my voice hoarse. The need to do something—anything to soothe his pain is overwhelming.

Brows drawn together, he nods toward the hall on the right. "Bathroom."

Leaving him standing in the entryway, I all but sprint to the bathroom. It was my fault he had to come after me tonight in the first place. If I'd have stayed sober, or, at the very least, insisted on a group versus one intoxicated she-wolf to walk me home, he likely wouldn't have been injured. And Cara wouldn't have been knocked unconscious or woken with a possible concussion.

In the bathroom, I fling open the cabinet and scan the contents inside. It doesn't take me but a few seconds to find the small red case, so I find my way back to Sutton as he's lowering himself on a stool in the kitchen. I drop to my knees and open the lid on the medical kit.

"You don't need to do that."

"Shut up," I snap. "Unless you want it to get infected." I tear open an alcohol swab and gently touch it to his side.

He hisses. "Shit. I think you made it worse."

I glare up at him.

Sutton smiles softly. "Serenity, it's okay."

"No. It's not." I sniffle, and he slips out of the stool to kneel beside me.

"I will be healed by the time you can finish cleaning it." He cups my cheeks and runs his thumbs over my skin. Then, he tilts my head to the side and narrows his gaze. "You, on the other hand…"

Grabbing some gauze and a small brown bottle, he brushes the hair off of my neck. I tilt my head to the side to give him access. Cold moisture hits an open wound I didn't even know I had, and I grind my teeth together against the sting.

"Sorry." He gently wipes it then pulls back, showing me the white gauze crusted with blood. After setting the gauze and bottle onto the floor, he takes my hands. "It's not too bad."

My throat constricts. "I'm so sorry I screwed up."

"How did you screw up?"

"I was drunk. Walking in the woods. Take your pick."

Sutton's mouth quirks. "Seems to me you're beating yourself up just fine for the both of us." Standing, he pulls me to my feet. "Now, I don't know about you, but I'd love a shower."

He hasn't mentioned my confession yet, or the fact that I killed a woman tonight, and I can't decide whether I'm relieved or pissed off at the elephant in the room. He wraps an arm around my waist and guides me toward the stairs.

"Why haven't you said anything?" I demand, settling on feeling pissed off.

Tell a guy you love him and he acts like nothing has changed. An especially frustrating response given he's been more than open about how he feels about me.

He doesn't try to deny or sidestep the topic of conversation. Instead, he releases me so I can face him. "I didn't feel like bringing up something that might have just been effects of the alcohol or adrenaline."

"It wasn't." The air around us shifts, and my heart begins to pound. "I meant what I said. Almost losing you—I can't lose you, Sutton."

"I'm not looking to play games, Serenity."

"Neither am I." To demonstrate, I take a step closer. His nostrils flare, his pupils dilating as he looks down at me. With a trembling hand, I reach forward and touch his blood-smeared chest. The muscles beneath my palm are warm, inviting, so I add my other hand.

Sutton's eyes close, and he breathes deeply. I know he senses my lust, and somehow, it only makes the moment even hotter.

Tired of waiting, I stretch up and gently press my lips to his. A tender kiss to test the waters. And, thankfully, lacking one cock-blocking blue spark. The moment Sutton realizes my spark isn't going to stop us, he reacts.

Sutton's hand grips the back of my neck, and he spins me, pressing my back to the wall behind me as he takes my mouth. Gone is the sensual savoring from a moment ago. Sutton is an animal, and I've just set him free. His hands tangle in my hair as his tongue traces the seam of my lips. His roughness triggers something in me, and my grief vanishes. In its place is a desperation that threatens to snap my own careful control. I don't want gentle right now. I want Sutton Hargrave.

I open beneath him, and he fucking consumes me.

Hands slipping down my body, he grips my ass and lifts me, his hard length pressing right against my center as he pins me to the wall.

I don't care that we're covered in dirt and grime. Don't care that tonight nearly went horribly wrong. Because right now, it's just me and him. And I want him. Desperately. Against the wall, on the stairs, the bed—I don't care.

Holding me tightly against his body, he ascends the stairs one by one, still fucking my mouth with a tongue that I *know* can work magic.

If he tries to stop now, I'll kill him myself.

Somehow, we make it into the bathroom, and he manages to turn the water on. It slaps the tile and Sutton pins me against the wall again, a low growl escaping his lips as he trails his tongue over my jaw, my neck.

Every nerve in my body is ablaze, every fiber of my being consumed by the man before me.

His fingers sear my skin as he carries me into the shower, me still fully clothed. Lukewarm water hits my back, but it doesn't cool the fire between us. Like gasoline on a flame, it ignites.

My hands grip the thick strands of his hair. He sets me on my feet and grabs my dress, ripping it open. I gasp as he throws the tattered remnants of my dress to the tile at our feet. His hand palms my breast, thumb and finger gently pinching the peak of my nipple.

Warmth burns me up from the inside, and I arch back.

"You drive me mad," he growls in my ear before nipping my jaw.

There has to be something wrong with me because it turns me on like nothing else, and I want him to bite me again.

Grabbing the waistband of his shorts, I shove them down, exposing every inch of his naked body.

My mouth goes dry.

My heart pumps.

Sutton is fucking *huge.* And why wouldn't he be? Everything about this man is larger than life. He cups the back of my neck and yanks me to him. I grip his length, squeezing gently. He thrusts into my hand, and I squeeze it harder, sliding my hand over his hard length.

He spins me, pressing my front to the shower. His hard body at my back, I'm pinned. Trapped. And so fucking turned on I can barely breathe.

Sutton's free hand goes to my hip, and he squeezes, sliding

down over my ass and between my thighs. He brushes his fingers over me, and I gasp.

"You are so perfect," he whispers in my ear. "I don't know where I should touch you. It feels like we've waited so long."

"I want you," I choke out. "Please."

Sutton chuckles, the sound an aphrodisiac. I slide my legs apart a little more. He cups me from behind, his hand so close to my ass I don't know whether to be nervous or exhilarated. "What should I do with you now that I have you?"

Here, at the mercy of an alpha, I've never felt so powerful. My body jerks when he slides a finger over my clit. Every muscle in my body tightens, preparing for what is promising to be the release to end all releases. "Sutton," I moan, his name a plea. "Please."

"Please, what?" he growls, his finger moving torturously slow over me. Every touch sets my blood afire.

"Let me—" I arch back, my head falling against his chest.

"Not until you ask," he growls. "What do you want from me?"

"Please," I pant. "Faster. Let me come."

He picks up the pace, sliding one finger inside of me. Then two. He fucks me with his fingers as his thumb caresses my clit. Stars explode in my vision, and I cry out, my hands grasping for the tile even as it offers no support.

My legs go weak.

He continues sliding his fingers in and out, in and out, slowing down each time to draw out all of my pleasure until I'm completely mindless.

Then, he withdraws his fingers and turns me to face him. Hair soaking wet, the water drips down over his body, each droplet caressing muscles I want to touch. Taste.

I want everything. All he has.

Sutton steps closer and lifts me again. I wrap both legs around his waist, kissing him with feverish passion. Cold air nips at my skin as he carries me out of the shower. He crosses the room and throws me back onto his bed, completely soaked.

His massive hands go to my knees, and he spreads my legs, chewing on his bottom lip as he stares at me. I'm fully exposed, completely open to him, and he looks hungrily at what I'm offering.

"You are so fucking delicious," he growls as he climbs onto the bed between my legs. Leaning forward, he aligns with my body, pressing his length against my entrance.

"Please," I choke out.

"I already told you my rule, Serenity. Tell me what you want."

"You," I whisper.

Sutton beams at me. With one thrust, he buries himself in me, and I cry out.

Sutton groans and stills. "You're so fucking tight."

"You're so fucking large," I shoot back.

He pulls back and drives into me again. Again. Again. Each thrust pushes me closer and closer toward the edge. "I want to see you," he growls and rolls over, taking me with him so I'm on top. My palms splay over his muscled chest, and he reaches up to cup my breasts.

I move, driving us at the speed of my own heart until—throwing my head back, I scream his name, the orgasm tearing me apart into a million tiny pieces. He flips me back over and drives into me faster, a furious, punishing pace, until he pulls out and rolls over to his back.

He strokes himself once before his own release takes over. Seconds tick by, each of us still reeling from what had to be an award-winning bang.

"That was—" I start, breathless.

"Worth nearly dying for?" he questions.

Cracking an eye open I glare at him. "You tell me."

Sutton chuckles and gets to his feet. "What I will tell you is that

I am nowhere near done with you, Serenity Kellis." Gripping my hand, he yanks me up and pulls me toward the bathroom for round two.

"Is that a threat or a promise?" I joke.

But the gleam in his eye holds no humor as he tells me, "Both."

He grins down at me. "Pun intended?"

"Ugh," I groan. "My point is you can make it up to me with an orgasm."

"Are you sure you're up for that? I could have sworn the last thing you said before you fell asleep was 'if I can't walk tomorrow, it's your fault.'"

I wiggle my legs out from under him, stretching and bending them for effect. "I'm not saying you didn't do your job, but..."

I yelp as he tickles me, both of us laughing while we sexy-wrestle our way toward round six... or seven. I've lost count. All I know is every single round has been toe-curling and delicious, and I really might walk with a limp when I finally get out of this bed again. His bed. Or ours. It's getting a bit hard to know for sure.

A problem that seems delightful compared to the true reality that awaits me when I come down from my sex high.

Am I using Sutton's body as a distraction from the horrors that await us when we're done? Damn right I am. Do I think he minds? Abso-freaking-lutely not.

The tickling turns to stroking. My laughter turns to heavy sighs as Sutton's hands grip my arms and yank them over my head, pinning them to the mattress. He trails his nose over my throat and inhales. "What to do with you," he whispers.

I arch up into him, pressing my center to him, and he groans. "I can think of a few ideas," I reply.

Sutton chuckles and releases my hands, pulling back until he's kneeling at my side. "So can I." Reaching forward, he flips me over so my stomach is pressed to the mattress. The covers completely leave my body, and his fingertips go to my spine.

A soft moan leaves my lips as he trails his fingers down my back. When he shifts his weight and nudges my legs open with his knee, a small bite of fear shoots through me.

Chapter Eleven

I wake to the feel of a hand trailing over my bare shoulder and up my collarbone. A zing of pleasure trails with it. I inhale deeply. The scent of sex and Sutton Hargrave reminds me exactly where I am—and what I've done. My eyes open, and I smile at the sight of Sutton's face staring back at me. His chin bears a layer of stubble I remember scratching along my thighs last night. And his long hair hangs in his eyes but not so much that I can't see the desire reflected in their depths. He's propped on his elbow and watching me with a look of reverence that touches parts of me I'm surprised to find haven't felt this way... ever.

"Good morning," I say sleepily.

"Mm, morning." He leans down and presses a kiss to my lips that's probably supposed to be chaste and quick, but one taste of him, and my body takes over. Lips still locked, I reach up and wrap my arms around his neck, pulling him down over me and reveling in the feel of his weight against me.

"I didn't mean to wake you," he says between kisses.

"Yeah, that was a real dick move," I murmur.

Falls Gazette

On my belly, I feel more exposed than ever. Especially when he cups my ass with both hands and then slides one down to the part of me that aches for him. I moan, arching my back to give him more access.

Sutton's hot breath fans over my thighs, and I still. He chuckles. "Am I making you nervous?"

"A little," I admit. This happens to be the closest any man has ever been to my ass, and, well, given his size, I can't say I'm jumping at the idea of expanding our sexual adventure.

"I'm not after that, Serenity. At least, not yet," he whispers as the hand cupping me grips my thigh, folding my leg up to give him better access. He runs his tongue over me, and I cry out, pleasure rocketing through my core. One hand pins my thigh to the side. The other slips between my body and the mattress to caress my clit as he slides his tongue into me.

"Sutton!" I cry out, my hands fisting the sheets as he continues driving me closer and closer to the edge.

Release shatters me, and Sutton moves quickly, sliding up my body and driving into me from behind. He grips my hips, each thrust drawing out every bit of pleasure from my body. We clash together, two pieces that fit perfectly together until—

"Fuck," Sutton growls and pulls out, rolling onto his back and pumping himself with his hand until his own release breaks free.

Together, we suck in deep breaths, one after the other, my heart hammering. I honestly cannot even put into words how amazing that was. And yet, I honestly believe I've only just scratched the surface of the pleasure this man can bring me.

"Shit." Sutton jumps out of bed and heads for the bathroom. I sit up against the bed, waiting for him.

"What is it?"

He steps out of the bathroom wearing sweats as someone pounds on the door. "You'd better cover up."

Panic claws at my throat as I imagine Myrtle here to rain down vengeance for what I've done to her sister.

I killed Yvette.

The events of last night come crashing down around me, and my mind fills with the horrific image of Sutton covered in blood, unmoving.

"It's okay," Sutton says, probably in response to the rapid thudding of my heart. "It's just Jasper. But if he sees you naked, I will have to kill him."

I cover up quickly, and Sutton pulls open the door, though I cannot make out what is spoken between the two.

He turns toward me. "Meet us downstairs," he says, wearing a grim expression on his face, then slips out and shuts the door behind him.

I scramble to catch up, grabbing whatever clothes I can find on my way to the door.

Turns out, I *can* walk and dress, but running while pulling on leggings is a bit harder. I nearly trip down the stairs as I struggle to get down them while pulling the leggings into place over my bare ass. At the bottom of the steps, I land hard and look up at both Sutton and Jasper watching me from the foyer.

Jasper's expression is grim, and Sutton doesn't look any better. The fact that Sutton doesn't tease me about my legs not working means something's up.

"What happened?" I ask, adjusting my shirt to make sure everything's covered.

"Harriet Patmore was found dead this morning," Sutton says.

Harriet? "The woman who sent us the basket of tea?"

Her gift had been among the others, along with a very kind note that didn't pressure me to do anything other than to "take care in these hard times."

"Yes," Sutton says.

A slow dread works its way through me. "How did she die?"

I pretend he's going to say heart attack, accident, old age—anything but what he says next. "Her throat was cut open and drained of blood. Near the old ward lines at the edge of town."

"Wait. You mean the boundary that separated the woods from the town? The one you couldn't cross before...?"

His non-answer is all I need to know. My stomach plummets.

Myrtle.

"She's trying to restart that part of the spell," I say.

Sutton and Jasper exchange a look.

"What?" I demand.

"My father tried coming to the house earlier," Sutton says. "He couldn't get through."

"Wards won't let him pass," Jasper adds.

"It's working," I realize. "Whatever she's doing with Harriet's blood, it's working." I look at Sutton, fear making it hard to breathe. "She's trying to cut you off from everyone again." The look in his eye is pure misery, and I realize how badly this will set him back if Myrtle succeeds in trapping him again.

"She knows we're stronger as a pack," Jasper says.

He sounds angry, ready to fight—but how can we do that when the enemy won't face us?

Yvette faced us out of anger—and lost. But Yvette is not Myrtle. Myrtle has proven to be calculated and incredibly patient.

I ball my hands into fists, feeling the magic surge inside me. I have no idea what made it stay hidden last night while Sutton and I... But it's back now, and I can't afford to hurt anyone else. Not until Myrtle is the one standing before me.

"We need to go into town," I say. "So she can't lock you out."

"And then what?" Sutton asks. "We'll be exposed. And that's what she wants ultimately." His expression hardens. "I won't put you in danger, Serenity."

"You can stay with me," Jasper says, but Sutton shakes his head.

"I won't put you in danger either. It's me she wants."

I bite my lip. "We'll figure it out. But we should get moving, or we won't be able to get out at all."

They both agree, and after a quick grab of the things I need, we meet back at the front door. It's a sad collection of items that I'm carrying. Most of them don't belong to me. Not really. A pair of jeans and a jacket Cara sent over. A few toiletries gifted to me by the pack. I bring the tea—mostly because it feels disrespectful to Harriet's memory to leave it behind.

I'm ready faster than Sutton and end up outside with Jasper while we wait.

He's quiet, though I get the feeling that's just his nature.

"You okay?" he asks finally.

"I mean, Yvette's no longer a threat, so that's … a relief. But—"

"Taking a life isn't for the faint of heart," he finishes. Then his mouth tips up in a haunted smile. "You're not faint of heart, though, Serenity Kellis."

Before I can ask how he knows that, Sutton returns. At the same time he steps outside, Cara appears from the trail, breathless.

I drop everything I'm carrying and throw my arms around her neck.

"Whoa," she says, catching me before I can take us both down.

"You're okay," I say, squeezing until she pries me off her.

"I'm okay," she confirms.

"You were unconscious," I begin. "And they said something about a concussion—"

"Already healed. Wolf power, remember?"

I exhale.

"Look, I'm sorry," she says, hanging her head. "I should have protected you—"

"Are you kidding? You nearly died trying to save me."

"Yeah, but I was stupid. Too many drinks. Not paying attention."

"Neither was I," I tell her. "Consider us even. I'm just glad you're all right."

She grins. "Yeah, thanks to you." She hip-bumps me. "Badass witch slayer."

"We need to get going," Sutton says. "Any trouble?" he asks Cara.

"Woods are clear," she tells him then hangs her head. "And... I'm sorry about last night."

"No need to apologize, I'm just glad you're okay." Though the way he says it is strained. Surely he's not actually mad?

"Thank you," she says, obviously relieved.

"Let's get moving." He takes my hand, and we set off through the trees.

No one says much on the walk toward town. I sense Sutton's thoughts have gone to a dark place, but mine aren't any better. So, I leave it alone.

All too soon, we've reached the outskirts of town. Up ahead, I can see a few pack members guarding an area they've marked off. And in the center, a figure lies prone in the patchy grass.

Harriet.

I slow my pace.

"You don't have to see this," Sutton says.

"Yeah," I say, taking a deep breath. "I think I do."

Harriet's body has been cut and drained—just like the Sheriff's. Just like all the others before.

Judging from the expressions everyone wears, it's a devastating blow. More so than the past victims. Because this time, Myrtle didn't wait until All Hallows Eve to renew the curse's magic. She's thrown out the rules. Making them up as she goes. And that's scarier than anything that's happened yet.

Predictability is what we relied on. If she's not acting as we expect, well, there's no way to know what's coming next. No way to prepare.

Which means Myrtle has all the power—and despite everything, we still have none. Even with Yvette gone, we have no way to stop this. No way to be free.

I hang back, waiting while Sutton talks to the pack members. I can hear them offering him a place to stay—offering us both. But he turns them all down. I don't blame him. He's protecting them in what little way he can. But we can't be homeless.

When it's clear they're wrapping up, Phineas arrives and embraces Sutton tightly. I can see the worry in both their eyes. They're terrified of being separated again. My heart aches for them. For all of them.

And that ache fuels my determination like never before.

By the time Sutton is finished, most of the others have cleared out.

"Everything okay?" I ask when he approaches me. "They all cleared out so fast."

"My father wanted to get Harriet to the coroner as soon as possible," he explains. "They were friends for a very long time."

"I see." My eyes fill with tears that I refuse to let fall. "Now what?"

He glances back toward the trees. "I've sent a couple of teams to run the perimeter. If Myrtle's out there, casting this spell again, she'll have to do it along the ward lines. If not here then farther out."

"Have they found anything?" I ask.

Before he can answer, a boom sounds. It's not very loud, but when I look up, I see a thin curl of smoke rising in the distance. Unease burns in my gut as my adrenaline spikes.

"Is that—"

"Yes." Sutton's answer is no more than a growl. He starts for the woods in the direction of the smoke, and I grab his arm, stopping him.

"What are you doing?" I demand.

"She can't get away. Not again."

He tries pulling away, which isn't hard because, holy hell, this man is strong. I have zero chance of stopping him if he's decided to go, and fear threatens to rip me apart at what might happen to him if he faces Myrtle alone.

"Sutton, wait," I call, but there's no need.

He makes it all of three steps before he smacks into an invisible barrier and stumbles back again. He straightens, staring at the spot where he was just driven backward. Slower this time, he approaches it again and lifts his hand, palm out. He presses against something, gritting his teeth with the powerful effort he puts behind the motion.

Whatever it is he's trying to move, it doesn't budge.

I step up beside him and press my own hands to what feels like a cold, smooth surface.

Then I yank them back again and stare at Sutton.

"She did it," I say. "She reconstructed the barrier. We're locked out."

Sutton looks torn between relief and misery as he says, "Or locked in."

Falls Gazette

Chapter Twelve

"Three large coffees, please. Black. Strong." My voice hardly wavers as I place my order.

From across the counter, Jolene nods at me, her typically stony expression softer than usual. With bloodshot eyes, she begins working on the coffees. *Bean There* is all but empty with only two patrons other than myself inside. Since word of Harriet's murder spread, most folks have retreated into their own houses or businesses. Even in broad daylight, the town looks nearly empty. I'm still surprised Sutton let me out of his sight long enough for me to get us coffee. He and Phineas went ahead to the morgue—an errand I decided to opt out of. Mainly because I've hit my quota of dead bodies in the last twenty-four hours. Two is enough and I don't need to see or stand around with any more than that.

"I hear Sutton can't return to his house," a woman whispers loudly in the corner to the man at her table.

"What if we don't have a year? What if this is the year that witch decides to end us all?"

My throat constricts, burning with emotion as I turn to face them. "You cannot give up hope," I tell them.

They simply stare back at me.

"I'm sorry. I didn't mean to eavesdrop." Turning back to the counter, I offer Jolene a twenty, but she shakes her head and hands me the drink carrier.

"Don't worry about it."

"Jolene—"

"Just stop this bitch." Her bottom lip quivers slightly, and the display of emotion is so unlike her I don't even know how to respond. Which is probably a good thing since she immediately turns around and starts letting steam out of a machine.

Drinks in hand, I step out into the dreary afternoon and head down the block toward the police station, which also happens to double as the city morgue. Nothing like a dual-purpose building, I suppose. It's close enough to the coffee shop that Sutton claimed he'd hear my screams if Myrtle tried anything while I was gone. It took everything in me not to make a crude joke about him enjoying my screams last night, but given the serious nature of what we're dealing with, humor doesn't feel appropriate. At least, not at the moment.

As I walk, I keep my head down, not meeting the eyes of the few people out and about. How can I? I have nothing to say to them. *So sorry I was having the best sex of my life while one of the beloved residents of this town was brutally murdered. Likely because I committed a murder of my own last night. Before said sex, of course.*

A tear slips free, and I angrily wipe it away with my empty hand. Yvette would have killed Sutton. She would have killed me and Cara, too. I will *not* feel guilty about what I did. Not until the rest of this threat has been dealt with. Then there will be plenty of time to focus on crimes committed during my time here.

My phone vibrates in my pocket, the *Bad Boys, Bad Boys, What You Gonna Do?* ringtone signaling just who's on the other end. *Perfect. Just what I need. An interrogation.* "Hello?" I ask, still walking down the street. With both hands occupied—something Steven would chastise me for.

"How's your vacation going?" Steven's tone makes it clear he's so far past believing this is a vacation anymore.

Forcing my fakest voice ever, I reply, "Peachy."

"Peachy, huh? Eating a lot of fruit?"

"Definitely. Peaches, apples, grapes. Virginia is known for its pawpaws."

"What the fuck is a pawpaw?"

"Part of the custard apple family. Delicious." I committed murder yesterday, and now I'm talking to my homicide detective older brother about fruit. What the hell has become of my life?

Steven is silent for a moment. Then I hear him mutter something before returning to the line. "Sorry, working a case where a wife killed her husband and his mistress after engaging in a three-way with them."

"Yikes."

"Understatement. Maybe I'll just take an extended leave of absence and travel to a remote Virginia town, too."

"No." The word comes out faster and harsher than I meant, and knowing Steven, he has now massively read into the response.

"What's going on with you?"

"Nothing is going on. I'm just tired. Lots of hiking."

"Ser—"

"I'm fine, Steven. I promise." Stopping just outside the door to the station, I set the coffees down on a bench and take a seat next to them. "I met someone," I say, hoping like hell it doesn't bite me in the ass.

"And that's fifty bucks for me."

"What the hell does that mean?"

"I bet Dad you'd met someone, which is why you haven't come home."

"You *bet* on me hooking up?"

"And won. That's the important part."

"Are you fucking kidding me, Steven?" For some crazy-ass reason, tears fill my eyes. I can't be mad at him, I know that. It's not like he can ever know I'm over here dealing with life-or-death situations, but shit. I'm facing off with murderous bitches and he's gambling on my sex life. I don't know if I've ever felt so alone as I do right now.

My entire life, I've had my family. I've always been able to be open with them. To ask for help when I need it. And now—now doing so would mean I would lose them, too.

"Why the hell are you so pissy? It's not like my bet was off."

"I'm not mad. I'm sorry." Pinching the bridge of my nose, I will the anger away. "It's just early, and we're still figuring things out."

"What's his name?"

"Nope."

"Serenity Kellis."

"Steven Kellis."

"Give me his name."

"Not yet. When I figure things out, I will."

"Social security number?"

"Nice try."

"I can't exactly run a background check on him without some details."

I snort. "Because a background check let me know Roscoe was going to be a cheating son of a bitch? I'd really rather keep this one quiet for now. Please? Can you just trust me?"

Steven sighs. "Fine. One week. Then I want a name."

I grimace. A week isn't exactly my preferred timeline for

dealing with all my problems, but I can't afford to argue either. "Deal."

"Serenity!"

I turn, surprised to see a red-faced Mable rushing toward me.

"I have to go, love you."

"Love you, too."

I shove my phone into my pocket and fully turn to face her just as she comes to a stop. Holding up a finger, she takes a few deep breaths, and I watch, half-amused even as my mood remains somber.

"I thought you were an agile wolf?"

"An out-of-shape one," she jokes. "It's been a while since I had to run." Straightening, her gaze meets mine. "How are you?"

"Not great," I admit. "We have another dead woman, and there was the whole murdering Yvette thing last night. I guess I'm trying to come to terms with condemning Audrey as a murderer and becoming one myself."

"You saved Sutton, Cara, and yourself from Yvette's wrath, you know. That's something to be proud of."

"Maybe."

"There's no maybe about it, Serenity. If it weren't for you and your abilities, we would all still be trapped in our human forms, and the three of you would likely be dead."

"Well, I appreciate your faith in me." I force a smile.

Mable hesitates and begins to fidget with the bottom of her sweatshirt.

"What is it?" I ask. I swear if it's another dead person—

"I have something I need to admit." Her chaste response makes me uneasy.

"What?"

Mable swallows hard and meets my eyes. Every muscle in my body tenses, prepared for her to admit that she's actually Myrtle.

Maybe she has been since the night of the ball. Fighting the urge to retreat, I hold my ground.

We're out in the open. Surely—

"I sent you the newspaper clippings," she blurts.

I gape at her. "You sent them to me?"

She nods. "I hired a messenger to deliver them."

"But...why? I mean, why me?"

"When Sutton told me he found the curse breaker, and he told me your name, I looked you up. After that, I followed your work for a long time, and it was so easy to see what a kind, good person you are."

"Wait a damn minute. You sent me those clippings? Are you the one who slipped them under my door at the B&B when I first arrived too?"

She nods again. "After I found out you were the curse breaker, I did research. I looked into you, your family—you are such a good person, Serenity." Reaching forward, she places her hand on my arm. "They believe you are the curse breaker because a witch cast a spell that gave your name. But *I* believe you are the one who will save us because of how strong you are. Because of the depth of your caring and kindness. Because of your heart."

Her words are a comfort, but just as quickly as they soothe me, I'm wary again. "You lied to me. From the moment I stepped into the library."

Mable's hand falls, her expression morphing to one of guilt. "I couldn't tell you. Not until I knew for sure you would stay. I tried, I gave you hints."

"Hints aren't the truth, Mable."

"I know," she says softly.

"Do you? Because everyone keeps lying to me. They keep hiding information that would be helpful."

"We were only trying not to scare you."

"Yeah, because scaring off the girl you want to tangle in your web in hopes she can distract the spider long enough for you to get free would be a bad thing."

Mable's brows draw together. "It's not like that."

"Isn't it?"

Her eyes well with tears. "We never meant for you to be trapped here with us."

I pause and force myself to take a deep breath. Life in this town is far too short for grudges. I've seen proof of that fact already today.

"I truly am sorry I hid the truth from you," Mable says. "I believed I was doing what was right."

"Don't ever lie to me again."

"Promise." She beams at me. Then her gaze shifts to someone over my shoulder. "He believes in you, too," she whispers. "Because when he looks at you, he sees what I see."

Glancing back, my gaze locks with Sutton's as he starts toward me. "And what's that?"

"A hero."

Falls Gazette

Chapter Thirteen

"Mable," Sutton greets as he and Phineas come to a stop beside us.

"Sutton, Phineas." She grins at them both then claps her hands together. "I should be off. Books to categorize. Come see me soon?" she asks me, and I nod.

"Sure."

"Great." Then, she turns and bounds back down the sidewalk in the direction she came from.

"Everything okay?"

I turn to Sutton. "Depends. Anyone else wrapped up in your plan to bring me here?"

He pales. "She told you?"

"Yes. How did you tell her my name, anyway? If you guys were trapped apart."

"Last year's ball," he explains. "It was right before that the witch came to see me."

"And it took almost a year to bring me here."

"I didn't want to at first," he admits. "When Mable started

adding your stories to the baskets they sent over the line, I decided to keep you out of it."

I stare back at him, shocked and sad all at the same time. "That would certainly explain why you didn't seem too happy to see me in the woods."

He steps closer. "I think I started feeling something for you the moment I saw your picture next to your bio."

Phineas clears his throat, reminding me that it's not just Sutton and me standing here on the sidewalk.

"This isn't over," I warn Sutton.

He grins. "I never would have expected it to be."

Clearing my throat, I do my best to shove this particular revelation down and change the subject. "Two coffees just the way you ordered."

"Thank you," Phineas says as he pulls out a cup.

"Thank you, Serenity," Sutton echoes, lifting his cup for a sip.

"No need to thank me. Jolene wouldn't even let me pay for them."

The men exchange glances that tell me I'm missing something. "What?"

"Harriet was Jolene's aunt."

Her swollen red eyes, subdued demeanor. I cover my mouth as tears blur my vision. "That's so awful."

"It is."

"I wish I would have known. I'd have—I don't know—given her a hug or something."

"Jolene's not exactly the type," Sutton tells me. "If you had tried to hug her, she probably would have shown you her teeth."

"Fair enough."

Phineas takes a drink of his coffee. "I need to run back into the station and add the coroner's preliminary report to my notes about the case. You two going to be okay?"

"You're working with the police?" I ask, surprised.

"Only until we can elect a new Sheriff," he says quietly. "With Arden gone, someone had to step up."

My chest pangs at the reminder. "Right."

"You sure you won't stay with me?" Phineas presses.

"Positive," Sutton replies quickly. "I won't risk anyone else. We'll find a place."

Phineas sighs. Sutton's comment hangs between us, and I can see Phineas' skepticism even as he turns and leaves us alone. I know he doesn't like us out here exposed like this. Neither does Sutton. Hell, neither do I. But I agree with Sutton. We can't put someone else in danger, not even if it means we're sleeping in a tent or a hotel.

An idea pops into my head, and I go with it before I can second guess myself, especially if it keeps me from sleeping on the ground tonight. Sure, I ran from the place last time I was there, but a lot has changed since then.

I've changed since then.

"I know where we can go," I announce.

Sutton turns to me.

"The B&B is empty, right? With Yvette gone—"

"No. Absolutely not," Sutton shuts it down quickly.

"Yvette is dead, though," I say.

"And Myrtle is not," he shoots back.

"Look, it's the only place available without tenants to endanger," I say. Or, not living ones anyway.

"We've tried entering," he says. "The magic blocks our access."

"That was before," I say. He doesn't ask "before what." We both already know. "Look, we go there, see if it's unlocked, and if it is, we have a place to stay. Plus, I can finally get my own underwear back."

"I think you've been doing just fine without them," he replies, gaze darkening.

Lust pools in my belly despite the fact that we're talking about squatting in a dead lady's house, which would have made me feel like the worst person ever if said dead woman was not an evil witch who tried to kill me. "I want my stuff back, Sutton. If Myrtle is there, or it looks like she's been there, then we can leave. But you've had people watching it, right?"

He nods. "They haven't seen anything."

"See? Perfect place."

Sutton's lips flatten into a tight line, but he nods. "Fine. But if anything is off—"

"We're gone," I finish. "Promise." Here's hoping he doesn't consider the resident specters as a reason to run.

SOMEHOW, THE B&B APPEARS EVEN MORE LOOMING THAN IT WAS the first time I saw it. Coffees in hand, Sutton and I walk up the driveway slowly. Jasper will join us soon along with a security detail, but for now, it's only Sutton and me. My car comes into view, and I nearly weep with joy. Rushing forward, I run my hands over the dusty paint. "I missed you, baby," I whisper.

"Did you just talk to your car?"

I glance back to find Sutton watching me, amusement on his face. "I did. What's it to you?"

He shrugs. "Not a thing. Guess I can start having my regular conversations with the coffee pot again."

Rolling my eyes, I follow him up the steps. He opens the door and peers inside. No magical wards block our entry.

"It's empty," he announces, moving inside then gesturing for me to follow.

I don't bother to ask how he simply knows we're alone here. But I can't help a twinge of jealousy. Wolf senses would be a nice perk in a moment like this one. Where my own fear makes it impossible to fully believe him until I can see for myself.

The air is stale as if the inn has been vacant for quite some time. If Yvette was hiding here, she closed herself in tight. I shiver, recalling how many nights I slept in the same house as the enemy. I'm lucky to be alive. Lucky and seriously confused about why she didn't kill me in my sleep.

"You okay?" Sutton questions.

"I'm fine," I reply, flashing him a smile. "Just weird being back here and knowing that she's..." I trail off, and he nods, knowing what I was going to say.

Footsteps on the stairs have us both whirling toward them. "I thought you said it was empty," I whisper.

Beside me, Sutton is a coiled spring. "It was."

Two people appear at the top of the stairs. When I see their faces, I exhale and grab Sutton's arm before he can attack. "Wait," I tell him. "They're not here to hurt us."

At least, I don't think so. We both watch as the couple descends the stairs and stops in front of us. Victoria claps her hands together. "Lance, look! New guests!" Still wearing her yellow puffy vest and black long-sleeved turtleneck, she looks exactly the way she did the last time I saw her. Which makes sense since she's dead.

Lance smiles softly at Victoria then turns to us. "How lovely to see you again, Serenity," he says. "I trust you've been well?"

"Serenity?" Victoria's brows draw together in confusion for just a moment before realization dawns on her. "Yes! Serenity! It is so good to see you! It's been lonely since you left. Have you seen Yvette? I was looking for her."

Awkward. "Yvette is—"

"Out," Sutton snaps. He looks torn between rage and murdery-suspicion. I get it. Victoria and Lance don't *look* like dead people. They look alive and very killable. Turns out, they're not. "You must be the apparitions Serenity spoke of."

"We prefer friendly neighborhood specters," Lance replies coolly.

Sutton shoots me a glance, and I realize up until now, he hadn't taken me seriously about the ghosts living it up like it's Groundhog Day.

"And you are?" Lance prompts.

"This is Sutton Hargrave," I say. "We're staying here until... well, until we can go home."

The word "home" sticks strangely in my mouth. It's true enough for Sutton, but for me? Where, even, is home anymore?

"Pleasure to meet you," Sutton says and extends his hand. He seems only mildly more friendly now that he's identified Lance and Victoria, but his body is angled in front of me as if to protect me from a threat.

Lance reaches for Sutton's outstretched hand, and my jaw drops as Lance's hand closes over Sutton's. They shake, and I take notice of Lance's furrowed brow as if it's taking every bit of focus to maintain his grip.

"Are you okay?" I ask.

"Must be full of specter go-go juice," Lance jokes.

I have to bite back a smile. Okay, maybe they're not so scary after all. "Specter go-go juice?"

"Energy," he replies. "If we're chock full of it, and are able to concentrate hard enough, we can touch people, move objects, but each time we use it, the energy wanes. It's a brief way to feel human for a time."

Sutton studies Lance as if re-assessing his threat level.

"Good to meet you both," Sutton says.

Some of the tension eases, but now my attention is drawn to the rest of the house. The utter silence of it still has me on edge. I know for a fact Yvette couldn't possibly be here, but I can't rest until I see for myself that it's truly empty.

Victoria beams, clinging to Lance's arm. Somehow, they're able to touch each other? "You two make quite the handsome couple. Don't they, Lance?"

"They do," he agrees.

"We must do dinner," she announces, making my heart ache for her. How many people has she asked to dinner only to never get to follow through on the invitation?

"We're not here for dinner," I say. Her face falls, and it makes me feel like an absolute asshole. "Or at least not *just* dinner." I glance at Sutton questioningly. "But maybe we can make that work?"

She beams at me. "Wonderful! If only Yvette were here," she adds solemnly. "She makes the best roast chicken."

Sutton starts to answer, but I cut him off.

"We'll cook," I blurt out. "Tonight, I mean." I avoid Sutton's gaze, looking instead at the happy couple. "How about it?"

"Sure," Lance says.

Beside me, Sutton lets out a low growl.

"Sutton is an excellent cook," I add as much for them as for my own amusement.

"Wonderful. It's settled then." Victoria looks ready to burst with excitement.

Before Victoria can talk us into any more plans, Sutton speaks up. "Serenity and I have already had a long day," he says. "Give us some time to get settled in, and then we can talk more about dinner."

He gives me a pointed look that dares me to argue. But he's right. My skin hums with the remnants of energy still hanging around this place. I pretended not to recognize it when we walked in, but the longer I stand here, the more I know exactly what it is teasing at the edges of my awareness.

There's magic here.

More than a little bit.

It's not doing anything right now. More like the leftovers from something else. It achieved its goal, and now all that's left are the crumbs. I don't know how I can feel it, but I have a feeling killing Yvette changed more than just my body count.

Sutton doesn't react to it, and neither do Victoria and Lance. So I don't mention it. But I nod at Sutton's suggestion.

"We'll be close by whenever you're ready," Lance says, which honestly freaks me out if I think about it too hard. Can ghosts peep without you noticing?

They retreat back up the stairs, leaving Sutton and me alone. "Well," he says. "That was..."

"Creepy?"

I brace myself for some disembodied voice to complain about the insult. But everything is quiet. Even their footsteps have faded to nothing.

"So," he says, "You want to have a dinner party?"

"I want to find out what they know," I say, "About Yvette."

He looks a little more into the idea. "I'll text Jasper," he says, giving in. "Ask him to bring some groceries."

"Thank you."

"Come on," Sutton says, "Let's check out the house."

Sticking close to Sutton, I let him lead the way. Together, we wander through the first floor. Kitchen, sitting room, a tiny library, and a dining room complete the floor plan. Every room is cute and clean—and very normal looking. As if their owner wasn't a diabolical hundred-year-old witch-bitch.

We ascend the stairs slowly.

Sutton doesn't speak, probably because he's listening to our surroundings, seeking out anything that seems off. I don't speak because, if I do, my voice will probably give away my nerves.

But there's no one around.

Not in what used to be my room—which looks completely untouched since the moment I left it, right down to the dirty clothes on the floor. And not in any of the other guest rooms either.

In fact, none of them offer a shred of evidence Yvette ever lived here at all.

"This is weird," I say.

Sutton murmurs his agreement.

"Weirder than having to go through a dead woman's things," I add.

In the last bedroom, my eyes linger on a painting that is large enough to take up nearly the entire wall on my left. Its gilded frame is ornate and outdated. Something that belongs in a past century. And then there's the portrait itself. The woman looking back at us from the forest background is young and not exactly beautiful but commanding somehow with her sharp, austere nose and high cheekbones.

Her eyes are captivating. Whoever painted this was talented. It's almost as if she's looking right at me.

I turn away, shuddering at the thought. We have enough creepy creatures in this house.

Sutton meets my eyes. He wears a strange look.

"What is it?" I ask.

"Nothing." He shakes himself free of what worries him. I should press him for more, but I don't. For some reason, the idea of discussing our fears out loud in this room, in this house, doesn't seem wise.

I join him in the hall. Reaching out, he presses a rough, calloused hand to my cheek. "You're braver than you think, you know."

His words nearly mirror what Mable said to me earlier. "You really didn't know Mable was bringing me here?"

He shakes his head. "I wanted to keep you out of it."

"Even if it meant damning your entire pack? You didn't even know me."

"Ever since I saw your photo," he says, thumb stroking my cheek, "I knew I had to protect you. Even if it meant spending an eternity trapped in this hell."

"Is that your way of telling me I'm a pretty face?"

"That's part of it." He offers a smile that vanishes quickly.

"And the other part?"

"I don't know," he replies. "But I feel a pull to you. An unexplainable connection that makes me physically ache when you are not around." He leans down and presses his lips to mine. I lean into the kiss, absorbing every moment into the recesses of my memory.

Truthfully, I understand exactly what he means. Because even though it makes no sense, I feel the pull, too.

Sutton pulls back and smiles at me at the same moment my stomach growls. "Come on, let's get you some food."

He pulls me downstairs and opens the front door just as Jasper arrives with an armful of grocery bags.

"Someone call for a delivery?" he asks, a half-smile on his face.

"Thank you." I reach out and grab a few bags while Sutton gets the rest.

"Anytime. How's the place look?" Jasper asks.

"Nothing out of place," Sutton says. "In fact, we couldn't find a single personal item."

"Well, at least you have the run of the place," Jasper says with a shrug.

"It's strange, though, right?" I say. "She would have had clothes or something left behind."

"Maybe she hid her belongings," he says. "She had to know

you'd get in here eventually and poke around. Maybe she has things she didn't want found."

I don't have an answer for that.

"The team's here," Jasper tells Sutton. "We're doing a perimeter check, and then we'll run regular patrols."

"Sounds good," Sutton says.

Jasper turns and heads back outside as Sutton and I reach for the grocery bags and begin unpacking.

After stocking the kitchen in silence, Sutton begins putting together some sandwiches. It's all so normal, which makes it easy to pretend—if only for a moment—that we're not shacking up in the enemy's lair with a couple of dead people as roommates.

The normalcy is relaxing, and by the time we're finished putting things away, I'm stifling a yawn. The last twenty-four hours have included little sleep for...reasons. It's catching up with me.

After topping the sandwiches, Sutton turns and offers me a plate. "Snack then nap?"

"I'm in."

After we eat, I try like hell to sleep, but it doesn't happen. Putting aside the whole "ghost" thing is a lot harder than I thought it would be. Especially when I want so badly for Sutton to get me naked, but I'm not convinced we aren't being watched.

A four-way is just not something I'm interested in. Sharing has never really been my thing.

Sutton's ringtone breaks the silence, and he offers me a smile as he answers it. "Hey, Mable." Then, he slips out of the room and into the hall.

Climbing out of bed, I stare out the window of my former bedroom, noting the security team stationed at the edges of the yard. Cara is taking a few days off, which Sutton made sound like her idea, but the hard expression he wore when he told me has me wondering if he isn't a bit irritated with her about our attack the other night. I don't ask him about it. Not because I don't care, but there simply isn't time for one more problem to solve.

My thoughts drift to Lance and Victoria.

Their presence here is another problem we don't have time for. But I can't help wondering if they aren't cursed just as much as the rest of us. Stuck in this house, doomed to repeat the same day over and over again. It sounds so … empty. Or maybe I'm thinking of my own future stuck in this damned town.

The only difference is that, for me, time marches on. For Sutton, the world stands still. Someday, I'll grow old and die. While the man I love remains the same.

My heart is too bruised to break in this moment, but it will. Eventually.

The bedroom door opens, and I turn to see Sutton watching me. I look him over in a way I haven't done since before this nightmare of a day started. He's wearing dark jeans and a shirt that clings in all the right places. The stubble dotting his jawline and the wild, unkemptness of his hair thrill me. My stomach flips at the sight of him, at the way he watches me like I'm the center of it all. I still can't understand how the hell my hormones can continue working in the middle of all this chaos. But they do not seem deterred in the slightest that sex as a priority makes zero sense.

Lust is a nonsensical little she-devil.

"I'm going to the library to give Mable a hand with the questionnaires," he says.

My sexy daydreams are splashed with cold water. "Oh."

"Give me a hand?"

I bite my lip. "Help with the interrogations?"

He arches a brow. "You don't approve?"

"It's not that. I just... I'm not sure I'll be of much use. I don't know these people like you do." I take a deep breath and add, "I think I need to take some time to work on my magic."

Words I never thought I'd say.

He nods as if it's the most normal idea in the world.

I don't bother to mention the fact that I've been feeling its pull stronger than ever since the moment we stepped foot in this house. Or that I'm mostly concerned with the fact that I killed a woman last night, by accident if we're being technical. And I damn sure don't want that to happen again. Especially with someone I care about. Someone like Sutton.

He hesitates, clearly debating the wisdom of my proposal.

"Don't look at me like that," I say. "I'll be fine." He doesn't look convinced. "You have half a dozen wolves stationed outside, right?"

"Yes." He doesn't look satisfied. "I'll call for a few more. And two on each door."

I roll my eyes but don't argue. Not when I think about reversing the roles. He almost died last night, and I can still taste the panic and absolute devastation I felt in that moment. I don't want to put either of us through something like that again. Even if it means a whole army of babysitters.

"Fine, but you have to take your own entourage too," I say.

He seems to understand my thinking and nods. "Deal."

I meet him in the doorway, and he pulls me into his arms. I wind my arms up and around his neck, clinging tightly. For a moment, I let myself forget what waits for me outside the safety of his embrace. All that matters is Sutton's heartbeat against mine. My hands release and slide down his chest. Underneath my palms, I can feel the rise and fall of his chest.

He bends down and steals a lingering kiss.

When it's over, he presses his forehead to mine, his eyes closed.

"Be careful," he whispers. "I can't lose you."

I pull his mouth back to mine, my lips meeting his like a promise. "You won't."

Falls Gazette

Chapter Fourteen

With Sutton gone, the silence is deafening. I half-expect Victoria and Lance to pop up and invite me to dinner again or compliment my hair, but they're nowhere to be found. Their absence is eerie now that I know they never actually leave these grounds. The longer I stand around thinking about it, the creepier their non-presence becomes.

I look down at my hands, noting their heaviness.

The magic clings to them as if attracted like a magnet. The more I use it, the more aware of its presence I've become. It seems almost unbelievable that, up until a few weeks ago, I didn't know I was capable of magic. And now, since last night, I can't stop noticing how much of it my body contains.

The only disconnect has been how to access it deliberately. But now, I have a theory.

With a deep breath, I concentrate, calling to the parts of myself I tapped into before—when I used it on Yvette. The fear that fueled my determination. The desperation. The depth of my desire to protect my loved ones.

Emotion, overwhelming and nearly uncontrolled, wells up inside me.

Without warning, blue sparks shoot from my fingertips. A bolt of magic hits the vintage lamp beside my bed and sends it crashing to the floor, shattering the glass top into tiny pieces. I flinch then press my hand to my mouth to keep from screaming. Something about the noise against utter quiet is terrifying.

Shit. "Sorry! I knocked something over!" I call out, hoping it's enough to keep the guards at bay. Given their exceptional hearing, the last thing I need is one running into the room in the midst of a magical panic attack.

Rushing forward, I stop again when my feet crunch over the broken shards. I step back and look around, trying to think through my racing thoughts.

Emotion. That's the key. Except, if I can't control my feelings, how can I possibly hope to control my magic? Unfortunately, the only other magic user in this town is intent on destroying us all. Not exactly someone I can go to for lessons.

My search for a broom and dustpan leads me downstairs. I poke around the kitchen and closets and am elbow-deep in a pantry full of canned goods and cleaning supplies when I hear a voice behind me.

"Have you decided on a menu for dinner?"

I jump, hitting my head on a shelf, and stumble backward into the kitchen. My hip bumps the large kitchen island, and I nearly topple over. Straightening, I stare at Victoria, wide-eyed and full of adrenaline. Beside her, Lance shoots me an apologetic look.

"You nearly gave me a heart attack," I say, still catching my breath.

"Sorry about that." She pauses. When I start to move away, she holds up her hand. "Don't go!"

I halt.

Her shoulders sag. “I’m just glad for company. It gets lonely here.”

“Oh.” Of course it does. Once again, my heart pangs in empathy. What must it be like to be a ghost with no friends? “Okay.”

I move away from the pantry and look between them. If I’m going to share this place with them for the foreseeable future, I might as well get to know them. And maybe see what they know about Yvette in the process.

“So, how do you like Midnight Falls?” Victoria asks brightly.

“It’s … different.”

She grins knowingly.

Lance steps forward. “This might be easier if we lay our cards out a bit. We understand the residents in this town are … a bit more than human.”

“I see. Yes, that does make it easier.” I don’t know why I feel weird outing a bunch of supernatural creatures when Lance and Victoria are otherworldly beings themselves. “In that case, the real answer is this town is unlike anywhere else I’ve ever visited,” I admit.

“We totally agree,” Victoria says. “From the moment we arrived, we knew something was different here. Didn’t we, sweetie?”

“There was a certain feeling about this place,” Lance agrees.

“Were you two… I mean, before… were you human?” I ask.

“Yes,” Lance says. “We were human.”

“We didn’t know about the wolves here either, not until after we died,” Victoria says. She frowns. “And even then, it’s been a bit of a roller coaster re-learning the truth all the time.”

“You mean the memory loss,” I say tentatively, but she just laughs.

“Yvette keeps things so hush-hush, but there’s no need. Hell, I don't know I'm dead half the time sooo," she shrugs, "Your secrets are safe with me."

"Was that a thing before you died?"

"Umm, not to be funny, but I don't remember," Victoria admits, her expression completely serious.

I should probably win an Oscar for keeping a straight face at what is clearly not a joke—but also totally is.

"No," Lance answers for her. "The memory loss came after. Part of the trauma, I think, of our crossing over to this side of things."

"And the whole Groundhog Day thing?" I ask.

"It's Groundhog Day?" Victoria's eyes widen.

"Well, for you, I mean, with the whole repeating thing..." I trail off, realizing the repetitiveness is probably just due to Victoria's short-term memory and not actually repeating the same day over and over again.

"It's true," Lance says. "Every day feels much the same. We can't leave the property, and we have no one else for company other than the residents of this house."

"That must be hard," I say. "I wish there was a way to help free you from this loop. Give you back your memories. Maybe you could even move on or whatever."

"We're together," Lance replies, taking Victoria's hand in his. "Who knows where we'd be if we weren't here."

"Yeah, but, what if you could be together somewhere that's not this lonely house?"

Lance looks at me sharply, and I can tell he knows something's up with Yvette's absence. He doesn't ask, though, and I don't offer it. Not until I'm sure they aren't going to haunt my ass for eternity as punishment. For all I know, they were all besties.

Victoria smiles softly at Lance. "We're soulmates," she tells him. "No matter where we go, we'll be together."

He gazes lovingly at her. "I just want to be with you."

My eyes prick with tears. Their love, it breaks my heart. Those who claim love is easy are wrong. Things with Roscoe? They were easy—for a time. But then, that wasn't true love. I know that now. With Sutton, things are never easy. We are creatures from two different worlds on a collision course. The stronger my feelings become, the harder it gets to imagine a future where we're together and happy.

As for Victoria and Lance, their love wasn't even given a chance before they were robbed of a future. It's heartbreaking and incredibly unfair. While I understand Lance wanting to stay with Victoria, what comes next has to be better than this endless loop, right?

"Do you really think you can help us?" Victoria asks. "A change of scenery would be nice," she adds, more to Lance.

He frowns but doesn't argue.

"Maybe. I mean, I'm happy to try." I may not have been able to break the curse, but surely helping a couple of ghosts move on is something I can manage. After all, there are fewer stakes with this one, right? And if I can help them, then perhaps it will atone for at least some of my failures.

Even if I know they will weigh on me for the rest of my life. However long that might be.

"Do you have time now?" Victoria asks, eyes lighting up.

"Sure, I—"

"Your husband left," Lance says; a statement, not a question.

"He's not my husband." My cheeks heat, and I look away.

"I see. You're here alone then."

For some reason, the way he says it puts me on edge. I straighten, squaring my shoulders. "There are men posted at all the doors. Probably listening and watching right now."

"Forgive me, I only meant..." He exchanges a look with Victoria, who seems to actually know what he's thinking. "We want to show you something."

"Okay," I say.

Victoria claps her hands in excitement.

"This way." He leads the way back upstairs, and I follow.

As we walk, I notice the way their feet click against the floor—the sound is so corporeal. It's weird. Part of me wants to ask them how it works, becoming solid and then... not. But before I can figure out how to do it without insulting them again, Lance stops in front of a door at the end of the hall.

"In here," he says.

It's the room at the end of the hall. The one with the larger-than-life portrait from earlier. I follow him inside, purposely averting my eyes from the woman on the canvas.

The magic is thicker in here. My skin tingles with it.

"Not much to see in here," I say, mostly as an excuse to hurry up and get the hell out.

The vibe in here is "creepy Victorian chic," and I'm not here for it.

"No," he agrees. "Yvette hid her personal spaces well."

That gets my attention. I watch as he crosses the room and opens a wardrobe.

"Hid?" I echo, confused.

He doesn't answer except to retrieve something from the wardrobe. He turns back to me and holds out a thick, leather-bound book.

"Where did you find it?"

"There. A false bottom." He gestures to the wardrobe shelf and I look from there back to the book he's holding out.

"What's this?" I ask.

He hesitates. I glance from him to Victoria, whose cheeks have gone pink with some sort of embarrassment.

"What's going on?" I ask.

"We heard you," Lance admits. "Earlier. With your— With Sutton."

"What did you hear?" I ask, instantly wary. Were they spying on us, after all? Gross. We're going to have a talk about boundaries.

"You've come into your magic," he says. "And you need help controlling it."

My eyes narrow. "What the hell do you know about my magic?"

He smirks, the little shit. "You're not the only one we've heard inside these walls, Serenity."

My heart beats a little faster. "Yvette."

He nods. "We know she wielded magic. And that you do too."

"We heard her talking about you," Victoria admits. "On the phone."

"What did she say about me?"

"At the end, she was afraid of you. Afraid of what you might be capable of. It must mean you're very powerful." He glances at Victoria again. "You said before that you wanted to help us. Maybe this book can help us all."

The book. Right.

I look down and brush off the dust that's begun to gather across the cover. Underneath is a symbol. A five-point star inside a circle. My hands tremble as I trace its lines. I suck in a breath and crack open the cover. Inside, Yvette's name is scrawled on the first page. I flip through, surprised to see most of the pages are blank, like a journal. The ones with writing are handwritten, and I can only assume Yvette herself put this together.

"What is it?" I ask, scanning some of the entries she left behind.

They read like instructions.

"She called it a grimoire," Lance says.

I look up at him sharply. There's no trace of deception, but then again, I'm not an expert on dead people's facial expressions.

A grimoire. I've watched Charmed enough times to know that basically means this is a witch's spellbook. If so, maybe Lance is right. Maybe Yvette left enough instruction in these pages to teach me how to use my magic.

I page through, faster now, scanning for some entry that's about me or about magic in general. Harnessing it, controlling it, maybe even getting rid of it. I don't necessarily want to give up the one thing I have to defend myself, but I also can't afford to harm anyone I love with it either. However, there's nothing quite as obvious as all that.

Instead, the pages are filled with specific spells ranging from simple to complex. How to bring a plant back from the brink of death. How to glamour an item by hiding it in plain sight. How to conjure a cat. The further I go, the more complex the spells become.

Maybe learning how to do some of these will help me understand my magic. If nothing else, practice makes perfect. I stop on a page titled "Release the Soul" and scan more quickly.

"Ooh, what did you find?" Victoria asks, noting my interest.

She comes to stand over my shoulder, and I try not to react to the fact that I can see her plain as day but there's zero sensation of physical presence. Not even a brush of her shirt against my arm. Apparently, her energy level is at zero.

I will never get used to this.

"Release the soul and set it free, As I will, so mote it be." Victoria sings the words like it's a child's rhyme, but my entire body reacts with an awareness that leaves me breathless and swaying on my feet.

The magic in the room seems to ripple.

I look from her to Lance. "This is it," I say. "If I can do this spell for you, maybe it'll free you from being stuck here."

A faint flair of hope lights in Lance's eyes. Victoria squeals and jumps up and down, clapping her hands in excitement. "Oh, that sounds so fun," she says. "Then maybe we can go to that fancy dinner place."

Lance's expression softens as he looks at his wife.

"And maybe it'll restore her memories," I say quietly. "For good."

He nods, expression tight. "Let's give it a go."

Lance helps me find and gather the items listed. A candle. A bowl full of water. Chalk. Every one of them is hidden inside this room. False bottoms in the drawers. A loose floorboard with a hole underneath. I have no idea how they just know where things are. Nothing better to do than spy on Yvette, apparently. I don't think too hard about it, though. I'm too busy reading over the instructions so that I'll feel mildly prepared for what I'm about to do.

Then again, what can possibly prepare a girl for her first spell?

Yvette's words are clear and concise, and I'm weirdly grateful. With such clear instructions, hopefully not much can go wrong. Still, I can't help worrying I'm about to send the future into some twisted version of itself. This isn't Practical Magic, I remind myself. I'm not manipulating anyone. I'm doing a good deed. Offering inner peace or whatever.

Following the spell's instructions, I use the chalk to draw a circle around me and the items I've gathered. Halfway through, I catch sight of the painting again and pause, wishing we'd picked a better location. Above me, straight ahead, hangs the woman whose eyes still seem to follow my every move. But we've come this far. I'm not going to derail us because of some dumb painting.

With a steadying breath, I begin.

The words are simple, the steps straightforward. I light a candle then dip my finger in the bowl and let it drop onto the floor. Then I recite the words. Over and over again until the magic that lingers in the room begins gathering itself to me. My hands grow heavy. Full of energy. Finally, a spark lights underneath my skin. The floor creaks, and the furniture shakes, and I have to swallow a scream because, hello, this is the kind of shit horror movies are made of.

Lance and Victoria step to the edge of the circle and join hands. Victoria grins at me. Lance looks desperate with hope.

There's a sound like something ripping, and I look past the ghostly couple to the painting.

The canvas has been torn in two. The halves hang loose now, blowing in the creepy-ass wind that gusts through the room. The problem isn't the fact that it's torn itself open, though.

Panic lodges in my throat as I realize the woman in the painting is gone.

Footsteps sound behind Lance, and he whirls, moving aside to reveal the absolute creepiest fucking thing I've seen yet. The woman from the painting is solid and alive—and standing directly in front of me.

Lance takes one look at her, and he and Victoria vanish.

My jaw drops.

Holy shit.

They just...did that.

I turn back to the woman. Holy shit, *I* just did *that.*

Her mouth curves in a smile that looks faker than a pair of newly purchased knockoff knockers.

"Well, can't say I expected you to do me that particular favor," she says haughtily, smoothing her dress and patting her hair as if she's just freshening up rather than coming to life. "But thank you, all the same, I guess."

I pick my jaw up off the floor long enough to ask, "Who the hell are you?"

She cocks her head as if surprised I don't already know the answer. "I'm Tabitha Augustus. Sutton's fated mate."

Falls Gazette

Chapter Fifteen

I stare at the ghostly form standing before me. You have got to be fucking kidding me. This cannot be real. I close my eyes, picture her gone, and open them again—only to see that she's still here and wearing the same sadistic smile from moments before.

Son of a mother fucking crackerjack. Did I help Victoria and Lance move on? No. Did I summon Sutton's ex-girlfriend? Fuck yes, I did. No, not even a girlfriend. His crazy, obsessed, psycho stalker and the very reason this entire town was cursed in the first place.

How the hell do I keep making things worse? I swear, if ever there were an award for situation escalator, I would win the grand prize, hands down.

I clear my throat. "It's, um, nice to meet you."

"I'm sure." She grins at me then begins to move about the room, her old-fashioned heels clicking against the hardwood floor. "I have to say, I'm quite surprised you are the one who freed me. I never would have expected aid from you, Serenity."

"How do you know my name?"

"I know quite a bit about you." She glances back at the ripped painting. "Wasn't much else to do but listen to my aunt gossip with my mother."

Aunt. Mother.

She means Yvette and Myrtle.

She's telling the truth.

My gaze travels to the torn canvas then back to her, and I groan. No fucking wonder Sutton was caught off guard by the woman in the painting. The last time he saw her, she was dead.

Sutton. He is *never* going to leave me alone again when he realizes I accidentally summoned his stalker.

"How are you here? *Why* are you here?"

"You summoned me," she replies, almost aggravated she has to explain it. Well, excuse the fuck out of me. Summoning spirits is not exactly something I do every damned Tuesday.

"And what does that mean, exactly?" I ask.

With an eye roll, she explains, "You freed my soul from the confines of that bloody painting." She spits the last word. At my raised brows, she explains, "Mother has a sick sense of humor when it comes to punishments."

"Are you saying your own mother killed you then imprisoned you in a piece of wall art?"

"Are you doubting her cruelty?" Tabitha demands.

"Not at all. Only her ability."

I've been a victim of Myrtle's handiwork for long enough. Still, what Tabitha is suggesting tops everything I've experienced so far. Then again, if I was ever tempted to feel sorry for this girl, her answering snarl squashes it.

"My mother is incredibly powerful," she says, rage contorting her expression. Then she blinks, and her anger cools, replaced by a calculating suspicion. "But so, it seems, are you."

"Whatever, look, you're free now. Move on. Go into the light or however it works."

She cocks her head to the side and studies me with scrutiny. "Why would I do that?"

"Because you're dead."

"That is nothing but a small hurdle for a love as true as mine." She moves across the room, gliding elegantly toward a writing desk in the corner. My gaze drops to the sharp letter opener gathering dust.

Can she hurt me?

Victoria has occasionally touched me…Lance shook Sutton's hand. What if—"True love knows no limits," she coos. Her fingers pass directly through the letter opener, so I breathe a sigh of relief. Seems you have to be dead-alive for a hot minute before you get that particular party trick.

"Love?" I snort, feeling a bit less threatened now.

Her eyes darken, and she bares her teeth. "I saw him kiss you earlier."

Oops. Here's hoping ghost bitches can't throw hands. "And your point is?"

"Sutton is not yours."

"He's not yours, either."

Tabitha snarls, her eyes glistening with the challenge I'm apparently giving her. "You truly have no idea what you've gotten yourself into, have you?" Moving forward, she stops mere feet from me, right on the edge of the chalk-drawn circle.

And since I'm not one to back down from a challenge—a personality trait I'm seriously starting to see as a flaw—I get to my feet and stand my ground. "If you're trying to intimidate me, it won't work."

"Intimidation?" She barks out a laugh. "There is no need to

intimidate you, witch, because you don't have a chance with him. He is mine. It has been written so."

This bitch is crazy. Straight up fucking nuts. Bonkers. Elevator doesn't go to the top floor. Lights are on but no one is home. "Isn't that the kind of psycho-babble that got you killed in the first place?"

"Did you ever hear the story of how I met my love?" she questions, tone almost wistful as though revisiting a happy memory.

"You mean the story of how you became obsessed with a man who never wanted you?"

She arches a perfectly shaped dark eyebrow. "Never wanted me? Is that so?" Tabitha bites down on her bottom lip and smiles, making my skin crawl. "Our paths crossing was not mere coincidence, little witch."

Good, we can add condescending to the crazy. "Oh, no?"

"In my family tomes, a prophecy was written. I stumbled across it in my studies of our ancestors. It was a long entry, a list of prophecies that had already come to pass about our family line. I'd tried my best to ignore it more than once, uninterested in boring historical accounts. But when I finally sat down to read it, I realized the end of it held a future prophecy; something that hadn't yet come to pass. And that prophecy was about me and Sutton."

"Give me a break," I say, rolling my eyes.

She ignores my interruption. "'The true mate of the Hargrave Alpha is the daughter of my line,'" she quotes, and my stomach drops.

The fuck?

Tabitha goes on while I wrap my head around what she's saying. "Since his father was already mated, it was simple enough to realize it was the son mentioned rather than the father. After all, he was destined to be Alpha, was he not?"

She begins to pace, and I watch her with wide, desperate eyes. I can't possibly let myself accept her crazy-ass claim.

"Even if what you're telling me is the truth, it could have been anyone in Sutton's line," I say. "Could have been Sutton's great-great-grandchild it referred to." I cling to that because surely she is *not* the true mate of *my* Sutton. She can't be.

"I considered that. But I was curious, so I went out looking. I waited in the woods outside their manor, watching, biding my time until, finally, he stepped out. So handsome." She stops pacing and presses both hands to her heart, practically swooning. "It was then I *knew* he was mine. It was then that I gave him my heart."

Okay, time to bring out the big guns to shut this insanity down. "I hate to break it to you, but Sutton never loved you."

Her eyes harden, and the floor beneath her feet creaks as if she's actually influencing physical reality with her anger. "He would have. But his mother..." She trails off, a snarl on her lips. "That bitch kept getting in the way."

I very much doubt that, but antagonizing an already insane ghost seems like it wouldn't be the smartest of ideas. "And why did she keep doing that?"

"I sent him letters, but his mother always intercepted them. She hid them so he wouldn't see."

"Sutton saw those letters, Tabitha. Hell, I've seen them."

She glares at me. "Those were not meant for you." And she completely glazes over the fact that I just told her Sutton did, in fact, see the letters. And that he chose to ignore them.

"You made a mistake," I tell her. "You misread, misinterpreted. It happens. In fact, I suggest you check out a movie called, He's Just Not That Into You. It might explain some things."

"I did not misinterpret," she hisses. "I am Sutton's fated mate. I am his, and he is mine. The great Seers of my ancestors foretold it."

"No—"

"I certainly hope you enjoyed your time with him, witch. Because it is over."

Below, a door slams. "Serenity?" Sutton calls out, and I freeze.

Tabitha lights up like a fucking bulb at the sound of his voice. Then, she turns to me. "I'll be seeing you soon, Serenity. Thank you for my second chance."

She disappears the same way Victoria and Lance did, leaving me staring at the place she vacated. Sutton's footsteps thud on the stairs as they carry him closer to me.

Oh fuck.

Oh shit.

What the hell am I going to do? Attempting to buy myself more time, I rush out into the hall before he can see the destroyed painting and chalked up floor. He looks exhausted. Completely and utterly worn down, which makes me feel even more like shit.

Because I'm about to make it a whole lot worse.

"How did the interrogations go?" I ask, the sound of my voice more high-pitched than usual.

He sighs. "I don't know why I expected them to yield anything. They never have before as I understand it."

"I'm so sorry."

He shrugs. "Eventually, she'll have to show herself. I just hate not being able to do anything. Inaction drives me mad."

Ugh. Wait 'til he hears about *my* action.

"How's Phineas?"

He looks physically pained. "Frustrated. Listen, until we know for sure who we can trust, it's just us, Serenity. You and me. We're the only ones we can be sure are not Myrtle."

"You think she's taken your dad?"

"I think anything is possible. And I want to be even more careful from here on out. We should have been cautious from the beginning. I never should have let you go out without me." He pinches the bridge of his nose.

"I took care of myself."

"But you shouldn't have had to." He moves forward and opens his mouth to speak again but then closes it again as his gaze drifts past me to the door I left open. Eyes narrowed, he walks into the bedroom. The moment he turns to the destroyed painting, his body tenses. "What the hell happened in here?"

"Listen. Before you get mad—"

Sutton whirls on me. "The guards said they heard and saw nothing out of the ordinary, which means I know this wasn't an attack—or was it?" He rushes forward. "Are you okay?"

"No, not an attack." *At least, not a physical one. I did, however, get a mini lashing for having my tongue down your throat.* "I'm fine. Promise."

Sutton crosses his arms. "Then what the hell happened? What is this symbol drawn on the floor? Why is the painting destroyed?"

"So you know how Lance and Victoria are stuck here?"

"Yes."

"Well, Lance brought me up here to show me where Yvette kept her belongings." Bending over, I retrieve the book of spells I dropped onto the floor. I show it to him, but he doesn't reach for it. "He showed me this. It's apparently a—"

"Grimoire," Sutton finishes. "All witch families have them."

I decide not to hate on him for knowing something I didn't.

"Yes, well, there's a spell in here to free a trapped soul."

Sutton's mouth falls open, and he gapes at me. "Tell me you did not practice magic when you have no idea how to actually use it?"

"How else am I supposed to learn?"

"For fuck's sake, Serenity!" He throws his hands in the air and turns away from me for a moment. When he faces me again, he's more composed. "Please tell me you were at least successful. Tell me that we're the only ones in this house now."

I bite down on my lip. "I mean, the spell did technically work."

"Serenity."

“I might have accidentally freed a soul I didn’t mean to free. But to be fair, I didn’t know she was trapped!”

He looks about two seconds away from losing his shit. A bomb about to go off, Sutton stares at me and then looks at the painting. It’s when his gaze returns to me that his face loses color. “Tell me it’s not her. Please, for the love of everything, tell me you did not free the same woman who was in that painting."

"Tabitha says hi.” My attempt at a joke is completely pointless, and I hate myself for making it the moment the words leave my lips.

Sutton explodes. He whirls around and slams his fist into the wall. The wooden boards crack beneath the strength of his hit and he turns to face me. Chest heaving, he takes one deep breath then another, finally gaining composure. “Tabitha’s alive.”

“Not alive, exactly. She’s a specter like Lance and Victoria.” He glares, but I keep going. “She was trapped in that painting. Apparently, it was her punishment from Myrtle for causing all of this. Which, by the way, you could have mentioned it was her when you saw it!”

“So, this is *my* fault?”

“No. That’s not what I’m saying.”

“Fine.” He forces out an exhale, but I can tell it’s not helping him calm down. “You freed her. And now she’s what—gone?”

I wince. “Not exactly.”

“You do realize that you just set loose the soul of a woman who has more reason than Myrtle to want you dead, right?”

“I do realize that, yes. And obviously, had I known it was a possibility, I wouldn’t have done it!”

Sutton shakes his head and closes his eyes for a brief moment. “She is a ghost, correct?”

“Yes.”

“And she didn’t harm you, which likely means she can’t.”

“No. I don’t believe so. At least not right now.”

"But at some point, it could be a very real possibility." His gaze narrows on me.

"Yes."

"Shit, Serenity." Sutton takes a deep breath. "Her not attacking you means she's an annoyance, not a problem. At least, not yet." He sighs. "Are you okay?"

I don't even mention the prophecy, though it stays in the back of my mind. I don't want to believe it, but I'm a reporter, which means I also know my denial doesn't make it false.

No. Tabitha is nuts. There is no way it's the truth. It can't be.

"I'm fine," I lie. "Just a bit shaken. Not every day you run into the ex-stalker of the guy you're sleeping with." Sutton looks unconvinced, but there isn't anything either of us can do about it now. "So, how about that dinner with our friendly neighborhood specters?"

Falls Gazette

Chapter Sixteen

Dinner with Lance and Victoria is strained. No one wants to talk about Tabitha or my failed attempt to help free my ethereal friends. To be honest, I'm surprised they showed up after bailing on me the moment Tabitha popped off the painting.

Either way, it's an awkward evening, and before we've even made it to dessert, I feign a headache. We end the night early with a promise to do it again soon. Something that'll probably happen sooner rather than later since, chances are, Victoria won't remember any of this tomorrow anyway.

Though, at least, they had time to confirm our suspicions. All Tabitha needs is to re-generate her spiritual energy and learn to concentrate. Then, she goes from annoyance to threat. Yet another problem we need to deal with.

As Sutton and I clean up the kitchen, it's all I can do not to jump out of my own skin every few minutes.

So far, Tabitha hasn't appeared, and I can only hope she stays away. But my movements are jerky, my nerves frayed, as I wait and wonder for the moment she'll pop up.

Sutton's silence feels deliberate. I'm still not sure where we stand after our argument earlier, but I can't stop thinking about what Tabitha said. And I can't stop wondering if she's listening right now.

A moment later, Sutton's arm brushes my elbow, and I yelp, dropping a clean plate back into the soapy water.

"Sorry," he murmurs then peers sharply at me. "You okay?"

"Just a little jumpy," I admit.

He frowns.

"Let's go upstairs," he says, taking my hand and pulling me toward the stairs.

"But, the dishes," I begin.

"I'll finish them tomorrow."

With a sigh, I let him lead me up the stairs and into our bedroom. I hesitate, unsure about changing when it's highly possible I have an invisible audience. Sutton's crumbling manor house sounds cozy as hell right about now. At least there, the only occupants are corporeal.

Sutton, apparently, doesn't give nearly as many fucks about it. He sheds his clothes and crawls beneath the covers, motioning for me to do the same. I change quickly into an oversized shirt and sleep shorts and join him, grateful for the warmth of his body.

He wraps his arms around me, holding me close, and I breathe him in, shutting out everything else.

"I'm sorry I yelled at you," he murmurs against my hair.

I melt a little. "Me too," I whisper. "It's not your fault."

"It's not yours either." He strokes my hair. "We're going to figure this out, Serenity. And I will keep you safe, I swear it."

There are so many reasons to poke holes in that promise, but I don't. Instead, I shut my eyes and pretend he can hold up his end.

Just before I drift off, I swear I hear soft laughter echoing through the walls.

A HARD BODY PRESSES AGAINST MINE, SCOOTING IN CLOSE TO SPOON me from behind. I'm not even fully awake as I scoot reflexively closer to the hardness pressing against my ass.

"Mmm," Sutton hums, his voice low and delicious against my ear.

His arms tighten around me so there's no space left between us at all.

My desire wakes me fully, and I tense against him. His hand, moving lazily over my hip, stills.

"What is it?" he asks.

Oh, nothing, just the idea of your crazy-ass ex-stalker watching us has me drier than the Sahara.

"I just … can't," I say, my own blue balls leaving me irritated at myself for those two words.

But Sutton just relaxes and continues to cuddle me. "It's okay," he says quietly.

I can feel how very much it is not okay, but I'm grateful he lets it go. The minute I stop caring whether ghosts watch me climax is probably the minute I join the crazy-pants category along with so many other residents of this town. Then again, if Sutton keeps waking me up like this, I'll probably give in sooner rather than later.

The man has a way with his hands.

Finally, he peels himself away to shower and dress. I groan, hating myself for my own sense of propriety, but the longer I'm left alone, the easier it gets to think about something else besides Sutton's chiseled abs and impressive... gifts.

Inevitably, I think of Myrtle. And Tabitha. And how much I

need to figure out a way to stop them both. Or, at least, lift this curse that has me trapped here inside their personal brands of torture. But the more I consider leaving, the harder it is for me to see a future for myself anywhere other than Midnight Falls. Or with anyone other than Sutton Hargrave beside me.

My gaze drifts to the door where he's showering. And I realize —what if he's not alone in there? Jumping out of bed, I rush toward the door and open it before scanning the room for any ghost bitches. While there is nothing but steam, I do notice a shape appearing on the mirror as if someone drew it there before the shower came on.

Stomach full of rocks, I move forward and glare at the single heart drawn on the mirror. I didn't do this, which means ghost bitch did.

"Coming in to join me?"

I glance back at Sutton as he peers around the curtain, hair wet, a grin on his face. "I think Tabitha was spying on you."

He looks to the mirror and arches a brow. "Maybe you should come in to protect me."

It takes me a moment longer than it should to realize he's messing with me. My nerves dissipate, and I fight the urge to punch him. "You asshole."

But Sutton's grin is worth every moment of misplaced anger. "You are the one who released her, darling. Consider that payback."

"Definitely not getting in there with you now," I reply with a grin as I turn and saunter out of the bathroom, shaking my ass with a bit more effect than normal.

Take that.

Nearly ten minutes later, Sutton re-emerges, dressed and ready for the day—whatever it holds. I watch from the bed as he gathers his things and puts on his shoes.

"You're leaving?" I ask.

"I'm going to check in with Mable. See if she has any books that might help us un-do your, uh, trick yesterday."

"Okay."

"Join me?"

"Maybe later. I'm going to read through Yvette's grimoire and see if there's anything I missed. I promise not to attempt anything until you get back," I add before he can argue.

He nods. "The security teams are doubled up just until I get back," he adds. "Will you be okay?"

"I'll be fine." I have a house full of ghosts watching my every move. "Not like I'm alone here."

He bends toward me and presses a kiss to my forehead. "Be careful."

I frown as he walks out, knowing full well he means I shouldn't try any more magic while he's gone. The fact that he's probably right irritates me enough that I form an idea. If I can't use Yvette's grimoire, that means I need a different sort of teacher. And if Myrtle, Tabitha, and Yvette are all from the same family line, and they are all witches, that means it's very possible there's another witch in my family too.

Reaching for my phone, I dial the one person who might know something. She answers immediately.

"Serenity!"

"Hey, Mom. How are you?"

"Me? How are you? I was beginning to wonder if you fell off the face of the earth."

I cringe. "I know, I'm sorry I haven't been great about keeping in touch."

"It's okay. I just want you to focus on yourself for once, sweetie. You deserve that after everything with, well, you know."

"You can say his name, Mom. Roscoe."

"Right. I didn't want to upset you."

"Believe me, I've gotten past it."

"So I hear." The smile in her voice is evident, and I groan. Steven.

"Ugh, what has that bastard told you?"

"Your brother simply mentioned that you met someone. I think it's great, honey. Truly. Even if it's just a passing—what do you kids call it?—rebound bang."

"Mom!" My cheeks flush, and she laughs into the phone.

"Seriously, honey, I am happy for you."

"I cannot believe you just said rebound bang. You've been listening to Sawyer too much."

"I'm no prude, my dear. How do you think you and your brothers got here?"

"And now I might vomit."

She laughs again, clearly proud of herself. "So, this time away has been helping, I take it."

"I'm focusing on myself," I say, using her words because it's safer than trying to describe what's actually going on.

"I'm so glad. You deserve all the happiness, sweetheart."

"Thanks." I take a deep breath. *Here we go.* "Hey, can I ask you a question?"

"Anything."

"Well, I have a friend who is kind of into the whole genealogy thing, and she thinks her ancestors were involved in the witch trials. Do we have anything like that in our family line?"

"Witch trials, wow, that's interesting."

It's a horrible lie, but it's the only one I could think of that wouldn't raise a red flag with her. My dad is a total history buff, so this, at least, will feel semi-normal to bring up.

"I'd have to ask your father but—"

"Ask me what?" his muffled voice echoes through the line.

"Oh, hold on." There's a shuffling sound, and then the audio changes a bit to sound hollow. "You're on speaker, dear. Now what was the question?" my mother asks.

I repeat my rehearsed lines, and this time, my dad answers. "I'm not aware of any witch trial affiliations," he says. "Our people came over from Ireland sometime in the nineteenth century, so I think we missed out on all that. What's your friend's family name, and maybe I can dig something up."

"Oh, you don't have to do that," I say.

"Your father thrives on these things, Ser, you know that," my mom says.

"It's just a silly idea," I say, "nothing to trouble yourself with, seriously. I just loved the idea of a real witch in the family."

I laugh it off, my attempt dry, but my mother is way more amused. She chuckles hard enough to make it clear she thinks this is weird and says, "Someone's been binging Charmed again."

"Right." I sigh, forcing out a response that will placate her and end this topic. "The reboot isn't the same."

"It never is," she agrees.

For some reason, her words hit me like a punch in the gut. I tell them I love them and hang up the phone. In the silence, all I can think about is my mother's response: *It never is.* Her words echo in my head, haunting me long after the call is ended. I turn the words over in my mind, trying to figure out why they're bothering me so much.

Finally, I realize with a sad jolt, it's me.

I'm the reboot.

Trying to pretend I'm as good or better for Sutton than Tabitha. But what if that prophecy is right? What if she really is his fated mate? I've read about mates before. Mostly fiction novels like Julie Trettel or Jaymin Eve. In those stories, every single mate is a destined pair. No one can tear them apart, not even a magical curse-casting bitch with the power of a hundred years in her hands.

Not even me.

My chest pangs, and the ache I feel is a bleak acceptance.

I want to weep for myself, for the loss of a man I never really had to begin with. I can't help but lick my wounds and silently curse Tabitha for being the cause of my heartbreak. That makes twice now I've lost the man I cared about to another woman. I won't make it three.

Maybe for me, love is off the table.

Maybe it was never on the table to begin with.

The only thing I have left is my magic. And even without a destiny that involves Sutton and me together, I know I can't forsake the people of this town who've been cursed. Nor can I sit back and let Tabitha haunt me forever—literally and physically.

If anything, her presence here only makes me more determined to end this curse and get the hell out of this place forever. If I can't have Sutton, I have to walk away. Living here with him every day, knowing she's the one who's meant to have him, is a torture worse than anything Myrtle could do to me now.

I have to master my magic. I have to break free. And I have to say goodbye to the only man I've ever loved. Battling a witch is one thing; battling fate is another.

SUTTON DOESN'T COME HOME FOR LUNCH. HE CALLS TO CHECK IN, and I can hear the worry and strain in his voice. Mable has nothing helpful for learning about my magic. But I know that's not the worry he fears most. It's been two days since Myrtle killed Harriet and used her blood to reset the wards. Two days of waiting for whatever it is she's going to try next. The longer she remains silent, the more worried he gets.

And the more desperate I feel to learn something that might help.

I shower and then settle back into bed with Yvette's grimoire. If nothing else, it can offer insight into the mind of a witch—even if she was batshit crazy. At this point, the list of who isn't insane in this town is shorter than the list of who is.

But two hours later, my eyes blur with exhaustion and I've learned nothing helpful. Sure, I could probably cast a spell to conjure a black cat, but none of the spells listed here can actually defeat someone like Myrtle.

I'm out of ideas and, I have a feeling, nearly out of time.

A creak sounds somewhere in the house, and I jerk toward the bedroom door. It remains closed. No more sounds follow. My heart thuds, and I brace myself for someone to just pop up in the middle of my room. But no one appears.

"Fuck this," I grumble and toss back the covers.

The moment my feet touch the floor, a single sheet of paper flutters before me. I snatch it out of midair, angry at the way Tabitha is clearly taunting me with her presence.

"What the hell is this?" I demand.

No answer.

I scan the paper, expecting a death threat or some other thinly veiled psycho-babble. But it's not. In fact, it has nothing to do with me at all. My heart sinks lower as I read it once then a second time, trying to convince myself I've misunderstood. But there's no mistaking the words printed on the page. I turn it over, noting the handwritten scrawl on the other side too.

Tabitha's family name.

Augustus.

Dated the eighth of January, 1745.

"I have seen many things with the Sight of the Goddess. Here be one. An Augustus daughter fated to mate a Hargrave son. The alpha

must choose his own destiny, but beware, son of beasts. If you refuse her, you will be destroyed by your rejection. The only way to be truly whole is if you accept the love freely given."

It's a journal entry of some sort.

Written by a woman named Constance.

And maybe I would have chucked it straight into the garbage if it didn't confirm Tabitha's screwed-up claims about Sutton being her mate.

The longer I stare at the words on the page, the sicker I feel.

Another creak sounds. This one from the hall. She's close, that bitch. Laughter echoes off the walls, and I snap. Folding the paper, I stuff it into my pockets and lace my shoes up. If Tabitha can't leave, I will. I'm getting out of this house. Now.

Falls Gazette

Chapter Seventeen

For the first time in what feels like forever, I run.

My shoes hit the soft ground with barely audible thuds as I move through the trees, my arms pumping. Behind me, the security team follows—close enough that I feel safe but far enough they can't see the tears steadily streaming down my cheeks.

All of this is too much.

I never wanted to carry the weight of the world on my shoulders. I was content with my little slice of life. But now that I've tasted Sutton? That I've become a part of something so much bigger than myself? How the hell am I supposed to go back to normal?

How am I supposed to move on without him?

My chest tightens, a vise that steadily squeezes the life from me.

A few miles in, I realize I have no idea where I am anymore. Glancing back, I see the security team still keeping up. Pressing on, I leap over a small fallen branch and push out into a clearing.

Removing the earbuds from my ears, I gape at the huge waterfall just ahead. It spills down into a crystal pool of water that laps softly at the bank. The sound of water roaring as it crashes drowns out even the heavy beat of my own heart.

I take note of the security team just inside the tree line before moving closer to the water and taking a seat. Drawing my knees to my chest, I tuck my face and do something I almost never do—I cry.

I cry for the woman I was, the naïve, heartbroken woman who ran away from her pain and straight into a nightmare. And I cry for the love I found here, love that will never amount to anything more than time well spent.

It can't.

Tabitha made me see that.

Even if we find a way to break this curse and free ourselves from Myrtle's torture, Tabitha's prophecy will remain. The fact is Sutton's destined for someone else. Maybe it is Tabitha, maybe not. But it's not me. And I refuse to hold him back from his true destiny.

This has to end. Now or later.

A hand goes to my back, and I sniffle, blinking back more tears. Sutton's scent fills my lungs as he sits beside me, remaining silent.

My mom always told me that crying was okay. That falling down was normal. But that once you do, you have to pull yourself back up. *Do not remain on the floor, Serenity,* she'd tell me. So, after a few moments, I take a deep, steadying breath, and lift my face to look out over the water.

"I forgot how beautiful this place is," Sutton says.

I glance around and realize the security team has vanished.

"Where are the others?" I ask.

"I sent them away."

His strong fingers trail down the side of my face before he grips my chin and turns my face so I look at him. His hazel eyes are full of questions—that much is easy enough to see. Gaze narrowed on my face, he strokes my cheek. "What is it? Did something happen?"

Pulling away from him, I shake my head.

"Then what is it?"

Shoving up, I get to my feet and cross my arms to keep the traitorous limbs from reaching for him. My chest constricts, my throat burning with emotion. "Did you know there's a prophecy written about you? About your mate?"

His jaw tightens, telling me all I need to know.

"You did," I whisper. "You knew, and you let me—" Closing my eyes against the tears, I try to keep at least a slice of composure amongst the heartbreak. "You knew," I repeat.

"It's a bunch of bullshit." He steps toward me, and I retreat.

"No."

"Serenity, Tabitha used that to try and draw me in. My mother—"

"So your mother did have a hand in keeping you apart?"

"She didn't want Tabitha to use it as a way to manipulate me into a relationship I didn't want. It's a lie, Serenity. Just like everything else she says."

"Tabitha certainly believes it's true," I tell him, and he turns away for a moment, muttering something under his breath I cannot quite make out.

He turns back to me, pain and accusation in his eyes. "So something else did happen."

"Actually, Tabitha filled me in on the fact that she is destined for you yesterday."

"Now who's keeping secrets?" he shoots back.

"It's not a secret if you already knew it."

"There's no proof—"

"Oh? Then what's this?" Reaching into the small pocket on my leggings, I withdraw the folded piece of paper. "Go ahead, Sutton, take a look."

He takes it from me and carefully unfolds it, his expression hardening as he reads the words scrawled on the paper. The words that cement what Tabitha has been telling him.

"Do you have any idea what this means? If it's true—"

"It's not!" he roars, crumpling it in his hands. "It's not true." But I can see the hesitation on his face, the brief instant in which even he is questioning its validity.

"If it is, though," I choke out, "You denying her could be what is causing all of this."

"Myrtle is causing this," he snarls back.

"Sutton. It says right here that rejecting your mate will destroy you. I can't be the reason you die." Tears spill from my eyes, slipping down my cheeks. "I can't go through this, I can't—"

"There is nothing between Tabitha and me," he urges, moving closer. His hands grip my arms, and he rubs them gently. "The prophecy is not true. It's made up. We know Myrtle is behind all of this."

"But what if it's not all her? What if part of the reason you're being punished is because you didn't choose your true mate? That paper says you will be destroyed if you refuse but whole if you accept."

"*You* make me whole, Serenity."

I shake my head, refusing his words. "The prophecy says your mate is someone from the Augustus family line, so it can't be me. Don't you see?" I choke out, gesturing between the two of us. "This is doomed."

"You don't believe that. Tabitha is wrong. That prophecy is nothing but a bunch of lies written by a troubled woman. Hell, she might have forged it!"

"She's not corporeal, Sutton. There is no way she could have written it."

"Then Myrtle—"

"Hasn't been in the house," I choke out, poking holes in all of the logical explanations he tries to throw my way. "And Tabitha. She would never write something that would push you together. "

"Tabitha could have written it before she died."

"Maybe. But how do you know? Is it truly worth the risk?"

"You are worth every fucking risk, Serenity. There is not a damn thing I wouldn't give up for you."

"In that, we agree. Because I will give you up if it means you survive."

Sutton throws the paper to the ground and closes the distance between us. My eyes flutter closed as he cups my cheek. I wish I could freeze this moment, preserve his touch. "You are who I want, Serenity. Not her. It's never been her." His lips press to my cheek as he kisses my tears away.

My heart breaks.

Shatters.

Explodes into tiny little jagged shards that pierce me to my very core.

"I love you, Serenity."

Tipping my face up to his, I see that he truly believes those words. And, who knows, maybe he does, but I'm not going to fall for this trap again. If Sutton and Tabitha are truly meant to be together, there is nothing that will keep them apart.

"Please. Believe me."

More time. I need more time. Or maybe just one last time, a final goodbye. So, tipping my face, I stretch up and press my lips to his. Sutton's large hands go to my hair, removing the band holding it back and threading through the strands.

I breathe him in, wrapping my arms around his neck as I taste him on my tongue. Kneeling, he takes us both to the soft ground beside the water. It roars, drowning out all sound. For a little while, I'm going to let it drown out reality too.

Sutton's hand slips beneath my shirt, his fingers scorching my flesh as he drives the fabric up, pulling away from me long enough to remove it from my body. Cool air hits my bare skin, and his eyes darken as he takes in the sight of me.

A moment later, he reaches down and strips his own shirt off, tossing it aside. He stares down at me, his masked expression giving nothing away. Chest rising and falling with heavy breaths, he crawls over me, lowering himself against me until his lips trail down my throat to my breast.

I moan, arching up as he draws my nipple into his mouth. Pleasure shoots through me, warmth burning through my body like a rogue flame. Yet, even as I am loved by him in this moment, the tears flow down my cheeks because I cannot help but remember this can't last.

Sutton's mouth trails up my face, and he presses his lips to my cheeks, kissing the tears away as he palms one of my breasts. Loving him has given me the best moments of my life.

And those are what I will cling to. Pushing him off of me, I stand, my gaze locking with his as I undo the laces of my shoes, slipping out of them before peeling my leggings from my body. Within moments, I stand before him, completely bare.

A low growl leaves his lips and he moves toward me, remaining on his knees to press a kiss to my stomach. My hands tangle in his hair as his warm breath fans over my skin.

"You are everything, Serenity," he whispers, staring up at me through thick lashes.

I swallow hard but don't speak, terrified that the words won't come out even if I try.

Sutton stands, slowly, then frees the button on his jeans. He pulls them off and then stands bared beneath the late afternoon sun.

If I can ever only have this moment—I'll take it. A greedy treat to myself.

We clash, skin on skin, his hands are everywhere as we drop to the ground again. I climb onto his lap as he sits up, one arm wrapped around my back. Holding his gaze, I lower myself onto him, pleasure shooting through my body as he fills me.

Sutton's lips part, and he swallows hard as I move—up and down—slowly. Drawing out every single moment I can, I torture the both of us with delicate movements. Here, surrounded by trees, we steal peace in the midst of chaos. Life in the presence of so much death.

And when Sutton leans in and kisses me, the tenderness confirms what I already know—this has to be goodbye.

For the safety of him and his entire pack.

We have to walk away.

Falls Gazette

Chapter Eighteen

Sutton doesn't comment on my silence as we get dressed. I can feel him watching me, trying to catch my eye, but I don't look over. Not even when I retrieve the torn page from where he threw it on the ground earlier and stuff it back into my pocket. What happened between us just now changes nothing. I don't want to argue about it anymore. The truth just is.

We head back the way I came, though I barely recognize the path from earlier. Sutton seems to know the way, and I let him lead me, telling myself it's the logical reason for letting him hold my hand. And why I cling to his in return.

"Mable and I spoke today," Sutton says, breaking a silence that's only getting more tense as we go. "She has an idea for a way we can lure Myrtle out. Set a trap. Go on the offensive instead of always playing defense."

"This sounds promising," I say. The sooner we end this and put it behind us, the sooner I can move on. Or try.

"We use the painting idea," he says. "If she found a way to lock her own daughter inside it, maybe we can do the same to her."

"You told her about Tabitha?" I ask, cringing.

"The pack needed to know."

"You told the entire pack?"

"We're all on the same side, Serenity."

I think of George and wonder how true that statement really is.

"Even if we wanted to, we can't. The painting is destroyed," I tell him.

"So we get another."

I decide not to point out that magical paintings probably aren't that easy to come by. Not that I would know. But if it were that easy, every portrait in the world could potentially be home to a ghost.

That thought makes me shudder.

"And who will you get to perform the spell?" I ask.

He cuts me a pointed look, and for some reason, it pisses me off.

"I'm nowhere near skilled enough for something like that," I say.

"How do you know? You brought Tabitha back from it. Who's to say you can't do the opposite if you tried?"

"Where is this coming from?" I ask. "Yesterday, you made it clear how reckless it is for me to do magic without understanding how it works. And today, you want me to just blindly go for it."

"What I want is for this curse to end," he says.

"So do I," I say, but the words feel hollow. When it ends, what then? What will I do? It's not like I have a job to go back to. That's long gone. And so is any semblance of a life I might have had back in New York. I can't even imagine trying to be happy in that city anymore—and that scares me just as much as being trapped here.

"Your sparks haven't burned me in days," he adds, and I jolt with surprise.

He's right. About that, at least. Since that night with Yvette, my magic's been just a bit easier to access—and easier to control.

I'm getting better at it, after all.

"I believe in you, Serenity. You're the curse breaker. Now you just have to believe in yourself."

I don't answer.

His words tug at me. It feels unfair, this push-pull we have with one another. Even if I refuse to give in to my feelings toward him, we're still connected. That has to mean something; I just have no idea what. Or if it's enough.

Sutton lets me have my thoughts. We walk in silence, and I try to pull myself back from the dark turn my mood has taken.

When Sutton's hand tightens suddenly, I look up sharply. One look at his intense expression and I know something is wrong.

"What is it?" I ask.

He's staring at something off the path. I follow his gaze to a pile of fur half-buried underneath the leaves.

Dread slams into me along with recognition.

That's not just a pile of fur. It's a wolf. Or the body of one, anyway.

Blood cakes its face and throat. And more blood stains the ground nearby.

"Is that—?"

"Jasper," Sutton says tightly. "Yes."

"Is he...?"

"I sense no heartbeat."

We both scan our surroundings, suddenly more alert. But if the threat is still here, I can't sense it.

"Come on." Sutton pulls me down the path, faster this time.

I have to nearly run to keep up with the strides of his longer legs.

But then, he's pulling me up short again.

I see it right away this time.

Another wolf, bloodied and still among the brush.

"Lyall." Sutton's voice is low. Full of grief—and rage. I don't have a chance to answer before he turns and nods at a third wolf. "And Salvador."

"The team," I realize. The wolves who'd followed me out here.

Sutton sniffs, attention darting left and right.

My heart thuds wildly.

We continue on, and in another horrifying few moments, I spot Fischer and Damon too. The entire security team—all dead. And we didn't hear a thing.

Guilt threatens to consume me right here, but Sutton's hand squeezes mine, pulling me along like a lifeline.

"Where are we going?" I ask.

"I need to get you back to the house," Sutton says. "Then I can call for the pack to—"

"Leaving so soon?"

I let out a short scream as a woman steps out from behind a tree. Sutton yanks me behind him but not before I see her face—and nearly vomit at the sickening familiarity of it.

"Audrey," I breathe.

"Hello, Serenity." She inclines her head. The move is jerky, unnatural. Which makes total sense because the woman standing before us, skin sagging like a pair of last century's tits, is dead and gone.

Except that she's here.

And alive?

What. The. Fuck.

"Myrtle," Sutton growls.

His body strains toward her. I can feel the indecision in him. He wants to attack her, but he won't tear himself away from me.

Judging from the smug smile she wears, she knows it too. "Yes, Myrtle is close by, but she's not inside me, not anymore."

Horror fills me at what she's implying. What I'm actually seeing.

It can't be.

It's impossible.

"What is this?" Sutton demands.

"A little reanimation spell." Her gaze zeroes in on me in some kind of silent challenge as she adds, "Nothing a seasoned witch can't handle."

Reanimation?

So it *is* possible.

"Do you mean this bitch is a zombie?" I nearly shriek.

Audrey-Myrtle offers a smug smile—as if my horror is a testament to her greatness. "That is one word for the magic, yes," she says. "A magic I can show you how to wield if you let me."

"Lady, you are crazier than a witch's tit. I want no part of your kind of education."

Sutton bends down and picks up a fist-sized stone. Before Zombie-Audrey can react, he hurls it at her. The rock strikes her on the cheek. It rips away a chunk of skin but otherwise does no damage. She doesn't even seem to feel it.

I grimace at the disgusting reveal of cheekbone.

"That was unnecessary," she says.

I actually happen to agree.

"What do you want?" Sutton demands.

"Serenity," she says as if it's obvious. "I thought I made that clear the night of the ball."

"I will die before I let you hurt her," he says.

"Intriguing idea," she says, "Especially considering the debt she owes for taking my sister's life." Her eyes narrow at me. "Your magic is powerful, city witch. More than even I imagined." She looks at me so intently I can almost feel the energy between us. "Tell me, what's it like?" she asks softly.

"It's..." I don't know how to answer. Or why she wants me to.

The truth is, it's empowering as hell. Just like that night in Sutton's library during the ball, I am drawn to the power of magic like a moth to a flame. But something about that truth feels too much like giving her what she wants.

"It's a handy little weapon," I say, "Especially against witch-sisters who fuck with my friends."

Audrey opens her mouth and screams.

The shrill sound is more than human. It's supernatural and hurts like hell. I cover my ears, wondering whether my eardrums will burst. But Sutton's answering growl is loud enough to match it, and a second later, Audrey falls silent again. Her jaw closes, but the hinge seems off.

"What the hell," I demand.

"Your betrayal pains me. My sister was important. But..." She pauses as if gathering self-control. Honestly, the woman moves like a puppet on a string. She's a skin sack, controlled by magic. It's disgusting. "What's done is done. If you agree to help me now, I will agree to peace between us."

"Help you," I say warily. "What could you possibly want my help with?"

"The magic necessary for the curse is no small thing."

"Are you saying your own magic isn't enough?" I challenge.

"I am more than powerful enough," she scoffs. "But your magic would make an excellent replacement for mine. And it would be enough to cast this curse permanently in my absence."

My jaw drops at the fucking audacity. "You think I'm going to help you curse these people? A spell that has also trapped me? You really are insane."

"It's true, you are trapped, but that's not what pains you most, is it, Serenity?"

Her words are sharp and knowing—and they slice me into silence.

"You and I both know the real pain is being forced to spend eternity with someone you can't have. Someone you aren't meant for." Her gaze flicks to Sutton, and he growls, but Audrey cuts him off. "I can take that pain away. If you let me, I can show you how to keep from ever feeling that kind of hurt again."

She pauses, confident in her offer. She thinks she has me. And honestly, what she's promising is tempting. A release from the hurt at letting Sutton go? At loving him and then walking away from him—forever? I'd be lying if I said I didn't want that.

"How?" I ask, and Sutton growls again.

Audrey ignores him. "Magic, of course."

I bite my lip. "And in exchange, what do you want from me?"

"Your blood," she says.

"What if I say no?"

"Then I will take what I want—by force. And you may or may not survive the experience."

Beside me, Sutton growls.

"I will have what I want, Serenity. One way or another."

"And I will fight you every step of the way," Sutton snaps.

"I have no doubt." She looks from him back to me again. "You can save him the heartache of losing the rest of his family in the process."

I can feel Sutton's eyes on me. I look over and let him see the temptation to give in written in my expression. He turns away, and when he does, it leaves a hollowness in my heart. This woman is offering to put me out of my misery—but at what cost?

No matter how much it hurts to love Sutton Hargrave, I won't save myself by cursing him. I will die a thousand painful deaths—or worse, live a thousand painful lives—if it means freeing the man I love from the grip of this crazy-ass witch.

"Yeah, I think I'm going to pass," I say.

Sutton's eyes whip to mine. Relief shines back at me, followed by fear. "She'll try to kill you," he warns.

"Emphasis on try," I tell him. Then I look back at Audrey whose cheeks have actually reddened with rage, which is kind of impressive, given the deathly pallor that clings to her. "You do what you gotta do, lady, and I'll do the same. But I will never, ever come to the dark side and help you."

Stuart would be quite proud of my Star Wars reference.

Audrey's eyes flash with barely controlled fury. "You will regret your choice, Serenity Kellis. If you won't offer me what I want, I will come and take it."

Audrey takes a step forward, but Sutton steps in front of me.

"Stay back," Sutton snaps at her. His chest heaves with labored breaths, his muscles straining against what's left of his control. "You won't harm her, not without me ripping you apart in the process."

She holds up a hand, her face blank of any emotion as she stares back at Sutton.

"Despite my desire for vengeance, the only one I'm interested in hurting," she says, eyes gleaming as her voice builds, "is you."

The last two words echo around us. As if Myrtle herself is speaking them through Audrey's decaying mouth. As if another mouth has joined the chorus.

The eerie echo ends as another woman steps out from behind the tree.

Sutton stiffens beside me. His reaction is worse than any I've seen. Worse even than finding his entire team dead in the brush. I look closer at the woman, trying to figure out who she is.

Her few remaining strands of dark hair are combed into an up-do my great-grandmother might have worn, and her old-fashioned dress and high collar are reminiscent of another era. Then there's the fact that her exposed bones are covered with very little skin. Even the dress' fabric—now riddled with holes—hangs off her bony shoulders like it would a hangar. Whoever she is, she's clearly been dead a long time.

Beside me, Sutton lets go of my hand and falls to his knees, his expression twisted in anguish.

"Hello, Sutton," she says.

"No," he chokes out.

"Sutton," I say, bending down to check for some unseen injury.

He only stares at the woman, more pain in his gaze than I've ever seen. It ignites a protectiveness in me that warms the magic swimming underneath my skin.

I let go of him and straighten, glaring at the woman. "Who are you?" I demand.

"Forgive my manners," she says with a jaw that creaks as it moves. "I'm Vivian Hargrave. Sutton's mother."

Falls Gazette

Chapter Nineteen

Vivian Hargrave? Is this chick for real? All the color drains from Sutton's face as Vivian shifts her attention from me to him. "Son. Just as I remember you."

"No," he growls, his fingers digging into the soft soil at his knees. "You're not her."

She ignores his accusation. "How is your father?" she questions. "I do miss you both." She sniffles, but the darkness in her eyes only deepens, the corner of her mouth lilting in amusement at Sutton's obvious pain. "You would reject me? Just as you rejected your own mate?"

"That's enough," I snarl, moving in front of him. "You are not Vivian."

Her grin spreads, a smile far too wide to be human. "But I am. Aren't I, Sutton?"

"We need to go," I urge Sutton.

He doesn't move. "We have to save her."

"Sutton..." I try to keep my voice as gentle as possible because my words certainly aren't. "I'm sorry, but that's not your mother. Your mother is dead, and you know it."

"I'm right here, Sutton." Vivian opens her arms. "Come give Mommy a hug, won't you?"

Sutton makes a pained sound.

I whirl on him and reach down to wrap both hands around his biceps. I try to tug him to his feet, but the difference in our body sizes is enough that the struggle is very, very real. Unfortunately, the magic I feel gathering around us is also real. Something tells me Myrtle's patience with this little game is about to end.

"Dammit, Sutton, get up," I hiss.

Something hard hits me square in the back, and I lurch forward, tumbling over Sutton and falling to the ground. A large stone lands beside me, and Sutton's control snaps. He shifts. Turning from man to wolf in a mess of torn clothing. Then, turning his face to the sky, he lets out a bone-chilling howl.

Hopefully, that means it's time to go because I am fucking done here.

Myrtle's apparently done, too. Playing nice, that is. Out of the corner of my eye, I see movement, and when I squint into the trees, I see what she's brought with her to take this to the next level.

More bodies.

Dozens, at least.

They're moving slow, but they're coming this way, every one of them disjointed and clearly … undead.

Apparently, Sutton's mother wasn't enough of a mindfuck.

This bitch has an army of zombies headed our way.

Despite the pain radiating from my back, I climb to my feet and take off at a sprint, Sutton directly behind me. Myrtle, wherever she is, sends magic aimed sharply at our heels. Jumping over tree branches and small fissures opening in the ground at my feet, I race, arms pumping, lungs burning. Twigs snap around me as more of the dead stumble through the trees, a sea of unknown faces all rushing toward us.

Shit.

My heart hammers in my chest as adrenaline surges through my veins—the only thing keeping me going as I race through a legitimate zombie attack. I saw I Am Legend and had nightmares for weeks over those undead assholes. Who the fuck would have thought I'd be right in the center of my own version of the story? Except, no virus created these fuckers. Unless you count Myrtle. That woman is a disease, for sure.

I stumble through brambles, zig-zagging past fleshless hands. They reach for me, bony fingers outstretched, and I barely make it through their lines without being torn to shreds.

Up ahead, the bed and breakfast comes into view, and hope blooms in my chest as I notice the crowd waiting for us there. The yard is packed with townspeople, and as soon as Sutton lunges through the tree line they shift. At once, dozens of humans change to wolves, their clothes flying in all directions as their bodies transform—twisting into their animal. Predators, every one.

They snarl but hold their ground. I glance behind me to the dozens of undead now at our backs and then nearly stumble in surprise as Sutton suddenly shifts back to human.

"What are you—?"

"We have to hurry." He grips my hand and yanks me back toward the B&B.

"Sutton! Let me go!"

"I can't focus if you're not safe," he roars, his naked body covered in dirt and a sheen of sweat.

"But they want *me*," I say, desperate to help fight. The thought of letting anyone else die for me is a crushing weight.

"That is exactly why I need you to wait inside. Serenity, please."

Maybe it's the zombies closing in on our heels. Or maybe it's the pure desperation in his dark, stormy gaze, but I give in and let him drag me toward the front door.

"If you think I'll leave you to deal with them alone, you're dead wrong," I shoot back as soon as we're inside the house.

Victoria and Lance pop into view right in front of us, both of them wide-eyed. "What is going on?" she questions, but my attention is on the man currently trying to hide me away when I should be in the middle of the fight.

"You cannot be out there, Serenity. You can't defend yourself like we can."

"I have magic," I argue, "or have you forgotten?"

"Have *you* forgotten that it's *your* blood she needs to seal us away forever?" he growls. "It's *you* she's after. So stay the fuck here, or you risk trapping us all."

I know he's right.

He knows he's right.

Dammit.

"Help her hide," he orders Lance. When he turns to leave, I know I cannot follow. No matter how badly I want to be out there. Who knows how much blood that bitch needs. A drop? Easy enough for a fucking zombie to get.

The door slams, and I turn to race for the stairs.

"Serenity!" Victoria calls out. "You need to hide!"

"No!" I yell back as I throw open the door to my bedroom and race for the window overlooking the yard. The dead line the trees while the wolves stand, ready to fight. Sutton's wolf—easily discernable from the rest thanks to his massive size—moves to the very front of the crowd, right next to a slightly smaller gray wolf I imagine is likely Phineas.

Phineas. Oh no. I cannot even finish the thought before Vivian herself steps from the trees.

He drops his head and whimpers before trying to move closer.

Sutton blocks his way, and my heart shatters. It's horrific enough to lose the person you love, but then to be forced to see them as your enemy— Myrtle is going to die for this.

"We've come for the blood of Serenity Kellis," Vivian says, and I'm not sure which is worse—her demand for my blood or the fact that her husband and son have to watch this grotesque animation of a creature who looks like—but isn't—the real Vivian Hargrave.

"You will leave without it—or you will die," Sutton says, his voice hoarse at the threat he's just tossed at the remains of his own mother.

She doesn't answer.

I clench my hands into fists and hold my breath as moments tick by.

And then, like a scene straight out of a war movie, they clash together.

It's chaos. Bodies moving too fast for me to keep up. Frantically, I scan the crowd for Sutton. Behind me, Victoria gasps, but I ignore her, my eyes glued to the scene below. Limbs and body parts fly as the wolves tear the dead apart—but not without casualties of our own. A white wolf—soaked in blood—falls to the ground as a trio of skinless women move on to another target. Their weapon? The pointed ends of their own bony fingers.

I press a hand to my mouth and will myself not to be sick. "This is bull shit. I can't stand here and do nothing!"

"Who says you have to do nothing?" I turn to Victoria, who gestures to the heavy history book on my nightstand. She tries to pick it up, and her hand passes right through it. "Throw the book at them," she declares before glancing at Lance with a cheesy smile. "I've always wanted to say that."

"Book? I can't throw the book!" But then my eyes land on the ceramic bookend right beside it. "Now *that* I can throw." Crossing the room in two strides, I retrieve it then rush back over and yank the window open. Leaning out, I scan the crowd for the closest victim—and find them. Directly below me, a dead man trots toward a wolf not paying attention, so I wait, one, two, three seconds until —I let it go.

It falls to the ground, crushing the skull of the already-dead guy.

The thing crumples, and I grin. "Who says I can't help?" I ask, turning to Victoria with a triumphant smile.

She grins at me. "Again!"

I scan my room for another makeshift weapon. But it's not the physical items I notice most now. Magic permeates the air around me, infecting my blood with potency, and I let it, embracing it instead of my usual attempt to ignore it. If I can throw something physical, I can certainly do more. Especially since I seem to be powerful enough to warrant an entire zombie army.

Giving in to my emotions, I channel it all into the magic, closing my eyes and imagining striking down the zombies below.

When I open my eyes, I wave my hand toward them—but nothing happens.

No blue spark.

No zap of electricity.

My heart falls.

"What is happening?" Victoria questions.

"I don't know." Throwing my hand out like the Scarlett Witch in every Marvel movie, I expect to see *something*, anything, but instead, the zombies and wolves continue to battle it out, uneffected by my magic.

It stings far worse than I care to admit.

A sharp howl echoes from the thick of the fighting, and I shift my gaze in time to see Sutton face off with his mother—or what used to be his mother. Vivian's smile is crooked, and the dress she wears is now hanging limply over her left arm. As if chunks of her limb are now completely gone. My stomach roils.

This is wrong. This is all wrong.

I turn and rush out of the room. I'm nearly down the stairs when Lance pops into view. I yank to a stop to avoid passing through him. Could I? Yes. But something about it seems...rude.

"You can't go out there," Lance insists.

"You can't stop me," I remind him.

"Sutton—"

"Sutton is currently engaged in a fight with his very dead, very decayed mother."

Victoria materializes with a gasp, and Lance's eyes widen.

"I will not leave him to face her alone," I add. "I can't."

Still, they don't move. I sigh. *Screw manners.* Running straight through them, I race down the stairs, outside, and directly into the fray. Almost immediately, I duck as a body is thrown past me and into the side of the house. Bones crunch, but the thing—I honestly can't tell if it was a man or woman at this point—gets right back up and charges toward the wolf who tossed it.

From here, I can't see Sutton through the chaos. I sprint toward where I saw him last, rounding the corner of the house, but a man steps into my path, blocking me. His uniform is wrinkled and covered in mud, dimming the shine of the badge still pinned to his lapel.

He grins, his familiar face looking completely alien to me now. His throat is missing patches of skin where it was cut to bleed him the night of the ball. And his eyes are hanging way too loosely in their sockets for my liking. I take a step back, unable to breathe at the sight of him. Probably a good thing because, up close, he smells like death.

"Hello, Miss Kellis," Sheriff Arden Rhodes says. "So nice to see you again."

Falls Gazette

Chapter Twenty

I stare in horror at the man whose death I've carried as my own failing since the moment it happened. Guilt settles against my shoulders all over again, but my disgust makes it hard to feel sorry. The fact that he's standing here at all is just ...wrong.

"Get out of my way," I say.

"I died because of you, and now you won't even spare a moment to speak with me?"

"You died because of Myrtle," I retort, ignoring the way his words stab at me. "She's the reason all of this is happening." I force myself to look him in the eyes and add, "I know you can hear me, Myrtle. Stop this. These people have done nothing to you."

"This town took everything from me," he hisses. From the venom and disgust in his words, I have no doubt this is Myrtle I'm speaking with now. "First my daughter and now Yvette. They deserve to suffer as I have."

"You killed your daughter. Not these people. Not Sutton."

"It would have never happened without his involvement. The

Hargrave family is a blight on this world. And now they feel the pain they caused me."

"Tabitha started this, but you can end it. Right now."

"So can you. Give me what I want. Your blood. And I'll go. Forever."

"You'll trap us forever, you mean. Just like you trapped your daughter."

"What do you know about Tabitha?"

"I know she's free now," I say. "Thanks to me."

"What are you talking about?"

"I found the painting," I say. "Or should I say 'prison'? What kind of mother doesn't let her own daughter's soul find peace?"

His eyes narrow and I know I've hit a nerve. Myrtle clearly didn't realize Tabitha's been let out to play. Rhodes casts a glance toward the house. I can feel Myrtle's desire to go see for herself. Good. That means my distraction is working. While I buy myself time, I gather what magic I can to myself, but like before, I can barely pull enough together for a single spark.

Dammit.

"She's still determined to have him, you know," I go on. Rhodes looks sharply back at me again. "Even after all this time, she's chosen him over you. Why do you think that is? Oh, maybe because you're the villain here. Not Sutton and not any of these people."

"You're wrong. These people are rabid animals," he replies. "And what do we do with rabid beasts, Serenity? We put them down."

"The only rabid one I see here is you," I spit back. Casting my gaze behind me briefly, I catch sight of the book stopper I threw out the window. I take a step backward toward it. "Using your victims as glorified meat puppets? Pretty fucking twisted."

"But it sure is a show stopper, is it not? Oh, come on, as a writer, I assumed you of all people would appreciate the theatrics. The plot twist as it is."

"I write non-fiction, you bitch." Reaching behind me, I retrieve the bookend and swing out. It slams into the Sheriff, ripping chunks of flesh from the side of his face. His head whips back toward me, and he reaches up, snapping his dislocated jaw back in place.

I gape in horror, the urge to vomit nearly overwhelming me.

"You pathetic little girl," he growls. "You truly have no clue just what you are doing, do you? Use your magic, Serenity. Go on. Show me what you're made of."

He reaches for me, and I stumble back, going down hard on my ass. My fear surges, and I let it loose. Magic shoots from my hands but it doesn't hit him. Instead, the shot flies wild and hits another zombie square in the back. The undead drops where it stands, crumpling and turning to dust in an instant.

Rhodes lunges for me, and I scramble to my feet, barely managing to escape before his hand has a chance to close around my throat. He grins, a savage smile that is so out of place it makes the bile churning in my belly rise to my throat.

What she's doing to these people—it's wrong on so many levels.

"Go on, Serenity," he taunts. "Hit me with your best shot. I'm waiting."

I reach for my magic and thrust a hand out, but nothing happens.

He laughs. "Pathetic. Give me what I want, and I'll go away," he says.

Somewhere behind me, a wolf whimpers, but I'm too afraid to look away to see who it is. *Please don't be Sutton.*

I bite my lip, fully aware I'm out of options for self-defense. "If I give you my blood, you'll leave and never come back?" I ask.

"You have my word," the Sheriff replies.

The word of a murdering, necromancing witch.

Like that means anything.

The offer is almost tempting, though. *Almost.*

"The word of a psychopath doesn't mean shit," I say.

With my magic on an unapproved vacation, I do the only other thing I can think of. I raise my leg and kick. My heel hits him square in the chest. Bones crack, but despite the horrifying sound, he is completely unaffected. Instead, he grabs my ankle and smiles as he yanks me forward.

A scream leaves my lips as I'm pulled from my feet. My head hits the ground, pain ricocheting through me as the injury leaves me dazed. Everything around me fades, the sounds of fighting coming through as if I'm underwater.

My arms scrape over the ground as Rhodes drags me closer to him. Then, he kneels. I throw up my hands to fend him off, but my movements are too slow. He grips my arms and pins them above my head with one massive hand.

Then, he reaches behind him and withdraws a silver blade. It glints beneath the light of the sun as he shows it to me. "You will beg me for mercy," he growls as his shriveled hand tightens its grip. The cold, dead fingers bruise my wrists as he leans down with the blade.

A menacing snarl pulls my attention as a massive wolf slams into the Sheriff. The two tumble to the dirt, and the wolf jumps to his feet, his gray fur matted with blood—and chunks of things I really don't want to think too strongly on.

Blinking rapidly, I manage to sit up, my head pounding.

Sutton's wolf gnashes its teeth as it stares at the Sheriff, who is already pushing to his feet.

"I will have her," Rhodes growls. Then, he charges.

So does Sutton.

The two clash, Sutton taking Rhodes back to the dirt.

Sutton brings his claw down and rakes it across the Sheriff's face. Skin shreds, falling away to reveal bone and tissue. But the Sheriff continues to struggle, and Sutton responds by sinking his teeth into Rhodes' throat and ripping it clean away.

Thick, black blood bubbles slowly from the wound. Not much. Hell, not nearly enough for him to seem alive though he continues to act like a newly dying man. His breath catches, and when he coughs, the dark crimson leaks from his mouth too.

Gross.

Sutton growls and closes his mouth around the Sheriff's throat again. He shakes his head, jerking the body until his neck snaps. The cracking sound it makes brands itself in my mind, and I know, without a doubt, it's a sound I'll remember for the rest of my life.

Finally, the Sheriff stops moving.

He's gone. A second time. Hopefully for good, this time.

I press a hand to my mouth as nausea rolls.

Sutton steps back, positioning himself in front of me, but there's no need. The rest of the zombies have already begun to retreat; what little there are left of them. Nearly all are lying dead—again—in the soft grass where the remaining wolves still bare their teeth at the ones animated enough to move.

"This isn't over," I hear a disembodied voice call out as the remaining zombies disappear into the trees. I cannot do anything but look at the dead Sheriff and try not to vomit. Bile rises as the adrenaline begins to wane, sending my body into uncontrollable shivering.

Sutton kneels in front of me, human once again. His naked skin is covered in blood, soaked in it. The overwhelming stench of death clings to him, and I scramble back, covering my mouth with one hand. He reaches for me, and I shrink back further, unwilling to be touched by the blood of a man I've seen die twice now.

"Serenity," Sutton says, his voice rough with emotion. Worry, pain, relief—it's all there, but I don't know what to say to any of it.

"Serenity." He calls my name again, this time rougher. His tone almost pleading with me to assure him that I'm okay.

Truth is I don't know if I ever will be.

Finally, I look up, but my answer is cut short by a crack of thunder.

No, not thunder.

I know that sound. And it means something much, much worse than a bolt of thunder.

"Get the fuck away from her, or the next one will be between your eyes."

Cold familiarity washes over me as the last voice I ever expected to hear in this cursed place registers. I whirl to see Steven behind me, the barrel of his weapon trained on Sutton's chest. Behind him stands Allison, eyes wide, face pale.

Panic claws at my throat, and I scramble to my feet, swaying when my head throbs in protest.

"Steven," I say, but he doesn't even look at me.

My brother's eyes are wide as he darts glances from Sutton to the Sheriff's body on the ground at Suttons' feet. And I realize with horror what sort of assumptions he's making right now.

"Steven, it's not what it looks like," I say.

"Save it, Ser," he snaps. And then to Sutton, "You're under arrest—for murder."

Midnight Bound

Falls Gazette

Chapter One

The ringing in my ears from the gunshot is deafening. I stand, heart in my throat, the business end of Steven's pistol aimed in my direction. Or rather, aimed at Sutton, who stands just beside me. The warmth of his body lets me know he's close, though I don't dare take my eyes off Steven to check.

My big brother is furious—jaw hard, eyes molten as he glares at me. But even with his firearm trained on Sutton, he's not the biggest threat. Around us, the pack gathers, their low growls a threat my brother doesn't seem to pick up on. Thankfully, though, they don't advance—yet. I have literally seconds before this turns into a bloodbath, and if that happens, no matter which side wins, I'll lose.

"Steven, listen to me," I urge, attempting a calm, steady tone despite the fear burning a hole in my stomach. "Sutton is not the bad guy here. Please put the gun down."

"Uh, why is that dead guy missing a cheek?" Allison's question rings out sharply against the silence, but no one answers her.

Steven's glare narrows on where Sutton stands behind me. "Sutton? Is that this asshole's name?"

Sutton growls low at the insult, but Steven is not in the least intimidated. No surprise there. My brother would rather die than show cracks in his armor. Which, unfortunately, is exactly what terrifies me now. He kills Sutton, the pack slaughters him.

There is no winning here unless he puts the damn gun down.

"It's not his fault," I tell him. "Please, believe me."

My brother's gaze shifts back to me. "He's covered in blood and surrounded by bodies, Ser. In my mind, that absolutely makes him the bad guy."

I don't think about it. I simply move my feet and step directly in front of Sutton, putting myself between Sutton and the gun.

"Serenity, get out of the way." Steven's voice is hard.

"No." I stand my ground, and Sutton's hand goes to my lower back.

"Get your fucking hand off of her," Steven snarls, cheeks flushing crimson. He adjusts his aim so the barrel is pointed at Sutton's shoulder, which is broader than mine and still exposed.

The wolves growl in unison, a terrifying sound that raises the hairs on the back of my neck. This is about to get ugly really fucking fast.

Heart pounding, I take a cautious step toward Steven. If I get close enough, maybe he'll lower the gun. "Steven…" I start.

"Not a fucking chance in hell I'm listening to anything you say until you get the fuck over here behind me."

Allison hurries out from behind Steven. Careful to remain out of the line of fire, she wraps blue-tipped fingernails around my arm. "This is crazy, Ser. Let Steven handle it. Everything is going to be fine." She tugs, but I don't budge.

Seeing her now, I want nothing more than to wrap my arms around my friend and squeeze. But I hold my ground. "No." I yank my arm away and step back again so that I'm still an obstacle between Steven's bullet and Sutton's body. Glaring at my brother, I say, "If you're going to shoot, do it, but you'll have to go through me."

A low warning growl rips through the pack of wolves who, during my distraction, have inched closer. If it weren't my brother currently in their warpath, it would warm my heart to know they're not just protecting Sutton—they're willing to step in for me, too.

Steven swings the gun toward the pack, and my blood turns to ice in my veins.

"Don't attack him," I scream, throwing my hands up. "He's my brother!"

The wolf closest to Steven stops in its tracks. Gone is the snarling expression, though his golden gaze remains trained on Steven.

"Thank you," I tell Phineas, my voice cracking on the words. And then I turn back to Steven. "You pull that trigger and they'll kill you. I won't be able to stop them." A tear slips from my eyes and falls down my cheek. "Please, don't put me through that. Please, don't make me watch you die," I whimper.

Steven glances back at me, and in eyes I know better than my own, I finally see that he recognizes the threat he's facing. "I won't let them hurt you," he says.

Finally, a crack in the armor. "They aren't going to hurt me, dumbass. They're protecting me. They've been protecting me this entire time." Well, maybe that's a half-lie given most of them hated me until Halloween, but my brother doesn't need to know that.

He scowls, clearly unconvinced.

"She's telling the truth," Sutton speaks out from behind me.

Steven swings back toward us, his weapon lower now but still ready to fire should he need it to. And I've seen how well my brother does on a tactical range—there's no doubt in my mind he'll manage to take a few wolves with him should things go south.

“You honestly expect me to take the word of a naked guy covered in blood and surrounded by bodies?”

“To be fair, those bodies were dead when they got here,” I point out.

Steven glares at me. "These animals are killers. This man is a killer. Take a look, Ser. The evidence is everywhere.”

The wolves snarl again, teeth bared as they take another step closer.

Spots invade my vision as my blood pressure skyrockets. This is going to end—soon. And I’m not entirely sure who I’ll be left with when it does.

“Stand down,” Sutton orders.

The wolves fall silent.

I glance over my shoulder, and Sutton offers me a nod.

“What the actual fuck,” Steven says, looking from the wolves to Sutton. “These your pets?” he demands. “They do your dirty work?”

“You have no idea what you’re talking about,” I snap.

“No?” Steven questions, taking a step closer to me. Sutton growls, but I ignore him. “I know what I see. And that is you protecting a killer. What did he say to make you feel the need to protect him, anyway?” Before I can answer, his expression twists in horror. “Is this the guy you’ve been seeing? Fuck, Ser, has he really brainwashed you this badly?”

“Sutton’s not a killer,” I say, my temper rising the more he talks.

He snorts. “You know, Stockholm Syndrome is a real thing.” I start to argue, but he goes on, “Let’s take a look at the facts, shall we? You came here to investigate cold cases no one else could solve. You tell me, you think you know who the killer is, and then, the next time I talk to you, you’ve decided you’re not going to bother investigating anymore. Instead, you’re going to stay because you met a man.”

"That's not—"

"From where I'm standing," he interrupts, "looks to me like you chose to stop investigating because you didn't like where it was leading. I was worried you'd get yourself killed or injured, but I have to say I never thought you'd be so fucking stupid as to let yourself get involved with an actual murderer."

That does it. I step forward, close enough that he can see my expression easily, but not so close that he can grab me and pull me out of the way. "You listen up, Steven Kellis. The only moron here is you. You're so hell-bent on focusing on what you think you see that you're missing a much bigger picture. Do not speak to me like I'm a child, especially when you can't know the half of what I've been through since coming here."

"Ser—" Allison starts.

"Not a word," I snap. Then, I turn back to Steven. "You might be the big bad detective here, but you're refusing to see the truth right now. And that makes me really fucking disappointed in you."

"Then go on," Steven says. "Go ahead, and paint the bigger picture."

"These wolves are protecting me. Something they have to do because a wi—woman," I correct, not wanting to drop the witch bomb just yet, "decided she wanted to bottle my blood."

Steven's color pales ever so slightly, and Allison's eyes widen almost comically.

"Now, if you want to hear the rest, you're going to put the gun down and have a civil conversation with me."

Steven continues to stare at me, dumbfounded. "Bottle your blood. That's what you want me to believe?"

"If you don't believe your sister or my son, believe all of us."

Steven jumps and turns. My stomach twists when I see Phineas in human form once again. "Where the fuck did you come from?" Though even as he asks the question, I can see the disbelief on his face. He knows full well a wolf was standing beside him before. And now that wolf is gone. Or changed, anyway. “And why the hell are you naked?”

“Oh my,” Allison whispers.

Nude Phineas holds up a hand. “None of us would ever hurt Serenity,” he says. “What you see here is our attempt to protect her. These bodies were sent to hurt her, and we fought them off.”

“You mean people?” Steven demands. “Show some respect for human life, man.”

“No, I mean bodies,” Phineas tells him calmly. “They contained no life when they arrived here today.”

“Bodies were sent to hurt her. Do you people hear yourselves? Bodies cannot be sent anywhere. They’re fucking lifeless!”

Before I can try to explain what Phineas means, along with the reason behind him being naked in the first place, Sutton mutters an order, and the entire pack begins to shift.

Bones pop out of place, fur recedes, and within seconds, a yard full of naked townspeople stare back at us.

Steven lowers his gun completely and stares at them. Then, he turns his attention to me. His shock leaves him with a haggard expression. “What the fuck are you involved in, Ser?”

“Listen,” I tell him, “I know it’s hard to believe, but these people mean you no harm.”

“People?” he echoes. “Is that even the right word?”

“Of course,” I say. “They might be able to shift into wolves, but they’re still people.”

He stares at me. “This is insane. You’ve officially lost your mind.”

“You’ve walked in on something unexpected,” Sutton says tightly, “and obviously at a very bad time for us all. Why don’t we go inside and discuss it?”

Steven’s disbelief turns to accusation as he looks at Sutton. "I’m not going anywhere until I get some damn answers. Who are you, and why have you dragged my sister into this chaos?"

Sutton's jaw tightens. Steven's hit a nerve.

"No one dragged me anywhere," I say. "But Sutton's right. We should take it inside so all of this can be cleaned up." I glance down at where the Sheriff still lies near our feet. Dead—twice over now. I'm not stupid enough to think his death will stop Myrtle from using him against us again, though. She could return at any moment. Hell, she could be watching us still.

That thought panics me even more. I have to get Steven and Allison out of sight before Myrtle realizes they're here.

"Fine," Steven says. "But if you blow any more smoke up my ass, I'll drag you out of here and shoot anyone who stands in my way." He holsters his gun, a huge win for me.

Sutton tenses at my back, but I reach back and touch his arm, nodding quickly. "Deal. Only the truth."

It's not like lying is an option at this point anyway. He's seen too much for that. And if I tell him the truth about the danger he's walked into, hopefully, he'll leave before anything else can happen. Though, knowing my brother? He won't walk away until I do.

And I'm not going anywhere.

Steven motions for me to lead the way, so I step around him, Sutton remaining close beside me as we make our way into the house.

Allison starts walking on my other side as I pass, and I glance over at my friend, relieved she's here yet terrified she came at the same time.

"You're not going to yell at me too?" I ask.

"Still deciding," she admits. "I am looking forward to hearing your story, though." She hip-bumps me as we near the front door of the bed and breakfast. "I get the feeling you left some important details out of our calls."

Falls Gazette

Chapter Two

Sutton opens the front door to Yvette's bed and breakfast and steps back to let us pass. I give him what I hope is a reassuring smile before leading Steven and Allison into the B&B. Phineas and the rest of the pack remain outside, but I have no illusions of privacy. Given all that's happened, they'll be listening to every word we say inside these walls, and I can't blame them for it.

What happens next doesn't just affect Sutton and me. It affects this entire town.

Once in the foyer, I stop and wait as Sutton closes the door and moves inside. His strained expression is the perfect representation of the level of shit we're about to have to deal with. My brother being in Midnight Falls is difficult enough.

But a homicide detective who just witnessed an entire town of blood-streaked wolves turn to men while surrounded by a sea of dead bodies? Catastrophe.

"Maybe you want to clean up first," I tell Sutton.

"Hell no," Steven snaps. "I'm not letting him out of my sight until I get some answers."

"Seriously, Steven? Where the hell do you think he's going to go?"

"I have no fucking clue, but I'm not taking any chances."

"Listen—"

"Serenity, thank goodness!" Victoria's words echo through the room several seconds before she appears out of thin air and rushes forward. She throws her arms around me, and I'm surprised to find I can feel them—sort of. Mostly, it's cold like a draft when someone leaves a window open.

I manage to recover quickly from the surprise, but Steven and Allison? Not so much.

"Oh, and you brought new guests," Victoria adds excitedly, drawing back to look at them.

Before I can answer, Lance pops into view, and Allison screams.

"Apologies," Lance says hastily. He looks at me, adding, "We were very worried when you ran out of here, into the fight."

Steven gives me a look that seems to say, *"I was right; you're insane. And now I am too because your crazy is clearly contagious."*

I ignore it.

"I'm okay," I assure Lance. He glances at Sutton, his eyes widening at the sight of all the blood coating his skin, and I add hastily, "We both are."

"I'm going to put something on," Sutton says, aiming a pointed look at my brother.

Steven opens his mouth as if to argue, but Sutton stops him. "Serenity's right. You know nothing about what you've just walked into. I don't owe you an explanation for it, either, but I'll give it anyway because I care for Serenity. Rest assured I will return in a moment. I don't make a habit of leaving the most important people in the world to me behind." Steven's expression tightens at that, but

Sutton turns and heads for the stairs, adding, "Besides, if we're going to fight over her, I'd rather do it fully dressed."

Steven doesn't say a word as Sutton disappears up the stairs. Then, one by one, everyone turns to look at me. A moment of awkward silence descends, and I hurry to smooth it—and buy time. My plan is to ask about their drive up or some other form of small talk, but what comes out of my mouth is: "What do you get when you cross a sports reporter with a vegetable?" When no one answers, I continue, "A common-tater."

Victoria snorts, but neither Allison nor Steven looks impressed. With that in mind, I decide to start laying it all out there. Might as well rip the bandage off. "Right. Lance, Victoria, this is my brother Steven and my friend Allison."

"Hello." Victoria offers her hand, and Allison reaches for it.

"*Best* friend," Allison corrects, clearly having recovered from the ghostly pop-in. But when her hand passes straight through Victoria's, she pales.

"Whoops," Victoria says, tucking her hand away with a sheepish smile. "Looks like I'm spent for now."

Steven looks ready to shoot something again. "Serenity."

"Would you mind giving us a bit of privacy?" I ask, looking at Lance. "Family business."

"Of course." He takes Victoria's arm and leads her around the corner. I'm grateful they've made a normal-looking exit, but when I turn back to Steven, I know it won't matter. The damage is already done.

"They're ..." He can't seem to finish the sentence.

"Specters," I finish for him.

Steven glares at me. "Ghosts."

I wince at the bite in his tone. "They prefer the first term, but yes."

"They're dead though," Allison says warily. "Like, actually dead."

I sigh, flicking a glance toward the stairs as Sutton returns. He's wearing a pair of sweatpants that hang low on his hips, and despite the tension of this moment, I can't help but notice how sexy he looks. He pulls on a t-shirt as he descends the last of the stairs, pulling it down over rippling abs that, even covered in blood and zombie guts, make my stomach flip in appreciation.

I swallow hard, shoving away the attraction and trying not to think too hard about what it says about me, considering he's coated in filth and my brother is literally a couple of feet away.

"Serenity?" Sutton questions. He's frowning at my expression, and I realize I've let my thoughts creep into my face.

My cheeks heat. *Right*. "Maybe we should start from the beginning," I say.

"Maybe," he agrees.

I turn to Steven, who is waiting impatiently.

"Well," I say, unsure what to say and especially how to say it. "You've already seen for yourself that werewolves are real. And specters," I add. "But the truth is: Lance and Victoria and the wolves aren't the only supernatural creatures in this town."

"You trying to tell me Big Foot lives down the block? Does the Chupacabra attend Sunday dinners?"

I do my best to ignore Steven's sarcasm. "No, but the house you're standing in belongs to a witch."

Allison's eyes widen, and she turns in a circle, scanning the room as though she's expecting someone else to have popped in. Honestly? Stranger things have happened in this damn town.

"What does this witch have to do with you getting involved with murderers?" Steven demands. The fact that he didn't laugh in my face bodes well, though, because it means he's not refusing to believe everything he saw earlier.

Sutton tenses.

"This town is cursed," I say because, fuck it, there's no going easy where Steven's concerned. I can see he's determined to make this difficult. In fact, if there was a level above impossible, it would be named after Steven Kellis' stubborn ass.

"Cursed how?" he asks.

"A hundred years ago, a witch named Myrtle got angry when her daughter fell in love with Sutton."

Steven puts up a hand to stop me. "Hang on, a hundred years ago? You expect me to believe this fucker is a century old?"

"I expect you to shut up and listen," I snap. He rolls his eyes but keeps his mouth shut.

I try again, silently bracing myself for Tabitha to show up. This is her story, after all. "Myrtle confronted them and tried to attack Sutton, but her daughter, Tabitha, got in the way. Tabitha died—" Allison gasps. "—and Myrtle blamed Sutton for it. After that, she cursed him and this entire town. Now, they're all trapped here, and Myrtle uses them to renew the curse by killing someone once a year on Halloween."

"The murders you came to solve..." Allison's expression softens as she puts it together. "This Myrtle woman killed them."

"Yes."

Steven's not quite so empathetic. His eyes flash with accusation as he glares at Sutton. "So, you broke a girl's heart a century ago, and her mom wants revenge? To top that off, instead of dealing with your problems, you dragged my sister into it and put her in danger."

"You know nothing about me. I would do anything to protect Serenity." Sutton's words are an angry growl.

I put a hand on his arm, and both men fall silent. Steven's gaze is locked on my hand where it touches Sutton.

"Sutton didn't drag me anywhere," I say firmly. "He tried to make me leave, in fact. More than once. But I stayed, and now... I'm trapped here too."

"This is insane," Steven says. "You know that, right? I mean, do you hear yourself? Witches, curses, trapped in a town?" He snorts. "I don't know what the fuck is in the water here, but you're coming home with me, and that's final."

He reaches for me, and I jump back, leaning into Sutton when it throws me off balance. He wraps both arms around me, and I don't miss the hurt in Steven's eyes when he realizes Sutton is protecting me from him—my own brother.

"Serenity—" Steven starts.

Rather than fear, it's anger I feel. "Okay, that's it." My patience, already worn thin, snaps. "Do you hear yourself?" I shoot back at him. "You literally saw those wolves shift into men outside. There are zombies littering the front yard. And you just met two of the three ghosts who currently reside in this house. Yet, you're still going to gaslight me into thinking I'm the crazy one?"

Steven tries to respond, but I'm not having it.

"You will leave," I say. "Now. Today. Both of you." I flick a glance at Allison, who's gone pale at my outburst. "You will not breathe a word of this to Mom and Dad or anyone else. And you will not come back, no matter what happens. I have a lot of shit going on, and I don't have time to hold your hand through the stages of big-brother-assholery while you process this new reality. You can do that back in New York. Do you understand?"

For a moment, no one speaks.

I take a deep breath, aware of the pounding of my own heart as I wait for Steven to do as I asked. This was a stupid idea on his part to begin with. Now, all that matters is getting him out of danger as quickly as possible. If I have to be a bitch to do it, then I will.

"This witch," Steven says slowly, and I brace myself for another declaration about how we're all insane, "she's the one who sent all those people—zombies—to kill you today?"

I don't answer.

Finally, Sutton speaks up. "Yes. She used magic to reanimate their corpses and attack us."

"Why?" Steven asks. He's infuriatingly calm now, and it makes me want to hit something. "What does she want with Serenity? With her blood?"

He's looking at Sutton now, clearly realizing he's pushed too far to get anything more out of me.

"She wants to use Serenity's blood to recast the curse," Sutton says. He hesitates and then adds, "As it turns out, Serenity has magic in her blood too."

Allison shoots me an incredulous look. Steven merely frowns, and I have to bite back a scream. Sutton should have left that part out. It's only going to make my brother dig in his heels that much harder.

"I see." Steven's expression is unreadable now, but he's looking at me again. "Do you know where I can find her? This witch who seems so obsessed with your blood."

"Why? So you can interrogate her for more proof that I'm crazy?" I snap. "Not going to happen."

"No," he says, his voice even and his energy deadly calm, "So I can kill her myself."

I'm caught between a weird sense of affection and buoying hope. "So, you believe me?" I ask.

Steven snorts. "I believe *you believe* this nonsense. And if I have to follow you down this rabbit hole to get you back, I will. You're my sister, Ser. I love you." He glances at Sutton, adding, "And I'll do anything to protect you—even if it's from yourself."

Hope and affection are ground to dust beneath his words. My temper flares, and I let it. It's either that or heartbreak. As much as I want him to be safe, I don't want us to part on such terrible terms. But it looks like I'll have no choice.

"If that's what you truly believe, then you won't have any trouble leaving," I say.

"Serenity," Allison begins, but I hold up my hand.

"Both of you. Now. You can let yourselves out."

I head for the stairs. Between their disbelief and the danger they're in just being here, sending them away is the only thing I can do, but I don't have to watch it either. Today has already been exhausting. I can't take much more.

"I won't leave," Steven says at my back, "Not without you."

I stop and turn back, trying to think of something else to say. Something terrible enough to chase him off.

"Why don't we go into the kitchen," Sutton offers. "You're probably hungry from the drive. And we can talk more after we've eaten."

I glare at him for trying to make peace. Normally, I'd appreciate it. Right now, it feels traitorous. Especially when Steven's been a king-sized asshole to him.

"No thanks," I tell him and begin climbing the stairs again.

"That's enough," Steven booms from behind me. I pause, turning back to see his face has flushed red. His patience has snapped too, and he looks a lot less stable for it than I feel. "Look, this is insane. You can either come with me now, or I'll bring enough police that even your little wolf pack can't stop me from dragging your ass home. It's your choice."

"Steven…" Allison begins.

"Don't," he says so forcefully that she takes a step back.

Sutton growls at that.

"You don't scare me," Steven says, which is probably the least safe thing he could have said just now. "I won't let you poison her against me."

Sutton's eyes narrow.

I return to his side and grab his hand before he can do something stupid.

"She's told you the truth, and you've rejected it and her," Sutton snarls at my brother. "I haven't poisoned anything. You did that all by yourself."

"You're both talking about impossible things," Steven says. And I hear it then. A small sliver of doubt has crept into his voice. I blink, shocked to realize what's really going on. He's not in denial. He's afraid. He won't admit any of this is true because, if he does, he'll have to accept how much danger I'm in. Slowly, I make my way back down the stairs and over to him.

"Steven…" I begin, reaching for him, but he yanks back.

"Werewolves, witches? What the fuck, Serenity? How can you possibly expect me to take this all seriously?"

"You've seen the proof with your own eyes," I say gently. "You both have."

"She's right, Steven," Allison offers.

She takes a step toward him too, but he backs away from us both, eyes wide, head shaking in more denial.

"It's not that simple," he says, and my anger drains away.

"It's okay to be afraid," I say.

"I'm not afraid," he declares. He looks at Sutton. "Besides, if what you're saying is true, this is all his fault for rejecting that poor woman to begin with. She's the real victim here."

"Tabitha is no victim," Sutton says vehemently.

The air around me turns suddenly cold, and I tense. No one else seems to notice, but the energy ripples and I know we're not alone anymore.

"Sutton's right. Let's go into the kitchen," I say, my stomach twisting as I realize there's only one resident we haven't laid eyes on yet. And I really wouldn't mind if I never saw her again. Unfortunately, Tabitha has other plans.

She appears just behind Steven, and our eyes meet. Her dress is the same dated gown she wore in the portrait, and her hair is still styled as if she's stepped right out of the early nineteen-hundreds. She looks from me to Sutton and back again. Then, she winks.

"I can't just accept all this," Steven is saying.

He falls silent as Sutton snarls.

Before I can speak, I watch as Tabitha leans in close to Steven's ear.

Allison squeaks in surprise then clamps her hand over her mouth in shock.

"What?" Steven demands.

"Don't freak out," I say, trying to remain calm for my brother's sake. But Tabitha's eyes are gleaming with mischief.

"Why the hell would I freak out?"

"Tabitha," I say, "Don't."

She grins at me and blows on Steven's ear.

He jumps clear off the ground, whirling to face her.

She raises her hand and wiggles her fingers in a coy wave. "Boo."

Falls Gazette

Chapter Three

Steven screams—like, legit screams—and stumbles backward, his body launching faster than his feet can keep up with. For a split second, I think he's going to catch himself, but no such luck. He lands on his ass with a grunt, palms bracing his fall, though probably not by much if the wince he gives is any indication. As quickly as he lands, he jumps up again, staring at Tabitha as if he's seen—well—a ghost.

"Who the fuck is that?" he demands, backing across the room to stand beside me. I can't blame him. Tabitha's form is much more ghostly than human right now. If I squint, I can see straight through her body to the wall on the other side. The mirror hanging behind her shows no reflection either. The effect is spooky as hell, but I'm guessing that's her goal.

I sigh. "Meet Tabitha Augustus. The girl who started all of this."

"Hello," Tabitha says, way too pleased with herself and the chaos she's caused.

Steven gapes at me, shifting his gaze to Tabitha and finally back to me. "She's the one whose mother cursed the town?"

"One and the same," Tabitha offers with a grin. "And you didn't tell me you had such a striking brother," she says to me. "For a mortal, I mean."

Steven looks like he might throw up.

Allison crosses her arms. "Steven prefers the living," she snaps.

Tabitha studies my friend then laughs softly. "Relax, I have a preference for immortals." She turns to the man on my other side. "Hello, Sutton."

"Tabitha," he greets stiffly.

"If you're still here, why the hell can't you just tell your mother to back the fuck up?" my brother demands, stepping forward. "If she did this for you, tell her to stop."

Tabitha arches a dark eyebrow. "My mother is not one to be told what to do."

"Tabitha's right," I say. "Myrtle locked Tabitha's soul in a painting as punishment for loving Sutton in the first place. She's not overly fond of her own daughter at the moment."

"Nor has she ever been," Tabitha replies. "Anyway, I heard my name so decided to pop in and introduce myself, but I'm bored now. Sutton, I'll be seeing you." She winks then fades away, disappearing, so both Steven and Allison turn to face me.

"How many ghosts did you say live here again?" Allison asks warily.

"Three."

"It was originally two," Sutton adds darkly. "But Serenity freed Tabitha from her painting."

I glare at him. "Whose side are you on?" I hiss.

"You did *what?*" Allison demands. Before I can answer, her shock transforms into curiosity. "Wait... How did you manage that exactly?"

Once a reporter...

"Magic in my blood," I remind her, sending a small spark of

magic shooting from my finger into Sutton's ribs. "Besides, it was an accident."

By the time I look over, Steven and Allison are still staring at my hand, but their disbelief is slowly turning to something not quite so skeptical. We fall into silence for a few minutes. I wait it out, knowing I need to give them both time to process it all. Finally, Steven clears his throat. "If all of this is real—and that's a big *if*—I'm staying until we get it sorted. There's no way in hell I'm leaving you here alone to deal with this."

"Steven. You can't stay," I insist, stepping forward. "You being here puts both you and Allison in more danger than you can imagine."

"I'm a cop, Serenity, or have you forgotten that? I'm in danger every single day I step out of my apartment."

"This is different."

"Maybe. But the bones of the problem are the same. You have a killer on the loose, and I am a homicide detective. Seems like I'm exactly where I'm supposed to be." He turns to Allison. "I'll get the bags. Keep an eye on her."

Then, without another word, he turns to leave.

Sutton speaks up even before Steven's out the front door. "I'm going to grab a shower."

I take hold of his arm. "You can't be serious. You're just going to let him stay here?"

He gives me a wry look. "I doubt anyone *lets* your brother do anything. A family trait, it seems." I scowl as he adds, "But no, I don't plan to stop him."

"Sutton, this is too dangerous--"

"That's his decision to make," he says and then more pointedly, "As it was yours."

He's got me there. Dammit.

Sutton presses a kiss to my temple then turns and disappears upstairs.

Allison, alone with me now, crosses her arms.

"You are a bitch, you know that?" Her words lack any and all heat as she throws her arms wide in a dramatic gesture. "I cannot believe you kept all of this from me."

"I'm sorry," I say, guilt tugging at me. "Next time I find myself trapped in a town full of werewolves, I'll be sure to let you in on it."

"Good." She crosses the room in two long strides and wraps both arms around me in a crushing hug. "I missed you like crazy."

I return the embrace, tears burning in the corners of my eyes. "I missed you, too." Even as terrified as I am with her and Steven being here, it also brings me a sense of relief. As if I'm not alone anymore. Not that I was ever alone with Sutton here, but Allison and Steven are from pre-curse Serenity's life, and it's been far too long since I felt like that girl.

She pulls away and squeezes my arms. "You found yourself a cursed town, a bunch of werewolves, and an incredibly sexy Roscoe replacement, all in a matter of a few short weeks. I'm quite impressed, Ser." She winks at me, and I laugh.

"Sutton is not a Roscoe replacement."

Allison considers my words. "You're right. He's a massive step up."

"Get out!" Sutton bellows from upstairs. His words are followed by female laughter. "Now, Tabitha!"

We both whirl toward the stairs as Tabitha appears, grinning. "Can't blame a girl for trying." She disappears, and Allison turns toward me with wide eyes.

Before I can figure out how to explain what probably just happened, Sutton appears at the top of the stairs in only a towel and a look of pure rage. "If that girl wasn't already dead, I'd kill her myself," he grumbles.

He stalks off, and a second later, a door slams shut.

I find myself biting back a smile. Honestly, I should be mad. But Tabitha's absolutely right. Sutton is sexy as fuck, and I really can't blame a girl for trying.

Allison looks like she might actually laugh too. Before either of us can say anything, though, Steven pushes through the front door with two backpacks and a duffel. "Your wolf friends all went home."

"Probably because they realized you didn't pose a threat," I tell him honestly.

Steven grunts. "Where are our rooms?"

"You want to stay *in this house*?"

"Why the hell did you think I was getting the bags?"

I stare at him, trying to figure out *why* I didn't put two and two together. "Steven, you know this place is haunted, right?"

"Can't say I missed that part."

"And was owned by a witch who is now dead?"

"I thought the witch was alive," Allison says.

"Not that witch. Her sister. Umm…" I trail off. How much do I tell them?

"Serenity, I swear if you're keeping more secrets I will throw you over my shoulder and make you fucking leave after all," Steven growls.

"The owner of this house was named Yvette. Tabitha's aunt. And I may or may not have accidentally killed her with my magic."

Allison's jaw practically hits the floor.

Steven's eyes harden. "You did *what?*"

"She attacked me and my friend in the woods—also with magic—and then when Sutton showed up, she almost killed him. After that, it just kinda happened; the magic was there, and it blasted her." I stare down at my hands as if that will serve as some kind of evidence.

“It blasted her? Seriously, Ser?” Allison asks.

I shrug and meet Allison’s gaze. “She would have killed us.”

“You killed someone.” Steven speaks the sentence like an accusation, which pisses me off all over again.

“Don’t judge me, Steven Kellis. I’ve been doing everything I can to stay alive, and you cannot tell me you wouldn’t do the same. Shit! You threatened to kill someone less than five minutes ago!”

“That’s different.”

“Why?”

“Because you’re my sister, and you were never supposed to experience this type of danger. At least, not while I’m alive.” He pushes past me. “I’ll find two vacant rooms myself.”

I gape at him as he stomps up the stairs. The bastard managed to piss me off *and* make me feel guilty in the same sixty seconds. That has to be some kind of record, right?

“He’s been pretty worried about you.”

Turning to face Allison again, I note her haunted expression.

“We both have,” she adds. “And when he mentioned coming out here, I insisted on tagging along, so I got a front-row seat to his panic the entire way here.”

“Panic?” I snort. “Steven doesn’t panic.”

“When it comes to you, he does.”

AGITATED, I PACE THE LIVING ROOM FOR WHAT WILL PROBABLY BE my only quiet time in the foreseeable future. After his shower, which remained luckily solitary after Tabitha’s initial prank, Sutton left to update the pack while, upstairs, Allison and Steven get settled into their rooms.

Their fucking rooms.

In a haunted B&B.

That is set in a cursed town.

Full of zombies who are trying to kill me.

And a witch who wants my blood.

Honestly, I'd laugh at the shit cards I've been dealt if I wasn't so terrified something was going to go wrong.

The wallpaper in here is nearly as horrifying as the reality I'm facing. Salmon pink—if you can consider that a pink—and covered in tiny green dots. Photographs and paintings make up about half the wall while oddly shaped mirrors, decorative plates, and more than a few shelves, complete with antique dolls, cover the rest.

It is literally the creepiest room in this house, and that includes the room I released Tabitha into. Up until now, I've mostly avoided the space, and now I remember why. I'm just about to leave for somewhere less gaudy when a voice behind me stops me cold.

"I see you're making yourself right at home." I stiffen, the all-too-familiar voice washing over me as I turn. *What the...*

It can't be. It's impossible.

An antique, gold-rimmed mirror hangs directly in front of me and, in it, the reflection of a woman I haven't seen since—well—I killed her. "Yvette? How is—" I turn to look behind me, but I'm alone. What I'm seeing in the mirror isn't a *reflection* of her form; it *is* her form.

"Scream for them and I'll kill everyone in this house."

Dread coils in my belly. "Does no one in your family stay dead?"

She chuckles. "When you killed me, you did nothing but set my soul free, and since this mirror is spelled with my magic, it called me home."

"Wait. You've been here the whole time?"

The ghost count inside this house just keeps going up.

Her grin spreads, a menacing smile that makes me want to hurl. "Your brother and friend seem awfully worried about you."

Magic surges beneath my skin, and I clench my hands into fists. “Leave them alone. They have nothing to do with this.”

“Wrong. They have *everything* to do with this. At least, they do now that they’ve arrived in our quaint little town.”

“What do you want?”

“You,” she says simply. But I know better than to think anything about this is simple.

“Your sister already tried coming for me. It didn’t go well.”

“You mean the part where you hid upstairs while Sutton and his pack fought and nearly died for you?”

I don’t answer.

She’s hit too close to home with that one. Guilt tugs at me, but I refuse to let her see it.

“My sister and I have a proposition for you.”

“A proposition,” I repeat then snort. “As if I’d do anything for either of you.”

But I don’t miss the fact that, despite being trapped in this mirror, she’s been in contact with Myrtle.

“You might if it’s the only way to save those you love,” she says. “You may be a lot of things, Serenity, and fortunately for us, obnoxiously protective is one of them.”

“I wouldn’t expect either of you to understand familial loyalty.”

“You wouldn’t, would you?” She grins. “Which is precisely why we’ll win. There is nothing we won’t do, no one we won’t sacrifice to put you down. Your brother, your friend, Sutton, Phineas…I can keep going.”

“What the hell do you want?” My stomach churns, my legs like lead as I stand here looking a woman I killed in the eyes. A woman who now apparently wants to make a deal.

When did my life become an episode of the X-Files?

“Give yourself up. Help us finish the curse—for good this time—and we’ll let your brother and friend leave here alive.”

"All I have to sacrifice is an entire town, huh?"

Yvette smiles. "They're going to remain trapped, one way or another, Serenity. There is nothing you can do for them. Your brother and friend, though, there is still hope."

"He won't leave without me."

"That's not our problem," she replies. "You will go into the woods tonight to turn yourself over."

"And if I don't?"

"Then tomorrow, this entire town and all those in it will burn. We will gut your wolf, slaughter your brother and friend, and make the entire town watch. That way, they know it was because of you they lost their alpha."

The images her words conjure terrify me. She has me right where she wants me, and she fucking knows it. The smile on her face, the way her eyes light up as she threatens me—they know I'll do what they ask. And I wish I could prove them wrong. But with Steven, Allison, and Sutton on the line? There's no way in hell I'll risk it.

Never.

"Tick, tock, Serenity. We'll be expecting you." She disappears from view, but I keep my brave face on because now, apparently, it's not just the ghosts we have to worry about watching us.

"You're not fucking going anywhere."

I whirl, heart hammering, to see Sutton standing in the doorway. "How long have you been standing there?"

"You're not going anywhere," he repeats, eyes murderous as he stalks toward me. "Tell me you're not seriously considering it."

"Considering what?" Steven questions as he and Allison come into the room.

"Serenity had a little visit from an old friend," Sutton tells them without tearing his gaze from me. "Didn't you?"

Falls Gazette

Chapter Four

I'*m so busted.* Their angry, accusatory glares are a triple-beamed laser aimed right at the secret I would have hidden if not for Sutton overhearing that damn conversation. *Freaking werewolves and their amazing hearing.*

"I just want to protect you all," I insist, hoping they can at least understand that aspect of it.

"Well, you don't do it by keeping secrets," Steven snaps.

I stifle a groan.

"Steven's right," Allison says. "I thought we were done keeping things from each other."

The hurt look she gives me is worse than any angry comment they could have made. My shoulders sag.

"Yvette's soul is apparently trapped here," I say quietly. I glance at Sutton, whose frown is etched deeply onto his handsome face. I hate seeing him so worried. I hate everything about this stupid, stupid curse. "She's watching," I add. "Through the mirror."

They all glance past me to the gold-framed mirror. It's empty now. Innocuous-looking in this outdated room. But I know better, and my heart still hammers from the way she just popped up like that.

"Then what the hell are we still doing standing here?" Allison demands.

"She's right. Let's talk upstairs," Sutton says.

"It's not like there aren't other ears," I remind him.

His frown deepens, which I didn't even think possible before. "We can't leave the house." He glances at Steven, and I'm assuming the conversation with the pack didn't quite go as well as he was hoping. "Not without setting off the pack."

"Then upstairs it is," Steven comments.

"First, I'm getting this thing out of here," Sutton says.

He strides over and yanks the mirror off the wall. Then he marches through the house, all the way to the back door. We all follow him out, and I watch as he sets the mirror on the porch, leaning it against the house with the glass facing inward.

I half-expect Yvette to return, squawking a complaint about being removed. But nothing happens. Sutton steps back and grunts, satisfied, and we each file back inside.

Silently, all of us make our way upstairs and into the bedroom I share with Sutton. My chest tightens as I recall everything Yvette said to me. No wonder they've always been two steps ahead, they've been spying on us!

As soon as we're inside, Sutton scans the room and crosses it to remove the one and only mirror hanging in the space—facing the bed. *Eww.*

"Do you think she's in there too?" Allison whispers.

"Better to be safe than sorry," Steven says.

Sutton sets it out in the hall and then closes the door, leaning against it as Steven studies the room.

"You're both sleeping in here?" my brother questions.

"Don't even think about starting with me right now," I tell him.

I swear if he starts in on me about my sleeping arrangements, I might actually implode. Surprisingly, he shuts up.

"Let's just cut straight to it." Allison crosses her arms. "What did this Yvette say to you, exactly?"

Quickly, I recap Yvette's "deal" for them. Even before I'm done, they all wear matching looks of disapproval. Shocker.

"You're not actually considering her offer," Steven states as if he's in my head. When I don't respond, his eyes narrow. "Because that would be the stupidest move you could make."

Letting out a breath, I cross to the window and look down at the still lingering carnage. While the bodies are gone—I don't even want to know whose job that task became— blood still stains the grass below. "You don't get it." Frustrated, I turn back to face them. "Today's attack was just a warning. If I don't give Myrtle what she wants, she'll come after you three next."

Steven scoffs. "The bitch can try."

His confidence is so absolute that I don't even bother to argue.

"We're stronger together," Allison says.

Even though her words are softer, it's clear she shares the same misplaced confidence Steven does. Or maybe it's their lack of fear that bothers me so much. They clearly have no idea what they're up against.

I turn to Sutton. "You know what Myrtle is capable of. I can't do nothing."

"Sacrificing yourself won't stop them." He flicks a glance toward my brother. "On this, we agree."

"Good for you two. Start a fucking club then," I snap.

"Ser, from what you've told us, this woman is clearly not going to stop. In fact, the moment she gets you, she'll have won," Allison attempts to rationalize with me. But it's difficult to rationalize when the consequences are terrifying. Still, I also know when I'm outnumbered.

And at the moment, I am. "Fine," I say. "But if we're going to stay here, we need to find a way to get Yvette's spying ass out of that mirror." I cut Sutton off before he can get the words out. "Not like I did with Tabitha."

His lips twitch.

For some reason, knowing he can still find humor bolsters me.

"Good, if we've settled that, I'm going to take a shower." Steven marches out.

Sutton makes a comment about needing more supplies for the extra people to feed, and then he leaves too.

Allison, however, flops down on the bed and looks back at me expectantly.

"What?" I ask warily.

"We finally have more than five minutes together," she says as if her intentions are obvious. "And I want to know everything. Start from the moment you got here. And no more secrets."

I almost refuse her. The idea of spilling so much is daunting. Not to mention she's still trying to wrap her head around so many impossibilities being actually real. But then I think about how many times I'd wished for a friend during the past few weeks. And the reality of finally having my bestie back is too good to deny.

"Okay," I say, settling on the mattress. "But you might want to get comfortable because this shit could take a while to tell."

"I'm not going anywhere," she says with a grin.

An hour later, we're both cackling, and my ribs hurt from how much I've laughed. Instead of being judgmental or lecturing me about my recklessness like Steven or Sutton might have done, Allison is supportive and, more importantly, always willing to find humor in the hard shit.

"You did not try to fight zombies with a ceramic bookend," she says, laughing through tears.

"Hey, I did some real damage," I say in defense. "I peeled away at least three layers of skin with the edge of that thing."

"Ugh, gross," she groans.

"Tell me about it. I think Myrtle's trying to disgust us to death."

That sobers her immediately. "She sounds truly horrifying."

"She's a bitch," I say, my anger quickly blotting out my light mood.

"And her daughter?" she asks. "Tabitha?" She lowers her voice to a whisper and says, "The ghost? She seems like a piece of work."

I wince, knowing damn well the subject of our conversation is probably listening in. Unless she's got Sutton cornered alone in a room somewhere. That possibility is much more likely, and I'm tempted to go looking for him now. He has been gone a long time.

"Ser?" Allison prompts, and I realize I've been silent too long.

"Sorry, yeah, it's a lot," I say on a sigh.

"Well, Steven and I are here now, so you don't have to deal with it on your own."

"I wasn't on my own," I tell her, and my heart warms as I say it. Because as much as I missed my best friend and my annoyingly protective brother, having Sutton to lean on through everything has made it almost worth going through all of it in the first place.

The look Allison gives me says she knows it too.

"You know," she says cautiously, "You haven't asked me once about how things are at the paper."

"Shit, I'm a horrible friend. I'm so sorry. How are things there for you?"

"Not for me, for you," she says.

"Oh."

Her brows lift. "You don't want to know anything about your old job?"

I shrug. "What would it change? I'm still stuck here. And even if I weren't... I'm not sure I'm the same girl I was then."

Her brows lift. "Are you saying you don't want to be a reporter?"

She sounds incredulous, and I can't blame her.

"I don't know," I admit. "It's kind of hard to think past the fact that two witches—actually, make that three, just in case—want me dead or at least drained of blood. In comparison, my career doesn't seem all that important."

"Not to mention a century-old werewolf alpha male is madly in love with you."

I shake my head. "How do you manage to make all of this sound so romantic?"

Her eyes gleam. "I mean, you *are* talking to New York City's most prominent Lifestyle reporter."

"Wait. Lifestyle?" I repeat. "What did I miss?"

"A lot," she says, tossing a pillow at me.

"First off, congratulations! Second, tell me everything," I order, catching the pillow and using it as a backrest. "Leave nothing out. Well, everything except the *cat* guy."

She wrinkles her nose, and we both crack up laughing again.

"Fine. But first, I want to know more about this magic you have. I mean, it's not every day a girl finds out her best bitch can move things with her mind."

I snort. "First of all, I never said I could move things with my mind. Nice fishing, though."

Allison grins at me. "Well? Let's see what you can do."

"Okay, hang on." I get off the bed and cross the room to retrieve the grimoire. As soon as it's in my hands, I rush back over and plop down onto the bed. "I've been practicing."

"Is that—shit, Ser! You have a fucking Charmed spell book!"

"It's a grimoire," I correct with a laugh. "So, yes, technically."

"That's so fucking cool!" My best friend's eyes light up as she takes it in.

Her enthusiasm is such a fresh change from the wariness I've felt and the worry Sutton has shown over me using this book. More confident, I run my hands over the leather cover and then crack it open to the first orange sticky note hanging out of the top.

"You tabbed a spell book?"

"Late night reading," I reply, cheeks heating.

"You are an organizational freak, you know that?"

"Maybe, but I never lose anything."

Allison rolls her eyes then claps her hands. "Show me what you can do."

"Okay." I take a deep breath and close my eyes, focusing only on the threads of power I've been trying to sense. They grow stronger with each attempt, and in this moment, they're almost too easy to grasp onto. I raise my hands, letting the power rise, then run my hands over my body.

"Holy shit!" Allison exclaims, but I focus only on the power.

Seconds tick by until every inch of my body tingles. Then, I open my eyes. Allison stares right past me, her head whipping to the left and right as she tries to find me.

"Ser? Where the hell did you go?"

My grin widens so much my cheeks hurt. *I did it!* This spell in particular is one I've been trying to master because it means hiding in plain sight. The best kind of camouflage. My own, personal invisibility cloak.

"Serenity?" Allison calls out. Her tone has an edge now; she's getting nervous.

I raise my hands again and snap, envisioning the strands snapping loose.

"What the!" At the sight of me, Allison throws herself backward and tumbles to the floor.

Unable to help myself, I bend over, laughing hysterically as she clamors back onto the bed.

"You just—you were invisible!"

"Yep! And that's just the start of what I'll be able to do once I master the magic."

Allison climbs back onto the bed and rubs the palms of her hands on her jeans. Eyes glittering with excitement, she smiles. "More. Right now. I demand more."

WELL INTO THE NIGHT, THE ONLY SOUND AGAINST THE UTTER silence is Sutton's light snoring as he sleeps beside me. After dinner, he'd admitted the pack was still unconvinced about Steven. The meeting earlier had revealed their distrust and then some. The compromise? An extra team watching the house. Now, there are double the guards outside. All of them listening to everything going on inside these walls. And that meant zero sexy times with my man. Between the pack of wolves outside and my own brother sleeping thirty feet away, I just can't. When I'd told him so, Sutton had chuckled. Then, he'd promptly kissed my forehead, assured me everything would be okay, and immediately fell asleep.

If only it were that simple.

Now, the clock at my bedside reads a little after two a.m. Despite the late hour, I'm wide awake, my thoughts racing. The later it gets, the fewer reasons I can come up with to ignore Yvette's threats earlier.

Myrtle wants my blood. She has a purpose; a use for me. Yvette, on the other hand, has already proven she'd just as soon kill me as use me for a damn thing. Not to mention Sutton.

She's already tried killing him once. And despite what I promised the others earlier, I refuse to let her get close enough to do it again. I'll die first. Even if I am willing to walk away from him,

Sutton Hargrave will survive this. Otherwise, what the hell was even the point to it all?

The problem is, Myrtle's always one step ahead. Like having her dead sister watch over us from a magical fucking mirror.

And I'm not stupid enough to think being trapped inside that mirror is keeping these twisted sisters from hurting a single person in this house.

Even the thought of her hurting one of them tightens my chest with absolute fear.

We could leave. But there's nowhere else to go. Sutton's house is still inaccessible, and now, with Steven and Allison here, we're even more of a target for Myrtle. Sutton's already made it clear he doesn't want to bring that kind of danger to anyone's home, and I don't blame him.

These people are already suffering enough.

Maybe we can hole up in the library. Mable would be willing enough. Especially since I learned she's the one who lured me to town in the first place. But I already know Sutton won't hide there. He won't bring this kind of danger down on the town he's spent a hundred years protecting. Not even with Tabitha here, stalking his every move.

Tabitha.

The moment the idea takes shape, I know what I'm going to do. Still, I lie here and pretend to think of another way. A way that involves less chance of me dying. But I know there isn't one. Going after Myrtle is stupid…that's what they'll say. And there's a very good chance they'll be saying it at my funeral. That my magic won't be strong enough to kill her without dying in the attempt. But if that bitch takes me with her, I'll go out knowing I saved them all.

I tell myself it will be worth it.

Sutton Hargrave is absolutely worth dying for.

When I finally get up, I move as silently as possible. The magic rises fluidly in my hands, and I brush my palms over my body, spelling myself into absolute soundlessness. It's becoming easier to wield, the magic. Despite having little training, the energy itself is instinctual. I tell myself that makes me stronger, more prepared for what I'm about to do.

I killed Yvette with less than half the skill I have now. Maybe I can actually do this.

With magic cloaking me, Sutton doesn't stir.

Once I'm dressed, I creep out into the hall, but I don't go downstairs. Not yet. Instead, I make my way quietly to the bedroom at the very end of the corridor. Steven almost chose it for Allison earlier, but I stopped him. They each took the rooms across from Sutton and me. And now this one, Yvette's old room —now, Tabitha's more or less—remains empty. Of living people, anyway.

I slip inside and close the door behind me with a soft click.

Moonlight filters in through the window, so I don't bother flipping the light switch. It'll only give me away.

"Tabitha," I whisper.

I pause, wondering how the hell to summon a ghost that refuses to take orders in the first place. But a few seconds later, something moves out of the corner of my eye, and when I turn to look, Tabitha stands in front of the armoire, her ghostly silhouette beautifully pale in the gloom.

"Careful," she says, "Sutton's half naked and alone in there. A girl could see an opportunity."

I ignore her threat and say what I came to say. "I'm leaving."

She frowns. "Leaving where?"

"I'm going to find your mother and put an end to this—one way or another."

There's a beat of silence between us. She doesn't ask what I mean, and I don't expect her to. Tabitha's flighty attitude is only a distraction. She's cunning, and I have no doubt she already knows exactly what Yvette demanded earlier.

When she does speak, her words surprise me. "You can't beat her. Trust me. I've tried."

I don't let myself think too hard about that. Not now.

"We'll see," I tell her, feigning confidence. "But before I go, I need you to promise me something. Protect the others while I'm gone."

She sniffs. "Your brother and his little pet are of no interest to me."

"I don't care about your interest. I want your word you'll watch over them."

"Why would I give you that?"

"Because if I leave, it means you'll have Sutton all to yourself. You get what you want. And in exchange, so do I."

I can practically see the wheels turning at that.

"Why me?" she asks finally. "You hate me."

"Maybe I do. But you love him."

"Isn't that a reason for you to want me far away from him?"

"Sutton can decide for himself who he wants close to him."

Even though I mean the words, my heart aches as I say them. Because I'm standing here taking that choice away.

Tabitha snorts. "Men never know what they want until we tell them."

I shake my head, in no mood to argue this. "Do we have a deal?"

"Deal," she says.

Her smirk is victorious and smug enough that I ball my hands into fists. Despite this being my idea, she has just made it seem like the win is all hers. I remind myself that punching her would only complicate our arrangement. If I could even make contact at all.

Ugh.

Cloaking the sound of my steps, I let myself out into the hall and down the stairs. At the bottom, I wait, making sure Steven hasn't positioned himself in front of the exit just in case. But there's no one else down here. Even Lance and Victoria seem to be tucked in for the night.

Carefully, I make my way through the darkened house. When I reach the back door, I hesitate. The pack is undoubtedly guarding this place, and I can't risk them spotting me. With another flourish of my hand, I call up my magic and perform the same trick as earlier. Invisibility settles over me, and I let myself outside. The back door makes a soft click as I shut it, and I hold my breath, scanning the backyard and the trees beyond. But no one comes to investigate.

I exhale.

The mirror still stands where Sutton left it earlier. With silent movements, I carefully lift the mirror and turn it around so the glass is facing outward again. Then, I crouch in front of it and hope the railing hides me from view of the patrols. Finally, I square my shoulders and let my invisibility fall away.

"I'm ready," I whisper.

Yvette's reflection winks to life immediately, and her lips curve into a sharp smile. "Yes," she says, "I think you are."

Falls Gazette

Chapter Five

I've never been scared of the dark. Not in the traditional sense, at least. As a child, I had too many older brothers willing to fight off anything that went bump in the night. Boogeyman? Steven could kick his ass. Monsters under the bed? Stuart vanquished them with his karate moves. On more than one occasion, I fell asleep to Sawyer cracking my door and making sure everything was calm and quiet. But now, as I move through the trees with nothing but the dim moonlight to guide me, the once-unfamiliar feeling of fear unfurls in my belly. I'd nearly brought my cell with me, except I have no doubt Steven knows someone who can track the damn thing.

And I cannot risk him finding me. Not until I know he's safe. That they're all safe. I wrap my arms tightly around myself as I trudge onward toward where Yvette instructed me. Above, an owl hoots. The abruptness of its sound makes me nearly come out of my skin. If not for the magic rendering me soundless, my shriek would have definitely busted me. I pause to exhale slowly, waiting for the panic to recede. My heart thunders in my chest as I continue walking in the direction Yvette told me to go.

I'm deeper into the woods than I've ever been and walking in the exact opposite direction of Sutton's house. Basically, I'm lost as shit. Yvette didn't give me much to go on. "Go down to the old church, and take the path behind it. Don't stop walking until we find you." It's not even the pitch-black forest I mind so much as the "we" part of her directions. Who is this "we" anyway? If I see a zombie missing half its face right now, I will literally die, which totally foils my plans.

Something crunches a branch behind me, and I jump, my heart hammering like a drumline picking up its beat.

For fucks sake. If I die out here—

"Serenity, so nice of you to join us this evening."

My back stiffens as the cool tone fills my ears. The fact that she can see me at all doesn't bode well for my plan. But more than that is the familiarity of the voice itself. *Please have a face, please have a face...* I turn to see Sutton's un-alive mother standing before me. Vivian Hargrave. Other than being pale, she looks normal. Alive, skin intact, which I am more than grateful for because zombie in the woods? At night? By myself? No thanks. I didn't even make it through the Resident Evil movie.

"Where's Myrtle?"

Vivian grins at me. "I am right here," she replies. Except I know from experience it's not Vivian talking. Nope. Thanks to a very macabre brand of magic, Myrtle's talking *through* Vivian. It's equal parts disturbing and impressive. "Follow me." Turning, she begins gliding through the forest, leading me deeper and deeper into the trees.

With a snap of my fingers, I let my magic recede. No point wasting it since it's obviously not working in the first place. I try not to panic about the way she clearly saw right through it just now.

Instead, I mentally run through all the other tricks I know. One of them has to help me beat her.

"You ever get tired of wearing dead people as costumes?" I ask to her back.

"As it happens, this magic is nothing more than a looking glass. I can see through these eyes. Move through these hands. All the while, my borrowed body is tucked away safe."

"And whose body might that be?" I ask, fishing shamelessly.

"Nice try," she says.

The fact is, Myrtle is hiding in someone in Midnight Falls. But even now, when I've delivered myself into her hands, she won't say whose life she's stolen.

"You're disgusting, you know. Hiding out in dead people."

"Means to an end, Serenity." She doesn't sound bothered by my tone. In fact, she sounds smug as hell.

The bitch thinks she's won.

Fine. I'll let her think so. For now. All I have going for me is the element of surprise. So I swallow back my smart-ass comment and let her lead me farther and farther away from the only people who can help stop what will happen to me if I fail.

Seconds tick by as we walk until, all around, the sounds of nature fall mute. No crickets chirping, no more owls hooting—nothing but my footsteps and the breeze rustling through the branches overhead. *Not creepy at all.*

"Where are we going?" I demand.

Myrtle doesn't bother answering, nor does she offer me a single glance.

"You can at least give me a heads up. Are more of your zombie buddies going to be joining us?"

Still, nothing.

I fall silent and go over my plan. Get in, kill this bitch once and for all, and get the hell out. If I'm lucky, I won't die in the attempt.

If I'm very lucky, Steven won't kill me for doing it in the first place. Idly, I wonder if Sutton would help him or fend him off. Then I decide I probably don't want to know.

Just ahead, the trees make way for a large clearing with a small cottage sitting directly in the center. Vivian walks straight for it, and I follow, slightly slower. The closer I get, the more sinister the place feels. The wooden boards making up the walls are cracked in some places and rotting in others. From what I can make out in the darkness, the roof is partially caved, and the front door is gone. But it's not just the age that has me on edge. There's a darkness here. A gross kind of magic that hangs like death all around me.

"Cozy," I murmur as Vivian's body leads me inside. The stench of mold fills my nose, and my stomach rolls in response. Dingy, mildewy, and the farthest thing from a sanitary location for a blood draw. I suppose if Myrtle doesn't kill me, something in this place might.

Vivian turns to me, her unseeing eyes sharp on my face. When she speaks, I know Myrtle's the one choosing the words. "I'll admit, I didn't think Yvette could do it. But you are here, which means you have accepted our terms," she finally says.

"No. I am here to discuss the terms," I correct. "Then, I'll decide whether or not I want to accept them."

Vivian arches a dark brow. "Very well. What are your terms."

"First, I want to know what you're planning to do with my blood." Of course, I already know what she wants to do with it, but I'm hoping this will give me more of an insight as to what happens after the curse is renewed.

Vivian clasps her hands behind her back and begins to pace, the hem of her skirt gliding over the floor as if she's merely floating. "We are going to seal this town for good," she says. "Using the magic in your blood. In casting a spell this powerful, you will become immortal and remain behind, thus sealing its potency forever."

"You keep saying 'we'," I point out. "But last I checked, Yvette was dead. Trapped in a mirror, sure, but very, very dead."

Vivian grins at me, and the lack of humor makes my skin crawl. "Not everything remains dead," she tells me. "The soul is all that matters, and in this case, my sister's soul is very much alive. When the curse is complete and I've found a new body, I'll find one for her too."

I swallow hard. *Peachy.* "Why? I mean, why include the entire town?"

Vivian's face contorts in hate. "The people here deserve to be punished."

"For what? They did nothing."

"They did everything," she snarls back. "My daughter was pulled in by Sutton's charm. She was manipulated by him and everyone in this town. Tricked into turning her back on me."

"Tabitha is the one who obsessed over Sutton. Not the other way around."

"Is that what he told you?" she questions, crossing her arms. "Men will say whatever is necessary to get between your legs. Something I'm assuming you've already allowed him to do."

Anger heats my face, but I don't pop off. Not yet. "As a matter of fact, your daughter was the one who filled me in on what happened."

A muscle in her jaw twitches. "You've spoken with Tabitha?"

"Given that your sister has been spying on me, I'm assuming you already know that, so cut the shit. Tabitha is obsessed with Sutton. You chose to keep them apart and, in doing so, drove a massive wedge between you and your daughter." Myrtle looks about ready to explode, so I keep it going. "Not Sutton. Not this town. You did this."

"You know *nothing,*" she growls. Then, by the next heartbeat, she's back to her usual cool-natured self. "He tricked you. Just as he tricked her. And you were so foolish you fell for it. The only thing he ever wanted was the magic in your blood. You were a means to an end as well, Serenity. A way for Sutton to break the curse placed upon him and his people for their poor treatment of my daughter."

"You're wrong." Deep down, I know she's lying. But even so, I can't help wondering... What was going to happen as soon as the curse was broken? Would Sutton have wanted to keep me? Or would he have dismissed me like nothing more than a used-up party favor? As soon as the thought enters my mind, I reject it. No way. Sutton and I are real.

"I see the doubt in you."

I play it up, letting her believe she has me. "Sutton loves me." I force doubt into my words.

"He made my Tabitha believe he loved her, too," she replies. "And this entire town stood by and allowed it to happen. They allowed my daughter to be made a fool of. To be treated like she was disposable."

Feigning sadness, I let the emotions she is hoping to see in me play out all over my face as I convince myself she's right just for good measure. Betrayal. Loss. Fear. I round them all up and hope like hell the one semester of drama I took in high school doesn't fail me now.

For this to work, I *need* her to believe she's gotten to me. Because then, I stand a better chance at getting out of this hellish cabin alive. "Fine. You want to seal the town. Punish them. But why me? Why do I have to be the one to stay and become immortal?"

"As your punishment," she replies. "You worked against me and killed my sister. You will remain here, with this town, for eternity. And once Sutton knows you're the curse-caster, he'll want nothing to do with you." Her eyes gleam in cruel enjoyment. "Or better yet, he'll try to kill you. And find out how useless that task will be."

Now, the fear is very, very real. Eternity trapped in one place? With people—no, werewolves—who are going to hate me enough to try to kill me until the end of time? I shake off the fear and refocus on what's important. I don't dare gather my magic. Not yet. Instead, I keep talking and look around for something to use as a weapon when my moment comes.

"My brother and Allison. They can leave when this is done?"

"Of course. As of now, they've done nothing to interfere with my plans. Therefore, my fight is not with them."

There. In the corner. My eyes land on a broom propped against the wall. It's not exactly deadly, but it's all I've got.

"There's no *as of now*," I reply, taking a step closer. "They get to leave. Period. No matter what."

Myrtle smiles. "You have no bargaining power here, child. The only reason you still breathe is because I am giving you a fair chance out of sentimental loyalty for my late brother."

"Brother? Sentimental loyalty?" I snort. "Maybe body jumping and obsessively cursing this town has made you crazy, but your dead brother has nothing to do with me."

She grins, a sick sort of stretching of skin on Vivian's zombie face. "You have no idea, do you?"

"No idea about what?"

Myrtle's grin spreads. "Whose witch blood runs in your veins." She tilts her head, watching me carefully as she says, "My brother, Maxwell Augustus, defied our family and married a human. When this happens, it's not uncommon for the offspring's magic to become dormant. A suppressed gene, I believe they call it. The magic can skip entire generations, in fact, before it reappears down the line."

Her words hit me like a ton of bricks. She thinks my witch blood is from *her* family line?

"You have no proof," I say, the broom forgotten.

"The proof is standing before me," she snaps. "Your great-grandfather Maxwell's blood calls to me even now.

Maxwell.

The familiar name makes my stomach roil. I've seen it thousands of times in my father's office. It's the signature on those damned maps he loves so much. My great-grandfather Max.

And that means I'm... Myrtle's niece.

My mouth falls slack, eyes widening. "No. That's not true."

"Denial serves no purpose here."

Her tone is incredibly patient to the point of bored. She doesn't care one way or another whether I believe her. She cares only for my blood—which makes more sense than ever. Who better to strengthen this woman's curse than a witch from her own family line?

"I'm an Augustus?"

"Of sorts," she replies. "Though that won't matter if you continue wasting my time. You wish for your brother and Allison to go free. I am allowing that. No harm will come to them as long as you give me what I need."

"Not good enough," I say, forcing myself to focus now more than ever.

I think of the broom. Imagining myself grabbing it, breaking its handle in two, and staking this bitch. Is she a vampire? No. Can I kill an already dead lady? Technically speaking, probably not. But all I have to do is distract her. And then my magic can do the rest.

Invisible. Soundless. I can do this.

Maybe she saw through me earlier, but if Vivian-the-zombie's eyes don't work, I might have a chance.

"You'll leave every member of my family unharmed," I add. "You'll get what you want, but they remain safe."

"Fine," she growls.

I can feel her patience thinning. It's now or never.

I let a bit of vulnerability creep into my expression. It's not hard. I'm terrified of what I'm about to do. "You're going to make me immortal?"

"Yes. The curse will need unlimited power to draw from as it has drawn from mine since it was cast." A trace of regret creeps into her tone as she adds, "If only I'd possessed the ability to make my own body mortal back then. But I've learned. And I won't make the same mistake twice."

"Will anyone else have to die?"

"No. The town will simply remain here, frozen in time. I'll place wards to keep the humans from venturing here, which means it will only be the wolves and you, for eternity."

"So, no more food supply trucks coming to the stores."

"You will be completely cut off," she confirms. "A necessary lesson you taught me, Serenity. You coming here was troublesome, though I suppose it is working out for the best." Tilting her head to the side, she offers me her hand. "Do we have a deal, then?"

Swallowing hard. I reach out and close my fingers around Vivian's cold, dead hand. A shiver runs down my spine as we shake. Then, she releases me and crosses to an old table against the far wall. The moment her gaze draws downward to gather her supplies, I make my move.

Leaping forward, my fingers curl around the broom. The wooden handle is cold and smooth in my hands. Whirling with it raised, I call upon every drop of magic I can muster. Invisible. Soundless. Deadly. Fear steals my breath. Or maybe it's the force of the magic I've called forth. The air stirs, an otherworldly wind toying with the ends of my hair. Energy—pure, potent, paralyzing energy surrounds me. I've done it.

The swing is clean and perfectly aimed.

The broom hits Vivian in the back of the head, and she staggers against the table, arms splayed out to catch her unbalanced body. But the magic packs a hell of a punch, and her face slams into the aged wood tabletop hard enough to make a sickening suction sound.

With a second swing, I knock her legs out from under her and watch as she falls to the dirt floor. She lets out a groan, and I know it's not pain evoking such a sound. Myrtle's pissed.

Good.

I don't wait for her to recover.

Instead, I break the broom handle across my knee. Then I grip the two halves, one in each hand. In unison, I bring them both down and bury them in Vivian's eyes. She screams so loud I fear she's woken the entire town.

I stumble backward, trying to regain my footing. To call up more magic. Something strong enough to cast Myrtle's spirit into the fucking ether.

Vivian's body goes quiet and limp.

With my hands brimming in magic, I let it loose on the entire space. A boom sounds, and the walls shake. If there'd been any glass in the windows, I'm sure they would have broken. I barely manage to stay on my feet as I stumble the last few steps toward the exit. If Myrtle's anywhere nearby, that blast would have knocked her sideways too.

I hope.

Before I can reach it, the door slams open harder than humanly possible. A gust of wind tears toward me, shoving me backward. A figure darkens the opening, the shadowy silhouette of a woman standing firm against my blast. Sparks drip from her fingers like liquid silver.

While I cannot see her features or make out her expression, the woman's rage is visceral—the energy coming off her more powerful than anything I've ever produced —and I know, in this moment, I've already lost.

But I refuse to give up.

One more blast of magic. She doesn't see it coming, and the surprise of it sends her off balance. Darting sideways, I move past her, nearly making it to the door when something slams into the back of my head, and the world goes black.

Falls Gazette

Chapter Six

Strong hands grip my shoulders. Through a very thick layer of fog and what feels like cotton in my ears, I hear my name called.

"Serenity?"

Softly at first, then more urgent when I don't respond.

"Serenity!"

The voice is deep. Male. It feels comforting. Safe even. I can't remember why that's important, but it is. Unfortunately, my tongue won't move to form a response. I can't seem to will my eyes open, not because I'm physically incapable but because I really don't want to face what I already know is the angry expression of the man attempting to rouse me.

"Ser, can you hear me?" another male voice asks. "Dammit, she's bleeding."

This one is equally familiar but not nearly as patient.

I hear shuffling and then, "I'm going to kill whoever did this," the second voice declares. The words draw me closer to consciousness until, all at once, the fog clears, and a new sensation slams into me.

Pain.

From the second my eyes open, my head throbs like it's been beaten with a stick. I groan and lift my hand to the back of my head, pressing gingerly against the sore spot. I suck in a breath when my own touch brings fresh pain that stings the back of my skull.

Forcing my eyes open, I lower my hand and look down at my fingers. My eyes widen as I stare in horror at the sticky blood coating them.

"She's awake," says the first voice. *Sutton.*

My eyes flutter as I look up into his drawn expression. He wears a deep frown, and in his eyes is real fear being chased off by a palpable relief.

"My head," I manage to say. My voice is more of a whimper.

"I see it," he says grimly.

On either side of him, Allison and Steven hover. They each wear expressions in varying stages of panic. When our eyes meet, Allison tries to smile, but it's weak and unconvincing. Steven doesn't bother. In fact, he looks furious—at me or for me, I can't tell. Honestly, probably both.

I look past them to where muted daylight streams in through the single window, and I realize where I am. And why.

The cabin. Vivian. Myrtle.

Our bargain.

And my failed attack.

My expression must reflect my horror because Sutton's hands on my shoulders ease up, soothing rather than gripping for dear life.

"It's okay," he says. "You're safe now."

"I'm not okay. None of us are. I failed. I—"

I stop short as I catch sight of my inner arm. Purple bruising in the shape of a handprint is clearly visible. But that's not what makes me quake. There, in the center of the bruising, is a tiny red mark marring the inside of my elbow. The kind that comes from being stuck with a needle.

My body goes cold as I realize what must have happened.

"She took it," I whisper. "She knocked me out and fucking took it."

Then a sob is rising, and my throat closes in an effort to hold it inside. My next breath is ragged and nearly chokes me.

"We need to get her out of here," Steven says.

Sutton doesn't argue. Without a word, he winds his arms more firmly around me and lifts me easily into the air.

Steven regards him briefly and then shrugs. "That works," he says.

"Come on." Allison leads the way, and we file outside. The sun is brighter here, sending the pounding in my head to a crescendo. I turn, burying my face in a shoulder I never thought I'd see again.

They'll want to know what happened. And I'll have to tell them what a fool I was to try something so reckless and crazy. I failed them. And I failed myself. I'm a damned moron. A fool of epic proportions.

Sutton marches us through the woods in silence. Steven and Allison whisper quietly behind me, but I don't bother trying to hear what they're saying. I probably don't want to know.

Finally, we emerge from the trees, but instead of the bed and breakfast looming ahead, I see the church. Right. The path started here. I'd forgotten.

I expect Sutton to walk past it, but he marches us directly inside. "There's a first aid kit in the foyer closet," he says to the others as we enter.

"I'll get it." Allison veers off, and we leave her behind as Sutton continues farther in.

Sutton's footsteps echo in the small, empty sanctuary. He sets me gently on the front pew and then perches beside me. Steven slides into the second row, his expression still full of barely checked rage.

"Why are we here?" I ask.

"I'm not taking you back to that house." Sutton's words are barely more than a growl, and I wonder if something else happened. Before I can ask, Allison rushes toward us with a first aid kit already propped open in her hands. She scoots in beside Steven, and, together, they go to work pulling out gauze and antibiotic ointment for my bleeding head.

The moment the cleaning gauze touches my wound, I hiss out a breath.

"Sorry," Steven mutters. "This is not going to feel great."

Sutton reaches forward and grips my hands, squeezing gently as I fight back tears, thanks to the stinging agony that is Steven and Allison cleaning my headwound. I breathe deeply, eyes closed, trying to focus on anything else.

But all I can focus on is the mess I've created. Some hero I am.

While they work, I remain silent, not offering any explanation or information.

It's not until my head is bandaged and no more injuries are left to treat that I know I'm out of time.

Sutton's gaze darkens, and he releases my hands. "What happened?"

Right.

Best to get it over with.

"I went to see Myrtle," I say quietly.

"Yeah, we got that part," Steven says drily.

Clearly, no one will be cutting me a single inch of slack.

I take a steadying breath and then tell them as quickly as possible everything that happened.

"I thought I could use my magic. That I could at least distract her long enough to take her out," I finish, misery and pain making it hard to hold my head up. I don't even try to look them in the eye anymore. "Anyway, obviously, it didn't work, and she knocked me out instead."

I wince at the mention of my head, and Allison digs back into the first aid kit.

"Here," she says, holding out two painkillers and a small pouch of emergency water.

I take them gratefully and down the pills before chugging the water. The relief from my dry throat is instant. When I lower the bottle again, Steven and Sutton are both glaring at me hard enough to raise my blood pressure with the force of their ire.

"You really went out there in the middle of the night alone to fight a witch." Steven shakes his head.

It's not a question, so I don't bother answering.

"And your arm?" Sutton asks quietly.

Damn.

I knew he wouldn't miss that.

Steven and Allison both look down, and I lift my arm to show them the markings.

"She must have taken my blood after she knocked me out," I say quietly.

Sutton's silence speaks volumes.

"So, what the fuck happens now?" Steven asks.

I flinch at the sharpness of his words.

"Now, she'll use it to re-cast the curse," I say. "This time forever."

"Oh God, Serenity," Allison whispers.

Steven curses again and then leans back, his nostrils flaring with every angry breath.

I look at Sutton. "Say something."

I don't know what I expect. Rage, maybe. A lecture. Instead, his expression twists into a pained sort of accusation. "You could have been killed," he says.

"No," I say. "She won't kill me."

His eyes narrow. He knows there's more.

"If you believe that, you're more naïve than I thought," Steven says with a snort. "You never should have fucking come here."

I glare at him then focus on Allison, the only one who doesn't look ready to throttle me. "Myrtle had a brother," I say. "His name was Maxwell Augustus." Then I glance back at Steven again, waiting for the recognition. "He married a human, and they had children. And those children had children." Steven doesn't reply, so I add, "We know him as Great-grandpa Max."

Steven's expression goes slack.

"Wait. You're related?" Allison pales. "To the witches?"

"You're an Augustus," Sutton says flatly. It's not a question, but I wish more than anything I could tell him no.

Instead, I look down at my hands, at the bruising on my arm—anywhere but at Sutton's face.

Steven leans forward, eyes narrowed. "We're really related to this bitch?"

"Unfortunately," I tell him. "But for whatever reason, she's decided that relation deserves mercy. She could have killed me. She didn't."

"And that's why she wants your blood," Allison says suddenly. "I mean, it's classic spellwork," she adds, cheeks flushing. "Using the blood of a relative makes the magic stronger. It was in Charmed and in Legacies—"

She stops, her cheeks flushing. "Except this is real." Her hands tighten into fists at her sides.

"Right," Steven says, "So that brings me back to my earlier question: What happens now?"

"Once she completes the new curse, the town will be sealed

forever. But the deal I made means you two can go, and she won't harm the family."

"The deal?" Steven snaps. "What deal?"

"I did what I could to save you all," I say, finally risking a glance at Sutton.

His expression is unreadable, but that in itself tells me how upset he is with me. My stomach drops, heart breaking.

"How did you even get past the guards?" Steven asks. "According to them, no one even left the house."

"I used magic," I say.

"The invisibility spell," Allison says, eyes lit with understanding.

"She's got centuries' worth of experience," Steven says, his voice rising. He's clearly not nearly as impressed with my ability as Allison. "How in the hell did you ever think you'd be a match for her?"

His tone is harsh, his words a slap in the face. The way he looks at me snaps my control, and I grab hold of magic without even thinking. The air trembles with it, and far in the back of the room, a pew cracks down the middle.

Then, everything is silent again.

I exhale, forcing my temper to calm before I bring the walls down.

"Whoa," Allison breathes. "No wonder you thought you could fight her."

Steven scowls, but he doesn't argue.

"Even if Myrtle isn't going to kill you," Sutton says grimly, "There are others who might try."

"The pack," I whisper as realization hits home. Despite my best intentions, I'm the reason they will be trapped in this damned town for all of eternity.

"They'll blame you," Sutton says.

"They'd have to go through me if they want to mess with her," Steven replies, and Allison actually rolls her eyes.

Sutton doesn't spare him a glance. He's watching me. Waiting to see if I'll understand the gravity of what my little midnight rendezvous has caused.

Unfortunately, I understand it better than he knows. "They won't succeed," I say quietly.

He looks ready to argue, so I add, "The deal I made included the pack. I wanted to make sure no one else had to die for the magic. No more yearly sacrifices. Myrtle agreed. Which means, when she casts the new curse, it will make me immortal, using my eternal blood to constantly renew the magic. It's the only way to stop the murders."

Emotions cross Sutton's expression like shadows.

Steven and Allison are both speechless.

Voices sound from outside, quiet at first then louder as they get closer. Steven gets up and hurries to the window. Whatever he sees outside sets his expression into something foreboding.

"We've got company," he says.

"Shit," Sutton swears, and the vehemence in his voice makes me shudder.

Guilt presses down around me. This is all on me. All my fault.

Sutton gets up and joins Steven at the window. He glances out and then turns to me, drawing a deep breath that does more to stoke his temper than calm it, judging from the look he wears.

"Is that what we felt earlier?" Allison asks. "She recast the curse?"

"You felt something?" I ask.

"A sort of earthquake," she says. "We thought it was just the bed and breakfast. That Tabitha had done something, but maybe..." She trails off as Steven shoots her a look.

Something passes between them.

"I'm not going to just let Serenity get attacked and find out," Steven says.

"Sutton?" I say quietly. "What do you think?" I'm all but begging for more than a three-word response from him. Something, anything to tell me where he's at in his mind.

"Steven's right. I'm not letting anyone hurt you." His words aren't an answer. Not exactly. But they tell me everything I need to know. "You might have saved us," he says, "But you've doomed yourself."

Falls Gazette

Chapter Seven

My stomach drops as Sutton and Steven rush toward the door. Allison moves in beside me.

"Stay inside," Sutton growls before he and Steven slip out.

Heart thundering in my ears, I make my way to the door as soon as it shuts behind them.

"Eavesdropping?" Allison whispers as she comes to stand beside me. Without responding, I press my ear to the door and will my hammering pulse to ease just enough that I can make out what they're saying.

Fortunately, I don't have to wait long.

"What just happened?" a man questions. I struggle to place his voice.

"We felt the magic shift!" A feminine voice I recognize instantly calls out. Mable. "Tried the boundary line, but we still can't get out."

"What's going on?" demands another voice. "And what's *he* doing out?"

"I left to find my sister," Steven tells them. His tone is already warning them he's not going to back down. Shit.

"What you felt was a shift in the magic just as you thought," Sutton's booming voice burns me from the inside out. Even from in here, shielded from view, I can hear the disappointment in his tone. The strain.

I fucked up—big time. And yet, here I am, cowering behind the man I'm sleeping with.

"A shift? That's all you're going to tell us? George said that Serenity gave her blood to Myrtle! He says we're stuck here for eternity now!"

Dread makes my limbs feel like lead. How in the hell does George know?

"Serenity did not willingly give up her blood."

"Then how the hell did Myrtle get it?" *Cara.*

She sounds pissed, and I can't blame her. Can I really sit here and let Sutton handle the fallout of my actions? Am I truly that cowardly?

"I—" Sutton starts.

I grip the door handle and rip it open. All gazes shift to me, including those of Sutton and Steven. Both men glare at me, but I clear my throat and make my way down the wooden steps to stand on Sutton's other side.

Allison follows me, caging me between herself and Sutton.

Mable stands between Cara and Phineas while George and his group glower at me from a few yards away. I recognize the men he was drinking with from the night Cara and I went out. None of their faces are even close to friendly. Clearly, they've all decided to hate me. The rest of the town has congregated just behind them—Jolene and Ernie, the bartender, are the only other faces I instantly recognize.

Out of the corner of my eye, something moves. I glance over

and spot Vaughn, Sutton's head of security, prowling at the edges of our gathering. Normally, I'd consider him an ally given that he's loyal to Sutton. But the fact that he's staying out of my line of sight speaks volumes. I have very few friends here.

"Well?" Jolene demands. "Is what George said true? Did you give Myrtle your blood? Did she re-cast the curse?"

Swallowing hard, I meet her gaze and repeat Sutton's earlier words. "I did not willingly give her my blood."

A man I don't know steps forward, his dark gaze all but shooting daggers in my direction. "Then how the fuck did she get it?"

"She stole it. Last night."

Gasps sound.

"How the hell did that happen when we had two full teams guarding that damned house?" Jolene demands.

"This didn't happen at Yvette's place," Cara says slowly. She's confused, but she doesn't doubt her own eyes.

She should, though.

"I used my magic to cloak myself and go meet with Myrtle," I say. "I thought I could corner her and put an end to the curse." I take a deep breath. "Unfortunately, I failed."

"And now she has your blood," Cara says.

"Yes."

Everyone starts talking all at once. Some ask me questions; some yell; some point and scream at me, and others whisper amongst themselves. It's impossible to make out what each and every one of them is saying, but the message is clear enough: Serenity Kellis fucked us over. She's ruined our lives.

"Why on Earth would you think you could beat her in the first place?" one of George's followers demands.

I can feel Sutton's eyes boring into me. He doesn't want me to tell them. But I'm done lying. "Because I'm a witch too. Descended from Myrtle's line."

There's a collective moment of shock as they all absorb my words.

"We should have just let Myrtle kill you," a woman near the back roars.

George sneers at me, his small gang all staring threateningly in my direction. Steven looks ready to shoot now and ask questions later. He hasn't drawn a gun, but I know, if he does, there will be no diffusing it like before.

"I tried to stop her," I yell. It's no use, though. No one's listening to me. Not anymore.

George and his buddies begin to move through the crowd. They stop several yards away. George crosses his arms. "I knew you'd damn us all, you city bitch."

Sutton snarls and steps forward, but I put a hand on his arm before shooting Steven a warning glare that he'd damn well better not start a fight over someone calling me a name. "Watch your fucking mouth when you speak to her," Sutton growls.

"Or what?" George questions. "You've already chosen her over your own pack. Some fucking alpha you are. We were better off when you were trapped in your fucking house."

"Watch your tongue," Phineas warns.

George doesn't even bother sparing him a glance. "And now, what, we're supposed to heel to you and your fucking human pets?"

"George," Cara starts, her hands tightening into fists at her sides. She turns to Sutton. "You are the alpha of this pack; we need you to stand with us."

Her tone is gentler than George's, and I know she means well, but Sutton's eyes flash at her words.

"Not at the risk of Serenity," Sutton replies. His tone is strained, every muscle in his body stiff.

"Sutton. We are your pack," Cara urges, looking hurt. Her gaze darts from me to George like she's willing Sutton to find a way to fix this.

Sutton doesn't immediately reply, leaving the opening for George.

He throws his head back and barks out a laugh that churns my insides. He's baiting Sutton, trying to get him to turn on his own people. And it's working. "See? He doesn't give a shit about us!" The asshole turns to face the pack and throws his hands up in the air. "We don't have an alpha; we have a fucking whipped little pup." He turns back to us and glares at me. "And pups occasionally need to be taught a lesson."

George charges, shifting as he moves. His human body is taken over as he becomes a large, bloodthirsty wolf. His gleaming teeth are aimed straight for me, and instead of jumping aside, I freeze, momentarily stunned by the suddenness of it all.

Allison rips me back just in time, positioning herself directly in the line of attack.

I scream, terrified of watching my friend get mauled to pieces. Before George can reach her, a single gunshot echoes off the trees.

Our attacker hits the ground with a heavy thud and doesn't move.

I whirl on Steven, who is still standing with his gun raised. He swallows hard and lowers it before turning back to the pack. "Anyone else want to fuck with my sister?"

The uproar is deafening.

"It's her or us," someone yells, and the others take up the chant.

"Her or us, her or us." They don't immediately come for me as George did, but I can feel the change in the air as clearly as if they are trying to kill me.

Mable and Phineas don't join in, but their helplessness speaks volumes as they stand among the others who do repeat the mantra.

Cara looks grim at the whole scenario, but she doesn't try to stop it either. Sutton stares back at his pack and then looks to me. I can see the battle play out on his face, the choice he feels he needs to make, and before I can tell him that it's okay to pick his people—he hauls me into his arms and rushes toward the trees.

"Stop," Phineas roars at our backs. "They are not our enemy!"

"Says you," someone shouts back.

"He killed George," another calls out.

Craning my neck offers a glimpse of where Steven and Allison still stand among the angry pack members. Fear clogs my throat. We can't leave them.

Struggling is futile, though. Sutton's grip on me is iron-clad.

I try to talk, to reason with Sutton, but he's running so fast my entire body jostles with every step. My teeth chatter together until I'm forced to close my mouth tight.

A wolf sprints into our path, and we stop. "Move, Cara," Sutton warns.

She shifts quickly to stand before us naked, her expression dark. "You can't turn your back on us, not when the curse was just reinforced."

"I go back and they will tear Serenity apart." His stoic expression crumples, and desperation leaks in. "She's my mate, Cara."

Cara looks at me, then back at Sutton, and finally nods. "I'll do what I can to maintain the peace. Keep her secluded until their anger dies down." She shifts again and bounds off toward the church. Luckily, our pit stop has given Steven and Allison time to catch up to us. I breathe a sigh of utter relief to see them unharmed.

Without another word, Sutton resumes our trek but, at least, he's only walking now while Steven and Allison trail directly behind us.

"Sutton, I can walk," I tell him.

He sets me on my feet so abruptly that I sway until I catch myself. Sutton grabs my hand in his. Then he's walking again, briskly, and I have to hurry to keep up. Just because he's chosen me doesn't mean he's forgiven me.

"Where are we going?" Allison questions. "Not like we can just check in at the nearest Holiday Inn."

"We're going to hope the boundary preventing me from going home is gone now that Myrtle has what she wants," Sutton replies. He doesn't look at me. I pull against his hold, and he releases me, still not sparing me a single glance.

I might as well be two inches tall for how shitty I feel. There's no coming back from this, no fixing things. I've damned an entire town all because I was arrogant enough to believe I'd come out on top.

On our way back to his house, we're met with no invisible barrier, but it's not until we're walking through his front door that I really let myself breathe again. Being here, despite the horrible state of this house, is comforting. This is where I first found myself caught—and first fell in love with the man currently so angry at me he can barely look in my direction.

Myrtle's prediction echoes in my mind. That Sutton will grow to hate me for being responsible for the curse. I hope she's wrong. That he can find a way to forgive me—eventually. Eternity in this town, without Sutton's love, is a hell I can't bear.

"This is your house?" Steven questions. "It's falling down."

"It's because of the curse," I reply softly. "Doomed to this state except for the one night a year when—" I stop short as I realize this house will never again be restored to its true glory. Not without Myrtle ever forcing a Halloween ball on these people again. As cruel as it was to do, at least then, this place became as beautiful as the memories it stores.

"That's horrible," Allison comments.

"It's home," Sutton snaps.

"I don't mean to sound ungrateful," Steven says warily. "But won't this be the first place the pack looks for you?"

"We're trapped," Sutton snaps at him. "There's nowhere they won't find us."

"Good point," Steven says. But I don't miss his quick glance at me. And I know he still thinks he could drag me back to the city if he tried.

"Cara will warn us if anyone tries to come for us," Sutton says.

No one argues at that.

"Find a spare room; make yourself comfortable." He stomps off toward the library, slamming the door behind him.

I wrap both arms around myself in an attempt to ease some of my nerves, but it doesn't help.

Allison clears her throat. "I'm going to go find somewhere to take a nap." After lightly squeezing my arm, she moves past me. I suspect she and I will talk later, but for now, she looks like a walking zombie. Okay, horrible comparison. She has all her skin.

Knowing what's coming, I turn to face Steven. "Go ahead," I tell him. "Scream at me. Tell me what an idiot I am."

His familiar blue eyes soften. "I'm not going to do any of those things."

"You had to kill someone because of me."

"I killed someone to protect you. And Allison," he replies. "And from what I've heard, the bastard had it coming."

"What have you heard? You've been here all of five minutes."

"Sutton filled me in last night." His eyes darken. "When we realized you were gone, I had him run me through all possible suspects."

My heart squeezes at the torture I've put him through. "Still, I'm sorry you had to pull the trigger. I know how hard that must be. I mean, you're a cop—"

"I'm your brother first," he interrupts, holding out both arms. "Now, come here so I can hug my baby sister."

Tears spill from my eyes as I embrace my brother, pressing my cheek against his chest. I breathe him in, the familiar scent like home to me. "I really fucked up."

"You did," he replies. "But I also know you'll do what you can to make it right. And in the end, that's what will count."

Falls Gazette

Chapter Eight

I pace the hallway outside the library, listening to the muffled sounds of Steven hunting for enough pantry ingredients to make a meal. Allison has yet to re-emerge from upstairs, and I have zero reasons left to avoid Sutton. Yet, here I pace, wracking my brain for the right thing to say. But there just aren't words.

I fucked up—massively. And his entire pack paid the price. More importantly, though, I betrayed him because it was my actions that forced him to choose between me and his pack.

It's that thought that has me walking to the library and opening the door.

Sutton sits behind the desk, a glass of something amber cupped in his large hand. He looks up at me then back down at the glass. My legs might as well be made of lead as I force my feet to carry me inside and then kick the door closed behind me.

The silence between us stretches.

Sutton picks up the glass and empties the contents down his throat. I watch, hypnotized by the way his Adam's apple moves as he swallows the double shot. It's ridiculous to be turned on right now. Completely inappropriate, given the circumstances. But I can't help myself.

He sets the glass down with a sharp clink.

"I can smell your arousal from here," he says in a rough voice.

My body freezes then relaxes again. "Of course you can." I offer a laugh that's too brittle to contain actual humor.

He looks up. Our eyes meet.

I lean on the door for support when the force of his stare threatens to knock me back. Oh yeah, he's still pissed.

"Look me in the eye, and tell me you wouldn't have done the same thing," I say.

"What are you talking about?"

"You know what I'm talking about. Myrtle. Slipping off to murder the bitch alone. You'd have done the same thing if you were in my shoes."

He looks away. "Maybe."

"Maybe." I snort and take a step forward, braver somehow, like I'm winning this awful argument. "You know I'm right."

He glares at me. "You think this is about being right?"

My shoulders sag with my exhale. Fair point.

"I want to say I'm sorry," I begin, my voice quiet again. "I should never have snuck away alone like that. You were worried—"

"I wasn't worried, Serenity. I was fucking terrified!" His roar is punctuated by the chair tumbling backward as he pushes suddenly to his feet. He slams his palms onto the desk.

"I've never seen you this angry." I whisper the words, afraid that any loud sounds might startle the predator lurking within him. A predator that's dangerously close to the surface right now.

"My wolf isn't something I can just turn off." His eyes are wild with fury. No—fear.

The moment I recognize it, my defenses are shattered.

My voice cracks. "I don't want to fight."

"I don't want you trapped, but it can't be helped now, can it?" he snaps. "Face it. Sometimes we don't get what we want."

"There are worse places to be trapped," I tell him, keeping my voice light. "Worse people to be trapped with."

"This isn't a joke," he says darkly. "Do you have any damned idea what it's like to be completely and utterly cut off from the entire world? You'll never see your family again, Serenity. Once Steven goes, that's it. Tell me, were you seriously prepared for that consequence?"

The lump in my throat grows substantially. I wish I could say I was prepared. That I'd fully thought through the fallout. But my thoughts were on the immediate threat to Sutton, Steven, and Allison. Saving their lives mattered more than being *in* their lives. And I stand by that now. "We're going to figure this out."

He scowls. "Did your brother tell you that? Does Detective Optimist have any special advice for us?"

I don't bother to respond to that. Especially since Steven is the furthest thing from an optimist. In fact, his only advice is to kill everyone, every time. I stop short as I realize that's probably the thing Sutton sees as optimism. "Your pack will come to understand, won't they? As soon as the initial shock passes, we can tell them—"

"I don't want to have to hurt them," he interrupts. "But I will. For you. If it comes to that. I will kill the people I vowed to protect in order to shield you from their wrath." He shakes his head angrily. "And I shouldn't fucking have to."

My chest aches for him, my soul on fire for the pain I've caused the man I love. Coming here was supposed to make things better. It was supposed to bring justice for those who'd been killed. Yet, all I did was make things so much worse. I open my mouth to respond, to tell him it doesn't have to be that way, but clamp it shut again when Sutton lets out a growl.

"You have no idea the position I'm in now, Serenity."

“I’m sorry,” I choke out, little more than a hoarse whisper.

Silence stretches until, finally, he sighs, suddenly looking exhausted. “I don’t want to fight either.”

“Sutton.” I make my way around the desk, grabbing his arm. He doesn’t let me move him easily. But I yank until he gives way, and then I slip in between him and the desk, wrapping my arms around his neck.

His arms come slowly around me in a stiff hug. I can feel his temper still simmering. And I know there’s nothing I can say. When I pull his mouth down to mine, he resists, hovering just above my lips.

“My wolf nearly lost its mind,” he whispers. “I’m trying to come back from that, but...whether you want to believe it or not, you’re my mate. And my beast can’t just logic its way out of this kind of threat. I need time. I need to...” His arms tighten around me, his forehead drooping until it touches my own. He closes his eyes. “I don’t know what I need.”

“I'm alive," I whisper, my voice a plea. “Feel me. Touch me. Let your wolf see that I’m unharmed. We can make it through this, we can find a way, Sutton.”

His eyes open, flashing with pain. “Serenity,” he warns. “If we start, I won’t stop. And I won’t be gentle.”

I push onto my toes and press a kiss to his jaw. “Good."

He lowers his head, but the moment his lips touch mine, the tenderness vanishes. Sutton’s breath is hot against my mouth, his hands gripping tight against my hips as he drags me against him. I make a sound—a moan of longing and relief—and he growls, his tongue shoving between my half-parted lips.

His kiss is angry.

And the ache between my thighs is instant.

Even at his most passionate, I’ve never seen Sutton like this.

Furious, aroused, demanding. He's a storm—a devastation. And I want him so badly that I can't think straight.

When I rock my hips against his, something in him snaps. He snarls, lifting me off the ground and setting me on the desk. His empty glass falls and rolls away, landing on the carpet with a muted *thunk*. Sutton ignores it. A second later, books go flying as he shoves them aside. His hands yank my knees open, and his body crowds in against my own. All the while, he grips my chin and kisses me furiously, prying my lips apart as if he's launching a full-scale invasion.

But you can't invade where you've been invited.

I part my lips willingly, and his tongue fucks my mouth with enough force to nearly make me orgasm right here, fully clothed.

In the moment I think I might come undone, he pulls back, and I gasp, sucking in oxygen before he can suffocate me with his sensory assault. I get a glimpse of his expression and note the glassy, unfocused look in his eye. This is a new version of him; one I very much want to experience.

Lowering himself to the chair, he clutches my shirt in his fists then rips the fabric away. I let out a short yelp. My bra is gone before I know what's happened. And then his mouth is closing over my already hardened nipple with such force my body quakes.

The nip of pain as his teeth scrape my sensitive skin is intoxicating.

I grip his hair, tangling it in my fingers and pulling him closer.

"Sutton." I barely breathe his name aloud before he's sliding a finger beneath my panties and slipping it inside me. His thumb strokes my clit, his rhythm perfectly timed to the need of my aching core.

My world spins.

My thighs pulse with need. I'm dimly aware of his mouth pressing a trail of kisses from my breasts to my abdomen. Then he's lifting my legs, propping my thighs in his large hands, and I have to catch myself on my palms to keep from toppling backward off the desk. His mouth closes over my clit, and I bite back a scream until I taste my own blood.

The orgasm rips through me—furious, like him. My body goes taut with pleasure. He doesn't stop licking and sucking until the wave passes. Then, he stands again and pushes me onto my back, his stormy eyes intent on my own as he looms over me, his palm splayed over my chest.

"You have no idea how much I love you, Serenity Kellis."

His voice is raw with emotion. The anger still flashes in his eyes, but I can see the desperation behind it. The fear. And for a split second, his wolf stares back at me. My heart swells with love for them both. I reach for him, pulling him close as he bends over me.

"Show me," I tell him, letting him see how much I want him. Even like this. Especially like this.

He pulls back far enough to strip out of his clothes then steps forward and drives into me, sheathing himself until I'm completely full. I swallow a cry at the pure pleasure-pain from it all. Slowly, he slips nearly out again. I bite my lip, trying to keep from cursing him for it.

His grin spreads slowly as he watches me, inching himself inside me again. So. Fucking. Slowly.

Bastard.

I buck my hips, trying to get him to go faster, but he doesn't.

His hand slides up to my throat, tightening just enough to apply light pressure. "Something wrong, love?"

I shouldn't be so damn excited, but the rougher he gets—the more animalistic—the greater my craving for him. "You know damn well what's wrong," I manage.

His grin widens. "Is this not what you want?"

"I want this," I tell him, letting anger edge my voice. "But harder. Faster."

His eyes gleam. "With pleasure."

He slams into me, and I gasp. His pace is so furious it's all I can do to hang on. It's exactly what I asked for, though—exactly what I know he needs.

Hard.

Fast.

Passionate.

Sutton gives me everything I want and more. Another orgasm builds until I'm desperate for it. When he leans over me, his hair in his eyes, I grab him with both hands and hang on as we both tumble off the edge together.

"Let's fight every day," I say when I finally find my voice again.

He leans over me, his torso shaking with laughter—and shaking me with it. Then he looks up, his palm pressed tenderly to my cheek. "I don't know what I did to deserve you, Serenity."

"Is that a compliment?" I ask. "You know what? Don't answer that. In fact, let's not talk at all."

He stiffens. "Did I scare you?"

I reach up and smooth the worry lines that mar his skin. "Of course not. But you're welcome to keep trying." I wink.

He stares at me, disbelief showing. And maybe a little awe. "You want to go again?"

"I mean, I'm willing to argue first if it helps."

Falls Gazette

Chapter Nine

By the time we emerge from the library, we've made a hot mess of the room, and we end up doing what feels like a walk of shame to the upstairs shower. However, since Steven and Allison are both nowhere to be found, I'm spared the awkwardness of their reactions. For now.

Sutton and I are just arriving back downstairs again when Steven and Allison join us from the back of the house.

"Where were you?" I ask, instantly worried there's been some threat.

"We made some soup and then ate in the backyard," Allison says. "It was kind of loud in here."

My face heats as I realize exactly what she means. I can't even bring myself to look at Steven.

"Any soup left?" Sutton asks, and I shoot him a glare that he completely misses. Of course he's not bothered by our loud performance.

Allison points him toward the pot on the stove. When I look over, Steven's actively avoiding my gaze.

"Want some?" Sutton asks.

"I think she's already had some," Steven mumbles.

Fuck my life.

"How about coffee," I suggest instead.

An hour later, a soft knock at the door has all of us looking up from where we've been lounging in the living room. After three cups of coffee and trying to plot a way out of this mess, we've come up near empty. Steven pulls out his firearm as he stands, a fluid motion that comes as a result of years of training. Allison and I stand as well, though it's Sutton who's at the door first.

He pulls it open without hesitation.

"What the fuck?" Steven bellows as he puts himself between Allison, me, and the door. "The entire town wants her dead, and you're just going to pull the door open?"

Sutton glares at my brother then steps aside as Phineas moves into the room. My relief is instant, my joy unparalleled. I rush forward and wrap my arms around the first friend I ever made in Midnight Falls.

"Serenity," he says softly.

"Are you okay? You're not hurt, are you?" I ask him.

"I'm fine," he assures me. "Tougher than I look."

"I'm so sorry, Phineas," I tell him. "So sorry that I made things worse." I pull back, and he gently squeezes my shoulders.

"You were trying to help," he replies as though it's that simple. "I do not hold you accountable for what happens. You are as much a victim in all of this as we are. Perhaps more so." After another squeeze, he releases me, so I step back.

"Put your damn gun away, Trigger Finger," Allison scolds.

Steven glares at her but slips his firearm back into its holster.

Phineas clears his throat and steps toward my brother. "I fear we got off to a rough start, Detective. My name is Phineas Hargrave."

After eyeing his hand for a moment, Steven takes it. "Steven Kellis."

"It is great to meet you. Serenity has mentioned her family quite a few times."

"I only wish she would have mentioned an entire town of werewolves to me," Steven retorts. The jab is a low one, but Phineas grins and releases my brother's hand.

"Yes, well, I cannot imagine it would have been taken well had she told you the truth." Before Steven can respond, Allison steps forward and offers her hand.

"Allison Summerhill."

He takes her hand and smiles. "It is a delight to meet you, Miss Summerhill."

"What are you doing here?" Sutton questions.

"Can't a man just come visit his son?" Sutton doesn't respond, so Phineas sighs. "Things in town are strained, and I was in desperate need of a break. I remember why I was so glad to step down as alpha…I'm too old for this shit."

I snort, and Phineas eyes me curiously. "Sorry, movie quote," I reply.

"Cara's managed to hold them off, then?" Sutton asks.

"For now. They won't come here … if you don't go there," Phineas says.

"So I'm not trapped here by magic," Sutton says darkly. "But I am confined to my home again."

"They're only afraid," Phineas begins, but he stops himself. "George's death hasn't helped matters. I fear they won't stop until they've drawn blood in return."

"Over my dead body," Steven declares.

"Yes," Phineas glances at him. "That's the idea."

That shuts Steven up.

"What can we do?" Allison asks.

"I'd say *nothing* is probably the safest bet," Phineas tells her.

Allison frowns. Steven looks ready to argue, but Sutton steps in. "And Cara?"

"She'll let us know if anything changes," Phineas assures him.

Sutton exhales. "I could use a bit of nothing." The look in his eye is weary and so much deeper than lack of sleep. Looking at him now, at what this day has cost him, I realize doing nothing is exactly what we have to do. At least, for a little while.

Besides, I already know what happens next. Steven and Allison have to go, especially if I'm going to expect Myrtle to uphold her end of the bargain and leave them unharmed. Maybe it's selfish, but I want one last afternoon together as a family before I send them both off forever.

Phineas offers me a slight smile before shifting his attention back to Sutton. "You interested in a game of chess? We haven't played together since before..." He trails off and clears his throat.

The heavy emotion is all over his expression, and my chest tightens. To have been cut off from his only remaining family member all this time, only to be reunited, then separated again… well…I'd say I can't imagine what that feels like, but I think I'm about to find out very soon. I glance at Steven, and the ache in my chest blossoms into something far more constricting.

"Sure," Sutton replies. "I'll grab the board."

"Do you really think a fucking board game is the best way to spend our time right now? Your entire town wants to kill my sister because a crazy-ass witch used her blood for some spell. Shouldn't we be figuring out how to stop her from getting away with it?"

"Now is the perfect time to play a game of chess," Phineas replies. "Because sometimes, when we face problems far bigger than ourselves, the solution isn't going to come until we've cleared it from our minds."

"Trust me," I say. "I know from experience that he's right."

Steven continues to glare at Sutton's father for a moment. I'm expecting him to argue, but instead, he simply lets out a breath. "Fine. But when you're done, I want to wipe the board with Sutton."

Chuckling, the aforementioned opponent re-enters the room, board in hand. "I'm looking forward to that matchup."

An hour later, Steven glares at Sutton from across the mostly full chess board. After Phineas did, in fact, beat Sutton within the first thirty minutes of their game, they reset the board, and Steven took Phineas' place.

Which is exactly where they've been ever since, both men unwilling to risk their pieces in order to gain even a square inch over their opponent.

"This is getting really boring," Allison groans and straightens. "Phineas, you want some soup?"

"Absolutely. I'll help." He gets to his feet and follows Allison into the kitchen while the three of us remain seated at the table.

"And here I thought you were going to wipe the board with me," Sutton says.

"After the ass-whooping your father gave you, I figured I'd go easy, give you a chance to redeem yourself."

Sutton chuckles and then moves his bishop to take one of Steven's knights. My brother mutters a curse and moves a pawn. Which, unfortunately, is a huge mistake for my brother. By doing so, he's left his king unprotected.

Knowing Sutton is about to clean him out, I force the grin off my face. But, Sutton doesn't. Instead, he moves his queen forward, and Steven captures it.

What. The. Hell?

Three more moves and Steven is grinning like an idiot. "Checkmate! Consider your ass whooped."

"Considered," Sutton replies. "But it won't happen again."

"That's what they all say," Steven grumbles as he stands. "I'm going to go grab a bite." He turns and heads for the kitchen, so I face Sutton.

"You let him win."

He shrugs. "It seemed important. Besides, I already have everything I need." Snaking an arm around my back, Sutton pulls me in close and presses a light kiss to my lips. I lean into him, accepting his gentle affection even as my heart aches for everything still facing us.

Yes, he has me. I have him. But for how long? Who's to say Myrtle didn't stick around once the curse was cast and is merely biding her time to kill us all?

Phineas steps into the room, so Sutton releases me.

"I fear we need to talk. Now," Phineas says softly.

"Talk about what?" I ask, shifting my gaze to Sutton then back to his father.

"It's my father's tactic," Sutton offers. "Distracting me with a game of chess before delivering unfortunate news."

Phineas shrugs. "It has always made the delivery easier for me."

My stomach drops. "What bad news? What's going on? I mean, aside from the entire town wanting my head on a pike."

Sutton's grip tightens around my waist.

"The pack is falling apart," Phineas says. "Fighting. Those who were loyal to George want the detective strung up for his murder."

"They can fucking try," Steven snarls from where he stands near the kitchen.

"No, they can't," Allison replies. She shoots him a withering look. "They are werewolves, and you're a man. You would lose, you idiot."

"Not before I took a fuck-ton of them out with me."

Allison looks about two seconds from strangling him.

"You're not going to war with my pack," Sutton says, tone flat. "Because it's not going to come to that."

"I wouldn't be so sure, son," Phineas says sadly. "I don't know how much longer we can hold the line before they're knocking on this door in an attempt to get inside. They want both Serenity and Steven."

"They're not getting either of them," Sutton snaps.

Phineas runs a hand over his hair. "I know that, but you need to be prepared to take a stand. Should someone challenge you for alpha and win..." He trails off, but we get the big picture.

If anyone in town were to take Sutton's place as alpha, both Steven and I would be up on the chopping block. There would be little anyone could do about it without bringing the fire down on them as well.

Basically, we're screwed unless we can find a way to break the curse. An impossible feat given that the woman who cast it is likely long gone by now.

Falls Gazette

Chapter Ten

The echoes of a muted scream and heavy banging rip me out of sleep. Beside me, Sutton jumps up and yanks on his jeans. Adrenaline already pumping, I'm grabbing for one of his shirts and a pair of leggings before bounding after him down the stairs. The time on my phone says just after three in the morning.

"What the fuck is going on?" Steven grumbles as he staggers from his room, shirtless.

Allison steps out into the hall behind him, eyes wide and glassy. It dawns on me dimly that they've both just emerged from the same bedroom. But my panic won't let me react to that.

Sutton doesn't bother answering as he continues down the stairs. We all follow, reaching the bottom right as he rips open the front door to a panicked Cara. "What is it?" he demands.

"The pack—Sutton, it's bad," she replies, breathless. She's still clothed, which means she ran here on foot. I search her for blood or any sign of injury, but there's none I can see. I exhale as she adds, "I couldn't shift because I couldn't risk them thinking I was a threat. I couldn't..." She trails off, eyes glazing over with moisture.

Shit. Cara crying? That can't be good.

"What happened?" Steven demands, ripping the door from Sutton's grasp and fully opening it so he can fit in the doorway.

"They all turned on each other." She shifts her gaze to Sutton. "Your dad, Sutton, he's hurt."

Sutton's entire body goes rigid, and I gasp, heart falling to my knees. Sutton and I exchange a look. "We need to get to town," I say.

"You can't go," Cara tells me, tone rising with fear. "If they see you, they'll tear you apart."

"She's right." Steven glances back at me.

I know she is, but I hate it. Sutton still hasn't spoken, but when he turns back to me, I see yet another war playing out over his handsome features. If he stays, he risks his dad, but if he leaves, he worries something will happen to me.

I step forward and place my hand on his chest, directly over his racing heart. "Go. I'll be fine here with Steven and Allison."

Sutton continues to stare at me, and for a moment, his eyes glimmer, changing to let me know he's fighting with his predatory nature. "Fine. But Cara stays here, too."

"I'm fully fucking capable of taking care of them," Steven growls.

Sutton stands toe-to-toe with my brother. Both men glare at each other, both of them trying to be an alpha when, in reality, only one of them is. At least in this town. "I don't doubt your capabilities, *cop*, but if a pack of angry wolves shows up, there's only so much you can do. Cara is a powerful shifter in her own right, and she *will* be remaining behind."

Steven glares back at him. "This isn't over."

"Never would have considered it to be." Sutton pulls away and grips the back of my neck to rip me forward and capture my lips with his. The kiss is possessive, claiming, and a promise that we'll both be back together as soon as he sorts everything out in town. "Stay inside," he orders.

"We will," I promise.

Sutton turns and runs out the door, shredding his pants as he shifts before reaching the edge of the trees and disappearing into the dark.

Cara shuts the door. "Don't worry," she tells Steven, "I won't take offense to you not wanting me to stay behind."

"I don't give a fuck if you do. Truth is I trust none of you." Steven turns to me. "Let's go prep some coffee. I have a feeling this is going to be a long night." He tucks his firearm behind him into the waist of his pants then heads toward the kitchen. Allison falls into step beside him, and Cara shakes her head.

"Your brother is quite the detective, isn't he?"

"He is," I tell her.

"Doesn't catch everything though."

Something about her tone sends a warning bell ringing in my head. Before I can figure out her meaning, the front door opens, and four men stalk in, each of them easily recognized as members of the late George's little band of misfits. "What the hell are you doing here?" I demand as they stride toward us with grim determination. "Get out," I add when they don't respond.

My heart pounds as they advance. I look to Cara for help, but her expression holds none of the alarm I feel. In fact, she looks pleased.

"Don't let her leave," Cara tells them.

"What the hell is going on?" I demand.

From the kitchen, Steven and Allison appear. They pull up short at the sight of the intruders. Steven reaches for his gun.

"Don't even think about it," Cara tells him, and I stare at her, horrified.

At Cara's nod, the men shift into their wolves, immediately baring their teeth at us. But my eyes remain glued to Cara as the reality of what's happening begins to dawn.

I open my mouth, desperate to warn Sutton he's walking into a trap. Maybe he's still close enough to hear me--

"Scream and I'll have them put your brother down before you're even done making the sound."

"Fucking try," Steven growls from behind her.

"If he moves, kill him," Cara tells the wolves. "But Serenity's mine."

Something about the way she says it—the way she's always said it—steals my breath. All warmth drains from my body, and I stiffen. "You."

Cara smiles, the gesture utterly and completely inhuman, and entirely Myrtle. Something I know because it's the same carnal grin I've seen on each and every one of the faces of those she controls.

"Where is Cara?" I demand. "The real Cara?" But I already know the answer to that one.

"Dead," she says flatly. "Has been since the night of the ball. Quite a shame she was so uninteresting that no one even questioned the change. Audrey?" She snorts. "People at least asked me why I was acting so strangely. But Cara?" She clicks her tongue and steps toward me. "No one even cared."

"I care." A tear slips down my cheek. How the hell did I not see? How could I not tell? "Wait. The night Yvette attacked us—"

"Oh, you mean the night you murdered my sister?" she growls. "I almost gave myself away if only to kill you then and there. But then I reminded myself what a perfect replacement you make. Not to mention how much Sutton will suffer to know you're the one cursing him.

"That's why Yvette didn't kill you." Anger burns hot through me, and I pull at my magic. It flares to life at my fingertips, sparking and snapping. "She knew who you were."

"Yes. And you were so damned stupid, so wrapped up in Sutton Hargrave that you didn't even piece it together." She glances at Steven then back to me. "Now, you'll know what it's like to watch someone you love die."

I clench my fists, letting the power build. I'm only going to get one shot at her. One chance to take her down for good. And this time, I'm determined to not miss.

"We had a deal," I say, alarm spearing through me. The magic surges inside me right alongside my own fear. I don't dare look over at Steven and Allison even as I know that's who she means. "You promised to leave them alone."

"The deal is off," she snaps, lifting her hands as her magic stirs. "The curse remains cast in my name. Your blood wasn't enough, apparently. But it will be this time."

Her words make no sense to me. The curse is done. We *all* felt the magic. Before I can spend too much time trying to decipher what actually happened, Cara takes a step closer, and my magic surges from beneath my skin, clearly sensing a threat where I once saw a friend.

"Now, we can do this the easy way, or the hard wa—"

With a scream of rage, I raise my hands and blast her with everything I have. This is nothing like the whispery threads I've used to become invisible or noiseless. This is violence. Pure and simple. The power slams into her chest, but she doesn't budge from where she stands. Instead, she grins up at me. "Ouch," she says and then raises her own palm.

A gunshot echoes through the house, and I follow Cara's gaze as she glances down at her chest. A smoking hole sits directly over her heart, but she doesn't stumble. Doesn't fall.

Because she's already dead.

Holy shit. There's nothing we can do to stop her. And that means there's nothing I can do to keep her from killing Steven and Allison right in front of me.

"Bad move, Detective," she replies sweetly.

I reach for my magic a second time, determined not to give up without a fight. Cara whirls on me, raises a hand, and light fills the room. I'm flung backward, a deafening crack filling my ears before pain explodes in my chest. I scream. My vision blurs, ears ringing, unable to hear anything but the muted gunshots that come next.

I try to sit up, but then Allison is at my side, face swimming into view as she's pushing me back. She says something I can't hear over the gunfire. My vision clears just enough that I can see a wolf lunging toward her.

"Alli—" I start, trying to warn her.

Acting quickly, she lifts a small side table and swings. It hits the wolf with a hard *crack,* and it's driven away from us.

Another gunshot rings out.

My vision blurs.

I try again to sit up, but Allison shakes her head. I look away, and my eyes catch on something in the open doorway.

A familiar black wolf lets out a bone-chilling snarl as he bounds into the room. Sutton's golden gaze finds me, and he growls, whirling on Cara, who still stands in her human form. She raises her hand to blast him with magic, but Steven aims and fires.

One shot.

Two.

Three.

Each bullet tears straight through Cara's chest, but they don't stop her. She barely even bleeds though she moves more clumsily now. She lets out an angry scream and then turns to run from the house. To my surprise, Sutton doesn't follow. Why isn't he following? My body feels heavy, but the pain from earlier is fading.

Allison says something to Steven that's lost to the roar in my ears.

Sutton shifts and kneels beside me on the floor. Blood stains his chest and arms. I realize with a jolt the wolves Cara brought with her are scattered around—all of them dead. "Fuck, Serenity." Sutton's voice is choked, grief taking over every part of his expression.

I try to reach for him, but my arm feels full of lead. Steven and Allison crowd in on my other side, their faces plastered with fake smiles.

"It's not so bad," I slur, trying to smile.

Based on the looks of horror from Sutton, Steven, and Allison, they don't agree. My gaze drops to my chest, and even with my blurred vision, I can see that I'm in trouble. A thick shard of wood protrudes from my body, its bloody splinters sticking out gruesomely from between my ribs. The fact that I feel nothing—no pain, no sense of being impaled by a foreign object—startles me. Adrenaline kicks in. Along with fear. Tears form in my eyes, and I buck.

Sutton and Allison each grab an arm, holding me down.

"I don't want to die," I choke out, throat hoarse.

"No one's dying," Steven snaps. "Don't touch it," he orders Allison.

"She's going to bleed out! We have to apply pressure!"

"You pull that out and she *will* bleed out. In seconds," Steven all but growls.

Allison whirls on Sutton. "Where is the nearest hospital?"

"Midnight Falls doesn't have one," Sutton says, his voice tortured. He's staring at my face, not the wound, and I know for sure I'm dying.

Steven curses.

"First aid station?" Allison questions.

"We're wolves," Sutton snaps, not looking away from me. "We don't need healers—at least, not in that sense. And this is too much for even our herbs. Fuck. I was so fucking stupid!" He jumps to his feet and slams his fist into the wall.

I sniffle, panic settling over my numb limbs. I'm not ready to go. Not ready to die. Especially not when I'll be leaving everyone behind. Leaving them to pick up the pieces of a curse—wait, the curse! "I shouldn't be dying," I stammer.

Allison sniffles.

Sutton drops to his knees beside me. "What?"

"I. Am. 'Sposed. To. Be. Immortal," I stammer. Vision fading in and out, I can barely focus on his broken expression.

"The spell didn't work," Allison tells Sutton. "Cara told her that her blood wasn't enough."

I try to nod but am unable to move. The irony isn't lost on me, however. The pack can be saved after all. Except I have to die to make that happen.

"There's nothing else we can do then." Sutton sounds ragged. No, he sounds beaten.

"So, you're telling me that we can't move her because she'll die," Allison cries. "But if we try to stop the bleeding right here, she'll still die?" Her words are barely audible over the sound of her sobs.

My body grows colder. Steven looks down at me with a stricken expression that hurts to look at almost as much as dying does. Before I can summon words to soothe him, the front door is kicked in. A woman storms in, hair wild around her face, as she drags a limp body behind her across the floor. She flicks her hair aside, and I stare in disbelief.

Jolene?

Sparks snap at her fingertips—magic! The sight of it coming

from the hands of someone I never expected is a jolt to my system, but before I can fully focus on what it all means, she yells, "What the fuck are you waiting for? Save her!"

Sutton stares back at her, clearly as shocked as I am.

"Surprise," Jolene deadpans. "I'm a fucking witch."

"Save her?" Allison looks from her to me and then finally to Sutton. "You can save her?"

"Is that—" I barely manage. But even with my vision wavering, I can make out the unconscious form at Jolene's feet: Cara. A twisted sense of purpose makes me smile. At least one of us got her.

"Sutton," Jolene snaps, and it seems to be enough to bring him out of his shock. He looks at Allison.

"Yes, I can save her," Sutton confirms.

"Then fucking do it!" my brother yells, tears slipping down his cheeks. I've *never* seen my brother cry, and the sight of it kills me faster than the gaping hole in my abdomen.

"She'll be different," Sutton explains. "I have to turn her. Make her like me. If she's not too far gone—"

"Just fucking do it!" Allison orders.

"It's that or she dies, alpha. And you fucking know it," Jolene adds. She shoves her boot at Cara's limp form. "Don't make this all be for nothing."

Sutton leans down over me. "Serenity, I need to know you want this. It's the only way—"

"Do it," I rasp.

"We have to pull her off of this." Sutton motions to the wood.

"She'll die, likely within seconds," Steven argues.

"She's going to die if we leave her," Sutton counters. The two men stare at each other for a moment. Then Steven nods.

"Okay. Do it."

"I need to shift," Sutton says. "Can you two move her?"

"Yes." Without any more hesitation, Steven moves to my shoulders and grips just under my armpits. Allison grabs my ankles. In a blur of movement, Sutton changes from man to wolf and stands beside me.

The animal turns his gaze to Steven and drops his head in a nod.

"See you soon, Serenity." Jolene smiles at me, turns away, and drags Cara's body out of view. Before I can respond, blinding pain sears through my entire body as I'm ripped up from the wooden beam protruding from my chest. I scream, but it's too much. All of it is too much. And as light fades to dark, I'm hit with the realization that I'm out of time.

This is the end.

———

WARMTH BEATS DOWN ON ME FROM SOMEWHERE ABOVE. SUNSHINE that seems to brighten … wherever I've suddenly found myself.

"What the—" I turn in a slow circle, only to find myself standing in the center of a beautiful meadow. One I've never seen before and certainly don't remember traveling to when I...

Shit. The last few moments filter back through my memory. My hands instantly go to my abdomen, feeling for the injury I know should be there, but there's nothing. My skin is solid, unmarred. This can't be good. I glance around again for some clue about where I am—and how to get the hell out. *Magic* is my only thought. "There has to be a spell to send me back," I mutter.

"Hello, Serenity."

I whirl, raising both fists and facing off with a man. His dark hair curls just above his ears, and despite the roughness of his handsome features, his eyes are kind. "Who are you?" I demand.

"Sullivan," he replies. "Or Rip. Someone recently gifted me with that nickname, and I have to admit, I don't hate it."

"Rip?"

"I'm a reaper," he explains with a charming grin.

"Reaper," I repeat warily. "As in..."

"Collector of souls." His smile slips, and sympathy washes over his face. "I'm afraid it's your soul I've come to--"

"Do not finish that sentence," I say. Dread coils in my stomach, but I force the question out of my mouth anyway. "Am I dead?"

"Yes and no," he says, shoving both hands into his pockets.

"What the hell does that mean?"

"It means you are currently deceased, technically speaking. However, I'm not convinced you're supposed to remain that way."

"Technically speaking?" I repeat, confused. "I mean, dead is dead, isn't it?"

He shrugs. "There's a gray area in everything."

" A gray area. You mean like room for negotiation? Because don't get me wrong, I definitely want to live, but what exactly are we talking about here? Is this one of those I have to give you my firstborn in exchange for bringing me back to life kind of deals?"

"No firstborn necessary," he says, clearly amused, but his smile fades quickly. "Unfortunately, lass, I cannot bring you back. That's up to him now."

"Up to—" *Sutton. "I have to turn her. If she's not too far gone —"* His words echo through my mind as though they're spoken through a damned megaphone. "Sutton."

"Yes. And you."

"Me?"

"You have to want it, lass."

"Of course I want it," I scoff. "Living is preferable to—well —not."

"Are you certain? There's joy waiting for you in life, but pain too. You can't have one without the other."

His tone is so serious that I hesitate, really considering his words. What he's offering is an out. An escape from the misery and torture of the curse and everything we're up against. But that escape means leaving Sutton behind. Forever. And that's something I won't do.

"I'm certain," I say.

Sullivan nods. "Very good, lass. You won't be sorry." He winks.

I tell myself that means he knows it all ends well for us. "So... now what?"

"Now, we let your mate do his best to save you."

"Will it work?"

His smile is soft as he says, "We'll wait a few minutes and see what happens—"

Before he finishes his sentence, agonizing pain burns through my body. I scream and fall to my knees while the sky above me darkens alongside my fear. The ground beneath my hands begins to shake, and I dig my fingers in.

But the grass vanishes.

The reaper disappears.

And I wake with a scream, every nerve in my body ablaze with pure agony.

Falls Gazette

Chapter Eleven

The sound of my bones snapping echoes in my ears. I grit my teeth, trying to brace myself against it, but the attempt is pointless. My body is breaking down into pieces, and I'm just along for the ride. Another snap. This one pulls a scream from me, and the force of it burns my throat. My eyes water, and I gasp, drawing in a deep breath before the next break steals my ability to inhale.

Some time during my ribs giving way, I pass out.

When I come to, the pain isn't quite so terrible. My body aches, my muscles sore and stiff as if I've pushed my body to within an inch of my life. Or maybe even beyond.

The image of a man—a reaper—swims in my mind before sliding away again. I have no idea if our encounter was real. All I know is I'm alive. And the pain has grown far more manageable.

My surroundings come into focus slowly then all at once. I'm in Sutton's house. Not his—our—bedroom. Another room. This one is empty and unused. It has no furniture to speak of, which makes me wonder why they put me here at all. It can't be comfortable.

Sure enough, I realize I'm on the floor.

I stretch, moving slowly as I test out the pain it'll cause.

But the moment I look down and catch sight of my body, I freeze again. Instead of bared skin, I'm covered in sandy-colored fur. My arms—no, legs, four of them to be exact—are covered in it. I take a step and note the giant paw with long nails that click when they land on the hardwood floor.

Then I look up—directly into an antique mirror someone has propped against the far wall.

The scream I make is more like a yelp.

I try again, but the second attempt is merely a howl that cuts off too soon.

The sound of it scares me so much that I stumble backward and fall on my ass.

What. The. Fuck.

I'm a wolf.

"I thought it might be better to just get it over with." The sound of Sutton's voice has me twisting around, and I have to fight the urge to attack out of sheer surprise. "Easy." Sutton's eyes meet mine, and the relief he wears is something I swear I can smell. I watch as he slowly raises his hands in front of him to calm me.

"I thought it best to show you what you are now," he explains. "Rip off the Band-Aid and all that."

His forehead creases with lines I never noticed before. In fact, every tiny detail of him is magnified like never before. I see things, notice small details my human self could have never picked up.

When I look back at the mirror again, my gaze catches on my reflection, and I can only stare.

I'm a wolf.

Holy shit.

I'm a … werewolf?

I open my mouth, testing the waters of communication. But when I try to speak, what comes out is a growl.

Sutton grins. "You're fucking amazing, you know that?" He shakes his head, his gaze sweeping the length of me. And there's plenty to look at. Glancing toward the mirror again, I'm shocked by my size. I'm probably not as large as Sutton when he shifts but close.

"You probably want to run," he says. But he doesn't move toward the door. Instead, his smile turns to a look of concentration. "I'm going to take you outside, but I need you to know we won't have long for you to stretch your legs. Cara's in a cell downtown."

At the mention of Cara's name, the memory of what she did washes over me. My hackles raise, and Sutton continues, realizing I need answers more than anything else.

"Steven and Allison are keeping an eye on her. Your brother's made himself quite at home in the Sheriff's office, by the way." I snort at that. Of course he has. But wow, Cara in a cell? "As for Cara's capture, that's all thanks to Jolene. Apparently, she's a hybrid. A descendant of witches who settled here even before Myrtle—born both wolf and witch. She kept that side of herself hidden, and I'm ashamed to admit she kept her true nature a secret out of fear of the pack." His expression darkens as his thoughts seem to stray a bit. "We'll need to be more accepting going forward. More welcoming to our own."

He clears his throat, refocusing. "Anyway, Cara's in custody, and Jolene's magic is apparently enough to keep her contained. The isolation of a cell will keep her from gaining access to anyone else, which means she can't body jump for now. But her army is still out there, and until we're convinced she can't animate the dead from inside that concrete box, I'm afraid I can't let your wolf roam far."

My wolf.

His words send a strange awareness through me. A second skin that ripples beneath my flesh. A creature. A beast.

And it wants nothing more than to be let free of this room.

I let out a strangled sound. A whine, really. And pace back and forth toward the door.

Sutton's smile returns. Despite the gravity of our situation, it's obvious he's enjoying seeing me like this. For some reason, that makes my wolf want to show off.

So weird.

I try to make sense of the instincts and urges coursing through me. It's not as simple as becoming a wolf, I realize. Or not in the way I expected. Because Serenity the human isn't gone. I'm still here. Still me. But now, there's a creature inside me too. A predator. And even though we're the same being, the same body, I can feel her separately. Like we're merely sharing the space inside my skin. Which means I have to contend with my needs as well as hers.

This should be fun.

Like having a live-in roommate. Who has the hygiene of a puppy.

Sutton stands slowly. "I've asked everyone else to steer clear," he says. "My father came by after you... after the fight. And the security detail's been up my ass." He scowls, adding, "Not to mention your brother breathing down my neck. But I told them to give you some space for now. And I want you to take it slow. Your wolf is going to distract you at first. The instincts are a lot to handle. If you catch a scent of something or someone, she might want to run off, but I need you to focus, okay? Stay with me."

I nod, sort of, and he seems satisfied. Still, he hesitates, his eyes locked on mine. Finally, he moves toward me, holding his hand out, palm-up, toward my face. I lean in and sniff. The scent of him intensifies so suddenly, and I react without thinking.

My tongue darts out, and I lick all the way up his hand and onto his forearm.

Sutton throws his head back and laughs harder than I've ever seen.

"Oh yeah, you'll do just fine. Come on."

True to his word, I don't see anyone else as we make our way through the house and out the door. The sun's up, but I have no idea what time it is or even what day. And since talking isn't an option right now, I put the question aside. As soon as I figure out how to get back to my human self, I'll ask everything I want to know.

Nerves dance in my belly. If one of Cara's zombies makes an appearance—I shove the concern down. If a threat shows up, we'll deal with it. Besides, knowing Cara—okay, Myrtle—is currently in a cell right now is monumentally reassuring.

Until then, Sutton's right. The longer I'm in this form, the stronger my wolf's urges become. And she really wants to run. Well, she really wants Sutton to chase her, but I'm not sure what happens if he catches us.

Maybe I'm not ready for that yet.

My paws pass from the house to the ground, and it's like I've just taken a Xanax. My wolf relaxes instantly. Despite the panic and pain from earlier, being outside soothes me. Sutton's scent changes slightly, and I have the distinct impression being out here soothes him too.

Before I can decide what to do next, the sound of cracking bones fills my ears. I whirl, far too excited to see that Sutton has shifted. His wolf is massive compared to mine, just as I predicted. And from the moment his large, gleaming eyes land on me, the beast inside me is thrilled with his attention. I couldn't keep her from running even if I wanted to.

My paws push off the ground, launching me into the trees with power and precision. My mind empties of thought, which is surprisingly easy if I just let my wolf call the shots. And then we're running—fast and furious. Sutton's at my heels.

I slow slightly, hoping to let him catch me, but he merely adjusts his stride.

My wolf huffs at that but decides winning the race is fun too. I push harder, pulling ahead.

The feel of the wind through my fur is invigorating. I never want to stop.

Every single smell and sound around me hits me at once. Somehow, I'm able to process them all in the space of half a heartbeat, never breaking stride. Birds, foraging animals, dirt, wind, the smell of rain—it's all there.

I catalog every one of them and then focus on the feel of my body. The lingering ache in my bones has already improved. With every stride, my muscles feel looser and stronger than before.

Sutton was right. I needed this.

Damn, did I need this.

By the time I know where I'm going, I can already hear the rushing water of the falls. When we reach the bank of the river, I finally come to a stop, eyeing the small clearing and the surrounding trees until I'm satisfied we're truly alone.

"How do you feel?"

Sutton's voice draws my attention, and I note he's shifted back to his human form. I stare hungrily at his naked body, suddenly wanting only to be in the same form he is.

Except, I have no freaking idea how to get back to two legs.

At my whine, Sutton nods encouragingly. "You can do this," he says. "Just focus on taking the lead. Let your wolf fade into the background of your thoughts. Feel her energy—and then let that sensation go."

I close my eyes, concentrating on his words. On feeling my

wolf's energy. And then on letting that energy fade in favor of—well—me.

The shift is not pleasant, but it's nothing compared to before. My bones twist sharply, knocking the oxygen from my lungs, but I grit my teeth and wait for it to pass. Finally, I feel the skin of my hands and knees scraping against the ground, and I open my eyes.

Flesh. Fingers. Hands.

Whew.

"You did it."

I look at Sutton, who stands several yards away, pride shining in his bright eyes. Slowly, I get to my feet as he comes forward and helps me up. I wobble, leaning hard on him for support until I get my bearings.

"It takes a few tries to get used to it," he says. "But you'll get the hang of it."

I stare down at my naked chest where an ugly pink scar has formed just above my breast. The sight of it startles me, and suddenly, everything my wolf had been able to shove aside during our run comes crashing down around me. I wobble again, this time out of fear and urgency.

Sutton grips me tighter. "Serenity?"

"I think I need to sit down."

He leads me to a patch of soft grass on the bank of the stream and pulls me down next to him. Despite the fact that we're naked, my mind is too caught up in the horror of what happened to fully appreciate the view of his muscled body on full display.

"What is it?" he asks.

"I can't stop remembering," I say. "Cara. She tossed me through a wall. I... I almost died." I stare at him with growing panic.

He grips my hands in his, squeezing reassuringly. But his expression is morbidly grim as he says, "You did die, actually. For about eighteen seconds, there was no heartbeat, and I thought..." He swallows hard. One of his hands lets mine go, and he brushes my hair back from my face, his touch feather-light. "I thought I'd lost you." He smiles softly as I think of the reaper, Rip. "But you're strong as hell. And you fought your way back." His expression falls again. "I'm so fucking glad you came back to me. I'm only sorry it came at the cost of who you were."

"He said I wasn't supposed to be dead. That I could choose to come back. And that you would save me."

Sutton's brows draw together. "Who said that?"

I meet his gaze. "Sullivan. Or Rip, I guess. He's a reaper. I saw him when I was, well—shit, I was *dead.*"

"You saw a reaper?"

"I did. He said it was up to me whether I lived or died. That my choice could bring me back. And that you would save me."

He shakes his head. "That's the thing, I took that choice away from you."

"Sutton." I grip his hand tight in my own. "I wanted this. I told you to do it. Hell, Steven told you to."

He exhales. "I needed to be sure you still felt the same—after."

"I do. In fact, I feel more alive than I ever did before," I tell him. "Besides, I might not have been able to take that bitch out with magic but now? One bite and I can end her."

Anger surges inside me, and I can feel my wolf stirring, begging to be let out again. We could hunt that bitch down and—

"I'm glad you feel that way," Sutton says slowly. "Because there's something else you should know."

"What is it?" I ask, immediately going through a list of possibilities. He said Steven and Allison were fine, but maybe someone else--

"The thing about becoming a shifter," he says, "is that you can only be that. You are no longer human, not really."

"Yeah, I kind of figured that out." I snort.

"But you are also no longer a witch."

I stare at him. "You mean, now that I'm a wolf, I don't have magic?"

He doesn't answer.

Determined to prove him wrong, I lift my hand and aim my palm at the nearest tree. But when I call my magic to the surface, nothing happens. "I don't get it. I feel more power now than I did before."

"That's your wolf," he says, nodding. "Your senses. Your physical strength. Your mental acuity. It's all heightened."

"But Jolene," I say. "She's both wolf and witch. You said so yourself."

"Jolene was conceived of both. Born with the blood of both in her veins. Learning how to balance those two together has taken her whole life. It's one of the reasons she hid her ability—and the reason it took her so long to harness her power enough to use it effectively against Myrtle."

"And because I wasn't born a wolf..." I trail off, and he nods. "I see."

For some reason, the knowledge that my magic is gone leaves me feeling strangely lonely. But then my wolf surges again, this time nudging me consolingly, and I decide to deal with my feelings on all this later. For now, there's a witch in need of a serious bitch-slap. And a town in need of saving.

Even if they do probably all want to kill me.

"So, what do we do about Cara?" I ask, snuggling in closer to ward off a sudden chill.

Sutton doesn't answer. I watch as his eyes glaze over and he glances at my mouth. *Oh.* My nipples react instantly to the sudden tension. He leans close, his mouth only a breath from mine now.

Yes. Do it.

We're already naked.

The desire I feel for him is stronger than ever, and I wonder if that's a wolf-perk too or if dying somehow gave me blue balls.

"Knock, knock."

The sound of Allison's voice ringing out tentatively from the trees startles us both. I pull back, a snarl escaping me. Before I can stop myself, I'm surging forward—toward the danger. My mind screams *threat!* while my wolf strains to attack. To defend.

Sutton grabs me around the waist, yanking me backward before I can attack.

His grip on me pulls me from my haze, and I blink, shocked to realize I would have attacked my friend.

"Sorry," I call out, breathless and stunned at my own behavior.

"Don't be," Sutton tells me. "It's to be expected." And then, he turns to Allison. "I told you to give her some time," he says in a clipped voice.

"I know, but we were worried," Allison says.

Now that I'm not trying to kill something, I pinpoint exactly where Allison and Steven wait in the trees. Their familiar scents are so easy to pick up on; it's as though they're standing directly beside us, not behind a shield of shrubbery.

"I'm fine," I call out.

"Yeah, I think I need to see for myself," Steven replies.

Sutton sighs. "Fine, come on. But slowly. No sudden movements."

"Uh, actually," I call out, my cheeks flushing as I hear leaves crunching beneath their feet. "This is awkward, but uh, I don't have any clothes on."

"Here." Allison rushes out first and throws a blanket my way. Sutton catches it mid-air. "I thought you might get chilly."

"Thank you." Seeing her brings me more relief than I could have imagined.

Quickly, Sutton hands me half of the blanket, so I pull it up over my chest, and he uses the other side to cover his waist. We remain sitting, but as soon as we're covered, Allison calls out. "She's decent!" She winks at me, and my attention turns to the trees as my brother tentatively steps out from behind the brush.

The moment he sees me, his expression softens. Steven moves toward us then sits down beside Allison and stares at me as if he's expecting me to Hulk out.

"How are you feeling?" he asks.

"Better," I say firmly.

"What was it like?" Allison asks, eyes gleaming with curiosity.

"Ali," Steven mutters, and I blink.

Ali?

When did he nickname her? The air around us shifts, and I sense something I can't quite pinpoint. Shaking it off—for now—I answer honestly.

"Being a wolf feels fantastic, actually," I tell them. "Well, minus the whole bone-breaking situation but I think that is supposed to get better." I look at Sutton, suddenly stricken with the idea that I could be wrong. "Right?"

"Right," he says, patting my knee.

"What about you guys?" I ask, looking back at Steven. "What happened after I...?"

"You mean after you died? Or after I did CPR to bring you back while Sutton bit and infected you with werewolf venom?"

His voice is harsh enough to make me wince. "Yes?"

"None of this is her fault," Sutton growls.

"It's sure as shit not mine," Steven fires back.

"Stop," Allison says in a voice so sharp and unlike her that everyone falls silent. "You two bickering doesn't help us at all." She offers them both reproachful looks, and they have the decency to hang their heads. "Now, Serenity is our priority at the moment. Making sure she's healthy and well again. And after that, we're going to band together and figure out how to deal with this bitch Myrtle once and for all because I am not in the mood for all this body-snatching, zombie bitch shit, and I really need to wake up tomorrow without worrying if anyone I love is dead or undead or anything in the vicinity of dead. No more arguing until we fix this, got it?"

"Got it," Sutton mutters.

"I'll do my best," Steven says, which earns him a death stare. "Okay, okay," he says.

I grin at my friend. "That was impressive."

"Ugh, I haven't had a decent latte in days, sorry."

Sutton looks at her like she might be crazy, and it's almost enough to make me smile.

A rustling in the trees shatters the moment, and we all jump to our feet. My heart pounds, and my inner wolf strains to be let free again. To fight. The rustling comes again. Strange scents reach my nose. Sutton grabs me.

"Fight your instinct," he says quietly. "Just hold on to me."

I do, barely breathing as I struggle to fight my wolf back.

Then a familiar figure emerges from the trees, and I exhale.

"Mable," I say, surprised to see her here.

Phineas is right on her heels. Beside me, Sutton tenses as more of the pack follow them toward us. I recognize Fred and Sylvia Gordon. And Ernie the bartender. Not to mention every one of Sutton's best warriors, including Vaughn, head of security.

"Relax," Phineas says when he sees his son's expression. "They're not here to fight."

"Then why are you here?" Steven asks, his voice laced with suspicion.

Mable ignores his rough tone and smiles at me, her eyes twinkling. "We're here to welcome the newest member of our pack."

"Serenity, we want to tell you how sorry we are about what

happened before," Mable adds. "And to you, Sutton. She's your mate well and truly now. The pack won't go against her ever again."

"You're one of us now, kid," Phineas says with a wink.

"So, my being a wolf changes things between us?" I ask tentatively, still eyeing the others behind them. The last time I saw this many residents in one place, most of them wanted to kill me. Sure, Mable's sorry, but what about the rest of them?

Fred Gordon surprises me by answering in maybe the friendliest voice I've ever heard him use before. "It changes everything."

Falls Gazette

Chapter Twelve

Moonlight cascades through the trees, illuminating the ground with a soft glow. There's a chill in the air, but, thanks to my recent change from human to beast, I barely feel it. Even in human form, the chill doesn't penetrate. Like my skin is tougher or my temperature runs hotter. Maybe both. The wooden porch railing creaks beneath my arms, but I still lean on it, listening to sounds I never would have heard before.

An Owl hoots from a nearby tree.

Rabbits rustle through the grass, likely heading to their burrows for the night.

Somewhere, a pack of deer grazes on the vegetation.

All things I can hear and smell now. It's overwhelming, to be honest. There's a whole world out there I never even knew existed, and now that I can sense it all, I'm not sure how to compartmentalize so it doesn't hit me all at the same time.

Inside the house, I can hear the soft sound of my brother snoring as well as the hum of Allison's white noise machine that she carries with her everywhere. Something I know she was grateful to get back from Yvette's place.

After our impromptu pack meeting earlier, I demanded to see Cara for myself. My wolf feels pretty confident in the fact that we're invincible, but human-Serenity knows better and needs proof the bitch isn't a threat. Unfortunately, Sutton refused to let me anywhere near her. Not yet, he'd said. Something about giving my wolf a little more time to adjust.

I'd agreed but only until the morning. After that, it was back to work until this shit was dealt with once and for all.

Once I'd promised to lie low a little bit longer, Vaughn and some others brought us all of our belongings from the B&B, a show of the new peace between us. They also apologized for turning on me at the church and pledged their allegiance to me—which was kind of weird, honestly—and swore to protect me like one of their own against any and all threats. Even those who seemed dead set against me before have come around to accepting me into the fold now that I'm like them. But while they may have forgiven me for my missteps, I haven't forgiven myself.

Eighteen seconds. That's how long I was officially dead. If not for Sutton, I'd still be a goner. Which means the curse was never recast. And I was never immortal. On top of that, Cara, my friend, is gone. And the loss of her hurts. But the betrayal hurts worse. Our girls' night, all those moments I thought Cara was truly supporting me against the others—it was all a lie. It was Myrtle. Using me and pretending to be Cara so she could get close enough to me to get what she wanted. Myrtle may not have succeeded in re-cursing the town, but she's still done her fair share of damage. And I've yet to find a way to stop her.

At least, the bitch is locked up for now. Thanks to our new surprise half-witch, Jolene, Myrtle will not be walking free anytime soon. The wards will keep her trapped, magically and physically, until we can figure out a way to break the curse and get rid of her for good. And so far, she seems unable to use her magic against us too. That means no zombies coming to rip us apart.

Even still, my mind is muddled. My anxiety at an all-time high. Sleep isn't even a possibility right now. In fact, I feel better standing out here than I did curled up next to Sutton in bed. Must be a wolf thing.

Footsteps creak against the wood floor inside the house moments before the door opens and Sutton steps outside. His scent invades my senses, burning me from the inside out. It's a double attraction—me to him, my wolf to his.

So potent it nearly brings me to my knees. I forget all about Cara and Myrtle and curses. All that exists now is him.

"You okay?" he asks as he comes to stand beside me.

"It all sounds so different now," I reply, turning my head to drink in the sight of him. The t-shirt he wears stretches tightly over his chest, the sleeves tight around his biceps. *Fuck, he's handsome*. My wolf surges in response to my attraction, her way of telling me she approves of all of the above.

"You get used to it." He leans against the railing. "For me, it's always been there, but there was a time it overwhelmed me."

"Really?"

He nods, hazel gaze finding mine. "How are you feeling about the pack?"

I snort. "Pretty damn grateful they don't all want to murder me now."

"That definitely eases things on my end as well," he replies.

"Can I ask you a question?" I turn to face him now, crossing my arms. "Why did you choose me? When the pack tried to come after me, I mean."

Sutton straightens and mimics my stance. "Do you really need to ask?"

"Yes. You chose me, a stranger up until a couple of months ago, over a pack you've known for over a century. Why? Especially after I screwed up so royally. Had Myrtle been able to cast that curse with my blood—"

"She didn't."

"But you didn't know that," I remind him. "And you still chose me over them. Why?"

"You're my mate," he replies, his hand cupping my cheek. "I can feel it in my bones. Which means I stand at your side no matter what. You are who I protect, my pack will always come second to you."

Even as swoon-worthy as that declaration is, the pit in my stomach grows. "They need you."

"They do," he replies. "But I need you more."

It's spoken matter-of-factly, as though this is the way of the world and I need to understand it. "We have to do what's best for them."

He smiles as he drops his hand. "We?"

"Yes. We." I return his grin then face the trees again, leaning my elbows against the railing. "And we need to decide what to do with Myrtle now. As a pack. Jolene's magic is holding her for now, but it won't last forever."

"We have her trapped," he says. "That's what's important. We've never gotten this far before. It's almost over."

"What next?"

"We find a way to kill her," he replies, expression darkening. "And put an end to all of this."

"And if killing her doesn't break the curse?" I ask, voicing one of my larger concerns. "We still don't know that will end it. We could remain trapped here forever."

The air shifts around us, thickening as he moves behind me, his arms slipping around my waist. Sutton pulls me back against his hard body, and I go willingly, taking comfort in the feel of him against me. "I can think of worse ways to spend my time."

My stomach burns with lust as Sutton slips a hand beneath my shirt and cups my breast. His thumb brushes over my nipple, and a soft moan leaves my lips. "Sutton, we're outside."

"It's just us," he whispers in my ear. "Use your senses. Can you hear anyone else?"

I try to listen, but all I can focus on is the feel of his hands on my body. His free hand slips to the waist of my shorts, and he slips his hand inside, cupping me. His finger slips through my wet heat, and I buck against his touch, every one of my senses intensified. The friction of his finger sliding over my clit is nearly unbearable in the best possible way. If I thought Sutton's touch was hot before, it's molten now.

"Can you hear anyone?" he whispers.

"No," I reply, breathless.

"Would you care if they could see us?" he asks, flicking my clit with his finger.

"No."

He slips his hand free and turns me so I'm facing him. Then he lifts me and carries me down the porch and right up to the tree line. Stopping just inside, he sets me down again. Over his shoulder, I can still see the lights of the house, but, thanks to the branches hanging over us, we're shielded from view should Steven or Allison decide to look out their window.

Sutton stands before me, gaze darkening with desire.

We stare at each other.

My wolf surges beneath the surface, and I wonder if his wolf is just as approving of this match. Reaching down with shaking fingers, I grip the hem of my shirt and pull it up over my head, revealing my bare breasts in the moonlight.

Sutton growls, low and deep, and my blood boils in response.

He rushes forward and crushes his mouth to mine. His tongue slips between my lips to tangle with mine. A primal hunger, unlike anything I've ever felt, surges to the surface. I grip the front of his shirt and yank him toward me and then bite his lip hard enough to draw a drop of blood.

Copper fills my mouth, and Sutton growls as he grinds against me.

I trail my hands down, grip the bottom of his shirt, and rip it up over his head. He pulls away long enough for me to drop the handful of fabric to the ground. Then, he takes my mouth again, his hands gripping my ass as he fucks my mouth with his talented tongue.

My hands slip into his hair, gripping the thick strands as I cling to him like the lifeline he is. Sutton Hargrave is *everything* to me. And what would have scared me before—has now become a thrilling source of constant pleasure.

He sets me down and shoves me so my back presses against a tree. Then, he strips out of his sweats and drops to his knees before me. He looks up at me, wearing a wicked smirk on his face. Gaze dark, he shoves my shorts down and helps me step out of them. Then, he grips one of my thighs and places it over his shoulder.

Hot breath washes over the inside of my thigh, and I moan softly. He takes his time, breathing over my tender skin before running his tongue over my center. My entire body shudders.

"Sutton," I gasp at the pleasure exploding through me as my orgasm grows to nearly unbearable.

"I'm nowhere near done with you yet," he growls against me. Then, he lies on his back, pulling me forward until I'm straddling his face.

His tongue slips inside of me; then he pulls out and draws my clit into his mouth. My hands go to my hair as his climb up my belly and cup my breasts. A sound escapes me, but I no longer care who can see or hear us. All that matters is this—our bodies joined. I buck my hips against him, riding his face as my orgasm continues to climb to dangerous heights. Every single inch of my body is on fire, every single nerve burning with pleasure.

I want more.

Harder.

Faster.

Stars invade my vision as I come on his face, the orgasm so fucking amazing it nearly shatters me. He gently pinches my hardened nipples and slides his tongue over me, successfully drawing out every single second of pleasure he's given me.

And still, I *need* more.

I climb off of him, my knees pressing into the soft ground below me as I arch my back and look over at him, an invitation that he quickly accepts.

Sutton positions himself behind me, his hands running over my back. This moment between us, it's so damned carnal, so primal that it makes me lose my breath. But I don't need oxygen nearly as much as I need Sutton inside me.

He grips my hips and thrusts into me.

I cry out as he fills me then pulls out and thrusts into me again.

"So fucking tight," he groans. He fills me and then reaches down and wraps a hand across my throat to pull me up so my back is flush with his front. I spread my knees and cry out, the new angle hitting me in all the right places. Sutton's free hand snakes around my front, and he trails his fingers over my sensitive nub.

He slides in and out, fucking me with the same rhythm he slides his fingers against my clit. Another orgasm builds, and I cry out as it overtakes me, every muscle in my body turning to liquid.

Sutton thrusts one more time. Two more times. Then releases me and pulls away, lying on his back. He starts to work himself with his hand, but I shove it away and lean down to take him into my mouth. I suck, drawing him in as deep as he'll go as his hands tangle into my hair. He clings to the strands and thrusts his hips up, groaning. A moment later, I feel his body shudder beneath me.

His release fills my mouth. "Fuck, Serenity," he growls, gripping me as I swallow him down.

When I pull away, he's watching me, gaze dark, expression unreadable. I lean back on my knees as Sutton sits up.

"That was—"

"It was," Sutton interrupts. He looks around, his eyes clearer than they were just a moment ago. Clearer and intense with something I don't understand. "We should get inside."

Something is off, I can feel it as the air shifts around us. Where I just experienced the best sex of my life, I can't help but wonder if I somehow let him down.

"Are you okay?" I ask.

"Of course. More than okay.

"Then what--?"

Sutton stands and reaches down to help me to my feet. He grips my arm and pulls me forward, pressing a kiss to my lips. When he steps away, he smiles though it doesn't reach his eyes. "I just want to keep you safe, Serenity. Always."

Falls Gazette

Chapter Thirteen

Despite the late night, I stir just after dawn. In the moments where I linger between awake and asleep, the connection to my wolf is so absolute I can't tell us apart. Her needs are my needs. The primal and the civilized tangle together. We both crave Sutton, and we both need food. But most importantly, we both have to pee. Badly.

Easing out of bed, I'm careful not to jostle Sutton, who's draped over his side of the mattress, one leg hanging over the edge like an enormous—and sexy as fuck—starfish. If starfish can be sexy. Smiling to myself, I tiptoe to the bathroom and take care of business. When I'm done, a noise in the hall draws me, and I bypass the bed—which is a shame because I had some really fun plans for Sutton's wake-up call—and slip into the shadowy hallway.

Allison is there—coming out of Steven's room.

She freezes when she sees me. Our eyes meet.

"I, uh, got lost," Allison says. She's always been a terrible liar, but this is just laughable. Her face is redder than I've ever seen.

I don't need wolf senses to know what's going on. In fact, my nose wrinkles, and, for the first time since changing, I wish like hell I didn't have such a strong sense of smell. My bestie reeks of sex, and there's only one eligible male left in this house for her to get it from. Which means... Gross.

"You hooked up with my brother?" I hiss.

Her eyes widen, and she glances at the closed door behind her then grabs my wrist and drags me into her room. When the door is securely shut behind us, she finally exhales, looking positively sick. Or maybe terrified.

"Look, we didn't want you to find out this way. I meant to tell you. No, to ask you. Well, Steven insists he doesn't have to ask you for shit, but as your best friend, I think it's only right. And—"

"What do you mean, *ask me*? You want to ask my permission to have a one-night stand with each other? Awkwarrrd."

She winces. "Not a one-night stand."

She stares back at me as if waiting for me to get it. When I do, I nearly lose my shit.

"This has happened before?" I screech.

"Ssshh!" She darts glances to the door. "Do you want an audience for this conversation?"

"Do you?" I cross my arms. "Because I'm not the one who just got busted doing the walk of shame."

She groans. "You're going to make me suffer for this, aren't you?"

"You're damn right I am. What happened to 'no more secrets,' huh?"

"I mean, this was the last one," she mumbles.

Her head hangs low, and guilt rolls off her in waves. I hesitate, sifting through the million things I'm feeling all at once, thanks to my heightened emotions. I could be pissed at her for this, sure. But I'm not that kind of friend. Or sister. Steven's more than capable of making his own choices. And since I want him to let me do the same, I need to chill.

"Look, if you want honesty, the truth is I've suspected something between you two for a while now," I admit.

"You have?"

I tap my nose. "Journalist and werewolf, babe. You had no chance."

Right."

She falls silent, and my thoughts turn to the humor in all this.

Before I can fully get a handle on myself, the hint of a smile creeps over my face. Allison's tortured look lightens with hope at the sight of it.

"You're not mad?"

"Of course I'm mad." I can't help it, I start giggling.

"But … you're laughing?" Her confusion has a hint of fear in it. Which only makes me laugh harder.

"I'm sorry, I just..." I take a deep breath and try to calm myself. "And I thought the guy with the cats was going to be the most awkward moment of your sex life."

Allison's lips curve, and our eyes meet and hold. Then, in unison, we both crack up laughing. For some reason, in the midst of so many near-death experiences, I find this revelation hilarious. Maybe it's the wolf instincts overloading my brain, or maybe I've finally snapped, but the laughter is uncontrollable. By the time Steven comes to investigate, Allison and I are in tears.

"What the hell's so funny at seven in the morning?" he grumbles.

I take one look at him, hair rumpled from sleep and who knows what else, and lose it again. "You," I finally manage to say, my hands clutching my stomach.

He frowns and looks over at Allison.

"I'm sorry," she says, wiping her eyes. "She caught me coming out of your room and figured it out."

"Figured what out?" Sutton asks, coming up behind him.

"Steven and Allison are banging," I tell him, "And it's so much weirder than her cat guy... which I honestly didn't think could be topped."

Sutton and Steven exchange a look that makes me snort-laugh.

Steven glares at me. "I'm glad you think this is a joke."

"Would you rather I pour us drinks and make Allison tell me every detail of your night together like she normally does?" I ask with mock innocence.

He scowls.

"Uh, no offense, Ser," Allison says, straightening, "but I think I'm going to skip the recap for you this time."

"No offense taken," I assure her with a shudder.

"It's too early for this shit," Steven mutters and walks out.

I grin up at Sutton, who shakes his head and turns for the door as well. "I'm going to make coffee," he says over his shoulder.

"You're a saint," I call after him.

When they're gone, I look at Allison, who watches me expectantly. "Thank you for reacting so... Thank you for not trying to kill me," she says. "Which, given the fact that you can change into an actual fucking wolf, would not be too difficult."

"Is that what you thought I'd do?" I ask, sobering.

"Hard to say. Before... it depends on your mood, maybe? But now... I mean, you're a wolf, Ser. Your instincts aren't exactly the same. So, I had no idea what to expect."

"I guess you have a point. My emotions are running kind of high. Hence the fact that I couldn't get ahold of myself once I got going. The laughter felt good though. I haven't done that in a while."

She grins. "I'm so glad my choice of--"

"Don't say booty call."

"Boyfriend could offer you such amusement."

My eyes widen. "Boyfriend?"

She bites her lip, nodding.

"Exactly how long have you guys been seeing each other?"

"He came to see me a few weeks ago. When you stopped checking in. He was worried about you and wanted to know what I'd heard from you. So, we had coffee." She exhales, and it's a content sort of sound. "From there, it just sort of...happened."

"Okay." I hold up my hand. "I don't need to know all the details, remember?"

She grins. "Deal."

"You really like him?"

"I do." She looks uncertain again. "I mean, if that's okay."

"I'm not going to lie and say I'm not shocked. But"—I grab her hand, squeezing reassuringly— "I want you both to be as happy as I am with my—"

Her brow arches. "Boyfriend?"

"That sounds so weird for us but sure."

She softens. "You love him, don't you?"

I bite my lip, a smile escaping anyway. "I do."

She beams. "I'm so happy for you, Ser. You deserve this."

"Thank you. Anyway, if you two are happier together, I'm all for it."

"Thank you." She squeezes my hand back. "That means a lot."

"But please understand he's still my brother, and the sibling code states I must give him a ration of shit for this. Nothing personal."

"I understand. Do what you have to do."

"Good." I stand and head for the door. "I'm going to let my inner predator hunt down some coffee. You coming?"

She stands too and ushers me out first. "Lead the way, beast."

AFTER COFFEE AND EGGS AND ENDLESS SHIT-TALKING TO MY brother, the teasing and banter turn serious as we all settle in to figure out what the hell we do next in the shit-show that has become our lives. The minute we bring up Myrtle, and by association, Cara, my wolf strains inside me, wanting only to be let free. She whispers promises of death and destruction if only I'll let her take the lead. Sutton seems to notice the undertone of my thoughts and reaches for my hand, holding it firmly in his as if to remind me I'm human—and he expects me to stay that way for now.

Party pooper.

"We need to take this slow," Sutton says. At my scowl, he adds, "Believe me, I want to rip her apart limb from limb too, but we all know killing the body isn't enough. And we need to find out more before we do something that makes it worse."

He's right, of course. Ugh.

"The problem is that time is not on our side," Steven says.

"What do you mean?" I ask, worry sharpening my words. "I thought Jolene had it handled."

"Jolene texted me this morning. The magic is getting harder to maintain. She's straining to keep Cara contained," Steven says grimly. "I don't know how long she can hold the bitch. But I have men assigned to watch her around the clock. If Cara so much as sparks, they'll plow her with lead."

"That won't kill her," I remind him.

"It'll sure as shit slow her down," he says. "Have you seen someone run away with no feet attached to their ankles?"

I shake my head. There's no use arguing.

"So, what's our next move?" Allison asks.

"Our next step is what it's always been," Steven says. "Kill that bitch and move the fuck on with our lives."

"Agreed." Sutton looks just as bloodthirsty and, for once, in agreement with my brother.

"The problem," I say, "is she's not exactly killable. I mean, she's in Cara, but she's *not* Cara. She's a soul. A spirit who inhabits bodies."

"I can't believe zombies are real," Allison puts in, nose wrinkling in disgust.

"I've never seen her in physical form. Have you?" I look at Sutton, but Steven answers first.

"Cara's body is physical," he says. "And I can riddle her with so many bullet holes she'll look like Swiss cheese."

I roll my eyes. "Bullet holes don't make a difference," I tell him. "Not when Myrtle will just jump to someone else—which we want to avoid happening since, at least right now, we know whose body she's currently inhabiting."

"Serenity's right," Sutton says. "If she jumps again, we'll lose her."

"There has to be someone who knows something about how to take her out," Allison says.

I meet Steven's eyes across the table. Even before he speaks, I can guess what he's going to say. "We're not the only relation. Maybe Mom--"

"We are not bringing the family into this," I say, eyes narrowing as I brace myself for an argument. This is one battle I'll fight to the end. But Steven puts his hands up.

"Whoa, relax. I don't want to involve any of them, okay? It's too dangerous. But she might know something. Even if she doesn't realize it."

I shake my head. "I already tried fishing for information. Family tree stuff, rumors of witchcraft. She doesn't know anything. Neither does Dad."

"Damn." He turns to Sutton. "I don't suppose you've come

across any other witches besides the bitch we're trying to eliminate?"

"I haven't exactly been able to travel the last, I don't know, century."

Allison snorts.

Steven sighs. "All right then. So how do we figure out how to kill the unkillable?" Steven asks.

No one answers, but I know we're all thinking the same thing: if we knew that, we would have done it already.

"I want to see her," I say when it's clear no one has an answer.

"Fuck no," Steven says at the same time Sutton growls, "Absolutely not."

I eye them both with raised brows, and they duck their heads.

"You'll both be there," I say. "And it's not like I'm going to get close enough for her to do anything. I just need to lay eyes on her. See for myself that she's truly trapped. And besides, I want to talk to Jolene. Thank her properly."

Sutton is the first to give in. Steven looks less willing, but he apparently realizes arguing with me is just as futile as me arguing with him.

"Fine," he says. "But if she so much as—"

"I know, I know, Swiss cheese."

Falls Gazette

Chapter Fourteen

Walking through downtown Midnight Falls is a strange sort of déjà vu. It feels as if ages have passed since I was here but also like no time at all because nothing has changed. Townspeople—aka pack members—stop when they see us. Mable, especially, takes one look at me and veers off course to flag us down.

"How are you feeling today?" she asks, pulling me into a hug before I can answer.

Her squeeze is tight, but she lets me go quickly, drawing back to study me as I tell her, "I'm good."

She looks unconvinced. "We haven't turned a bitten wolf in ages," she says, shooting Sutton a reproachful glare. "You can tell us the truth. If you're struggling, we want to help."

"I appreciate that," I tell her. "And Sutton has been helping."

"Yes, I just bet he has."

I bite back a smile at that. Sutton huffs, but I pat her arm. "My wolf is taking some getting used to, but I'm adjusting. Running helps." Not to mention moonlight sex. I don't tell her that part. "And we're on our way to see the prisoner, which will settle my wolf even more."

"Yes, I can imagine your instinct to fight is high, what with the drama."

The drama.

Yes, that's one way to put it.

"Well, I won't keep you," she says. "But I will expect a girls' night once this has all calmed down." Her expression clouds, and I know we're both thinking about the last girls' night. The one with Cara—or the person we thought was Cara. "I'll buy the drinks this time," she adds.

"You don't have to do that," I tell her.

"Are you kidding? I'm the reason you're here, and... well, it's the least I can do."

"In that case, I'll let you buy me one if you let me do the same." I smile at her. "I wouldn't want to be anywhere else."

She exhales as if relieved at my words then glances at Sutton again, softening. "Yes, I can see some good did come out of this after all."

She smiles, squeezes my hand, and hurries off again.

We resume walking, and I feel a lot lighter than earlier, despite the looks we're getting from the others.

The majority of them stare, and it reminds me of when I first arrived in Midnight Falls. They stared at me for being a stranger before. Now, they stare because I'm one of them.

I offer tight smiles as we pass by, but otherwise, I'm more than happy to let Sutton usher me past them all and into the Sheriff's office. Inside, Steven takes the lead, surprising the hell out of me by issuing orders to everyone we pass. What shocks me more is that they listen.

The bitchy receptionist I first encountered all those weeks ago is back at her post, but her expression is much different than I remember. She's still a bit short with us, but I suspect it has more to do with Steven firing off questions—to which she hurries to answer—than it does me being—well—me.

Steven leads us straight back, past the conference room where Sheriff Rhodes once blew me off like some nosy, unwanted reporter. To be fair, I was a nosy, unwanted reporter. My, how things have changed. We move past the large hub of empty desks where the rest of the staff has all but abandoned their jobs. I can't blame them, considering what we're up against now. At the back of the room, he stops in front of a door marked "Restricted."

"The cells are just through there," he says. "Ali and I will wait out here. It's kind of close quarters in there. Remember, no getting too close."

"I got it," I say impatiently.

He grumbles something about "reckless sisters" and steps aside. Sutton follows me through the door, his chest pressing close against my back. I don't know if it's worry that has him sticking so close or just a not-so-subtle reminder that he's not leaving my side, no matter what.

Inside, a handful of cells line a narrow hallway. Jolene sits directly in the center of the walkway in a metal folding chair. She's reading a book that she quickly lowers when she sees us coming. I catch sight of the words Dragon and Mate on the book cover before it's all tucked out of sight, and it's all I can do not to let my eyes widen in surprise. I'm pretty sure Jolene's reading a dragon romance, and it's the last thing I ever expected. But I know better than to utter a word about it just now.

Her sharp gaze zeroes in on me.

"Glad to see you up and around," she says.

"Thanks," I say. "You too. And with magic, huh? Who knew?"

She snorts. "Guess it's all on me now, eh?"

I feel a pang of sympathy for her—and for the loss of my magic. Power I hadn't even begun to understand before it was ripped away from me.

"Not at all," I tell her. "That's why I'm here."

"But your magic--"

"I may not have magic, but I'm still ready to kick ass," I tell her.

She nods and gets to her feet as if she understands what I'm doing here. "She's there," she says, pointing at the cell just beyond where she stands.

I slide past her and make my way to the cell, peering in at the woman whose face is so familiar it still pricks at my heart to see it worn by such a monster. She's lying on her back on the steel bench welded to the wall. The only other item in the room is a stainless-steel toilet in the far corner. The whole place reeks of waste. My wolf cringes at the disgusting sensory overload.

As if she has heightened senses of her own, Cara's eyes open, and she sits up to look directly at me. I tense, watching her warily despite Jolene's claims about wards and shackles. But there's no sign of animosity or even a threat when she looks at me. Exhaustion lines her features, and while the eyes that stare back at me are full of venom, when she speaks, her voice is tired.

"You lived," she says flatly. "Pity."

"I thought you'd be glad," I say. "Another chance to use me for your curse."

"I'm done with you," she says with a dismissive snort. "The moment I'm free, I'll kill you all and be done with it. I've grown weary of this game."

"Is that because your magic didn't work on me?" I ask, unable to keep from taunting her. Mostly, though, I just want answers. And asking straight never works with Myrtle. You have to bait her into it, which is the real reason I've come in the first place. We need answers only she has. "You tried to make me immortal. To recast the curse. But it didn't work. Is that why you're giving up?"

"Your blood was weak," she spits at me, her eyes glimmering with a disgust I can practically taste on the air. "That's why the curse didn't work. My brother took a human wife, and with every human generation that came after, our family's power became diluted. Immortality weighed you and rejected you. And now, so do I."

Her words sting, which is ridiculous. I shouldn't give two shits what this woman thinks of my blood or any other part of me.

"Maybe you haven't heard, but immortality accepted me just fine," I tell her, crossing my arms. "Instead of the weak-ass witchy powers I inherited from you, I'm a wolf now. A predator who can't wait to rip you into tiny pieces."

"Are you really still naïve enough to think a wolf is any match for me?"

I grit my teeth at that. "You're beaten, Myrtle. Just admit it," I say.

"Please. I'm biding my time," she says, and that gleam in her eye grows. "Your little hybrid is weakening by the moment. And when she gives in to my power, I'll kill her for this. I'll kill you all."

"Keep talking shit, old lady," Jolene warns.

But I glance back, concerned. Jolene hasn't mentioned Cara fighting back at all. And to look at her, you wouldn't even know it was happening. But I know better than most that magic isn't about what you can see. It's mostly about what's happening under the surface. And apparently, there's more going on here than meets the eye.

That's not good.

Jolene steps up beside me, hands fisted, eyes blazing with a hunger for blood. I recognize it because my wolf wants that same thing right now. Cara merely smiles.

Jolene bares her teeth, and the air crackles with energy. A push and pull that leaves no doubt Cara's not bluffing. She's battling Jolene as we speak.

"Soon," Cara croons, "I'll be free, and you'll all be sorry."

At that, I finally lose it. Snarling, I lunge forward, gripping the bars in my hands and pressing my body against them as if I'll just pass right through. Every nerve in my body burns with a thirst for spilled blood that eclipses every rational thought.

My wolf surges to the surface, and I squeeze my eyes shut, barely hanging onto my human form.

"Let's go," Sutton says in a low voice.

He's at my back in an instant, his hand lightly pressing against my side as he steers me toward the door. "Now," he adds, prying my hands off the bars and pulling me toward the exit.

"That's right, Sutton," Cara calls. "Take your little wolf, and be gone from me. I don't need to destroy you. I've only to wait long enough for you to destroy yourselves."

Sutton growls and then grips my arm, propelling me toward the exit. Jolene follows, and we all file back into the station house. Steven and Allison hurry up, and I do my best to catch my breath and cool the raging fire in my veins.

"I won't ask how it went," Steven says flatly.

"Are you okay?" Allison asks me nervously.

"I will be," I say, trying to catch my breath.

"She needs to be destroyed," Sutton snarls.

"On this, we agree." Steven nods for us to follow him. "Let's go into the training room. There are a few others who want in on this little meeting."

"Others?" I ask as we all follow Steven.

The more distance I put between Cara and my wolf, the better.

As we near the training room, Sutton glances down at me expectantly. "It's my father," he explains. "Can't you smell him?"

As soon as he says the words, I realize I can. I'd been so busy fighting my wolf off, thanks to Cara's taunting, I hadn't noticed. Now, I inhale and let Phineas' familiar scent wash over me. I've just begun to relax when I notice there are two other signatures along with his. Luckily, my wolf recognizes them all and doesn't label them threatening.

I step inside and spot the three familiar faces waiting for us.

"Phineas. Mable. Vaughn," I say, looking back and forth between them. "What are you all doing here?"

"You didn't think we were going to let you have that bitch all to yourself, did you?" Mable asks, shocking me into silence with the vehemence in her tone.

I blink at that. "I, uh..."

Phineas grins at that and leans in for a quick hug. "Mable's a fighter when she wants to be," he whispers in my ear before stepping back again.

"Well," Jolene says, coming up behind us. "We caught the bitch. Now what?"

Vaughn eyes her with open distrust. "You tell us. You're the one who apparently has magic."

Jolene glares at him. "I don't care if you're pissed I hid my magic," she says. "I did it out of survival, and I don't regret it for a second. The important thing is it's working to keep her contained. But she was right about what she said in there," she says, gaze flicking to me, "I can't hold her forever. She's attacking me constantly with the little magic she can push through my wards. And once she's free, she's going to level this fucking town. I can feel her need for it."

"Why are we even having this conversation?" Vaughn demands. "Let's go in there right now and kill her and be done with it."

"Don't you think I've tried that?" Jolene says, and Steven shoots her a look that puts them on the same team for once. "Or did you think I wanted to simply lock her away and then spend every waking moment watching her and fighting her magic with mine until I slowly lose and she kills us all?"

Vaughn scowls. There's obviously a history between them that has made him feel betrayed in all this.

She doesn't give him a chance to answer as she says, "Believe me, I tried killing her the other night—we all did—but that bitch has no 'off' switch. Not with the kind of magic she's packing." She glances at the pistol attached to Steven's hip. "We're going to need a different approach if we're going to end her."

"Except we have no clue what approach that is," Steven says.

"What about the library?" Allison asks suddenly, turning to Mable. "Maybe there's a book that has some ideas."

But Mable shakes her head. "Believe me, child, I've looked. There's nothing. Myrtle made sure of that."

Allison sighs.

Across the room, I meet Sutton's eyes. "There is one person who knows how to stop her," I say.

Sutton looks confused, but at my expression, realization dawns, and he grimaces.

"Who?" Allison asks hopefully.

I sigh. "Tabitha. Myrtle's daughter."

"Tabitha's dead, sweetie," Jolene offers, her voice patronizing like she thinks I might be crazy.

"And you'll join her if you don't watch your tone," Allison shoots back, and I have to hide a smile at the shocked look Jolene gives her. Not one of fear but rather appreciation for the balls my friend is clearly packing for threatening her.

"She is dead, but she's still around," I tell them. "At Yvette's place."

Phineas looks intrigued, but Vaughn looks wary. Considering all of the security runs he's done around that house, I have zero doubt he's heard of our interactions to know I'm serious. "Not sure that's safe," Vaughn says.

"It's not," Sutton agrees, and I give him the stank eye.

"Nowhere's safe," I point out. "Not until we finish this. And Tabitha might be the only one left who can tell us how to do that. But she definitely won't talk to all of us."

"Right," Mable says. "We'll hang back."

"If you're going to that house of horrors, I'm for sure coming with you," Steven says.

"Actually, you're for sure staying here," I say.

He glares at me, opening his mouth to blast me, but Sutton steps in. "Serenity's right. Tabitha is volatile on the best of days. One comment from you and she'll let us all rot."

"Are you trying to say I have a less than charming personality?" Steven asks, feigning insult.

At that, Sutton snorts. "Understatement," he says, and Steven grins.

I stare at them, wondering when they reached the bantering stage of their frenemy relationship.

"Fine. You may have a point." Steven doesn't look happy, but he doesn't argue, which I consider a huge step in the direction of civility for those two. But Sutton's not done. "Jolene," he begins, but she cuts him off.

"Yeah, yeah, I got it. Stay here, and don't open the bitch's box."

"We all appreciate what you're doing for the pack," he tells her.

She flicks a glance at Vaughn and says nothing.

Steven scowls. "Just hurry up," he grumbles.

"Will do," I say.

"Vaughn and Phineas, you two stake out the perimeter, and don't let anyone in or out of this building," Sutton says. "But no coming inside unless there's trouble. We need to limit her contact with people."

"What should I do?" Mable asks.

"Update the security teams," Sutton says. "And assemble the pack."

"What should I tell them?" she asks.

"Gather in the library. Everyone. No exceptions other than essential personnel here to guard the prisoner. And no one in or out. If the witch does somehow manage to break free from her host, we're going to make it impossible for her to choose another body. This ends today."

ALLISON AND STEVEN SWEAR TO STAY AT THE STATION TO WATCH over our prisoner with Jolene holding the wards. Phineas and Vaughn both hang out in front of the station to stand guard just in case. And Mable heads outside to rally the town. Finally, it's just me and Sutton.

His hand finds mine, and he laces our fingers together. The contact is reassuring, and the silence becomes more comfortable.

"You okay?" he asks as we walk.

I shoot him a wry glance. "Define 'okay'," I say.

He snorts. "Your wolf, I mean. That was a lot of sensory information back there. Not to mention the bitch herself. Your predator can be strong-willed. Sometimes, it takes a lot to keep it in check."

"Sensory information?" I lift my brows. "That's a nice way of saying I nearly Hulked out, isn't it?"

He grins. "You're really sexy when you Hulk out if it helps."

For some reason, his words remind me of the way he took me so roughly in the library a few days ago. My thoughts wander to what it would be like now that I'm strong like him. Now that I can be rough right back.

"Serenity?" he asks, a growl lacing the word.

I shudder, knowing full well he can scent the direction of my thoughts. "Sorry. Sensory information."

He laughs. "Later," he promises.

"Later," I agree.

A beat of silence passes.

"And now?" he asks when both of our beasts—and our hormones—have quieted.

I nod, knowing exactly what he means. "My wolf definitely wants to get her claws on Myrtle. But she trusts me." I squeeze his hand. "And you."

He offers me a smile that lights his eyes more than curves his lips. "I trust her too," he says quietly.

As we walk, my senses hone in on the sights and sounds of the forest. Pushing farther, I realize I can hear so much more than ever before. Small, foraging animals. The wind in the trees. Birds nesting. It's amazing.

I also note that each sound comes with its own impression from my wolf. Threat or no threat. Tensed or relaxed. And I'm relieved nothing I hear feels like a danger to her. That means we're safe. For now.

Up ahead, the bed and breakfast comes into view. We turn down the driveway, and I'm struck by a sense of nostalgia. This place was my first home in this town—however short the stay. And in that little time, so many memories were formed. The first moment I saw Sutton, both as wolf and man. The moment I realized specters were real. And along the way became friends with them.

Despite my reluctance to enter, and the crazy bitch who once owned it, I'm sort of fond of the place too.

"There's no movement or heartbeats from inside," Sutton says, then turns and looks at me. "Ready?"

"Let's go see your ex."

He shakes his head at that.

We head for the door, my heart hammering.

Inside, the air is stale. As if the place has remained undisturbed since we left it. Unfortunately, the shattered dishes and broken lamps littering the floor suggest otherwise.

"Uh, what happened?" I ask.

Sutton shakes his head. "No idea."

"Has anyone been in here?" I ask.

"No one from the pack," he says. "And I don't scent anyone but the four of us."

We exchange a long look.

Sutton creeps quietly through the foyer and main floor. I follow, careful to stay out of sight of any mirrors. Yvette's gaudy parlor mirror is still on the back porch as far as I know. Apparently, Vaughn wanted to shatter it, but Allison put her foot down about it while I was busy transforming to wolf status.

Her superstition about bad luck prevailed, and the mirror remains untouched. For now.

"Hello?" Sutton calls out as we climb the stairs.

No answer.

He looks dubiously back at me.

I shake my head, unconcerned. "Tabitha's always been most active in the bedroom where I accidentally summoned her. If she's going to show herself, it'll be there."

He seems to accept my words and we keep going. Silently, I wonder if I'm right or if she's going to make us work for it. I don't exactly have the magic it would take to summon her forcefully right now. And the house is so still that I wonder if she's somehow found a way to leave after all. Though I am disappointed that I don't see

Victoria or Lance anywhere. Where the hell could they be? Doing ghostly things in whatever realm they hang out in when they're not here?

At the top of the stairs, Sutton turns and leads us to the end of the hall. To Yvette's bedroom. Now Tabitha's. The door is cracked open, so Sutton pushes it wide, and I follow him inside, only to realize we won't have to do anything to summon her at all.

She's already here.

Falls Gazette

Chapter Fifteen

Tabitha looks up from where she sits on the bed, shoulders drooped, head hung low. Tears streak her pale cheeks, and her lashes are wet from crying. Instead of acting surprised at the sight of us, she only looks ready to dissolve into more tears.

Instead, she reaches over and grabs a crystal from the nightstand and hurls it at Sutton's head.

He ducks, and it hits the wall with a harmless clink before falling to the floor.

I look back at Tabitha, impressed at her corporeal ability in this moment.

"What was that for?" Sutton demands.

"You know exactly what it's for. Bastard!" She reaches for another crystal, this one heavier, but her hand passes through. She makes a sound of frustration and tries again. This time, she manages to pick it up before it falls right through her palm onto the floor.

She whirls on us again, eyes blazing now. "How could you?" she asks, gaze trained on Sutton. "After everything we meant to each other."

"What are you talking about?" He already sounds exhausted by her antics.

"Were you the one who destroyed the downstairs?" I ask.

She glares at me briefly then back to Sutton.

"You were supposed to be my fated. My mate. And then you go and choose *her*. Like I never meant anything at all."

"You and I were never mates," he tells her quietly.

She ignores that, her gaze swinging to me. "And you," she says, her words an accusation. "You're a... a..."

"A wolf?" I offer.

"Not a witch," she finishes, looking horrified.

"I'm stronger than a witch," I say, not liking the disappointment she's aiming at me. I expected jealousy or rage, but that's not what this is. Not entirely, anyway. It reminds me of Myrtle's taunting. Like I'm somehow less for not having magic anymore.

Tabitha scoffs at my words. "Not even close, you idiot. How could you have been so stupid? Now you'll never beat her."

My eyes narrow. The urge to snap back at her is strong, but I take a deep breath and let it go again. "Tabitha, we need to talk."

"I'm done talking to you. Both of you," she adds, sniffling at Sutton.

She turns away, petulant. Hurt. Maybe once upon a time, I would have given in to empathy. Taken a soft approach, coaxing her to our side. But between Myrtle's shit-talking and my wolf wanting to eat someone's throat, I'm not in the mood for soft.

"Listen, Tabs, we have your mommy in a cell across town and exactly one chance to break this curse by breaking her face. Now, we can do this one of two ways, but you are going to help us figure out how to end her—"

She cuts me off, expression heating. "I thought you'd figured it out by now. My mother can't be killed. That's the beauty of the curse. Her immortality is woven right into the DNA of the magic itself. And that's unfortunate for you two because, as long as she exists here in the Falls, so does the damned curse. And that's why you'll never be free—not from her and not from this wretched town you're stuck inside."

"That's bullshit," I snap. "She's in a body. Across town. We have her imprisoned. If I kill her without another body to use, she'll cease to exist."

Tabitha's expression is a challenge. "Will she?"

I groan, and Sutton nudges me, stepping up to try instead. "Listen, we all want the same thing," he says, and Tabitha snorts. "You hate your mother," he adds. "I know you do. And you're stuck here, unable to get revenge for everything she put you through. Put *us* through. But I can get that revenge for you. Let me get justice. Tell me how to stop her."

Tabitha eyes him, considering.

Silence stretches as I bite my tongue, waiting for her response. Hope leaps into her eyes, and I think she's actually going to help us. But then Sutton shifts his weight closer to me, and her gaze zeroes in on our closeness, eyes narrowing to slits.

The hope vanishes.

"If you kill the body, my mother will continue to exist," she snaps. "Or did you miss the whole 'immortality' thing?"

My hands fist in frustration.

"And you're wrong about me. I can cross over whenever I want. I just preferred to remain in this place a bit longer."

"Wait. You can leave?" I ask. "Why didn't you tell us this before?"

She smirks. "Because *before*, I still had a chance at stealing him back."

"Tabitha," Sutton says, a warning in his voice.

Her smile vanishes, her expression clouding as she looks back at him. For the first time ever, I see vulnerability in her eyes. "That's not going to happen now, is it?" she asks softly.

"No," he says, quiet but absolute.

"Yeah," she says sadly. "I figured."

There's a beat of silence, and despite everything, I find my heart is heavy for her loss. For all her losses. Not just Sutton but her own life. Her future. Any chance at happiness.

Suddenly, her gaze flicks to me, and her eyes narrow. "Don't you dare feel sorry for me, you little man-stealer. If it weren't for you, I'd have my happy ending by now."

My jaw drops. "Are you kidding me? You're going to make this my fault?"

She huffs. "Not entirely, but you're not blameless either."

"You're insane," I say, and her cheeks flush.

She tilts her head, taunting me now. "And yet you came to the insane girl for answers."

She has a point. Taking yet another deep breath, I square my shoulders. "I'm sorry, Tabitha. Truly I am."

She glares at me. "I don't believe you."

"You don't have to." I step forward, and Sutton reaches out to grab my arm. I glance up at him and shake my head to let him know I'm not losing my shit like I did earlier. Reluctantly, he lets me go. "But it's the truth. You've suffered just as much as—if not more than—everyone in this town. Murdered by your mother for loving someone? That's a steaming heap of shit if ever I've heard one."

Tabitha sniffles. "Let's not forget being trapped in a painting and forced to watch as the man I love falls for another."

My chest tightens. Shit, she really was dealt a crap hand, even if she is bananas. "Exactly."

Sutton steps up beside me. "I am sorry as well," he says, "for the part I've played in your misery. It was never my intention to hurt you."

I glance up at him, constantly in awe of the type of man he is. Not many would apologize to their stalker. Not to mention the fact that it was her obsession that led to his entire pack being cursed for a hundred-plus years. How did I get this lucky?

"While I appreciate your apologies," Tabitha sneers, "I fail to see why you think I have any answers for you."

"Don't you?" Sutton asks. It's a simple question. Two easy words, but her reaction holds weight. A lot of it. Tabitha's brow creases, her jaw hardening. She knows something—maybe a lot of somethings.

"You can't stop my mother. She is unkillable," she says. "And I should know."

"Why is that? Because you were so—" My jab is cut short as realization dawns on me. The hair on the back of my neck prickles in response. Has the answer been literally staring us in the face this entire damn time?

"Serenity?"

Sutton's voice cuts through my thoughts, and I refocus on Tabitha. She's watching me angrily, eyes damn near burrowing holes through my body. "She is virtually indestructible," I breathe.

Tabitha rolls her eyes. "Which is literally what I've been saying this entire time."

"And you were, too."

She pales. "Clearly, I was not."

I grin. She's trying to evade, to make this difficult for us, but I've already pieced it together. Turning to Sutton, my smile spreads. "I know how we stop her."

"How?"

"Tabitha was indestructible too, thanks to Myrtle's magic—so after killing her body, Myrtle trapped her soul. And she's not the only one. Yvette's soul is trapped in the mirror downstairs." Gripping his arms, I urge him to make the connection with me. "Sutton, we trap her ass. We confine her to something, and then we bury it so damn deep no one will ever find it. Like Jumanji but hidden better."

"Jumanji?"

I shake my head. "Later. What do you think? It could work."

Sutton considers my idea, and I can all but see the wheels turning in his head. Meanwhile, my wolf is just as excited as I am—maybe even more so. She is desperate to act, to get this done and over with so we can put Myrtle behind us for good.

Tabitha remains completely silent, her gaze trained on Sutton as though he is the air she breathes. Shit, he kind of is.

"It could work. If we can find the right spell to trap her while still freeing us."

"That's the beauty of this whole thing. All we need to do is get her there. The curse will do the rest." He doesn't answer, but I can see him beginning to understand. "Tabitha says the curse is tied to Myrtle. And vice versa. So, wherever she goes, the curse goes too. Meaning--"

"Wherever we trap her, the curse will keep her confined in that place," he says, "Just like she's confined here. And then we'll all be free."

I grin. "Two birds, one stone."

"But where do we trap her, and how do we put her there to begin with?" he asks.

"Yvette's grimoire," I say. "It's at your house. It has to have the spell in there." I'm so excited that I'm nearly bursting at the seams, my heart racing a million miles a minute because, for the first time since this entire screwed-up situation started, I feel like we might actually stand a chance at winning.

"Look at how absolutely heartbreakingly adorable you both

are." Tabitha's sneer might as well be a bucket of cold water on my good mood. But I force myself to ignore her and press on.

"We can iron out the details when we leave here," I tell him, tugging him toward the door. "Let's see if we can say hi to Vic—"

"Did you figure it out yet?" Tabitha calls out.

Sutton stops in his tracks and turns to face her. "Figure what out?"

"Why, even though she's a wolf now, it didn't work?"

Sutton stills.

"What in the crazy hell are you talking about?" I demand, still edging toward the door. Whatever this is, it's a waste of our time.

But when I look at Sutton and take in his pale complexion, the way his hand tightens on mine, my heart begins to race. "Sutton?"

Tabitha's grin turns savage as she looks over at me. "You don't know, do you?"

"Know what." A vise tightens painfully around my heart, and it's all I can do to keep from freaking out because my wolf is screaming at me. The scent in the air has changed so drastically. I can't understand it, but whatever Sutton's feeling, it's not good, and my wolf responds accordingly. Her emotions are all over the place, making me wonder just what Sutton is keeping from me.

And I cannot help but think it's going to change everything.

"You've slept together since you became a wolf, have you not?" Tabitha asks, clearly aware of my answer already.

"I don't see how that's any of your business," I growl, my fingernails lengthening to claws. I take a deep breath and force my wolf back down. Sutton remains quiet beside me. He doesn't even seem to notice I'm about three seconds from shifting and attacking a ghost.

Tabitha shifts her gaze from me back to Sutton. "You didn't tell her. I wonder why that is?"

"Let's go." Sutton grabs me and yanks me toward the door, but I stand firm.

"Tell me what?"

He hesitates then drops his eyes from mine. "The mate bond did not happen."

Despite my confusion, I can feel the blood drain from my face in one fluid motion. Mate bond? What does that mean? Is that the thing that cements the two of us? The connection my wolf feels whenever he is near? "Sutton and I are mates." Though even as I speak them, a voice inside my head questions the words.

"No," Tabitha says. "You're not. Isn't that right, lover boy?"

"Sutton?"

He turns toward me, shoulders sagging. "She's right. We did not bond like we should have."

His words are a punch to the gut. I rip my hand free of his. "What the hell do you mean we didn't bond? When should we have bonded?"

"Last night," he says. "In the trees. When we... I expected it to happen when we claimed one another in that way. But it didn't."

Last night. When we joined ourselves together, heart, body, mind. And I realize this is what's been up his ass all day. Worried about our mate bond and keeping those worries a secret. And now he's going to let Tabitha use it against us like I give a flying fuck what some supernatural magic has to say about the man I love. Ugh. Her last-ditch effort to fuck with me from beyond the grave.

Tears blur my vision as I spin on my heel and march down the stairs. Secrets and more secrets. That's all this damned place has to offer. What's worse than the secrets themselves is the fact that Tabitha is the one who told me when it should have been Sutton.

Victoria and Lance appear at the bottom of the stairs. "Serenity, we've missed you!" She raises her hand and smiles until she sees my expression. "What is it? Is everything okay?"

"Men suck," I snap. "Except you, Lance."

He smiles apologetically as I storm outside and down the porch. Without looking back, I know I'm not alone. That he's right behind me. Always right behind me.

"Serenity," he calls.

Instead of answering, I let my wolf surge forward, and within seconds, my clothes are shredded, and I'm sprinting through the trees on four legs instead of two. The rightness of it settles me despite the churning of my emotions. Sutton doesn't try to stop me, doesn't rush in front and block my path, though I sense him when he shifts and follows me. One half of my soul calling for the other.

Just like the first time we ran, he lets me keep the lead. But this time, it's not excitement driving me forward; it's anger I need to burn.

Up ahead, the roaring of water fills my ears, and it's only once I'm standing beside the falls that I come to a stop. My paws dig into the earth as I work to catch my breath. My wolf is practically beaming with glee at the afternoon sprint, so much so that I feel far more relaxed than I was earlier.

I turn just as Sutton's massive wolf steps into the clearing, its obsidian fur shining beneath the bright sun. He's magnificent, and my wolf lets out a low growl of appreciation.

Easy, girl. We're still pissed, remember? Shifting back to two legs, I wait as Sutton follows suit until we're both standing beside the glistening water in nothing but our birthday suits. Instantly, I regret this decision because being mad at him while he's standing beneath the sun, all taut skin and hard muscle, is really freaking difficult.

"Say something," he says, sounding pained.

"You should have told me," I say, crossing my arms.

Sutton swallows hard. "What difference would it have made?"

I look over at him incredulously. "Are you serious?"

"Would you have decided that the lack of an official mate bond was evidence that we aren't supposed to be together?"

I gape at him. Surely, he's not serious. "If you think for a second that I would allow anything—especially that bullshit to come between us—then you don't know me at all."

He takes a step closer. "It doesn't matter to you? That the bond was not formed when it should have been?"

"You do realize that up until I came to this cursed town, I had no idea what a mate bond was, right? That I was engaged to marry someone because I thought I loved him, not because of some supernatural connection."

At the mention of Roscoe, Sutton's nostrils flare. *Good.*

"You were never meant to be his."

"Oh, I know that now. And I don't need some supposed mate bond to tell me what I already know, Sutton Hargrave." I close the distance between us now and reach up to stroke his cheek. Closing his eyes, he leans into my touch. "You're mine. In all the ways that count. And not because some stupid bond says so. Because I say so. I get to choose my mate, and I choose you."

He opens his eyes again, his gaze searching mine. "You're not mad?"

"Of course I'm mad. But only at the fact that you didn't tell me what was bothering you all day." He exhales, clearly relieved as I add, "I love you, dumbass. But if you lie to me again—including lies of omission—I will kick your ass."

He grins and snakes a hand around the back of my head to bring me closer. "I love you, too, Serenity Kellis."

"Great. Now that that's settled." My blood is still pumping, though, like it needs a release...

Leaning down, Sutton presses his lips to mine gently, a tender kiss with the promise of forever—mate bond or not. "Shall we go find your brother and tell him our plan?"

I reach up and wrap both arms around Sutton's neck and lean into him. My bare breasts rub against his chest, and lust heats my blood. "I'm not exactly interested in thinking of Steven at the moment."

Sutton chuckles. "Neither am I."

Falls Gazette

Chapter Sixteen

Hand in hand, Sutton and I make our way back to the Sheriff's office. Outside, Phineas and Vaughn raise their hands in greeting as we approach, and I offer the tray of coffees. Not a single body was left inside the coffee shop, which means everyone's gathered at the library per Mable's instructions. Sutton and I helped ourselves to the last of the fresh brew at Bean There. Because if you're going to trap a witch's soul inside an inanimate object thus, saving the world, caffeine is key. "We come bearing gifts."

"And good news, I hope?" Phineas adds as he takes a coffee.

"We think so," Sutton replies. "But we want to talk to everyone at once."

"Mable called and said she had everyone in town gathered at the library," Vaughn says.

"Good. Serenity and I will go in and grab the others." Sutton steps inside, and I follow. The moment the door shuts behind us, he freezes. I do the same as the overwhelming scent of copper fills my lungs.

"Blood," he whispers.

Steven. Allison. Jolene. Heart pumping, I race past Sutton through the offices and toward the jail cells in the back. I don't see any of them, and panic races through my veins as I reach the door that leads to the cells. I shove through it, ignoring Sutton calling for me to wait.

If something happened to them—

"Steven," I scream and slide to my knees at his side. Blood drips from a wound on the back of his head, but the steady rise and fall of his chest brings me a bit of ease.

And as I focus intently, I can hear the regular beat of his heart. Unconscious, not dead.

Jolene is unconscious too and slumped against the far wall, blood coating the corner of her mouth. My stomach churns. "Is she—"

"Alive," Sutton interrupts. "But—"

I glance up at Sutton. Expression hard, he's watching me carefully. "What is it?" I question.

My gaze flicks to a figure prone on the floor beside Jolene. Recognition dawns, and my gut coils with true fear. "Cara is lifeless," he answers. "And Allison is missing."

My blood runs cold, body turning to ice as I set my brother aside and get to my feet. I can feel nothing but the pain in my chest as it constricts, the blood pumping through my veins as the panic sets in. Sweeping the space, I see that he's right. Allison isn't here. But—

Cara's body lies limp in the cell near the bars. Eyes wide open and glazed over, she stares up at the ceiling. There's no sign of life coming from her discarded body. And that means Myrtle has found a new host.

"How did she get out?" I somehow manage despite the grief suffocating me. Allison had no part in any of this. She's innocent, a bystander. And now—my throat constricts as tears make it near impossible to see anything.

"We need to warn everyone," Sutton says. He slams a fist into the wall. "Fuck!"

Behind me, Steven groans.

I start toward him, but Sutton grabs my arm. When I look up at him, I can practically read his damned mind. "He's my brother," I growl back.

"He might not be," Sutton replies.

"Let. Me. Go."

He glares at me a moment longer then releases me with a muttered curse. Closing the distance, I drop to my knees at my brother's side again. "Steven?"

"Ser?"

"It's me. Can you sit up?"

With a grunt, he's able to lean back against the bars. Then, he reaches back and touches his head. His hand comes away bloody. "Shit, that hurts."

"What happened?" Sutton demands. His tone is harsh, and even though I can understand his reason for mistrust, it pisses me the hell off.

"I don't..." He trails off, and then his eyes widen. "Allison. She knocked me out! Why the fuck did she— Shit! Is that Jolene?"

"She's alive," Sutton tells him.

"Where is Allison?" Steven demands.

"She's gone."

I watch as his gaze lands on Cara's lifeless body, and the color drains out of his flushed cheeks. "No." The word comes out as no more than a growl, and he pushes to his feet, swaying as he stands. Reaching out, he grips the bars of a cell to steady himself.

Jolene lets out a soft moan. We all turn toward her as her eyes flutter open. Sutton rushes over and kneels beside her, but I stay near my brother, determined to keep him on his feet.

"Do you know what happened?" Sutton asks her.

"Fucking magic gave out," she groans. I watch as she quickly assesses the bodies in the room—and what they mean. "I'm so sorry." Her eyes widen, and for the first time, she looks genuinely afraid.

Steven glares at her. "You said it would hold!"

"It should have," she screams back. "The bitch has a century of experience on me," she adds, and Steven's face morphs from anger to panic.

"We have to find her," he roars.

I inhale sharply, catching Allison's scent lingering in the air. But when I try to follow it toward the exit, it vanishes. "I can't catch her scent," I say to Sutton.

His eyes are blazing with a wild desperation. "Magic," he says flatly.

"We have to do something," Steven yells.

"We need to make sure he's really Steven," Sutton tells me.

Jolene stands with Sutton's assistance. "And how do we do that? We haven't been able to figure it out in a century."

At Jolene's reply, I let my gaze drop to Cara. She fooled us for —shit, who knows how long, and while I don't believe Steven would have knocked himself out if Myrtle had in fact taken over him, we can't rule it out.

"Can't you tell?" I ask her. "Use a spell or something?"

Jolene pins me with a glare. "That magic is beyond me. I'm not exactly formally trained, remember? And even if I could do it, that's not how her magic works. Only a witch of her bloodline can do a spell like that."

She gives me a pointed look. I grit my teeth. Jolene's right. We have no way to know who's the enemy anymore. And that makes our entire plan useless. The grimoire won't matter. Neither will the entrapment scheme. Not without magic. And not without knowing where—or who—Myrtle really is.

Unfortunately, there's only one witch left in this town, and she's the last person I want to ask for help ever again. Especially after earlier. "Tabitha," I say.

"Because she was so helpful before," Sutton snaps.

"What choice do we have?" I hiss.

"She's not going to help us," he says. "She's too selfish for that."

"Where the fuck is Allison!" Steven roars.

I turn toward my brother. "We don't know. But we're going to find out." I gesture to Cara. "Bring her, please."

Sutton doesn't move, just continues to stare at me. "Why?"

"We're going to make Tabitha an offer she cannot refuse."

I expect him to argue, but he doesn't. Instead, he reaches down to gather Cara's body. My heart hammers, and I take a deep, steadying breath, only to freeze in place as another scent hits me. This one is almost more terrifying than the blood lingering here. *Smoke.*

"Fire!" Phineas yells at us from outside.

Sutton drops Cara. Abandoning our current plan, the four of us race for the front doors, sprinting down the halls of the Sheriff's office until we're bursting out onto the smoke-filled street. The thick, choking cloud assaults my lungs, and I cough, covering my mouth with the back of my hand as I search for the source.

Thick, black smoke billows from the library. Glass shatters, a second-story window blowing outward, and someone screams. My blood ices, the hairs on the back of my neck standing on end. We sprint toward the library as the screams grow deafening in my sensitive ears. I listen, confused at the sheer number of voices coming from inside, but then I remember Sutton's orders. *Everyone* in town is in that library.

Flames rage, licking from the inside out. Phineas and Vaughn are doing what they can to put it out, spraying it down with a hose from an emergency hydrant across the street, but the flames are only growing hotter against the stream of water.

"Stop!" Jolene screams. "You're only making it worse!"

They freeze and look from her to Sutton, helpless.

"We can't just do nothing." Sutton's tortured tone shatters what is left of my heart. First Allison and now this? "The entire fucking town is in there!"

"I know! But that is magic, not real fire." She closes her eyes, and the air around us charges with energy. I can feel it buzzing along my skin, and within seconds, the flames barring the entrance shrink down. "Go. I cannot hold it for long," she growls the words as if they pain her. Already, the color that had begun to return to her pale cheeks is draining away. Sweat dots her brow, and I can feel the urgency of her words.

"Come on," I say.

We waste no time. Steven, Sutton, and I race toward the entrance. We reach the stairs as Phineas and Vaughn sprint inside. Two walls of flames shoot up on either side of us, Jolene's magic having only given us a brief passageway.

The stench of charred flesh fills my lungs, and I fight the urge to vomit. To cry. To scream. But none of those things will be helpful—not yet anyway.

"Mable," I call out.

Someone coughs. "Here!"

A hand waves at us through the smoggy air. We rush forward and find Mable and the rest of the pack—or what's left of them—huddled in the kitchen area where I once searched for a meal.

"You're here," Mable says, her voice trembling with relief. "I didn't think you'd come."

"Where are the others?" Sutton demands.

She gestures to the people around her. "This is it," she says sadly. "Everyone else is lost." Their faces are covered in soot and ash that coat nasty red burns.

But they're the lucky ones. My eyes water as I glimpse the forms of those already lost among the charred and burning shelves. Their faces are unrecognizable, and the smell—it's enough to roil my stomach.

Outside, Jolene screams at us to hurry.

"Let's go." Sutton reaches forward and lifts a woman off the ground. She moans in pain as his hands close over her burns. Mable and the others stumble to their feet while Phineas and Vaughn lead them back outside. Steven and I bring up the rear, keeping our eyes out for any stragglers. Anyone we missed.

But when my gaze lands on a completely burned body near the doors, I know that everyone else is already dead.

Falls Gazette

Chapter Seventeen

I cough until I can't breathe then gasp for air, lungs burning, heart wrenching. Beside me, Sutton helps the woman in his arms to a bench near the sidewalk. She is covered in burns that aren't yet beginning to show signs of healing. Even with her wolf's heightened power, I suspect it will be days before she's back to normal. The others aren't in much better shape.

They're alive, though.

And as the last person exits the library, Jolene collapses, and the magic she'd held at bay snaps back to full force—the flames eating at the library just as horribly consuming as the real thing.

Wood cracks as the upper half of the building begins to cave in. Paint and shingles melt right into the fire as the entire building is engulfed.

I stare up at it, struck mute by the horror before me.

Vaughn helps Jolene to her feet. Phineas disappears into Bean There, only to re-emerge seconds later with bottles of water for the others.

Sutton appears beside me, his expression a twisted mask of rage and determination.

"We have to find Allison," he says quietly.

I start to agree until I realize his intention. "This isn't Allison's fault," I say. "She's the victim here."

"Myrtle must be stopped—no matter what."

"I won't let you hurt my friend," I say, my gut twisting at the idea that this fire—as horrible as it is—might have put us on opposite sides at last. I can see it in his eyes. He's finally been pushed too far.

Judging from the haunted look everyone wears, we all have.

"She *will* be stopped," I add with much more conviction than I feel in this horrific moment. "But Tabitha's the only one who can tell us where she is. We stick to the plan."

He starts to argue, but I don't let him. "We don't have time for a full-scale search," I say. *Or the manpower.* But I don't say that. I can't bring myself to form the words. Grief threatens to consume me if I do. Besides, the lives we lost inside that library are about far more than having enough bodies to fight this war.

They are why we're fighting at all. They are why we aren't simply giving up.

"Sutton," I say forcefully enough that he looks at me instead of the burning building. "We need Tabitha to tell us where she is. And for that, we need a bargaining chip. Bring Cara, okay?"

He nods, his face blackened from the smoke. "Okay."

Within minutes, we've dispersed. Phineas and Mable remain behind to help care for the wounded. Jolene tries to come with us, but I talk her into staying behind and using what magic she can to help speed up the healing of the injured.

"We'll let you know what we find out," I promise her. "Stay by your phone."

Vaughn has taken charge of the security team, or at least those still strong enough to fight, and sends them ahead to secure the perimeter of the bed and breakfast as Steven, Sutton, and I head for Tabitha.

Sutton has Cara's body tossed over his shoulder like a sack of potatoes, and I have to avoid looking at her face as it bobs at his back. She was a friend once. And then she was the enemy. And now she's dead. But if my plan works...she'll be something else entirely when this is over.

I have way too many feelings to unpack over that possibility right now.

Steven doesn't speak as we make our way up the drive to the bed and breakfast. I cast glances at him, but the muscle ticking in his jaw lets me know he's not okay, so I don't bother to even ask. Hell, I'm not okay either. All we can do is keep moving forward.

And hope there's some way to save Allison from what Myrtle has done to her.

The house is eerily silent as we push through the door. The shattered dishes still litter the floor and crunch underfoot as we pass over the shards. A soundless movement catches my eye, and I look up to see Lance and Victoria staring at us from halfway up the stairs.

"We could see the smoke from here," Victoria says sadly, her eyes on Cara. "Oh my. Is she—"

"Where's Tabitha?" Steven demands.

Lance frowns. "We haven't seen her since you were all here last. Not on this plane or the other."

My heart lurches at that. "What do you mean?"

"She seems to have disappeared," he says.

I stare at him, horror creeping in. Slowly, I turn to Sutton. "Maybe our last conversation was her way of saying goodbye. Remember how she told us she was never trapped here after all? She could have crossed over—"

"No fucking way," Steven roars.

He takes the stairs two at a time, barreling straight through Lance's ethereal form. Lance frowns, but Steven doesn't slow down as he disappears up the stairs.

"Tabitha," he yells.

No answer.

"Tabitha!" His scream is unhinged enough to make me wince.

Sutton grunts and sets Cara's body against the parlor doorframe.

Victoria and Lance come closer, concern etched into their kind faces. "Something bad happened," Victoria says quietly. "Didn't it?"

"Yes." I swallow hard but can't bring myself to explain about the library and those lives lost. It's too soon. Too horrible. "My friend Allison has disappeared. Myrtle has her, and we need to get her back before—"

"She's gone." Steven reappears at the top of the stairs. Instead of anger, he looks stunned. Lost. And it breaks my heart all over again. "She's just fucking...gone." He stares blankly down at me, and I realize everyone else has turned to me too.

This was my plan, and now it's useless.

I try to think of something else, but there's nothing. "Only a witch of her line can locate her," I say, unsure what to do next. We'll never find her on our own. Not without a scent. Or a hell of a lot more wolves to help us do it."

"Pardon the intrusion, but it sounds like you could use some help."

From near the back door, Yvette's voice rings out, and we all go still. Steven is the first to react, barreling down the stairs and past me before I can stop him. At the end of the hall, Vaughn stands, holding the mirror so it faces outward at us. Yvette's face is reflected through the glass.

"She's part of their line," he says. I can see the indecision in him. He doesn't like this, but he knows there's not another way.

"She is," Sutton reluctantly agrees.

I shoot him a sharp look, not at all excited about this twist in the plan. Tabitha was one thing. She's always been a firecracker. But Yvette is a wild card I don't want in our hands.

Steven marches up and takes the mirror from Vaughn. Then he returns to the main room and sets it against the mantel so it sits at shoulder level.

Yvette simply looks back at us, waiting. My muscles tense, and I hover just behind Steven, ready to grab him or shove him aside should she try anything dangerous.

"Can you help us?" Steven asks her.

"Steven, no," I say, but Yvette brightens, ignoring me.

"I can do a great many things, young man. But whether I choose to…well, that depends on what you're offering." She casts a glance at me. "Hello again, Serenity. How are you feeling?"

My temper flares. "We don't want your help," I snap. Reaching for Steven's arm, I tug him toward the door. "Come on."

He yanks away from me and plants his feet. "I want to hear what she has to say."

"Steven." I stare at him. "She tried to kill me. More than once. She's Myrtle's sister. She's the enemy."

"I don't care. This is about saving Allison. I'll do anything." He turns back to Myrtle. "Tell us where we can find your sister."

I turn to look at Sutton so he'll back me up. He stands close by, arms folded. But he shocks me by saying, "I want to hear what she has to say."

Behind him, Victoria and Lance are gone, and I can't blame them for making themselves scarce. Yvette-in-a-mirror is not a fun house I want to hang out in.

With no other choice, I turn back and brace myself for Yvette's mind games.

"I can tell you exactly where my sister is right now," she says. "No spell work required."

"How is that possible?" I ask, instantly suspicious, especially when she's not even putting up a fight about helping us.

"Spells are for the living, child. What I am now is pure energy. I know all. See all. Hear all."

"But you can't touch all." Sutton's glare is threatening, and Yvette merely nods.

"You're right about that. And I'll admit I yearn for a body. For a physical experience. Being human is so much sweeter than I appreciated before." Her gaze turns wistful, and her eyes flick to where Cara's body is slumped against the doorframe.

Shit.

I realize now why she's offering to aid us at all.

She wants what I would have offered to Tabitha. A chance to be alive again.

"Hell no," I announce, sharp enough that Steven startles. He turns to glare at me.

"What are you talking about?" he asks roughly.

"She wants to trade. Her help for Cara's body. No freaking way," I say.

His eyes narrow, and he turns back to Yvette. "You say you know all. Prove it. Is Allison alive?"

"For now," Yvette says.

This time, it's my turn to step forward, hope driving me. "How?" I ask. "How is that possible when Myrtle has killed everyone else she's taken over?"

"Her escape from that cell was a bit improvised, was it not?" Yvette asks. "At any rate, it seems there was no viable way to end your friend's existence before taking over her physical body. Which means they both exist inside it now. Until one manages to evict the other."

My hope is stabbed through at her words. "Evict?"

"Myrtle will eliminate your friend, and then she will have her revenge." Yvette's gaze flicks to Sutton, but I see none of the venom that used to exist where he's concerned. "She'll come for you now. She's done playing. Or, she understands the game is over. Either way, she's ready to end it, once and for all."

Sutton takes a step forward, hands clenched. "Let her come," he says, his voice so deadly calm that I shudder.

"Why are you helping us?" I ask. "I thought you hated Sutton just as much as she does."

"I love my sister," she says, and a shadow flickers in her eyes. "And for that love, I was willing to endure a lot of things. To hate, to kill. All in the name of loyalty. But her vengeance has run its course. And I won't continue to suffer for a revenge that's gone on long past its due date."

"All right," Steven says. "You have a deal--"

"Wait." I step between them, my heart pounding.

"Serenity, move." Steven's voice is urgent, but I stand my ground.

Every cell of my being is telling me not to trust the crazy bitch in the mirror, but Steven's right—we have no choice. Not if we want to save Allison. Still, magic has taught me a lot, and I'm not so easily tricked anymore.

"If you want Cara's body, you have to tell us where Myrtle is now. And you have to come and help us get rid of her. Those are the terms. Take it or leave it."

Steven looks ready to explode, but he keeps silent. Beside me, Sutton is practically radiating with the need to kill something. I understand. My wolf is losing her shit too, and being inside this room with a ghost-bitch who's tried killing me and my mate multiple times is not helping.

But I wait. It's up to Yvette now. And sadly, she's our only hope.

I expect her to use that to her advantage. Or to somehow manipulate the terms. But instead, she smiles disarmingly and says, "When you say get rid of her, what exactly do you have in mind?"

Falls Gazette

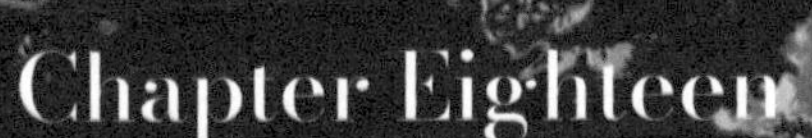

Chapter Eighteen

"This would be easier if you would let me have the body first," Yvette says for the third time.

"Not until we have confirmation that you're not lying," I snap back, glancing at Yvette's reflection as Steven carries her.

She glares back at me, clearly unhappy with the current restrictions. But given that she's been nothing but loyal to Myrtle in the past, I'm not planning on taking any chances that she's lying. Granted, she could still be playing both sides, but that's a problem for when we have confirmation that Myrtle is where Yvette claims she is.

Behind us, Sutton carries Cara's limp body as Phineas, Vaughn, Mable, and Jolene remain in the distance between. We're all silent, all of us wrapped up in our own thoughts of what's to come.

We could win, end the curse forever, and put Myrtle down for good.

Or, we might lose. Unfortunately, a loss no longer means simply being cursed and trapped. If Myrtle intends to be done with this game, losing means death. For us all.

So here we are. Marching through the trees toward what could very well be our end.

I swallow hard and try not to focus too strongly on that possibility, but even as I attempt to remain hopeful, I can't help but think of my family.

My mother and father will not just be losing one child but two. My brothers losing two siblings. Will they even find out what happened to us? Our cars will be found in town, sure, but our bodies? How will they ever figure out where we went? And all because I couldn't keep my nose out of business that wasn't mine

But then I think of Sutton. Had I not come here and forced my way into this town, I never would have known what 'sacrifice-everything' love felt like. He is my everything, my hope, my strength. And even with all we're facing, everything that might happen in the next hour, I would never want to change that.

"Get out of your head, Ser," Steven says softly.

I glance over at him, tears burning in the corners of my eyes. Reaching out, I gently squeeze his forearm before letting my hand drop again. My brother forces a slight smile, though it's haunted. Broken. Because of what's on the line. Not just me but Allison. A woman he only just recently began to care for. But I can see the depth of his feelings reflecting back at me now. He loves her. And this is breaking his heart. "Difficult to do that right now."

A muscle in his jaw tightens. "We need to be focused, as clear-headed as we can be."

"I'm working on it."

And doing a shit job.

"Siblings. No bond quite like it, wouldn't you say?" Yvette questions.

"Don't even start comparing your twisted-ass relationship to ours," Steven growls.

"Would you not kill for your sister?"

He doesn't respond.

"Not if they were innocents," I reply. "Just as I wouldn't slaughter and curse an entire town in the name of twisted revenge."

"So you say. An easy thing to claim when you're not put in that situation."

"I'm not even going to dignify that with a response," I retort. In the next instant, I freeze in place as a familiar scent fills my lungs. *Allison.* My wolf strains to be released, but I hold her back, waiting, listening.

"What is it?" Steven whispers.

"I smell Allison. Just ahead."

"That's where the cabin is," Yvette tells us.

I study the surrounding trees, trying to catch a glimpse of her.

"We've been here before." Steven mutters a curse.

I turn to him, surprised. "You have? When?"

"This is where Sutton and I found you the night you ran off to give yourself up."

"Yes. Though I imagine you didn't realize the significance of the location." Yvette clicks her tongue. "Now, I helped you get here, so hold up your end. Put me in Cara's body."

Ignoring her, I turn to face Sutton and the others. They've stopped walking, and his gaze is locked on me. In this moment, these few brief heartbeats, memories of our time together flash through my mind. Our first meeting in the woods.

Me running into him a second time.

Seeing him shift from wolf to man after he saved me from that bear.

Our first touch.

First kiss.

First…everything.

I am fighting for an immortal lifetime of these moments. "We're ready," I tell him.

He moves closer and sets Cara's body down on the ground. Steven places the mirror beside her, and Jolene steps up between the two of them. I don't ask if she's ready or if she still has enough magical juice to get this thing done. Mostly because I can't afford for the answer to be "no." None of us can. She closes her eyes and holds out both hands—one over Cara, one over the mirror—and begins to whisper.

Magic simmers in the air around us, it sizzles and pops along her skin. Then, in a flash of fog and spark, the mirror is empty. Jolene drops her hands and stumbles back.

Sutton reaches for her, but she shakes her head. "I'll be fine."

"Did it work?" Steven questions.

Cara—no, Yvette—groans and stretches. Her bones pop as she stands, eyes opening as she moves, stiffly at first and then much more fluid. "This feels…different."

I flinch. Something about hearing the voice of a woman who was once my friend haunts me now. Mostly because, instead of her soul looking back at me, it's the spirit of a woman I killed. A woman who tried more than once to murder me. And, more importantly, a woman who doesn't deserve the privilege of a second chance but is getting one anyway.

"Yeah, enjoy the new body later," Vaughn comments. He turns to Sutton. "We ready?"

Sutton crosses the distance between us and cups the back of my neck. He pulls me forward and slams his mouth to mine in a breath-stealing promise of tomorrow. "Let's end this." After releasing me, he turns to face the trees. Eyes narrowed, he glares. "Do you smell that?"

There's no need to ask him for clarification because, at that exact moment, the stench of the dead fills my lungs. Dread coils in my stomach. If I wasn't sure we were in the right place before, this confirms it.

Where her pets are, so is Myrtle.

"Get ready!" Sutton announces, remaining in his human form while Mable, Phineas, and Vaughn shift.

"I'm out of fucking energy," Jolene growls as she straightens and balls her hands into fists.

The dead march out of the trees, a twisted marching band of rotting flesh and twisted bones. They stop at the edge of the clearing and glare at us. But it's not the imagery that is troublesome. It's that in each of their literal cold, dead hands is a weapon.

Knives.

Axes.

They're prepared for battle. Ready to slaughter us where we stand. We just have to get to Myrtle first.

"This is new," Steven says.

"This is it," I tell him. "Myrtle is done toying with us."

"Then let's not give her a chance," Sutton replies.

The three wolves move in front of us, all of them dropping their heads and growling as they prepare for what will likely be the bloodiest fight we've seen. Here's hoping it will be the last one.

Steven raises his weapon and aims it at the nearest dead. He fires, and the gunshot echoes through the trees. Birds shoot toward the sky, and the dead charge. Mable pounces first, her wolf lithe and quick despite her years.

Still human for now, Sutton backs away toward the cabin. He keeps himself between me and the enemy, and I don't bother to tell him not to. It's useless to convince him I can protect myself. Besides, I know what he's thinking. If we can get there and stop Myrtle before anyone gets hurt—

A wolf lets out a blood-curdling howl.

I look over as Vivian rips her blade out of Phineas' side. His wolf lets out a second howl, this one more strangled, as he falls to the ground at his dead wife's feet. Vivian's expression is blank of any emotion as she looks down at him. Horror rips my heart out and the entire battle seems to freeze as we wait to see whether or not he'll get up again. That is until a second anguished howl rips through the clearing, and I watch in complete and utter horror as Mable is impaled by an axe-wielding zombie I don't recognize. She screams as her stomach is ripped open.

"No," Sutton bellows. He turns to me, hazel gaze full of agony. I can see it—his internal fight. His desire to protect me warring with his need to avenge his father.

"Go," I cry out. My wolf strains beneath my skin, desperate to join the fray. But if I do that, I risk losing not just this battle but the entire fucking war. So I stay the course, even though it kills me. And I send Sutton into the worst of it—hopefully to kill them all before any of them can do the same to him. He races straight for Vivian—for Phineas—and I force myself to turn away so I can focus.

So I can end this. There will be time for mourning later. But for now, it's up to me to stop any more from dying if I can.

Gunshots continue to fill the clearing as Steven does his best to even the fight, but with so few wolves fighting—

A woman screams from inside the cabin.

My blood runs cold at the sound.

Allison.

"Go," Steven urges us, bringing up the rear and pumping lead into anything that gets too close. Jolene and I sprint toward it, reaching the porch at the very moment Allison stumbles out. She falls to her knees, blood dripping from her lip and forehead. Eyes full of tears, she looks up at us.

"Ali!" Steven starts toward her, but Jolene grips his arm. "Let me the fuck go," he snarls.

"You don't know if that's her."

"Shoot me," Allison cries, eyeing the gun in my brother's hand. "Please, Steven." She balls her hands into fists and presses them to her temples then looks to the sky and screams. "It hurts so much, and I can't fight her anymore. Shoot me!" My breath catches as Steven levels his gun at her. But then he quickly lowers it again, closing his eyes in anguish. "I can't," he says, his voice hoarse.

Allison lifts her head and glares at him, tears gone from her eyes. "Because you're weak," she snaps.

Myrtle.

Anger pours through me. Rage and grief and sorrow and desperation, each one swelling over the other until all I see is red.

"Get out of my friend," I scream, hands balling into fists.

My wolf begins to rise, and I let her come, holding her close to the surface, willing her to lend me the strength to see this through.

Jolene steps in front of Steven and raises her hands. "I'll kill you where you kneel," she says, magic skimming her skin as she calls it forth. "Unless you release—" Jolene stops speaking, body going rigid at the same instant Allison falls limp to the ground.

Even without magic of my own, I can feel the shift in the air. The change in energy.

Myrtle is jumping from Allison to Jolene.

"Steven—" I start to warn him, but my brother seems to have caught on as well. He lifts his gun and slams it into the back of Jolene's head. She falls limp, collapsing to the ground. Guilt pricks at me for the move. I should be helping her. Helping Allison. But there's no time.

This is our chance.

Behind me, the battle between wolf and zombie still rages.

Howls and grunts mix with the sound of weapons swinging, and I can't think past the need to end it all.

I whirl on Yvette now in Cara's body. "The mirror! We have to trap her—now!"

But Yvette doesn't reach it before Myrtle makes her next move.

Blinding pain shoots through my head and down my spine. I collapse to my knees as my entire body goes rigid. Every muscle freezes, and every bone turns to cement. I'm unable to move, to breathe, frozen in a twisted scene as I'm forced to watch the bloody battle taking place mere yards away.

Slowly, as if gathering like a storm cloud, a new consciousness takes form in my mind. A different set of thoughts. A voice both familiar and foreign inside this space I once held sacred. But there's no way to fight it. No time for resistance.

She's already here.

Hello, Serenity.

Falls Gazette

Chapter Nineteen

Let's have some fun, shall we?

The voice isn't mine.

It doesn't belong in my head.

I order my arms to move, to push me up, but nothing happens. And then I stand—but not me. No, I'm not the one moving my body. I'm certainly not the one raising my hand and aiming my palm at Yvette.

A palm that suddenly hosts more magic than I ever had before I turned.

The knowledge of what my body is suddenly capable of horrifies me. More than that, the realization that there's nothing I can do to stop her from wielding it. From using me to hurt people. What's left of me nearly chokes on a sob as I think of what she'll do next.

"Serenity, stop!" Steven roars.

"Traitorous bitch," I hear myself say. Our gaze swings to Cara's body. To Yvette.

Yvette meets my gaze with only a small flinch. "You've ruined both our lives," she tells Myrtle, "seeking this twisted vengeance for a daughter who never wanted it to begin with."

"You're my sister!" Myrtle roars using my voice.

"And you were mine," Yvette replies as she lifts the mirror and begins to whisper.

Hope flutters in the depths of my soul. But then the magic begins to gather inside me. And I know Yvette is no match for us.

"Goodbye, sister. There's no coming back this time," Myrtle whispers.

Stop! Run! I try to scream, to warn them, but in the next instant, magic pours from my hand and slams into Yvette. The mirror shatters, and Yvette's newly reclaimed body slams into a tree and then falls limp beneath it.

My heart aches for another life lost, but that's not what threatens to break me now.

My attention is stolen by the mirror. Or rather, the broken shards of it that remain. *No*! Fear burns hot in my soul as Myrtle turns my body to where Steven now stands. He aims his gun at her, at me, tears shimmering in his eyes.

"Don't make me shoot you," he says.

Laughter falls from my lips. "You don't have the balls to shoot your own sister, Detective. You're held hostage by your petty feelings of love. It really is a flaw you humans share."

Something begins to build within me, and I struggle to maintain my grip on my own consciousness against the onslaught of whatever this is filling me. The magic—it's eclipsing—streaming up through my feet from the ground below. This isn't Myrtle's magic. This is … more. This is a magic even she could not hold before today. I shove against pure panic as power unlike anything I've ever felt seeps into my bones, my blood. Energy surges through my body, bringing with it a consciousness all its own. Memories. Truth. Visions from a century ago. Myrtle in her own skin. Tabitha standing between Sutton and her own mother's magic. Death.

A hardened heart and a blackened curse. The cabin before me haunts each scene as it replays in my mind. In her memory. Inside the heart of this new magic.

And it hits me. This is why we're here. Why this place is so special. This is where the curse was first made. Where latent hateful magic has sat for a century, waiting. Quietly building.

And now, the ground here is full of power, power that Myrtle is pulling into my body. To use against everyone I love.

Before I can find a way to warn them, energy slams into my brother, and he's thrown across the clearing.

Steven! I scream his name, but nothing comes out.

Then, Myrtle turns to Allison. "Little human bitch," she spits out. "You're stronger than you look. A pain in my ass. If you'd just given in, this would have all been over so much sooner. And now you'll pay for fighting back."

"Fuck you," my friend replies then spits blood onto the dirt and stands on wobbly legs. "Give me back my friend," she orders, "or I'll rip you apart."

More laughter that is not mine. Harsh and cutting.

Behind me, a wolf yelps, but Myrtle doesn't so much as blink. Terror grips my heart as I try to convince myself it wasn't Sutton. That everyone is okay. But it's getting harder to believe that. Especially considering the amount of power flowing through me now. It's like a faucet. And there's no turning it off.

"I think I'll take my time with you," Myrtle tells Allison. "Since you seem so determined to beat me, I suppose it would only be right to show you just how pathetic your fight was." She kicks Allison in the face, and my friend falls backward.

Then she kneels beside her and wraps my hand around Allison's throat.

I try to pull at the energy, to bring even a little into my soul so I can shove hers out, but it's no use.

"Any last words?" Myrtle asks her.

The question is purposely cruel considering Allison's ability to speak—and breathe—has been cut off by Myrtle's strangling hands. I watch as my best friend's face turns red then purple.

No.

This can't be how it ends.

"You always did have to have the last word, didn't you?" The voice is one neither Myrtle nor I expect, and our shock is mutual. Myrtle looks up, and our eyes lock on Cara's body, now restored and standing upright several yards away. But Yvette is no longer inside her. Myrtle and I know it at once.

Tabitha.

"Hello, Mother."

"What the hell did you just say?" Myrtle demands.

"What, you don't recognize your own daughter?" Her smirk is familiar, even on this new face.

For a second, Myrtle's just as frozen as I am locked inside my own body.

Then she abruptly releases Allison and stands, completely ignoring my friend as she scrambles away, gasping for air. Out of the corner of my eye, I see Allison crawling toward where Steven lies still in the dirt. A second later, she chokes on a sob, but it's a sound of relief rather than sadness.

He's alive. I let that be enough for now.

"How?" Myrtle demands of her daughter.

"Hitched a ride with Aunt Yvette," Tabitha says, gesturing toward the shattered mirror. "But she was so focused on saving you, she didn't even notice me in there with her. Fun fact, did you know when a spell is cast to remove a soul, it works on *all* of the souls trapped?" Tabitha shakes her head, looking side-to-side at all the carnage. "You always were a grudge holder, but this is screwed up, even for you."

"Tabitha? It's really you?" my voice whispers as my eyes fill with tears.

"In the flesh." Tabitha's expression darkens. "No thanks to you."

"You're angry," Myrtle says. "I understand why you would be. But you must know the painting was only a temporary hold. Once I'd exacted my vengeance—our vengeance—I would have come for you."

"Spare me the lies," Tabitha says, glowering.

Myrtle's temper sharpens. "You were always too soft for this kind of work, daughter. It's why I sent you away in the first place. Once my work was done, you would have been free to create the life you wanted."

"And on that psychotic note, reunion over. Let Serenity go."

Myrtle scoffs. "Don't be ridiculous. This has to end."

"I agree," Tabitha replies. "Give it up, and go find peace. These people—all of us—have suffered enough at your hands."

Myrtle's inner battle is a strange feeling to witness, and as her hesitation stretches, I find hope rising fast in what's left of my own psyche. But then, at the last moment, her decision is made. Heart hardening, all of her emotions have turned cold as she glares at her daughter through my eyes.

"Not enough," Myrtle says softly and then with more conviction, "It will never, ever be enough to account for what I lost. For what was taken."

Tabitha shakes her head. "You're the reason for your pain, Mother." She takes a step closer. "Everything that has happened has been because you couldn't let go."

"No. Sutton—"

"Sutton didn't do anything," Tabitha urges. "I loved him, and it took dying for me to realize he never really loved me back. Something he told me—repeatedly."

"No. He tricked you. Manipulated you," she roars, my voice ringing through the trees.

The echoes of war rage around us, but it's as though we're in our own world. My soul trapped, Myrtle in my body, Tabitha in Cara's. The people I love hanging by a thread.

"Please stop this, Mother." Tabitha starts forward, closing the distance as she pleads. "Please. Let go. Move on."

"Never! The only way this ends is when this entire town burns to the ground!"

Tabitha stops moving forward, expression faltering. "I wish you hadn't said that." She raises her palm, and magic swirls around her. I feel a tug on the magic Myrtle has gathered to herself. The curse's power suddenly funnels away from us. Tabitha's eyes gleam with the energy she's somehow stolen right from our grasp.

Myrtle starts to protest, to wield the magic against her own daughter, but it's too late. Tabitha's already sucked it all up for herself.

Tabitha smiles—an expression that's both sad and twisted with victory. Then, she unleashes the magic on her mother. It pummels my body, battering me and throwing me to the ground. I arch up as the pain grips me, burning my body from the inside out.

My scream builds and then is ripped away again as more magic shoves its way into my head. My heart. My very soul. It's a suffering unlike anything I've ever known. Even during my shift from human to wolf, I never hurt like this.

Trapped in my own mind, I scream in my silent, tortured agony until, finally—it fades.

My gasping is the first sign I might be me again.

Twitching my fingers, I'm overcome with relief to find the mental order to move my hand is met with success.

"You'd better get something to contain her, or she's going to keep body jumping," Tabitha orders. I blink, forcing my eyes open in time to see Tabitha moving slowly away from where I lay on my back. An orb of light hovers just above her outstretched palm, and I know what it is without even having to ask.

Myrtle's soul.

Tabitha meets my gaze, her expression strained. "I can only hold her for so long."

It takes me another beat to realize she's talking to me. That I'm the only one left capable of helping her finish this. With a groan, I lift myself onto my elbows, gritting my teeth against the pain that threatens to overwhelm me.

One glance toward the others reveals Jolene still prone on the ground where she fell earlier. Steven lies near her, and Allison bends over him, whispering softly. She looks back at me, tears streaking the dirt on her face.

"Is he--" I can't bring myself to finish the question.

"He's okay," she manages.

I nearly go limp with relief.

"And Jolene?" I ask, refusing to even mention Sutton's name. I don't see the wolves anymore, but the trail of zombie bodies leads straight into the forest, so I can only imagine--

"Alive," Tabitha snaps. "Now hurry the hell up and find me something to trap my mother in before she heads back in for round two and we're all done for."

At that, I force myself to stand.

Once I'm upright, the pain recedes quickly to a stiffness and soreness that's more manageable. I feel for my wolf, automatically reaching to be sure she's safe.

She snarls inwardly with a grumpy sort of relief, and I exhale.

Slowly, I turn, scanning the ground for something to contain Myrtle for good.

"What am I looking for?" I ask Tabitha.

"How should I know? I was dead before today," she snaps back, her usual sarcasm on full display. Not surprising, considering the stress but still... it doesn't help.

"Tabitha," I warn.

She sighs. "Something touched by magic. Something capable of holding a witch's soul."

A strange sort of energy stirs inside me. I'm drawn forward by a pulsing in my veins; a sort of beacon calling me closer. Following the call, I race into the cabin, casting right and left in frantic desperation. And then I see it—a massive leather-bound tome open on the table. It looks similar to the one Yvette left behind though much more used.

Myrtle's personal grimoire.

I close the distance, reaching for the only thing left that already holds enough power to contain a wicked witch's soul. It pulses with magic as I lift it into my hands and race back outside.

"Will this work?" I ask as I hold it up.

Tabitha grins. "That'll do. Set it down."

I do as she orders and then step back.

Tabitha nods toward where the shattered mirror is strewn. "Use the glass, and cut my hand."

Rushing over, I retrieve the glass and run it over the milky skin of her exposed palm. Dark crimson beads on the surface.

"Why?" I ask even as the blood begins to spill from her.

"My soul's magic is in the host's blood now," she explains.

"You mean your magic is in Cara's blood," I say, and she nods.

"And as you've likely discovered," she explains as she kneels down and smears her blood over the cover of the grimoire. It springs open, pages whirring by. "Blood magic is stronger than anything." She whispers something as she hovers her palm over the open spell book.

Blinding light shoots off the page as power surges in the ground beneath me. The Earth shifts, an earthquake that takes me to my knees. The orb floating just above Tabitha is suddenly sucked right into the open grimoire.

Then the book slams shut.

For a few heartbeats, there are no sounds, nothing but me waiting for the next shoe to drop.

Power sparks at my fingertips as an electric charge shoots through my body. Strength, emotions—grief, love, fear—grip me one after the other.

"What is..." I trail off and turn.

Sutton stands behind me, his bare chest coated in blood and dirt. Eyes shimmering with emotion, he watches me. And what's more is that I can *feel* everything he feels right now as his gaze holds mine.

Grief. Pain. But above all, I feel love. Blinding, heart-stopping love.

"The mate bond," Tabitha says from behind me. Her voice is soft. There's a trace of jealousy in her tone, but it's not nearly as much as I might have expected. "The curse is broken, and Sutton is yours. Turns out the prophecy was right. I suppose I was just a hundred years off."

I bite my lip, hope threatening to drown me as I look back at the man I was prepared to kill for. To die for. Again.

Sutton closes the distance.

When I reach him, he scoops me into his arms and lifts me off my feet. He spins me, burying his face in my throat. I wrap my arms around his neck, clinging to him like my life depends on this moment. This man.

I hear a sob and realize belatedly that it's my own. Sutton whispers soothing words. He sets me on my feet again, his hands smoothing my hair back so he can kiss my temple. Finally, I lift my face to his and meet his eyes.

"Your father?" I force myself to ask.

He shakes his head, deep grief etched in his strong features.

My heart aches, and tears slip down my cheeks.

"And Mable?" I whisper.

Again, he offers a shake of his head. When my chin trembles, he takes it between his thumb and finger. "We will mourn later," he says quietly. "There are those who need us still."

Nodding, I take a steadying breath and brace myself for whatever aftermath I'll need to accept next.

"He's right, you know," Tabitha says, and I follow her gaze to where my brother still lies in Allison's arms.

"Serenity, you better come," Allison calls suddenly. I rush toward where Steven's head rests in Allison's lap. Despite her earlier assurances, he remains completely still. Fear claws at my throat.

"What happened?" I ask.

"He started to come around, but then the earthquake happened, and now he won't wake up," she says as she cups his cheek with her shaky hand.

My brother is pale, far too pale. "Steven? Steven?" I choke out his name as though saying it will somehow rouse him.

Tabitha kneels beside me and tilts her head to the side as if she's studying him. Then, her hand goes to his chest, and Steven's body arches off the ground once. Twice.

"What are you doing," Allison demands, but Tabitha ignores her.

"It's okay," I say, and Allison falls silent.

Another heartbeat passes as I remain completely still, terrified of doing anything to interfere with whatever it is Tabitha is doing. Then, finally, the color returns to Steven's cheeks, and he groans.

Tears spill from my eyes, and Allison smiles down at him, smoothing his hair with her trembling hand.

"What the fuck happened?" Steven stares up at us.

"We got her," I tell him, grinning like an idiot, thanks to the relief I feel at seeing him alive.

"Damn right," he mutters to himself, and Allison silences him with a kiss.

Tabitha moves to Jolene next. She makes quick work of the magic, but when she's done, her expression is worn thin. I wonder if she's exhausted herself or if there's anything left to help the other injured. My eyes catch on Vaughn limping toward us from the trees.

Sutton pulls me to my feet, and I look over at Tabitha. "You saved us. We would have all died if you hadn't shown up. You did it knowing you'd lose Sutton forever."

Tabitha shrugs. "Someone finally convinced me it was time to move on."

My brow furrows. "Who?"

Before she can answer, a man appears at the edge of the clearing. He lingers by the trees, but even from here, I know him. Rip. The man I met while I was dead. Or maybe not quite dead but in between. He raises a hand and grins at me, but when he looks at Tabitha, his expression softens. His feelings are unmistakable. So are hers.

I gawk at her, noting the hungry look she gives him. "You and the reaper?"

Tabitha grins at me. "He is quite a looker, isn't he?" She turns to my mate and pouts. "So sorry, Sutton, but you and I are over. We had a good run."

Sutton starts to answer, but I squeeze his hand to silence what I already know will be enough to ruin this beautiful moment.

Rip comes to meet us, his clothes and skin pristine compared to the grime of battle we're all covered in.

"Who the fuck are you?" Sutton demands, positioning himself

between me and the reaper. I press in close, ready to stop him from whatever attack he's about to launch.

"Name's Sullivan, though my friends call me Rip. I'm a friend of Serenity's," he replies.

"You know him?" Sutton demands of me.

"I do," I say softly.

"I've never seen him before," Steven puts in, and I roll my eyes. Of course, the two of them would side together for once—now of all times. Before Sutton or Steven can interrogate Rip any further, Cara's body falls to the ground.

"What the fuck," Steven demands.

"I guess she's not one for goodbyes," Allison says.

Jolene mutters a curse as she sits up, rubbing the back of her head with ginger fingers. Vaughn reaches down to help her to her feet just as Tabitha's ghost appears beside Rip.

"Actually, I like making a notable exit," Tabitha says to Allison.

Steven and Jolene both curse in unison.

Suddenly, two forms pop into existence just behind Rip.

"It worked!" Victoria cheers.

I inhale sharply at the sudden appearance of my specter friends. Clutching my chest, I exhale and look between Victoria and Lance. "What worked?" I ask.

"The curse broke, and now we're free," Victoria says.

"Tabitha and Rip told us it might not work," Lance adds. "But it looks like the curse holding us inside the bed and breakfast has lifted."

"We can go home," Victoria says, clapping her hands.

Lance grins down at her, then they both shift their gazes to me. "Thank you," Lance says solemnly. "You risked so much to help us. We're in your debt."

"Your friendship meant a lot," Victoria adds, sniffling.

Their emotion tugs at my heart. "Yours too," I tell her.

Beside them, more people appear—ghostly forms that pop into view from thin air. My heart hammers as the clearing fills with forms that I actually recognize.

Cara is the first. She floats closer, looks down at her body, and shudders. "Unfortunate end to our friendship," she says, glancing up at me. "And to life I guess."

"I'm so sorry," I all but whisper, eyes misting. "So sorry that I couldn't save you. That I didn't know—"

Cara smiles. "Not your fault," she says softly. "You only came here to help. In fact, you were faced with a fight that wasn't yours and stayed anyway."

"You did good, kid." I whirl to where Sheriff Rhodes stands just behind me. His body is partially translucent, but seeing him is a gut punch nonetheless. "But I knew you would."

Before I can apologize for not figuring it out in time to save his life, Sutton lets out a strangled cry.

Phineas and Vivian stand just in front of him—both of them ghosts. Despite Sutton's earlier words, I'd hoped there was a way to save him. But seeing him standing here now, I know it's far too late for that.

"Son," Vivian whispers. Unlike her zombie form, this one is perfectly intact. Beautiful and radiant and full of love for her son.

"I'm so sorry," Sutton chokes out, tears streaming down his face. "I couldn't save you," he stammers. "Either of you." I rush over and take his hand, determined to be a show of strength even as I'm breaking apart.

"You did nothing wrong," Vivian says.

"You are the best son anyone could have ever asked for," Phineas says softly. He shifts his gaze to me. "And you, you are the daughter I always yearned for. The mate I always hoped Sutton would find."

I choke on a sob. "I'm going to miss our chess games."

He grins. "It's up to you to beat Sutton. Boy needs to be put in his place from time to time."

Smiling through my tears, I nod, unable to say another damned word.

"Don't mourn for us," Vivian adds. "We're together again. At last."

Phineas takes her hand. She looks over at him and smiles softly. I can feel their happiness radiating, and it does comfort me to know they'll be together.

Still, tears threaten to overtake me at the loss I feel. When Mable's ghost appears, a smile on her face, I completely lose it. Sutton's arm slides around my shoulders, and he holds me close.

"It's okay, Serenity," Mable says, eyes shimmering. "Don't cry for me. I've lived a long and happy life, and now it's your turn. Thank you for saving us."

"But I didn't save you," I choke out.

"You did," she smiles. "You saved my entire town. Even the people who tried to turn you away. You are the reason we're all free, Serenity. You granted our eternities back to us. In this realm or the next. And we are so grateful for your courage. For both of you." She glances at Sutton, and he nods.

Around us, the clearing is full where the rest of the pack has made their way over from town. Everywhere I look, I see people saying goodbye to loved ones lost. The emotion is overwhelming, but there's hope too. A happiness that has come from finally being free of the darkness Myrtle brought down on these people for so long.

A darkness that has finally lifted.

"All right, everyone, I've got another world to save," Rip claps his hands together. "We need to get going."

While the specters begin to gather around him, he bends down and grabs the grimoire.

"What are you doing?" I ask, suddenly nervous as I eye Myrtle's cage.

"Figured I'd deliver it somewhere for safekeeping," Rip says.

"That stays here," Sutton says, stepping up beside me with fire in his eyes.

I hesitate, not sure I disagree with his sentiment.

Rip shrugs. "I can leave it here," he says. "Which leaves you to guard it for all eternity. Or I can take it somewhere it will be safe, guarded by those trained to do so. Sworn to keep evil like Myrtle in check."

"And where is that?" Sutton demands.

"A library," he replies.

"A library," Sutton repeats warily. "We have one of those."

"Not like this one, you don't," Rip says. "The creature in charge of this particular library is trained in guarding objects such as this." He holds up the grimoire. "He'll keep this one locked down tight, I assure you. Unless you'd rather spend the rest of your life babysitting Myrtle yourself..."

Sutton and I exchange a look.

I can read his thoughts as easily as my own. Hell no, we don't want to do that. We just freed ourselves from her. I can't imagine a lifetime shackled to making sure she never escapes.

"We don't know you," Steven says as he stands and wraps an arm around Allison's shoulders.

Clearly, he's not willing to just give up the grimoire so easily. But the more I think about it, the less I want the job for myself—or for any of us.

"I think this is Serenity's decision," Jolene says. "And Sutton's."

Steven looks like he wants to argue, but something in my expression stops him. "All right," he says slowly. "Serenity?"

Rip turns to me. "Do you trust me?" he asks.

Holding his gaze, I try to search for a reason to say no. For any instinct to be off, but there is nothing. Honestly, even my wolf seems to trust him. "I do."

"That good enough for you?" he questions, turning to Sutton.

"Yes." Sutton's reply is instant. "But if the bitch ever gets out, I will hunt you down first."

"Ditto," Steven puts in.

Rip grins. "As much as I love a good challenge, I can assure you she will not escape." He backs away and stands beside Tabitha. "Ready, my love?" he asks.

She grabs his hand, holding tight. "I died ready," she tells him, and he laughs.

They turn for the trees, but before they've gone more than a handful of steps, Rip and Tabitha vanish. Then, one by one, the ghosts begin to disappear too. Until no one but the living remains.

"Sutton," I whisper, turning toward him. In the wake of their departure, I'm hit with the grief I'd contained up until now. "I'm so sorry."

He looks into the distance where Phineas and Vivian have disappeared and then closes his eyes.

His emotions surge through me. Pain. Grief. Acceptance. And—if I'm not mistaken—hope. "They're together now," he finally says. "And I know my father wouldn't want to be anywhere else even if he could."

I nod, hugging him tightly.

"Is that it?" Jolene asks, breaking the silence.

I turn to the tough-as-nails hybrid. She leans against Vaughn, his arm around her waist. "Is the curse really broken? We're free to come...and go?"

Turning to Sutton, I reach up and run a hand over his cheek. "Only one way to find out."

My wolf surges beneath my skin at the same instant magic

sizzles along the hand currently cupping my mate's face. I gasp, staring at my skin where the magic sparked.

"What...?" I breathe.

Sutton reaches up and gently grips my wrist, bringing it down to look at the sparks still dancing between my fingers.

The sensation I felt earlier. My quick healing from Myrtle's invasion. The way I was drawn to the grimoire in that cabin...

It wasn't just my wolf coming back to me.

When Sutton's gaze meets mine, I smile. "Seems Myrtle left me a present when Tabitha ripped her out," I tell him.

"I think," Jolene says slowly, "the magic chose you instead of her."

"So, it wasn't an accident then?" I ask.

She shakes her head, forehead wrinkling with uncertainty. "I don't know. But something tells me the power felt the break between you two—and chose you over her."

While I can't prove it, her words feel right somehow.

I close my hands into fists, silently thanking the magic. And promising it to try my best to be worthy of its choice.

"If that's the case, I'll make sure to use it for our good," I say. Jolene nods at me, a kinship forming in the unspoken words between us. "We'll use it to restore this place," I add. "Together."

Jolene grins. "Hell yeah," she says.

I turn back to Sutton. "Race you to the boundary line?"

"No head start this time," he warns me, his excitement growing along with my own.

This is it. The last piece of the curse we've yet to confirm is broken. Stepping away from him, I let my wolf take over, shifting in seconds until I'm standing before him as my wolf.

He follows suit, but before he finishes shifting, I turn and bolt for the trees. His answering snarl makes me laugh as I practically read his thoughts about no head starts. Heart pounding, my paws hit the soft dirt as I race toward town. Wolf free, magic in my veins, and the mate bond strong in my heart, I've never felt stronger than I do right now.

When I reach the boundary line, I stop and wait for Sutton.

Now leaving Midnight Falls, the sign beside the road reads. Something that hasn't been true for anyone in this town in over a century.

If anyone's going to take that first step, I want it to be Sutton.

But a moment later, Sutton comes to a stop beside me. He stares at the sign, and I can feel his uncertainty. His fear that the curse is still intact, that this test will fail.

So, I take the leap for him.

As soon as I'm across the boundary line, I shift back to my human form and smile at him, tears falling down my cheeks. "Your turn, mate."

He shifts to his human form and stares back at me. Hope burns brightly in his gaze, and my heart hammers as he steps over what used to be an invisible wall, joining me on the other side for the very first time.

"You're no longer bound to this place, Sutton. We did it. You're free."

He lifts his hand to tenderly cup my cheek. The depth of love and emotion shining in his eyes makes every single thing worth it if it meant getting us here to this moment. "I may be free, but I'm still bound, my love. Bound to you."

Falls Gazette

Epilogue

One year later

The front door opens and closes with an unmistakable *click*. The sound of it reaches me over the music spilling out of the speakers wired throughout the house. My stomach flutters with anticipation, and I hurry around the corner from the kitchen, abandoning the party tray of hors d'oeuvres I've so carefully begun to arrange.

Sutton stands in the entryway, his faded black jeans and flannel shirt stirring something in my belly. Something definitely not appropriate, given what day it is. And, shit, what time it is too.

He closes the distance between us, planting a kiss on my mouth that suggests he's having the same thoughts I am. My pulse races, and by the time he lets me go, I'm breathless and stuck trying to remember why we shouldn't just go upstairs and finish this in our bedroom.

Then the oven timer beeps, and I remember.

"How'd it go?" I ask, noting he's alone.

I frown, wondering if something happened. Even after nearly a year of pure happiness and complete normalcy—whatever that is—sometimes, my internal panic meter still points toward "shitstorm."

But Sutton smiles reassuringly—and there's a knowing in his eyes. An understanding. He gets it. "It went fine," he assures me. "They're—"

The door opens behind him, and a familiar face pokes her head inside. "Serenity?"

"Mom!"

I rush forward as she pushes her way fully into the house, and we wrap our arms around one another. My heart fills with the excitement of having her here. After two trips up north to visit them, they're finally getting to see where I live now. Where Sutton and I live. It's a big day.

One I've looked forward to for months. And now it's finally here. *They* are finally here.

Movement draws my gaze. I let my mother go and step back to take it all in. Behind her, coming up the front walk is the entire Kellis crew. They each carry at least one bag in their hands, except for Stuart, who looks like he's carrying an entire circus between Samuel on his back and a pile of suitcases in his hands.

His wife Kim is right behind him, wrangling their eldest, Sarah, who is attempting to run straight into the woods that border our house so she can play "knights and damsels," as she ineloquently keeps yelling.

My brother, Sawyer, reaches me first. He envelops me in a bear hug that lifts me clean off my feet and spins me around dramatically before setting me down again. "Sis, you look like a real housewife," he says, and I swat him.

"Don't call me names," I pretend to pout.

He laughs and passes me off to Melinda, his wife. "You look

gorgeous as always," she says, hugging me tight and then stepping back.

"Back at you," I tell her. "What do you serve at that restaurant, Sawyer? I need some of that."

"A good chef never reveals his secret recipe," Sawyer says with a wink.

Melinda laughs and squeezes my hand. "It's so good to see you," she tells me before Sawyer pulls her inside and kisses her noisily. Stuart walks up, shaking his head. "He's still a dumbass, all grown up," he says, earning a snicker from Sawyer. I reach for the bags in Stuart's hands, but he refuses to let me take them and instead plants a kiss on my cheek before passing inside. The moment he does, I hear him whistle.

"Damn, sis, this place is impressive." His voice nearly echoes in the large, open foyer.

I smile to myself. If he only knew. We've spent a year putting off my family's visit because I refused to let them see the house until it was finished. Now, it finally is, and the anticipation and pride are overwhelming.

"Come on," Sutton tells him from the entryway, "I'll show you around."

"How about a place to drop all this first?" Stuart asks.

"Kid's playroom is this way," Sutton says.

"Oh my," Melinda exclaims, her neck craning up to take in the spiral staircase and patterned ceiling. My memory flashes to the first time I ever saw this place restored to its intended glory. I can still see Sutton standing at the top of the stairs, dressed in a formal tux that accentuated every single detail of his muscled form. His dark eyes glowering, already pissed at my stubbornness.

It was a moment I'll never forget.

Restoring the house to the way it looked that night was my

wedding gift to Sutton, but it's also a living memory of the moment I fell in love with the man I get to spend the rest of my life with.

Blinking back to the moment, I watch as Sutton plucks Samuel out of my brother's arms and hauls him up high as he pretends to fly him through the house. Samuel crows his enthusiasm, and Sutton goes faster. My heart warms as I watch him play "uncle" so effortlessly.

Miranda, Sawyer, and Stuart follow more slowly, disappearing toward the back where we've remodeled the ballroom into a series of cozy living areas and a guest wing. One of the spaces is a game room, complete with a foosball table and a theater-style screen for playing movies.

Steven and Sutton have spent entire evenings "testing" the foosball table while Allison and I worked on the décor in the rest of the guest suites.

I turn at the sound of footsteps and see Kim and my dad coming up the front walk. She's finally gotten Sarah to agree to come inside, mostly because she's terrified Samuel is having more fun than her with the uncles. Kim hugs me and then chases after Sarah, who barely stops long enough to high-five me hello. My father is just behind them, Stuart's youngest nestled in his arms. My dad smiles big at me, and I lean in, pressing a kiss first to my father's cheek and then to the infant he's carrying. Baby Jack.

"You look good, Grandpa." I wink at him.

He beams then glances up at the two-story manor at my back. "Back at ya, kid," he tells me, his gaze sweeping up over the house, taking in the dark siding set against white and gray accent colors. The house is hauntingly beautiful way out here surrounded by trees. But it gleams where we've replaced nearly every plank and shingle over the last few months.

Now, instead of austere and grim, Hargrave Manor is inviting and cool. Like the shadows of a shade tree on a blistering summer day. Even the long, narrow drive that winds through acres and acres of Hargrave-owned forest is manicured and lovely. And, thanks to having it paved, the brand new 3-car garage that sits adjacent to the house now holds a shiny black Jeep for me and a truck for Sutton.

My old car, Diamond, is in there too, though she doesn't get out much anymore.

"Married life suits you," my father adds, and my cheeks warm in happiness at the compliment—and the reminder.

Even from out here, I notice Sutton's wolf scent change subtly at the comment. And despite the fact that my husband is nowhere in view, my own inner wolf preens for him. His hearing is impeccable, as always. And he apparently agrees with my father. I have a feeling he'll bring it up later. Since the moment our ceremony was complete—a backyard affair at my parents' house last fall, his dirty talk has expanded into all things "wife" and "marriage." It's adorable. And hot. Who knew being called "wife" could turn me on so much?

Baby Jack stirs, and my dad adjusts his hold on the little guy. "Better get this one inside," he says and slips past me into the house. The enjoyment radiating from him at playing grandpa makes my heart feel full.

"Well-well, the witch in her natural habitat."

I look back at where Stone is moseying toward me, a brown bag slung over his shoulder.

"Hilarious," I deadpan.

His brow lifts. "No snapping comeback?"

I shrug. "I've been called worse."

Besides, can't argue with the truth.

He grins at me, plants a noisy kiss on my cheek, and then stares up at the house. "It's a whole mood, isn't it?"

"And what kind of mood is that?" I ask, genuinely curious what his impression is.

"Well, let's just say, if any ghostly activity happens after dark, I'm hauling my ass over to the bed and breakfast instead."

I laugh at that, more entertained than he could possibly know. "I promise you there are no ghosts living in this house. Or anywhere in this town. Including the bed and breakfast—which you already know isn't open to customers for another month."

"So you say." He snorts. "Maybe they just don't show themselves to you. Maybe they'll like me better. And besides, we both know Allison will give me a room if I ask. I'm her favorite Kellis brother."

"You mean besides her own husband?" I ask pointedly.

"Eh, I mean, I guess," he says with a shrug. "But I wouldn't force her to choose, you know? Steven can be a real dumbass."

I shake my head, refusing to explain how wrong he is. "Come on. I'll show you the inside. Maybe it'll change your mind about the ghosts."

He lets me pull him into the foyer and then stops short, gawking at the ornate molding and patterned gold and white wallpaper that gleams underneath the polished chandeliers. When he spins to look at it, his boots squeak, and he looks down sharply, only to stare further at the solid marble floor. Swirling patterns sweep toward what used to be the ballroom and is now the guest wing.

Sutton's voice drifts toward us from where he's giving the others a tour of the downstairs.

When I look up again, Stone is eyeing me with outright awe. "This place is fucking ridiculous, Ser. You guys sleep under blankets made of hundred-dollar bills then or what?"

I smack his arm. "You're an idiot," I say, and he grins.

I stiffen at the sudden scent that reaches me from the kitchen. "Shit! The brownies!"

Racing back, I yank the oven door open and pull the brownies out, sliding them onto the stove to cool. They're overly done but not burnt. Still, I mentally kick myself for ignoring the timer. Magically restoring a house to its former glory? No problem. I've got this. Successfully baking a dessert? Ugh. I'm still a work-in-progress.

"Uh, Ser? Are you okay?"

Stone's words hold a note of wariness that makes me tense. I realize, way too late, my mistake. By the time I turn around, his gaze is locked on my hands. Specifically on the fact that they're not burnt or even remotely injured. Definitely a problem considering I just took a hot pan of brownies out of the oven without an oven mitt to protect my skin.

I wince at the mild redness coating my fingers. It's already fading to nothing—healing, thanks to my wolf's supernatural abilities. Dammit. Sutton and I both agreed we'd be extra careful this weekend, and here I've already let the cat out of the bag.

Or the wolf.

I look at Stone, floundering for an explanation he'll actually believe.

"Well, the thing is..."

Footsteps sound, low heels clicking against the marble floor.

"Don't mind Serenity," Allison says as she sweeps in, wedging herself between me and Stone. "She's burnt herself so many times this past year her nerve endings are shot." She lowers her voice to a conspiratorial whisper as she tells Stone, "Don't eat her squash casserole if you value your life."

He grins, and I can't tell if it's the distraction Allison provides or her insult to my cooking that he so approves of, but either way, it's all forgotten as he pulls her into a loose hug.

"Sister from another mister," he says, putting his arms around my best friend.

"Watch the belly," she warns him.

"Speaking of cooking," Stone says with an affectionate rub of her growing belly, "how is the little guy?"

"Or girl," Allison reminds him.

"Of course," Stone says, solemn-faced. "You feeling okay?"

"I feel great," she admits. "The first couple of months were hell, but now, at almost seven months in, I have all the energy."

"Good thing too," I say, "She's been working like a crazy person at the newspaper."

"First of all, we both have," she says, eyes narrowing on me—a look she gives me any time I suggest she should slow down and rest. "That's what co-ownership means."

We took over the paper together about six months back when it was clear no one else could run it as well as us. And it's been a blast getting it off the ground, hiring journalists and photographers, training them. Exhausting, too, on top of everything with the house, but well worth it to see our names as co-editors. Not to mention the jobs we've provided the community as we hire our staff.

"And you still look ravishing," Stone puts in, sweeping Allison into his arms and humming dramatically while he attempts to waltz her around the kitchen island.

A figure steps into the kitchen doorway and glowers.

"Stone, kindly take your hands off my wife." Steven's threat is met with a smile and a wink from Stone, which he aims at me.

I roll my eyes, knowing full well he only did it because he heard Steven coming this way.

"I guess I can try. It really is your fault for marrying someone so gorgeous," Stone tells him, leading Allison back to where they started and bowing gallantly.

Allison practically glows at the compliment. I shake my head. She eats this shit up, my brothers' rivalry. Considering the fact that she's an only child, she's pretty great at stirring the pot and then stepping back to watch the fallout.

I have to admit it is entertaining. And the rightful duty of any sister, in my opinion.

Even without his official uniform, Steven looks every inch the sheriff as he glares at Stone. "You touch her again and I'll arrest you."

Stone snorts. "You could try. But your donut-eating ass would have to catch me first."

Steven goes rigidly still—a tell we all know means he's about to launch his attack.

But Stone knows it too, and he's fast as hell, thanks to his military training.

They both launch into motion at once, Stone doing a hot lap around the island before slipping past Steven and racing down the hall, hooting loudly.

Allison laughs, and Steven pins her with a look. "You're encouraging this," he says.

"Of course not," she says.

Instead of chasing after Stone, Steven stalks toward her.

"Ugh. I'm just going to give you two a minute... gross." I give up on the pretense of a polite exit and hurry out as Steven grabs Allison and begins kissing her.

They've been extra gross lately, thanks to her pregnancy sex drive.

I swear wolves aren't as horny as those two. Well. Okay. That's a bit of an overstatement.

Even as I consider the thought, a figure steps into the hall, blocking my path. Sutton looms over me, snaking an arm around my waist and pulling me through the nearest doorway. The scent of books hits me first, and I relax in the familiar setting of the library. A room that's definitely seen its fair share of action.

Sutton spins me, shutting the door behind us with his heel in a smooth movement before pinning me against the wall and claiming my mouth with his.

"What are you doing?" I ask when he releases me.

"What does it feel like, wife?" he whispers then trails hot kisses down my throat to my collar.

Goosebumps race across my skin. But I brace my hands on his shoulders and push. "Sutton. We have company."

"They're busy settling in," he says, his breath deliciously warm and inviting against my collarbone.

"We can't just..." His hand trails my thigh and then dips between them to rub at my already-hot center.

"Five minutes," he whispers. "I want to be inside my bride."

Wife. Bride.

He's ridiculous with the way he uses those terms constantly. A reminder of what I am to him. And him to me. It's even more ridiculous how much it thrills me to hear them from him.

"Sutton."

But even as my desire climbs, my stomach roils.

Ugh, not now.

The nausea is sudden and gripping.

My hand tightens on his shoulder, and I'm no longer embracing him so much as clinging to him for support. The change in my demeanor makes him instantly tense. He draws back, studying my expression with concern in his dark eyes.

"What is it?" he asks.

I clutch my stomach, for all the good it does. "I'm going to be sick--"

He grabs the trash can and holds it underneath me just in time for me to empty the contents of my stomach into the bin.

When I'm done, he sets it aside and hands me a tissue. After all we've been through together, my capacity for embarrassment is nearly non-existent. Still, I feel a faint warmth in my cheeks as I take the tissue and wipe my face.

"Thanks," I say quietly.

"Are you sick?" he asks. The energy rolling off him is nervous. Unsure.

I shake my head. "Not like you think."

"You've been doing so much lately," he says, frowning deeply, "with the paper and the house and your magic. You've been over-doing it."

"It's not that," I say more firmly this time.

The magic is actually probably what's kept me most sane. The challenge—and excitement—of using it to restore rather than destroy has been indescribable. Unfortunately, it won't help stave off the effects of what I'm dealing with now.

"Then what?" Sutton asks, urgency driving his tone.

I sigh. This wasn't the preferred moment to drop this bomb, but I also can't lie to him. And I can't let him think the worst. Or worry needlessly. I won't. Not after everything.

Secretly, I had hoped this news would wait for the perfect moment. But then I realize that's exactly what this is. My wolf hearing tunes into the hum of voices coming from various rooms throughout the house. My family. All of them together in one place. Safe. Happy. Loved. And my incredible husband staring back at me with complete devotion.

In the end, I relax, and my heart softens to a puddle as I drop the magic I've been using to shield my secret.

Sutton's eyes narrow, and he tilts his head to the side as though listening to the slight shift in the noise around us.

"Is that a heartbeat?" he asks, eyes widening.

I grin, my eyes filling with tears as I think about this moment and how different my life looks compared to my plan. When I first drove into Midnight Falls, I expected to stick around just long enough to prove myself by solving the unsolvable. The last thing I ever expected was to find my own happily ever after.

And yet, here I am. Standing in front of the man I love. A man who I'd once believed to be a murderer. My-oh-my how things have changed.

"Serenity, is that…are we?" he trails off, as though he's afraid to be wrong.

"Sutton, darling, I'm pregnant."

His eyes go wide and he crushes me against his body, wrapping both arms around me. "How did you hide it from me?"

He doesn't sound angry at my subterfuge. If anything, there's awe and a sort of reverence in his tone.

"Magic," I reply, my cheek pressed against his chest. "I wanted to wait for the right moment."

"I love you so fucking much, Serenity Hargrave." He pulls away, though he keeps his hands on my arms. "Thank you." Eyes shimmering with emotion, he stares at me like I'm his whole world.

"Thank you?" I ask with a laugh. "It takes two to tango, you know."

He grins widely. "Oh, I remember." Leaning in, he presses a kiss to my cheek. "You're going to be an amazing mother," he says as he draws back.

"And you're going to be such a fantastic dad."

The emotion in his eyes deepens, and I can see uncertainty swimming in his dark gaze. "You think so?"

"Absolutely." I soften. "Phineas would be so happy if he were here. And so proud of you. They both would."

He shakes his head. "I never actually thought..." He clears his throat, his voice raw. "After a hundred years alone, I gave up." He looks at me, and I can see that this news has really rocked him. "I've wanted a family for so long, and I just worried it was too late for me."

"Not too late," I say, rubbing my nose against his affectionately. "We're right on time."

"Yes," he agrees, lowering his forehead to mine. "You were."

I push gently against his chest. "Okay, Mr. Hargrave, I need to brush my teeth now. And I want to keep this between us for now."

"Are you sure? Your family will be so happy--"

"That's what I'm afraid of. My mom will be beside herself. And my brothers? They'll probably tie me to a chair and not let me get up again until I've given birth. It's going to be ridiculous."

He grins. "Tying you up doesn't sound so bad."

I smack him playfully. "I mean it. Let's keep this secret for ourselves, for now, deal?"

Sutton cups my cheeks. "Deal. You are my life, Serenity. My forever."

"I certainly hope so." With a wink, I move away and start out the door.

Sutton playfully slaps me on the ass. "We're picking up where we left off later, mate. Now that I know it worked, we should get started practicing for the others."

"Others?" My voice pitches high as I think about all that morning sickness.

Sutton just laughs and leads me back to the party, hand in hand, exactly where we're supposed to be.

THANK YOU SO MUCH FOR READING! TURN THE PAGE FOR EXCLUSIVE bonus chapters from the series.

Falls Gazette

Bonus Scene #1: Sutton POV

Sutton (after Book 1, chapter 10 when he & Serenity talk in the woods and agree to work together)

I pace the first floor blindly. The house itself seems to moan and creak with my heavy steps but I stopped noticing the state of my surroundings ages ago. What does it matter when I have no one to show it to?

For decades, I've lived alone. Trapped inside a cage I never deserved and can't seem to break free from.

Somewhere along the way, I stopped caring about my own limitations. My priority is my pack. Their lives—and deaths. Their pain. But today, in a single moment, all of that changed.

Finally.

After over a century of waiting, I've found my mate.

After Rina's predictions with the blood augury, I doubted. But one look at Serenity today and I knew. All the way to my fucking bones, I knew it was her.

In the beginning, this news might have thrilled me. Even a decade ago, I would have felt differently. Maybe even been happy —if I can still feel that emotion anymore. But now? With the threat of *her* safety hanging in the balance and with me no more able to protect her than if I'd already succumbed to this damn curse?

My fear for her is an agony I've never known before now.

Fate's a cruel bitch.

I've known that all along.

My hands ache to return to the woods and find her, grab her. To carry her back here where I can protect her. Watch her. Touch her.

She's not safe in town.

She's not safe here either.

From the curse, maybe but not from me. Revealing my feelings would only scare her off and if she ran? My wolf would chase. In fact, the beast inside me wants nothing more than a pursuit. He wants her to fight, to resist. So he can catch her and claim her for his own.

Lowering her to the dirt and taking her right there underneath the stars...that's what my beast wants with Serenity Kellis. The human side of me might see the logic in using her to help me end this curse but in this moment, none of that matters so much as my desire to be inside her.

Just imagining her body against mine is enough to harden my cock. My vision blurs as the blood rushes from my head and rational thought becomes nearly impossible. My breathing turns ragged. For a long moment, my control hangs by a thread.

In the silence, I grip the wall and grit my teeth, waiting for the urge to pass.

A large chunk of plaster breaks free where I've used too much force. It crumbles in my hands and a frustrated howl rips from my throat.

This isn't working.

I take the stairs two at a time and go straight into my master bathroom, stripping out of my clothes. Then I step into the shower and turn it on. Frigid water hits me with a shock and my lusty thoughts are instantly drowned out.

I force myself to stand there, head bowed, focusing on the chilled water as it hits my head and runs down my back. Letting it chase away the need for her.

But nothing will do that. Not completely.

Even in the cold, I long to go to my mate.

No.

I growl the word out loud.

Serenity is safest not knowing how important she truly is. If she doesn't know she belongs to me, maybe Myrtle won't figure it out either. It's the only way I can keep her safe at least until I have the strength to send her away from this place.

Even considering it causes me pain but I know it's what I'll have to do. Besides, I have a feeling the hardest part will be making her listen.

My mind drifts back to our conversation earlier. The snarky way she told me off. Her mouth is sharp—and inviting. I wonder what it would feel like to have that mouth wrapped around my cock.

With my control slipping again, I wrap a hand around my erection—still fully hard despite the cold water. *Dammit.*

Slowly, I stroke myself, letting my thoughts give in to the urge to imagine it's her touching me. What she'd feel like. How she'd taste. My balls tighten and I stroke faster. The water no longer feels cold. All my senses are tuned to the fantasy now.

Serenity—here, naked.

Me—inside her.

My muscles strain with need. I prop my free hand against the wall and pump myself into my hand as if it's her body I'm filling now.

Finally, with a groan, I tip my head back and lose myself to my own release.

In the wake of pleasure, one thought remains absolutely clear: Serenity Kellis will be mine.

Falls Gazette

Bonus Scene #2: Steven & Allison

Allison (after Serenity first goes to Midnight Falls, VA)

"Yeah, yeah, I'm coming!" I call out as I walk toward the door. I run a hand through my short cap of hair and yawn, then rip my front door open in annoyance.

Damn near seven feet of toned muscle stands on the other side, a familiar blue gaze narrowed on me. "Why the fuck wouldn't you ask who it was?" he demands.

"Who is it?" I ask sweetly as I pin Serenity's brother, Steven with a glare.

His gaze narrows. "Not funny."

"Sue me. It's not even seven in the morning, logical thinking doesn't kick in for another three cups of coffee." I stretch, then notice the way his gaze rakes over my barely clothed body. Steven and I have met a grand total of one time before today, and it was over the body of a dead woman. Romantic? Hardly. But the man left an impression. And in this moment, I can see that I'm leaving one too.

"You sleep in that?" he questions, eyeing me.

I look down only to realize I'm not wearing pants. Then again, it could be worse, I guess, and I've never been one to get embarrassed about my body. "Underwear and a tank? No. Usually I sleep naked." I step away from the door. "Since I imagine whatever has brought you to my apartment is not a hallway conversation, why don't you come in."

"You're going to get yourself killed answering the door in your damned underwear." Steven moves into my space, brooding male wrapped in tight jeans and a leather jacket. He's seriously delicious, in an 'Officer please arrest me, I've been a bad girl' kind of way.

But, since he's my best friend's big brother, that's a tree I've yet to climb and probably shouldn't ever try. Moving into the kitchen, I yawn again, then fill my electric kettle with water before pressing the *coffee* button. As soon as the water starts heating, I turn back to Steven. "Maybe. But Momma said to never change, so here we are." I cross my arms. "What brings you to my door this morning?"

A muscle in his sharp jaw twitches as his gaze flicks to my now boosted rack. I drop my arms again and warmth pools in my belly. Seriously, the guy is a damned lollipop and I'm looking to become the next owl. Bet I can get to the center in less than three licks.

"Have you heard from Serenity?"

The lust drains from my body, only to be replaced with the heaviness of dread. "No. Not in a couple of days. Why?"

"I can't get ahold of her. She's not answering any calls, no texts. And I called the Sherriff's—"

Irritation for my friend flushes my cheeks. "You did *not* call the cops to check up on her."

His steely gaze narrows again. "I *am* the cops. And you're damn right I did. She's my sister."

I roll my eyes. "No wonder she's dodging your calls, Steven. She's a grown ass woman who, last I talked to her, managed to find a bit of happiness in the form of a sexy local."

He groans. "Gross. Don't say that."

"Based on the look of disgust on your face? You already knew that." I move out of the kitchen and head down the hall.

"Where the hell are you going?" His heavy footfalls tell me he's following me, which is fine. I've never been overly modest. I'd rather he watch me lose clothes, but if he wants to witness me putting them on, then more power to him.

"To put pants on. Is that okay with you?" I turn to face him in my bedroom doorway, hands on my hips.

The way his gaze travels from me to my bed, then back to me makes my blood heat. The tension between us grows in a way that I cannot even begin to put words to , but if I'm not mistaking—the detective is seriously eyeballing my goods. Again.

"Fine," he replies.

"Great." I slip into my closet and pull on a pair of cotton shorts, then run my fingers through my hair before heading back out into my bedroom and grabbing the phone off my nightstand. "Now, let's try and call Ser, shall we?" After unlocking my phone, I tap her name and hold my cell up to my ear.

"Hi! You've reached Serenity Kellis. Leave a message and I'll get back to you as soon as I can!" Her voicemail fills my ears and I try not to be annoyed as I hang up the phone.

"The service there is spotty," I say before Steven points out that it's weird her phone is going to voicemail. Before he can argue, I move past him and into my living room where I retrieve my laptop and carry it to the kitchen. The kettle beeps, so I stretch up to pull some fresh beans and my grinder down.

Behind me, Steven groans. "Can you not wear something longer?"

With the sweetest smile in my arsenal, I turn toward him. "I'm sorry, Officer, are my legs offensive to you as I stand here in my own home?"

He scowls. "My sister is missing."

I turn my back on him and scoop some beans into the grinder. "Correction, your sister has turned off her phone because she's currently enjoying her vacation."

"Right. Vacation. Is that before or after she investigates cold case murders?"

Pressing the button to the grinder, I try to remember if she told me that she'd confessed anything to Steven. While she's hit me up for info here and there, even I don't know the full scope of what she's doing—not that I want to admit that to Officer Asshole. As soon as the beans are ground, I put them in the mesh basket and start pouring hot water over the top.

I turn back to Steven and pretend not to notice he was clearly checking out my ass. "What do you mean, investigating?"

Steven narrows his gaze. "You and I both know what she's doing there, so cut the shit."

"Fair enough." I set the kettle down as water drips through the coffee into the carafe. "Serenity is a big girl, Steven. She can take care of herself."

"She's in over her head."

"Because she's not answering her phone?"

"Exactly." He closes his eyes for a moment, and when he opens them again, I see passed the leather-clad police officer and to the worried older brother. "She's my responsibility, Allison. And she had a shit go of it before she left. I need to know she's okay."

I grab two mugs from the cabinet and set them out, then cross toward him. I cover his hand with mine, then instantly regret it. Heat churns in my belly at the casual touch. It's like I'm one of those plasma globes and Steven's touch sets off the lightning within me.

Immediately, I pull my hand back and remind myself the sexy man in front of me is off limits. "I'll send her an email. Give her today to respond, then if she doesn't, I'll drive with you out there so we can both kick her ass."

He battles with the idea, the conflict plain as day on his face.

"If you show up and kick her door down with no warning, she's going to be pissed at you," I add, knowing full well that's probably what he's thinking.

Steven sighs. "Fine." His gaze shifts past me. "Why don't I finish the coffee and you send the email." Without waiting for a response, he moves into the small kitchen. The two of us barely fit, but I can't bring myself to move aside.

Because, dammit, I want the closeness.

I open my laptop, log into my email, and pull up a new composition.

"Serenity, your brother is holding me hostage, please write me back because he won't release me without proof of life," I read out loud as I type the words.

"Very funny." Steven presses down to send the coffee grinds to the bottom of the French press, then moves up behind, his front pressing directly into my back.

I go completely still at that. Or try to. It's almost impossible not to lean back against him, to rub against the man's chest like I'm a cat and he's the only one who can scratch my itch.

Shit, did I just compare myself to a cat? I blame that horrible, horrible date—No, wait. I'm not thinking about *that awkwardness* right now.

I need to get laid—desperately.

"Um, do you need something?" I ask in a breathy voice.

"You forgot to hit send," he says, voice low and deep.

"Yeah, well, I'm a bit distracted right now." Because my pride won't allow me to press back against him, I hit send, then turn around.

Steven, however, doesn't move. He simply continues glowering over me, a tall drink of water. "Why didn't we meet before the food truck park?"

"No idea. I guess I'm Serenity's dirty little secret," I joke.

His brows draw together and he cocks his head to the side.

"Not like that." I push against his chest—big mistake. Because instead of pulling my hands away, they linger. "More like she was afraid to introduce me to her brothers."

"Why?"

"Because I'm a hopeless romantic, and if the rest of you are anything like your sister, I probably would have fallen in love with one of you since Serenity's only downfall is that she's a woman. If she were a man, I'd have married her already."

He snorts at that. "I'm nothing like my sister."

"Then I guess we have nothing to worry about."

"I guess not."

He steps back and I take that opportunity to slide toward the cabinet where I stretch up and retrieve two mugs from the top shelf.

"Fuck, Allison. Go put some real pants on. Please."

"Nope. If you can't stand the sight of my skin, you can kindly fuck off." I set the mugs down and pour dark liquid into each one. Then, I turn to offer him a full mug. "If you want creamer, you'll have to go somewhere else."

He eyes the cup a moment, then takes it and immediately sets it aside. "Your skin doesn't offend me," he replies. "Quite the opposite, actually. The sight of it is driving me fucking wild." He steps closer which I didn't think was possible in the already cramped space between us. My breath hitches at the way he watches me now.

Shit. Shit. Shit. Serenity will kill me for this. My phone

dings so I set my coffee aside, then jump up to grab it. I'm expecting to see Serenity's name... Instead, it's a text alert letting me know my rent payment went through. "It's not—"

I turn and run straight into Steven. Out of pure panic over being singed by the heat he's putting off, I jump away hard enough to make me lose my balance, and Steven's massive arm shoots out to catch me from falling. Pressed in tight behind me, he holds me up at the waist, my back bent over, him folded forward as he keeps me from face-planting onto the tile.

Embarrassment wars with a rush of desire that nearly sends my knees buckling. But Steven won't let that happen. In a single smooth move, he pulls us both upright and spins me to face him.

My gaze locks on his and when I see the lust swimming in his own eyes, that heat turns into a blazing flame. "Uh, thanks."

"Not Serenity?" he asks in a husky voice.

"No. Not yet."

His stare is intense as he asks, "You really think she's all right?"

"I do," I say, still trying to recover from the feel of my ass pressed against what felt like a very impressive erection. "Why?"

"Because I'm a bastard for this." He yanks me up by the shoulders and slams his mouth to mine. I go rigid, the blaze devouring my body as it shoots through my blood.

Oh, fuck. I sink into him, gripping his biceps as I part my lips to give his tongue access. It slips in and slides against mine. The moan leaves my mouth but is swallowed by his. Steven's hands go to my ass and he lifts me, sliding me back against the countertop and stepping up between my thighs.

I should definitely stop this right now. Instead, I wrap both legs around his waist as sparks I've never felt shoot off in my body.

My brain.

Fuck me, Steven Kellis *is* passion.

Before I can think to strongly on it, I reach up and shove his jacket down off his shoulders, then grip his biceps and pull him closer. His hands go to my thighs, slipping up and gripping me in a way that has me aching for more. And when he pulls away, I'm fairly certain I've had an out of body experience.

"This probably shouldn't happen," he whispers. "You're my sister's best friend."

"Yeah. You're probably right," I reply. "Though, maybe we should just try that again. You know, see if that was a one-time sexual explosion or if there's more."

"Sexual explosion?" he questions, arching a brow.

"Yep." I snake both arms around his neck and drag him back to my mouth. It's hotter this time. Feverish as his mouth claims mine. "Yes. This—" I kiss him again, then grip the bottom of his shirt and pull back long enough to rip it over his head.

He steps back enough for me to take in the sight of his muscled chest. I run both hands over it, my fingers sliding over warm flesh stretched over taut muscle. "Fuck, that jacket doesn't do you justice."

"We should stop," he says as he grips the bottom of my tank and rips it up over my head.

"We really should," I agree as he tosses it to the floor, his hungry gaze going to my bare breasts.

Steven drops his head and captures my nipple in his mouth, and pleasure rockets through me as my orgasm builds from this simple contact alone. I arch back, a moan escaping. He draws the taut peak of my nipple into his mouth, sucking gently before nipping ever so slightly.

I wrap my legs around his waist and pull him toward me. His hard length presses between my legs and I practically weep with relief. This. This is the passion I've been missing. The connection that every date I've had over the last five damn years has lacked.

Steven releases my breast and captures my mouth again. He

cups my ass and lifts me, then carries me across my apartment and into my bedroom. When he dips, the mattress meets my back and he thrusts up against me, his erection tempting me even through the denim he wears. I moan again, my fingers slipping between us and undoing the button of his jeans.

I shove my hand down the front of his open pants and grip his dick. It's silky smooth, and so fucking hard. I squeeze gently and Steven groans against my mouth. "I don't think we can stop now," he murmurs between kisses.

"It would be a crime."

"And I'm a cop."

"Exactly," I reply as I release him. He steps back and kicks out of his boots, then shoves his pants down to the floor. Within seconds, Steven is standing before me. Naked, and the very mental picture of a woman's wet dream.

I want to lick him.

Bite him.

Let him do things that are probably *very* illegal to me.

I start for my shorts, but Steven shakes his head. "I want to take them off." He grips my legs and yanks me toward the edge of my bed, then slips his fingers beneath the waistband of my shorts. With slow, teasing movements, he pulls them and my underwear down my legs, then tosses them to the floor.

When he looks back at me, it's with a slow perusal that makes me shiver in anticipation. Shit, I could kiss past Allison on the mouth for remembering to shave her legs.

He leans down again, his massive hands run up the length of my legs, then he grips my thighs and spreads them open. "So fucking sexy," he growls as he drops to his knees beside my bed and buries his face between my legs. Passion and pleasure burn through me, scorching every inch of my flesh as his tongue slides over my clit.

He draws it into his mouth, and I grip his hair. "Yes!" I call out as I'm driven up to the crest of the biggest fucking orgasm I've ever had. Seriously, it's like even the hair on top of my head can feel the pleasure rocketing through me.

Steven drives his tongue into me and I come undone, exploding into a million tiny pieces and floating back down to the bed for part two. He steps back. "I don't have a condom."

"Top drawer," I say, breathless.

He rummages through it and pulls one out, then slips it onto his dick and climbs onto the mattress. I grip up and pull him down to my mouth as he positions himself at my entrance. The taste of me on his tongue drives me crazy. And when he drives into me in one fluid movement, I see stars.

"Fuck, you feel good."

"Same to you, big guy," I moan as I dig my fingers into his back.

Steven pulls back then slams into me.

He gives without remorse.

Fucks like an animal.

A direct contradiction to the restraint he seems to wear like a second skin any other time. The fact that I get this side of him only turns me on further. His large hands encompass mine and he pins them above my head as he thrusts into me. Faster. Harder. His solid length filling me to the very brink. And when I come undone for the second time in the last five minutes, I nearly weep with relief.

"Yes! Fuck yes!" I cry out.

Steven captures my lips again, his hips rocking back and forth until he groans against my lips and stills. His dick throbs within me as he comes, his release filling the condom.

We remain this way for a few minutes, entwined together in our passion.

Then, breathing ragged, he rolls off of me and lands on his back beside me.

"That was a sexual awakening," I say, my voice ragged. "Seriously, I think I died and came back to life."

"That was amazing," he agrees. "And unexpected."

"Yeah, I can't say I expected to get fucked into oblivion by Serenity's brother today." I sit up on my elbows and look down at him, a satisfied grin on my face. "But thanks."

He stares up at me incredulously. "Did you just thank me for having sex with you?"

"I did." I stand and cross to my bathroom to turn on the shower.

"You thanked me."

I turn to see Steven standing in the doorway. He pulls the condom off and tosses it in the trash.

"I did. Should I not have?"

"No woman has ever thanked me before."

"Then you were with the wrong ones. Because where I'm standing? You just gave me a massive orgasm. And if that's not worth a thank you, what is?"

"You did the same for me."

"Yeah, I did." I grin and Steven crosses over to yank me against him. He captures my lips again, turning my muscles back to putty.

"Thank you," he says.

"You're welcome." I kiss him again, then step back. "Now. Even though this was totally a one-time thing, how about a shower and a round two for good measure?"

Steven grins. "Definitely a one-time thing." Then, he captures my lips with his and proceeds to go a hell of a lot more than two rounds.

Want more delicious bonus content? Join the Patreon, where you'll get early access to new releases, special Patreon Exclusive books, and spicy bonus scenes!

Looking for your next read? Dive into One Dark Spark, a dragon shifter romantasy about a clumsy librarian who accidentally conjures a (naked) king, and four gnome warriors who battle monsters on their trust steed, a raccoon named Kitty.

About Heather Hildenbrand

Heather Hildenbrand lives in coastal Virginia where she writes paranormal and urban fantasy romance with lots of kissing & killing. Her most frequent hobbies are truck camping with her goldendoodle, talking to her plants, and avoiding killer slugs.

You can find out more about Heather and her books at www.heatherhildenbrand.com, by subscribing to her Newsletter, or joining her Facebook group!

Or find her here:
TikTok
Patreon
Facebook group
Instagram

Also by Heather Hildenbrand

One Dark Spark

Two Blazing Hearts

Three Scorched Kingdoms

Dark Wolf Soul

Deadly Wolf Bite

Broken Wolf Heart

Protect Me (Immortal Vices & Virtues)

Hunt Me (Immortal Vices & Virtues)

To Hunt A Wolf

To Kiss A Wolf

To Keep A Wolf

Midnight Cursed

Midnight Hunted

Midnight Bound

Wolf Cursed

Wolf Captive

Wolf Chosen

Wolf Revealed

A Witch's Call

A Witch's Destiny

A Witch's Fate

A Witch's Soul

A Witch's Prophecy

A Witch's Hope

Twisted Tides

The Girl Who Cried Werewolf

The Girl Who Cried Captive

The Girl Who Cried War

The Winter Witch

The Spring Witch

A Witch's Heart

Midnight Mate

Goddess Ascending

Goddess Claiming

Goddess Forging

Kiss of Death

Knock Em Dead

Death's Door

Dead to Rights

Dead End

The Girl Who Called The Stars

The Girl Who Ruled The Stars

Alpha Games

Alpha Trials

Alpha Chosen

Dirty Blood

Cold Blood

Blood Bond

Blood Rule

Broken Blood

One Hour: bonus novella

Imitation

Deviation

Generation

Guarded by the Alpha

Alpha Undercover

Mated to the Wilde Bear

The Bear's Fated Mate

Protected By the Bear

The Badge and the Bear

Tragic Ink: A Havenwood Falls story

Small Town Contemporary Romance (Heather Hildenbrand writing as Violet Stafford)

Stay for Summer

The Breakup Bet

Contemporary RomCom (writing as Moxie Rose)

Quarantine Crush

Corporate Crush

www.ingramcontent.com/pod-product-compliance
Lightning Source LLC
Chambersburg PA
CBHW021624030826
48979CB00038B/2542/J

* 9 7 8 1 9 6 1 4 5 5 1 9 1 *